TRAVIS

The Texans

Previous Books by Georgina Gentry

Cheyenne Captive
Cheyenne Princess
Comanche Cowboy
Bandit's Embrace
Nevada Nights
Quicksilver Passion
Cheyenne Caress
Apache Caress
Christmas Rendezvous (anthology)
Sioux Slave
Half-Breed's Bride
Nevada Dawn
Cheyenne Splendor
Song of the Warrior
Timeless Warrior
Warrior's Prize
Cheyenne Song
Eternal Outlaw
Apache Tears
Warrior's Honor
Warrior's Heart
To Tame a Savage
To Tame a Texan
To Tame a Rebel
To Tempt a Texan
To Tease a Texan
My Heroes Have Always Been Cowboys (anthology)
To Love a Texan
To Wed a Texan
To Seduce a Texan
Diablo: The Texans
Rio: The Texans
Colt: The Texans

Published by Kensington Publishing Corporation

TRAVIS

The Texans

GEORGINA
GENTRY

ZEBRA BOOKS
KENSINGTON PUBLISHING CORP.

ZEBRA BOOKS are published by

Kensington Publishing Corp.
119 West 40th Street
New York, NY 10018

ISBN-13: 978-1-62090-935-5

Printed in the United States of America

*This story is dedicated with
respect and thanks to the Texas Rangers,
those legends of the Lone Star State who
have fought and died for almost two centuries,
laying their lives on the line daily to
protect Texas and its people.*

Chapter 1

Red Rock, Kansas
April 20, 1889

"What the hell is going on here?" Texas Ranger Travis Prescott reined in his dusty gray stallion and looked around at the bustling crowd on the main street. He'd never seen so many people, all rushing about. His spotted dog lay down next to the horse.

"Hey, son," Travis yelled at a passing boy. "What's going on here anyway, some kind of town festival?"

The boy paused in pushing his rusty hoop down the street, his freckled face incredulous. "Ain't you heard, mister? The big land run is Monday."

"Land run? What land run?" Travis shifted his tall frame in his worn saddle.

"Where you been, mister? Everyone's talkin' about nothin' else." The boy stared up at Travis.

Truth of the matter, Travis had been tracking a killer for more than a month and he didn't know much about anything that had happened in that time. "Am I in Indian Territory?"

"No, sir, you're just across the line in Kansas, Red Rock."

Kansas. As a Texas Ranger, he didn't have any authority here. He probably didn't even have any in the Territory, but hot on the trail of the Grande Kid, who had killed a fellow Ranger, Travis hadn't even thought about state lines.

The boy turned to walk away.

"Hey, son, what day is it?" He'd lost track in all the weeks he'd been trailing Grande.

The boy sighed. "Mister, it's Saturday. Don't you know anything?"

Travis grinned at him. "I reckon not. You seen anything of a fine Appaloosa stallion wearing the fanciest saddle you ever seen?"

The boy thought a minute. "Yep. There's a horse like that in town. I think I saw it tied up in front of the Diamond Horseshoe Saloon."

Travis tossed the kid a dime and the kid caught it, grinned with snaggleteeth, nodded his thanks and started his hoop again down the crowded street.

So the Grande Kid was here after all, probably enjoying the women and drinks in this bustling town, convinced he'd lost Travis back along the trail. But Travis was half Comanche and he could trail a bug's tracks across the rocks.

Diamond Horseshoe. That made him think of Emily. Even now it hurt, even though it had happened more than five years ago.

You got too much pride, he thought and brought his mind back to today's problem.

"Okay, Mouse," he muttered to his weary stallion. "Let's find this hombre and cuff him, take him back to Texas."

He nudged the dusty gray horse forward and with a

snarl, old Growler reluctantly got up out of the dirt and trailed Travis down the street.

He carried his Ranger star in his pocket because it reflected light and could get him picked off by any outlaw he was pursuing. Now he took it out of his vest pocket and pinned it on his shirt as he rode, looking for the Kid's Appaloosa. What was he going to do if the Kid decided to make a fight of it? Travis couldn't risk hitting all these settlers who were coming in and out of the stores, filling their wagons with supplies for this land run. He had some vague recollection of hearing about it weeks ago, but then he'd started trailing the Kid through north Texas and capturing that killer was all that mattered to him.

People turned now to look at him and the star on his shirt, curiosity in their eyes. Travis looked straight ahead, his mind on the man he had come to take back to Texas. The Grande Kid was supposed to be fast with a gun and he'd have no qualms about shooting up the main street, even with women and children all around.

Then he saw the Appaloosa with the fancy saddle, lots of silver reflecting off the fine leather. There couldn't be another horse like it. Travis reined in and looked up at the sign above the saloon. The Diamond Horseshoe. Did he want to try to take the Kid inside or out in the street? Either way, other people might get hurt.

He sat on his horse a long moment, frowning. Maybe it was his expression or his badge that caused people to pause and look at him. Then they began to clear the street, melting into doorways or scurrying away. Women grabbed their small children by the hand and ran into stores. Men in buggies and wagons whipped up teams and pulled off down the road.

A bearded drunk lounging against a post out front of the

saloon looked up at Travis. "They don't allow half-breeds in their purty fancy saloon." He blinked.

Travis glared at him. "Go inside. Find a blond gunslinger wearing a fine black Stetson. Tell him a Texas Ranger is waiting outside for him."

The drunk's eyes got big. "He might get mad."

"I expect him to." Travis leaned on his saddle horn. "Now just do it."

The drunk stumbled into the saloon as Travis dismounted and led Mouse over to the horse trough for a drink. "You want a drink, too, Growler?"

The spotted dog, whose mama had been a ranch stock dog and his daddy a passing stranger, stuck his shaggy muzzle in the trough for some water.

Then Travis tied up his stallion to the hitching rail and stepped out in the middle of the dusty street, which was rapidly emptying of settlers and wagons. He had a feeling he was being watched as he checked his Colt, reholstered it and waited for the Grande Kid to come out. He hoped he came out. Travis would hate to shoot up a nice saloon where hombres were simply enjoying a few drinks and a hand of cards.

From the upstairs window of the Diamond Horseshoe Saloon, Violet La Farge watched the street scene with interest. She ought to go downstairs and mingle with the customers, but business wouldn't pick up until later in the afternoon. Anyway the action outside looked like it might soon be exciting. Brushing back her soft brown hair, she leaned her small face on her hands, elbows on the windowsill, and studied the big man who had just dismounted and tied up his gray horse. He looked to be a half-breed and too rugged to be called handsome, but he must be something special because he wore a lawman's star. He had an easy gait as he stepped out into the middle of the street and checked the pistol tied low on his lean hip. He looked like he knew how to use it, too. Maybe he'd come into the saloon later, if he didn't get killed, and she'd have a chance to meet him.

Travis picked his position carefully so that the late afternoon sun would be in his opponent's eyes. He stood there, feet wide apart, hands loose at his sides, waiting to find out if Grande would come out or if he'd have to go in after him. The Kid might try going out the back door, but his horse was tied up in front of the saloon and besides, the gunman had a reputation to protect. Travis could feel people watching him from behind wagons and boxes stacked out on the wooden sidewalks; women crowded behind shop windows to see the drama. The street was almost completely clear now.

Travis wiped at the sweat on his grimy face and tipped his Stetson to shade his eyes. He was bone tired after more than a month on the trail and he was eager to arrest this varmint and get him back to Waco. Once he got Grande across the state line and into Texas, Grande wouldn't have the excuse that Travis had no power outside the Lone Star state.

It was a nice spring afternoon, Travis thought, a good day to die. Well, for Grande to die. Travis was a crack shot and he thought he could outdraw the Kid.

He heard a murmur of excitement from just inside the door of the saloon and then the Grande Kid came out of the Diamond Horseshoe and paused on the wooden sidewalk, sneering. "You can't arrest me, Ranger. You got no authority outside Texas."

Travis kept his hand free and nodded, moving slowly so that the blond-haired bandit would be facing into the sun when he came out to face Travis. "I'm taking you back to stand trial for killin' a damned good Ranger, a whole lot better man than you are."

Grande laughed and leaned against the post in front of the saloon. "You followed me all this way to tell me that? You're more stubborn than I thought. I didn't think you could follow my trail."

Travis's voice was a soft but determined whisper. "I'm half Comanche, remember? Now drop your gun belt unless you want to die in the street here in Kansas."

The other's cruel face slowly lost its smile. "We'll see who's gonna die in the street, half-breed." Slowly he stepped out into the road, his blue eyes squinting against the sun.

Travis watched him warily. He'd heard the Kid was a fast draw, but he was fast himself. "Grande, I don't want to kill you, I'd rather watch you hang, so drop your gun belt and step away from it."

"I don't intend to hang, Ranger." The other threw back his head and laughed. "Everyone will see I killed you in a fair fight. Now quit jawin'. I got a good hand of poker and a fresh bottle of whiskey waitin' for me inside."

"You'll never live to drink it," Travis promised, watching the other man's hands.

"Hell, I won't!" Just the smallest tremble of his fingers signaled his intentions as he reached for the Colt tied low on his hip.

The Kid was fast, Travis thought as his own hand slapped leather and both pistols roared at the same time. He thought he heard a woman scream and then Travis felt the bullet hit his wrist so hard, it almost knocked the Colt from his hand and then indescribable pain and numbness as he tried to keep his grip on his gun.

The blond gunfighter looked at him with surprise in his blue eyes and then his pistol fell from his nerveless hand. He took two steps forward, grabbing at the sudden wet stain on his denim shirt. The crowd gasped a deep, audible breath as the outlaw took one more step and then collapsed into the street, his blood making a widening pool around him.

Travis stumbled forward, feeling like his arm was on fire. He managed to put his Colt back in its holster and saw that blood ran from his wrist down into the leather of his holster. He stumbled over and leaned against the hitching rail, feeling so faint he gritted his teeth. "Someone get the sheriff," he muttered, "and find me a doctor."

The spell was broken. People ran, shouting in excitement. "Did you see that?"

"Ranger shot the Grande Kid!"

"Is he dead?"

"Dead as a doornail. Is the Ranger hurt?"

A crowd began to gather.

Travis sat down hard on the wooden sidewalk and old Growler scampered over to lick his sweaty face. Travis patted the dog with his left hand. "I got him, boy," he gasped through clenched teeth. "He made me shoot him. Oh God, where's that doctor?"

"Coming through."

Travis craned his head and saw a plump old man carrying a small black bag coming down the sidewalk. "Out of my way. Someone been shot?"

Travis nodded at the old man gratefully. "Caught a slug in the wrist, Doc. Can you do anything to help me?"

The doc took Travis's big hand in his, frowned at the blood. "I think I'd better get you over to my office. That looks bad. How's the other man?"

Travis sighed. "Dead resisting arrest."

The old man stood up. "Can you walk?"

He wasn't sure he could, but he wasn't going to pass out

in front of all these women and children. "I—I think I can make it, Doc."

"Here, lean on me," Doc said and tried to help Travis to his feet. "My, you're a tall drink of water, aren't you?"

"Just like my daddy." Travis leaned on the doctor as they walked. He realized then he hadn't had anything to eat since some dried jerky yesterday. He'd been too intent on his tracking to think about food. Travis glanced back to make sure Growler was following them and saw he was leaving a crooked trail of blood. His wrist screamed in pain like his hand had been cut off. "I—I need to stop at the telegraph office," he whispered through gritted teeth, "let 'em know back in Waco I got the Grande Kid."

"Let's get your wrist bandaged up first and then you can do that," Doc insisted. "Didn't think anyone could outdraw that outlaw. The whole town'll be talkin about it."

Travis bit his lip and kept putting one boot ahead of the other. "It's my gun hand, Doc—"

"I know, I know. Here's my office." He half led, half carried the big man inside and sat him down in a chair. "Now don't you bleed all over my office. Let me get a pan of water and some bandages, see what I can do."

Travis stared down at his shattered wrist. It looked like raw meat. "You—you think the bullet went through?"

Doc turned on the light and put on his glasses. "Hmm. Let me wash it off and we'll see."

Travis closed his eyes as Doc worked on his wrist. It didn't feel like the bullet had gone through. He tried to move his fingers and flinched in pain.

Doc washed the wrist off and peered at it, shaking his head. "Just what I was afraid of, young man. Looks like the bullet shattered." He paused. "You need some painkiller?"

"Naw, I'm fine," Travis lied. "What about the wrist, Doc?"

The old man paused, peered at Travis over his glasses,

hesitated. "Well, I'm not sure. I don't think it's anything a country doctor can fix."

Travis looked up at him. "Can't you just cut the bullet out? I can take it. I've had more than one slug dug out of my hide."

"Here, have some of this laudanum, Ranger." Doc walked over to his medicine cabinet and poured a small bottle into a glass.

"Damn it, I don't want any painkiller." However he took it when Doc handed it to him. "Just give it to me straight. Can't you just dig the steel fragments out?"

Doc sighed. "Frankly, I'm afraid to. You got feeling in your fingers?"

Travis moved his fingers very slowly and then there was a flash of pain that almost doubled him over and the fingers of his right hand went numb.

"Just what I thought," Doc said, peering again at the wound. "Drink that, young man. I can tell you're in a lot of gut-wrenching pain."

He could feel the cold sweat dripping down his dark face. Reluctantly Travis drank some of the mixture. "I can take it, Doc. Tell me."

"Well, it looks to me like you've got a shard of steel, or maybe more than one, deep in your wrist."

"So take it out."

"I could, but to tell you the truth, I'm not a hifalutin back-east surgeon, and I think that's what you need. I'm afraid I'll paralyze that hand completely if I go to diggin' into those nerves in your wrist."

"You mean I wouldn't be able to use it?"

The old man looked at him and nodded. "If I leave it alone, maybe it will be all right if you're careful."

"Won't it just heal up?"

"It will heal over, but every once in a while, if you move

that hand wrong, the shards of steel may cut into those nerves and your hand will go numb."

"How numb?" Travis stared down at his bloody wrist.

Doc eyed the star on Travis's chest. "You're a lawman?"

Travis nodded. "Texas Ranger."

"Tough. Well, I'll give it to you straight. It might be numb enough that you won't be able to pull a trigger or even draw your pistol."

Travis began to curse. "What good is a Ranger who can't handle a gun? You're telling me I'm finished as a lawman?"

"It ain't the end of the world, son."

"It is for me. What the hell can I do with only one good hand?"

Doc patted him on the shoulder. "Now, son, I might be wrong. That wrist may heal up and you never have any trouble with that hand."

"But you can't promise that?"

The old man shook his head. "There's specialists back east that could probably operate on it and fix it, but it would cost a lot."

"More than a poor lawman has," Travis grumbled and now he drained the laudanum. "I reckon I'm man enough to face the truth. Do what you can, Doc. Bandage it up so I can go report in to the captain and see what he says."

Doc poured alcohol over the wound while Travis gritted his teeth. "Maybe it'll get better on its own. You can always hope so."

"A lawman can't take chances like that. He can get his partners killed."

Doc finished the bandaging, put the arm in a sling. "You looked a little pale, son. I'll give you some more painkiller and you go get something to eat. Things will look better tomorrow."

"Sure," Travis snapped and stood up. "What do I owe you?"

"Uh—a dollar."

Travis suspected it should be more than that. "I don't want your pity, Doc."

"Pity?" the old man snorted. "Look, you young whippersnapper, you've just rid this town of a gunfighter who's been tearing up this town for a couple of days now. I hope they give you a big reward."

"I'm a lawman. I can't take a reward for doing my job."

Doc walked to his medicine cabinet and poured a small bottle, handed it to Travis. "Fifty cents for the laudanum."

The drug was already working. The pain had lessened. He fumbled in his pocket for money, took the bottle and started unsteadily for the door.

"Son, if you don't feel better tomorrow, come back."

"Thanks, Doc." Travis went unsteadily out onto the wooden sidewalk where Growler waited patiently. With his arm tied up in a sling, his mood was worse than his wrist's throbbing. Old Growler wagged his stubby tail and followed Travis's uncertain steps.

Travis thought as he walked. *I'm finished as a lawman. What in the hell do I do now? I'm past thirty and have to look for a new job. The ranch can't carry anyone else, so I can't go home, although Mom and Dad and my younger brothers would welcome me back.*

Food. He should get some food. He didn't feel hungry, but he knew his animals were. He walked with unsteady feet to a butcher shop with Growler following along behind and bought some cheap hamburger and then went down to get his horse from the hitching post in front of the saloon.

He looked at the Appaloosa. No telling how long it had been tied here. He hated to see animals mistreated, so he took its reins along with his own stallion. He didn't think he'd make it to the livery stable, but he did. Just because he was in bad shape didn't mean his animals had to suffer. He sat on a hay bale and watched Mouse and Grande's horse eat the oats in their stalls and fed Growler the meat. He wanted a drink in the worst way. Maybe it would make his wrist stop throbbing. What was the name of that saloon? Oh, yes, the Diamond Horseshoe. But first, he had to wire Captain Shipley.

After asking directions to the telegraph office, he stumbled toward it, Growler trailing along behind. Once inside, he wondered how to word the wire. He couldn't bring himself to tell the truth, that he was finished as a Ranger. There was always that small glimmer of hope.

He licked the tip of the pencil and thought a minute before scrawling awkwardly with his left hand:

CAPTAIN SHIPLEY, TEXAS RANGERS, WACO, TEXAS.
FOLLOWED THE GRANDE KID UP HERE TO KANSAS.
STOP. KILLED HIM WHEN HE WOULDN'T SURRENDER.
STOP. TAKING A FEW WEEKS OFF BEFORE I COME BACK
TO WORK. STOP. MAY RETIRE. WAITING FOR YOUR
REPLY. TRAVIS PRESCOTT, TEXAS RANGER.

He sent it and stood around waiting for a reply. If he was lucky, the captain might be in his office on a Saturday afternoon. While he waited, he took another slug of laudanum. He was in such despair, he didn't care if he ever got any dinner.

It was late afternoon when the reply came:

CONGRATS ON GETTING GRANDE. STOP. WHAT THE
H--- ARE YOU DOING IN KANSAS? STOP. HAVE YOU
BEEN EATING LOCO WEED? YOU'RE MY BEST RANGER.
YOU CAN'T RETIRE. STOP. DON'T KNOW WHY YOU
WANT A VACATION, BUT GO AHEAD. STOP. UNTIL I CAN

GET YOU A PAYCHECK, SELL GRANDE'S HORSE AND
SADDLE TO GET BY. STOP. SINCERELY, MACK SHIPLEY.
CAPTAIN, TEXAS RANGERS.

Of course. Grande's horse and fancy saddle would bring
a pretty penny for someone wanting to make that land run
into Indian Territory. On the other hand, why couldn't he
make that run himself? With two fast horses, Travis had a
big advantage over the others. He could start his own ranch
on that free land. It would be better than going back to
Texas with all his pride crushed and letting everyone pity
him because he was now crippled and useless. He was
much too proud for that.

The thought of his own ranch cheered him a little. He
should go eat something, but what he wanted first was a
drink. He turned and strode slowly toward the Diamond
Horseshoe, wondering at the same time about that high-
pitched scream he had heard during the gunfight.

He walked unsteadily through the swinging doors,
the loud piano blaring at him as he stumbled up to the
bar. Around him, men backed away and he heard the
whispering: ". . . Texas Ranger . . . yeah, that's the one. . . .
Heard he killed the Grande Kid . . . Jesus! He must be
really fast with that Colt. . . . Not so fast the Kid didn't
manage to get a slug in his arm. . . ."

"Whiskey!" Travis ordered, slamming his left fist on
the bar.

The fat barkeeper looked him over with a slight curl of
derision to his lip. "We don't serve Injuns or half-breeds.
There's a bar for your kind on the outskirts of town."

And here it was again. The shame and scorn he'd dealt
with all his life. He reached his left hand across the bar as
fast as a rattlesnake strikes and grabbed the fat man by the
collar, lifting him off the floor. "I said, give me a drink or
I'll wipe up the place with you!"

He saw the sweat break out on the man's pale face as the barkeeper looked past him, gesturing helplessly.

Behind him, a cold voice said, "Frenchie, give the gentleman a drink. After all, he's a hero."

Travis let go of the barkeep, who hurried to get him a glass and bottle. Travis turned slowly to look behind him. The man standing there had a face chiseled from stone and his gun belt hung low. A gunfighter, Travis thought. *"Mucho gracias."* He nodded. "You join me?"

"I'm Slade." His smile was like a slash in his ugly face as he shook his head. "I never drink with customers."

Or maybe not with half-breeds, Travis thought. He shrugged and turned back to the bar as the fat man slid the glass and bottle in front of him. Behind him, he heard the sound of boots echoing over the music as the gunman walked away. "Who is that?"

Frenchie wiped his hands on his soiled white apron. "Slade? He's Duke Roberts's hired gun."

"Who's Duke Roberts?"

"He owns the place."

Travis drained his glass, feeling the bitter whiskey wash down his throat, wondering if he should be mixing alcohol with laudanum. At least it was numbing the pounding pain in his swollen wrist. He poured himself another as the other cowboys and settlers elbowed back up to the bar now that the threat of trouble had vanished.

Maybe it was the mixture, but now he was feeling pretty good. He leaned against the bar with a sigh and looked around.

In the distance, he heard the wail of a train whistle. He turned in time to see a man and a girl coming down the stairs. The man wore a fine broadcloth coat and carried a satchel. The brown-haired girl wore gaudy scarlet. Travis only got a quick glance before the couple was lost in the crowd, headed for the swinging doors where the stone-faced gunfighter stood. The three went outside.

Travis was getting a bit bleary-eyed and swayed on his feet. *Take it easy*, he warned himself. *A drunk can't defend himself if he has to.*

Not as if he could right now, even if he was sober, he thought bitterly, not with his right wrist in the shape it was in. Travis turned with a questioning look to the barkeep. "Who's the fancy dude?"

Frenchie wiped beer mugs with a dirty rag. "Duke, the boss. He's going to St. Louie to get some new roulette wheels. Business is really booming with this land run."

Travis merely grunted. The whiskey was beginning to slow his pain and he decided he'd better leave before he fell facedown on the floor. He made sure he still had his laudanum as he headed unsteadily out of the saloon. Outside, Growler, who had been patiently waiting for him, greeted him with a wag of his stubby tail.

Travis bent over to pet him and almost lost his balance. "Well, old fella, I reckon we'd better go see how the horses are doing and try to get a little rest. God knows it's been a long day."

He ambled down the dusty street toward the livery stable with the dog keeping the same pace behind him. He heard some shouting and then some shots, paused, decided it was the local law's job, kept walking. In the distance he heard the train chugging into town.

Walking toward the train station with Duke and Slade, Violet turned slightly to see the big Texas Ranger stumble out of the saloon and start down the street. She wondered if he'd make it.

Duke snapped at her, "What the hell you lookin' at, Violet?"

"Nothing." She turned back around as they walked. "You'll be back in a week?"

"I told you that, didn't I?" he said and made a snide remark to Slade about stupid women.

Slade laughed. "They're only good for one thing, Boss."

"Well, at least they make me a lot of money, especially this one." He reached out and familiarly pinched her breast through the low-cut scarlet dress.

Violet felt her face burn. She was ashamed of working in a saloon, but it was the only life she'd known since she'd been a child on the streets of Memphis.

A man stepped out from behind a building. Violet looked at him. He was drunk and unsteady on his feet, some poor clod-buster who had come in for the land run. "Hey, you, boss man," the man yelled and stumbled toward them.

"He's drunk, Duke," she whispered under her breath. "No need of killing him."

However, the pair of men with her had already stopped.

Duke said, "You talking to me, you hick?"

The red-faced man had a rusty old pistol in his belt and his clothes were faded and ragged. "Yeah, you. I lost all my money at your card table so now I can't buy supplies to make the run."

Duke laughed without mirth. "Farmer, that ain't my problem. You can't afford to lose, you should stay away from gambling."

People gathered to watch and now Slade had moved around next to the clod-buster as he stopped within a couple of feet of them.

He was very drunk and had tears running down his face. "You cheap card sharp, you cheated me—"

"You can't say that to me!" Duke challenged.

"Let him go," Violet whispered under her breath. "He's drunk, Duke."

The diamond horseshoe stickpin on his tie flashed in

the sunlight as Duke shook his head. "I'll overlook it this time. Take that back, clod-buster, and walk away."

"I want my money." The ragged farmer stumbled toward them, very close now.

She knew it was going to happen, she had seen it before. "No!" she yelled even as the farmer fumbled for his old pistol.

Slade, standing next to him, knocked the barrel up as the man drew so that the shot went wild and then Duke reached under his fine waistcoat for the Remington derringer he carried and shot the farmer in the heart. The man looked at them with wide eyes, stumbled forward and then fell dead in the street.

"You seen it!" Duke yelled to the crowd. "The farmer drew first."

Everyone nodded and Slade returned to Duke's side. A curious crowd gathered to look at the body lying in the street as the train chugged into the station behind them.

"Let's go," Duke ordered, shoving the tiny gun back under his fine frock coat, and grabbed Violet by the elbow as they walked. "What the hell you doing shouting out like that? He might have killed me."

"That poor clod-buster didn't have a chance against you and Slade, and you know it."

"Hell," Slade snickered. "Boss, your favorite whore is getting soft."

"Aw, she's just a woman, that's all." Duke grinned at her and slapped her bottom familiarly as they walked up on the station platform where the train waited. "Gimme a kiss, doll." Duke pulled her to him roughly and held her so close, the diamond stickpin in his tie cut into her soft breasts. She let him kiss her because she knew she had to unless she wanted to be slapped around right here in public.

The train whistled again and Slade took the carpetbags and swung up on the coach. "Come on, Boss."

Duke grinned and winked at her. "Now you make me some money while I'm gone, honey, and I'll bring you something pretty from the big city."

"That'll be nice," she said without enthusiasm. A plan began to form in her mind. Maybe with Duke and his gunfighter gone, she might figure out how to get away, maybe escape to a new life somewhere. She'd dreamed of it a hundred times. But how? Duke made sure she never had more than a few dollars in her purse. "Bye, Duke."

"See you in a week." The gambler swung up on the coach as the train began to move. Violet waved as the train pulled out and she stood there a long moment, watching it leave the station. She should get back to the Diamond Horseshoe. The evening crowd would be coming in and it was her job to get them to gamble and buy her expensive, watered-down drinks.

She turned and walked down the length of the platform, thinking wistfully of the big Texas lawman. Now there was a man who looked like he would love and protect his woman. He probably had one waiting for him back in the Lone Star state.

She rounded a corner and stopped. Sitting on a bench on the now deserted platform were four forlorn children sharing a small bag of crackers. They looked up at her as she paused.

"Lady, do you want to adopt us?" The oldest, a boy of about eleven, asked. He was bone-thin and held a crutch.

She shook her head and saw the gloom descend over the four little faces. There was a Chinese boy who might be ten, a red-haired little girl of maybe seven or eight who was chewing her nails, and a small blond girl hardly more than a baby. The blond one began to cry.

"I'm sorry." Violet knelt down in front of the quartet. "But I don't have a home or I'd take you all."

The red-haired girl sighed. She had freckles and buck

teeth. "Everyone's got an excuse. No one wants us, we're all rejects." She began to chew her nails.

Violet's heart melted. "I'm sure that's not true."

The Chinese boy said, "Yes, it is. They're sending us back to the orphanage."

The little blond baby began to cry again.

"Hush, Boo Hoo," the oldest boy said. "Crying won't do any good."

"You're going to an orphanage?" Violet asked.

"Nobody wants us," said the red-haired girl.

"I do," Violet said before she thought and all the children stopped eating crackers and looked up at her with hope in their eyes. Now what? She had no plan and no money to speak of, and was trying to get away herself, yet she couldn't let these pitiful children be sent to an orphanage. What on earth could she do?

Chapter 2

Violet's mind was busy as she knelt by the children's bench in her red satin dress. The bright feathers in her hair touched the littlest one's nose and the child stopped crying and laughed. "Feathers," she said.

"No, my name is Violet," she corrected. "How did you four get here?"

"Well," said the little red-haired girl with the buck teeth, "we're part of an orphan train."

"An orphan train?"

"Yes." The thin, oldest boy nodded and for the first time, Violet noted one of his legs was shorter than the other. "We got no parents. They gathered us up and put us in an orphanage in New York, and then they put us on a train and brought us west."

"Where are your parents?" Violet asked kindly.

"We don't know." The Chinese boy shrugged. "We're lost or maybe they're dead. The train stops at each town and they parade the children and people pick one or two."

"But nobody picked us," said the red-haired girl, "and you can see why."

"Nonsense!" Violet said. "You look like great kids to me."

"I'm crippled so they call me Limpy," said the oldest

boy, leaning on his crutch. "I wouldn't be much help on a farm."

"I'm Harold," said the Chinese boy.

"Harold?"

"I picked it myself," he answered proudly. "Nobody wants an Oriental kid. That one there is Kessie." He pointed to the redhead. "She's not pretty and she wants to be a suffragist, so nobody wants her."

The baby was crying again.

"Why does she cry?" Violet asked.

"Nobody knows. Boo Hoo cries all the time," Limpy put in. "She wets her drawers, too."

Violet looked at the little sack of crackers. "Who's looking after you?"

"The orphanage people," Kessie said. "They've gone to have a fancy dinner with the town's mayor. They said they'd be back in time for the late evening train."

"Then," sighed Limpy, "we'll be headed back east to the orphanage."

"Not if I can do anything about it," Violet said with determination and stood up.

The three older children looked hopeful and the toddler waved her pudgy hand toward Violet's head again and stopped crying. "Feathers."

What to do? She'd just made a promise she had no idea how to keep, but these four were looking up at her with such hope in their thin, sad faces.

"Come along with me." She motioned to them.

"The orphanage lady told us to sit right here until she came back," Harold informed her.

"Well, no, you're going with me," Violet said with more determination than she felt.

"Are you adopting us?" Kessie asked.

"Well, sort of. Now come along."

The children dutifully got up off the bench and followed

along behind Violet as she started off the train platform
and out into the bustling street. They must make a strange
sight, Violet thought as she walked—a saloon girl in bright
red satin with scarlet feathers in her hair and four thin,
ragged children trailing along behind her.

People turned to stare, but no one said anything or tried
to question her. At any moment, she expected to hear the
sheriff yelling, "Stop! You're kidnapping those children!"

Or worse yet, the orphanage lady running after them,
having her thrown in jail for kidnapping and putting the
children on a train back to New York City.

What the hell had she been thinking? They'd be expecting her back at the Diamond Horseshoe by dark, but as
busy as they were tonight with all those people crowding
in for the run, maybe they wouldn't miss her for hours.

"Slow down," Kessie called. "Boo Hoo can't walk fast."

Violet paused and turned to look. All the children were
puffing and the little blond baby was crying again. Limpy
had fallen way behind but was trying manfully to catch up,
walking with his crutch.

Harold looked up at her with his big almond eyes. "I'm
hungry. Have you got any food?"

She tried to remember what she had heard about Oriental people. "You want rice, right?"

He made a face. "I hate rice. I'd go for some fried potatoes."

"I don't have anything right now." Violet tried to think.
She couldn't take them back to the saloon to feed because
Frenchie, the bartender, would toss them out in the street.
She opened her tiny reticule and searched through it; just
what she'd thought, not more than a dollar, so she couldn't
take them into a café. Besides, they'd attract too much attention in a restaurant and someone might call the sheriff.
How could she have gotten herself into such a mess? She'd
been making plans to get away while Duke and Slade were

gone, but she had no chance with no money and all these extra mouths to feed. Why had she taken them on? Then she looked down into four sad faces and knew. Three large, lurching wagons passed, stirring up dust, all headed for the south edge of town to wait for Monday's land run. Then she had a thought: was it possible she could beg a ride into the Indian Territory for herself and four little urchins? Right now, she didn't have a better idea.

People didn't seem to be staring at the children as much as they were at her. After all, there were a lot of children with the settlers, but one seldom saw a saloon girl in red satin walking down the street leading such a bedraggled parade. She had to blend in. How?

"Kids, I'll figure out something."

Limpy smiled up at her. "You're pretty. How come you aren't married?"

"I'd like to be," she blurted before she thought. Who would marry a saloon girl? Maybe if she got to a new town where they didn't know her, she could start all over again.

They began walking again and passed a wagon parked out in front of the general store. A pretty young girl stuck her head out the back. "That's an awfully pretty dress, miss."

Violet paused and looked up at the country girl, thinking she was being sarcastic, but the girl looked friendly. "Would you like to own it?"

"Sure," said the girl, "but I reckon it cost a lot. I don't have any money."

Violet thought fast. The girl in the covered wagon was about her size and wore a plain blue gingham dress. "I'll trade you even up," Violet said. "Your dress for mine."

"You must be joking," the girl said. "Your dress is so fancy."

"I'm not joking," Violet answered. "I'll climb up there and we'll just switch clothes."

The girl hesitated. "I don't know what Pa will say when he comes out of the store."

"Well, put on something else and hide it from him," Violet said. "Just think, when you get to your new town, how pretty you'll be in this dress."

The girl giggled. "I'll do it!" She reached down, took Violet's hand and lifted her into the wagon.

In minutes, Violet clambered down to the street wearing the blue gingham and plain black shoes, looking like any country girl.

Boo Hoo looked up at her. "Feathers." She smiled.

"Oh, those." Violet reached up to yank the scarlet plumes out of her brown hair and handed them to the girl in the wagon.

Boo Hoo started crying. Violet picked her up. Her bloomers were wet. "Feathers," Boo Hoo wept.

"My name is Violet, like the flowers," she corrected. "Folks say my eyes are just that color. Now come along, before her pa comes out of that store."

They walked a little farther. It was late afternoon now and would soon be dusk.

"Gosh," said Kessie, "you look almost like a kid yourself in that dress, Violet."

"Yes, I know. Men always said I could pass for a kid if I needed to." She stopped dead, an idea beginning to form in her mind. She set Boo Hoo down on the edge of the wooden sidewalk and the child promptly began to cry.

"Please stop," Violet begged.

Limpy leaned on his crutch. "You're wasting your breath, ma'am. She cries all the time; that's why no one wanted to adopt her even if she is pretty."

"And she wets her drawers," Harold added.

"Oh, Lord." She had half a mind to take them all back to the train station and leave them. She might manage an escape by herself, but dragging along four orphans made it nearly impossible.

Kessie looked at her intently, still chewing her nails. "You taking us back to the train?"

That one was too smart.

"I didn't give it a thought," Violet lied because all four looked so sad. She walked over and looked at her reflection in a nearby horse trough. Kessie was right, she did look much younger in the plain blue dress, except for all the face paint and eye kohl. Maybe, just maybe, her new idea might work. She leaned over and began to wash her face, shoving aside a bay mare drinking there and trying not to think of how many horses had drunk out of this trough.

Now she turned back to face the children as she dried her face on her cotton skirt. "Better?"

Harold pursed his lips. "You didn't quite get it all."

Back to the horse trough.

"What about now? Do you think I could pass as a kid myself?"

The children eyed her critically.

Kessie said, "You better do something about your hair. It's too fancy up on your head. Little girls don't do that."

Violet knew her hair was fancy. Didn't the Diamond Horseshoe have a black maid who kept all the whores' hair looking good?

Violet took her hairpins out and her brown locks fell well below her small shoulders. She began to comb it with her fingers. Then as the children watched, she braided her hair into two pigtails. "Now how do I look?"

They all stared at her. "Young," they said in unison, except Boo Hoo, who said, "Feathers."

Violet sighed. "Okay, I am just like all of you; I came off the orphan train and I'm thirteen years old, going on fourteen."

Kessie looked up at her. "You want us to lie?"

Oh, dear, she had gotten an orphan with scruples. She'd make a good suffragette all right. "We'll just pretend for a while, okay? You see, there's a bad man looking for me, too, and I need to run away just like you do. Maybe all five of us can do it."

Limpy drew a circle in the dust with his crutch. "Now just how are we going to do that?"

"I haven't quite figured that one out yet, but I'm working on it, okay? Now remember, I am Violet and I am thirteen years old."

All the children nodded. Could she pull this off? And even if she could, how was she going to get all five of them out of town when she didn't have enough money for even one train ticket? She leaned over and looked at her reflection in the horse trough. She was short and slight. Duke had always complained about how small her breasts were. Maybe, just maybe, she could convince people that she was only thirteen years old, but then what?

It was turning dusk now on the bustling street.

"What are all these people doing here?" Limpy asked.

"I'm hungry," Kessie said.

"We're all hungry," Violet answered. "All these people are here for the big land run day after tomorrow. They'll all line up and the army will fire a cannon and they'll race into Indian Territory."

"And then what?" Kessie asked.

Boo Hoo was crying again and Violet picked her up, wet drawers and all, and hugged her close.

"Everybody races in," Violet said, "and the ones who get there first will win a farm or a town lot so they can start a business."

Limpy looked wistful. "That would be nice, if we had a farm or a ranch where we could all live as a family. I always wanted to be a cowboy."

Kessie said, "You can't be a cowboy, you're crippled."

"Hush," Violet said. "That isn't kind. Cowboys ride horses and in the saddle—it doesn't matter if you've got a bad leg."

They started walking again.

Harold said, "Why don't we race and get a farm?"

"That's silly." Violet shrugged as they walked south along Main Street. "We don't have any horses or equipment and besides, you have to be twenty-one to stake a claim."

Kessie asked, "Are they allowing women to race or is this another thing just for men?"

Yes, this kid would make a great suffragette.

Violet shook her head. "No, I think women can race, too, but we don't have any horses." Besides which, Violet thought, she was only nineteen, going on twenty, so that let her out.

"I'm hungry," Boo Hoo sobbed against her shoulder. The blue gingham was getting sodden and the child was heavy for a slight girl like herself to carry, but Violet gritted her teeth, adjusted the weight and started walking south again. They were almost to the edge of town. In the distance, she saw the wagons lined up by the dozens, the owners camping under the trees by the creek, waiting for Monday's race.

She was hungry, too. Violet felt like weeping with Boo Hoo, but she knew crying didn't do any good. She had to take action, just like she had when her mother died of yellow fever back in Memphis. After that, she and her little brother begged and stole food along the docks to survive. Then in desperation, she'd started picking up men on the streets to feed herself and Tommy. Poor Tommy. She choked back a sob. After three years, he got yellow fever in the summer and she had only herself to look after. She thought she could better herself by coming west, but no one wanted to hire her except saloon owners. She'd listened to Duke's promises of marriage, but he was like the others, only wanting to use her himself and make money off her body. Well, now was her chance to escape, but she was weighed down with four children. What to do?

"I'm hungry," said Kessie behind her.

"So am I," Limpy echoed.

Boo Hoo began to cry again.

"I'll get us some food," Violet promised, but she wasn't sure how. "Let's walk over to all those wagon people. Maybe someone down that line will offer to feed us."

They started walking and had to stop once for Limpy to catch up. "I'm sorry," he said, shame-faced. "One of my legs is shorter than the other and I just can't keep up."

"It's all right." Violet patted his thin shoulder. "We can slow down a little."

There must have been a hundred buggies and covered wagons stretched out along the creek and some men with just a horse and a blanket spread out by campfires.

They approached the first wagon and Violet gave the lady her saddest smile. "Please, ma'am, we're all orphans and we're hungry. Could you spare us a little of that bird you're cooking?"

The woman shook her head. "Sorry, honey, I got five kids of my own in the wagon and this might barely feed them."

Boo Hoo began to cry again as they walked to the next wagon. A middle-aged farmer was stirring a pot of chili.

"Please, mister," Violet said, "we're orphans and we're hungry. Could you spare us a little?"

He looked Violet up and down in a way that made her skin crawl. "How old are you, honey?"

"Thirteen."

The man grinned. "Young, just like I like 'em. You

crawl into the wagon for a few minutes with me, kid, and I'll feed all of you."

Limpy grabbed her arm and stepped in front of her. "No, she ain't doing that."

"Then starve, you little beggars!" The man cursed them and they hurried away.

It was growing dark now and Violet was getting a headache. There was food aplenty for her at the Diamond Horseshoe, but she shuddered at the thought of going back there and besides, she couldn't abandon these kids.

They next came to a buggy where a young man and woman sat by a campfire eating bread and butter.

Violet said. "Please, ma'am, we're hungry orphans. Could you spare us a little?"

The lady had a kind face. She stared up at little Boo Hoo. "Why is she crying?"

"Because she's hungry, ma'am," Harold said.

The lady said to her husband. "Isn't that the cutest baby you ever saw?"

"Now, Lucinda, don't even think—"

"She's an orphan, too?" the young woman asked.

"Yes, ma'am," Violet said.

"Then why don't you give her to me?" The young woman stood up and held out her hands. "We don't have any children and we'd love to take—"

Boo Hoo set up a howl that could be heard a mile away and clung to Violet like a baby monkey. "No! No! Feathers! Stay with Feathers!"

Kessie, Limpy and Harold all presented a front, stepping in front of Violet. Violet said, "I'm sorry, we can't give her away. You see, we're all family."

"I'd give her a good home," the woman said.

Violet shook her head and began backing from the couple. "No, we just can't do that."

The five scurried away with the woman calling after

them. Violet's heart was beating hard. Maybe the couple would have given Boo Hoo a good home, but suddenly this seemed like her own little girl and she couldn't let her go.

They walked a little farther and found an older couple with a sad-looking wagon with two worn-out old horses.

Violet hated to even ask. "Ma'am, we're orphans and we're all hungry. Could you spare anything? Maybe some milk for the baby?"

The old woman looked sad. "I can give you a little bread, that's all. If we don't get some land in this run, I don't know what we're gonna do." She held out a partial loaf, and Violet took it and divided it among the children.

Kessie looked at her with a keen eye. "Violet, you ain't gonna eat none?"

"I—I'm not hungry," Violet lied. "You four eat it. There'll be something better along the way."

It was dark now as they started back down the line of campfires. They paused at another wagon and two men hunched over a campfire scowled at them. The smell of brewing coffee wafted to Violet's nose and she wished she had a cup of it. The men appeared to be eating a hunk of beef they had roasted over the fire.

Violet said, "Please, we're orphans. Could you spare just enough for the little ones?"

"Orphans, huh?" one man snarled. "Why are you begging? Why don't you get jobs instead of asking honest citizens for handouts?"

"Never mind," Violet said. "Come on, kids."

As they walked away, Violet felt the heavy responsibility of her big, new family. Just how was she going to feed these kids? In desperation, she decided if she had to, she'd wait until the camp was asleep and try stealing food. She'd hate doing that, but these kids were hungry.

Up ahead was another camp. There were two horses tied away from the campfire, a gray and an Appaloosa grazing contentedly. A big man lay stretched out under blankets by the fire. A black pot boiled merrily and it smelled like stew. What's more, she could smell coffee.

They walked up and stood by the sleeping man, who was still in shadow. A spotted dog with a stubby tail raised its head and began to bark at them. The man stirred slightly.

Violet cleared her throat. "Please, mister, would you be willing to share your food? We're awfully hungry."

"Huh? What?" The big man sat up suddenly and stared at her, evidently having trouble focusing his eyes.

Oh, dear. Violet recognized him. It was the Texas Ranger she'd seen in the gunfight earlier this afternoon.

The dog rose up from beside the fire and growled at them, but Violet was too hungry to be deterred. "Please, mister, we're all orphans. Can you help me and my brothers and sisters?"

Travis had a tremendous headache as he tried to focus his eyes. Growler ran toward the children. "Watch out," he yelled. "Growler don't like people much."

The young girl in the blue dress put the blond toddler down and the baby stopped crying and walked uncertainly toward the dog. "Puppy. My puppy."

As Travis watched in amazement, the old dog looked at the toddler, then began to wag his stubby tail. Growler walked over to the baby and began licking her tear-stained face.

"Well, I'll be damned!" Travis said.

"Please, sir, I must insist you don't cuss in front of the kids."

He took a good look at the straggly crew: an indignant brown-haired girl about thirteen, a thin crippled white boy leaning on a crutch, an Oriental kid, a homely little girl with frizzy red hair and buck teeth, and the blond toddler who now had her arms wrapped around Travis's dog, her eyes all swollen and red.

"What's wrong with her?" he asked.

"Nothing." The oldest girl shrugged her shoulders. "Maybe she misses her mother, that's all."

"Where are your parents?" His wrist was throbbing and he wished they'd all go away and let him sleep.

"We don't have any," answered the oldest girl. "We're hungry. Can we have some of your stew?"

He hesitated. Feeding stray children might be like feeding a stray dog. That's how he had ended up with Growler. He sure didn't need a ready-made family.

"Are you deaf, mister?" the girl asked.

"No. I don't feel like talking. Why don't you take your little brothers and sisters someplace else?" *Any place else*, he thought.

"We got no place to go," said the thin boy with the crutch.

The oldest girl was now by his fire dishing up a bowl of his stew.

"Hey, I didn't say you could have that."

"You didn't say I couldn't." She handed the bowl to the Chinese kid, who began to gobble it.

"You got a lot of gall," Travis said.

"We're hungry," the girl said, "and you aren't eating it." She took the empty bowl away from the Chinese kid, filled it and handed it to the baby. "Here, Boo Hoo, eat up."

He'd never met a kid like her. Here she was defying him and the hungry horde was gobbling up his stew.

He had a sinking feeling that he'd just become the owner of five orphaned pups like Growler. Damn, he didn't need any more problems than he already had, but the young girl looked determined.

Now what was he going to do?

Chapter 3

Travis woke and looked up in the dawning light. A small white flag flapped from a branch just over his head. Had he surrendered? Or had someone surrendered to him? He couldn't remember anything. His head felt like an iron anvil that a horseshoer was pounding hard with a steel hammer.

He blinked and focused his eyes on the white flag and realized it was actually a very small pair of white drawers flapping in the wind.

What the—? He sat up, his head aching, his wrist hurting, and tried to remember what had awakened him. Instinctively he grabbed for his pistol and leveled it at the shadowy group by his fire.

"Don't shoot!" yelled a small voice and he identified it coming from a pretty young girl in a blue gingham dress, bent over his campfire.

"Kids?" Travis blinked and lowered the weapon. "What the hell—?"

"You really shouldn't swear in front of children," said the small voice.

He tried to focus. The girl was probably the oldest of the

lot, maybe thirteen. Her brown hair was tied in pigtails and her eyes were a smoky lavender blue.

"Then you ought not sneak up on me like a pack of Mexican pistoleros," he muttered and laid the Colt down. "Who are you and what do you want?"

"Don't you remember us from last night?" The pretty young girl asked.

He shook his head, "I don't know—maybe."

The five looked at him and the blond toddler began to cry.

"What's wrong with her?" Travis stared at the sobbing baby.

An Oriental boy who might have been eight or nine said, "She's hungry. We all are."

"Are you still drunk?" the pigtailed girl picked up the toddler. "We explained who we were last night. Now I'm making breakfast. Is that okay, mister?"

The girl had a soft Southern accent and looked determined. Besides her and the toddler and the Oriental kid, there was a scrawny white boy who might have been ten or eleven leaning on a crutch, and a homely little redheaded girl with crooked teeth.

"Looks like you're already helping yourself to my groceries." His wrist throbbed so badly, he wished they'd all go away and let him sleep off his laudanum and whiskey, but judging from the set jaw of the oldest girl, they weren't leaving.

Travis took a deep breath. "Well, I'll be damned."

The oldest girl squared her shoulders. "You probably will be, sir, but I wish you wouldn't swear before the kids."

"You tell 'em, Violet," said the fiery-haired girl.

Travis started to stand up, decided he couldn't manage it. "It's just that Growler never takes up with anyone and just look at him now."

They all stared. The baby had stopped crying but had

not released her grip on the dog's neck. She grinned at everyone. "Doggie. My doggie."

Violet took a deep breath of relief and looked toward the bacon frying in the skillet and took a sniff of the hot coffee. She looked the Ranger over carefully, thinking he was big enough and tough enough to take care of a woman and a bunch of kids. "Please, sir, I'm an orphan and so are all these children. My name is Violet. We joined up with you last night. Maybe you'd like to share some breakfast?"

Travis was hungover and his wrist throbbed. He wasn't hungry himself; he just wanted to go back to sleep and forget the pain. "Look, Violet, I got no time for a bunch of tramp kids. Why don't you beg on down the line?"

The young girl glared at him. He decided she would be a pretty woman someday. Her eyes were a smoky, almost lavender color, and she was slight but defiant. She definitely had grit. With that accent, she must be from somewhere in the South.

Violet squared her shoulders. "Sir, you are a Texas Ranger. You're wearing a badge. That means as a true Texan, you are obligated to help the helpless and look after unprotected women and children."

"Now that's a fact," Travis admitted. "All right, help yourself to my food and leave me in peace."

The children were all watching that skillet like a pack of starving wolf pups. The one called Violet lifted the skillet from the fire with the hem of her dress and set it on a stone. "I got bacon and eggs."

The thought made his stomach roil. "Just forget it, young lady." He waved her off.

The soft Southern voice said, "May I have some of your coffee?"

"Yes, just drink it and go on," he muttered.

"You look like you could use some coffee yourself," Violet said. "You smell like a brewery."

"No, thanks." He opened one eye and stared at her.

The little redhead piped up. "Violet, I do believe he's inebriated."

"What?" Travis asked. He had no idea what the word meant.

"Yep, he's drunk as a boiled owl," Violet answered and sipped her coffee.

"I got a right to be," Travis snapped.

Violet stepped over and knelt down. "Your wrist hurt? I saw the gunfight yesterday afternoon."

"Hell, yes, it hurts. Doc says there's a bullet fragment lodged in it and he couldn't take it out."

"It looks swollen. Want me to take a look at it?" Violet picked up his wrist. She had small hands.

"Aw, no, you're hurtin' me. Look, you kids just finish up my grub and go away."

He yanked the blanket up over his head. He was getting sober and his skull felt like his horse was stomping it.

But the one called Violet didn't move. "You going on the run Monday?"

"That ain't any of your business, young lady."

"You must be thinking about it, you got two good horses." She was a persistent child, he thought.

The Oriental kid said, "Why aren't you going back to the Rangers?"

"None of your business. Go away, all of you," Travis ordered.

"Yep, you've got two fast horses there," Violet said. "That'll give you a good chance of winning a claim. That is, if you're sober enough to ride."

"I got 'til Monday noon," Travis grumbled. "And anyway, young lady, didn't your ma teach you any manners? It ain't polite to comment on a stranger's condition."

"I got no ma," she retorted. "She died in the Great Fever outbreak in Memphis."

He had dozed off again. Violet watched him. He was barely sober, of course, and his face was etched in pain and his arm was swollen and discolored. If he had a shard of steel in that wrist, he might never be able to use that hand again. A Texas Ranger with a crippled gun hand was worse than useless. That must be the reason he'd decided to take part in the run.

She leaned over him and touched his shoulder. "We don't even know your name, mister."

"Travis," he whispered, "Travis Prescott."

"And is there a Mrs. Prescott who's coming to join you on that claim?"

Travis opened one eye. "For a little girl, you are the nosiest thing I ever met. No, there is no Mrs. Prescott except my mother, thank God, back in Long Horn, Texas."

"Go on to sleep, Mr. Prescott," Violet said softly, looking around at the children, who had eaten most of the bacon and eggs. Not only was Boo Hoo not crying, she was smiling as she shared her portion with the grumpy old dog.

Violet sat down on her heels by the fire and poured herself another cup of coffee, smiled at the sleepy children as she ate the last few bites of the food. Then she took the little drawers off the tree branch above Travis's head and led Boo Hoo behind some bushes to put them on.

Violet smiled to herself as she returned. She had a plan now. This Travis Prescott, even wounded, was more man than any she'd ever met and he wasn't married. She'd already decided that she and the children were going to latch on to the Ranger and go on the run with him. He might be a confirmed bachelor, but he was about to get a ready-made family, whether he liked it or not.

* * *

Travis tried to sit up and his head hurt so bad, he flinched. He reached to touch his aching skull and his wrist felt on fire. Then he remembered all of yesterday. He was no longer a Ranger; he was a cripple with no future.

"Well, Mr. Prescott, it's about time you woke up, it's past noon. I'm cooking you some breakfast. Would you like your eggs over easy or sunny side up?"

He blinked. "Who are you?"

"Don't you remember?" The young girl smiled and he thought someday, she'd be a pretty woman.

"He was snoggled," said the red-haired girl who ran over from her play. "He doesn't remember anything."

"Kessie," the older girl admonished, "that's not polite."

He remembered then. His camp had been invaded by this pack of starving orphans last night, and they'd still been here early this morning. "Where'd you get the eggs? I didn't have anything but bacon and coffee." The girl smiled back at him as she tended her skillet.

"Well"—she hesitated and gave him a fetching smile—"I got up early and saw there wasn't enough food to feed all of us, so I began trading down the line."

He needed a drink. He stumbled to his feet and began going through his saddlebags. "All right, young lady, or Violet or whatever your name is, where is it?"

"Well . . ." She didn't look at him as she poured a cup of coffee and brought it over. "I figured you'd drunk enough to last you a month, and I had to have something to trade for food—"

"You traded my whiskey?" He took the steaming cup in his left hand. "You traded my whiskey?"

"Please don't raise your voice, Mr. Prescott. You're scaring the children."

"Scaring the children?" His voice rose higher. "You traded off my whiskey without even asking me and—"

"You were out cold and you couldn't ask Boo Hoo to do without milk, could you?"

"Boo Hoo?" He couldn't even remember who that was until the little blond girl began to sob and Growler licked her face.

"If you've forgotten," the pretty young girl said patiently as if dealing with an idiot, "I am Violet, I am thirteen years old, the baby is Boo Hoo, the smart redheaded little girl is Kessie, the boy with the crutch is Limpy, and the Oriental boy is Harold."

"Harold?" Travis blinked.

"I chose it myself." Harold smiled at him with big almond eyes.

It was too much information to deal with since he had a hangover. Travis took the coffee in a shaky hand and sipped it. Violet made good coffee, he thought, strong enough to float a horseshoe, just the way Texans liked it.

"Sunny side up?" Violet asked.

"What?" he blinked.

"Your eggs."

"That's fine," he answered as he watched her break eggs into a skillet. "Wait a minute, I didn't have any eggs—"

Violet smiled. "You do now."

"Oh, yes, my whiskey—"

"I'd better check Boo Hoo," the older girl said and felt the toddler's bottom, sighed. "Here, take them off, honey, and I'll wash them out."

No one was paying the slightest attention to him. The kids had gone back to playing tag, the toddler and Violet had gone done to the creek to wash out the little white drawers.

The bacon and eggs smelled good, even though his stomach was queasy. He looked around at the children, who all came to sit down in a circle staring at him. The redhead chewed her nails and Boo Hoo returned to her spot next to the old dog, who wagged his stubby tail at her.

Now Violet returned and hung the freshly washed little drawers on the tree branch, then handed him a skillet full of bread, bacon and fried eggs and a fork.

"You got a lot of nerve, trading off my liquor without my say-so," Travis grumbled and set the coffee cup on a rock and put the skillet there, too. He began to eat. He hadn't realized how hungry he was.

"You already drank enough to last you 'til Christmas." Violet said.

"I reckon I ought to be the judge of that."

She shrugged and sipped her coffee. "Mister, after breakfast, I'll re-bandage your arm."

"I can do that myself, young lady."

"Not very well with one hand," she pointed out.

"Look." Travis stopped gobbling and glared at her. "I've now fed your bunch twice and I'll thank you to be on your way. I travel alone, just me and Mouse and Growler."

"Don't you get lonesome?" the Chinese kid asked.

"I do not." He returned to his food. "A Ranger is alone a lot of the time anyway, tracking outlaws."

"Are you an Injun?" the crippled kid asked.

Travis winced. His mixed heritage had caused him trouble his whole life. Even now in his mind, he could see big bullies chasing him at school. "Half-breed!" they would taunt. "Half-breed!"

He started to speak, but Violet said gently, "Limpy, that's not polite."

"It's okay." Travis shrugged. "I'm half Comanche."

"Wow!" Harold's almond eyes grew wide. "Did you ever take any scalps?"

"I'm a Texas Ranger, not a savage," Travis snapped. "Now, young lady, what are your plans?"

"Well, we haven't got any," Violet admitted. "We don't have any money and no place to go. Besides, the authorities are looking for us to put us all in an orphanage."

"An orphanage can't be that bad," Travis said as he sipped his coffee. "At least you wouldn't starve."

Four of them looked at him like he was kicking puppies and Boo Hoo began to cry again while Growler licked her little face.

Violet sighed and gave him a pitiful smile. "Well, sir, we were hoping to go along with you."

"With me?" Travis touched his chest in surprise, "Not a snowball's chance in hell."

Now tears came to all the children's eyes and he felt like he had just told them Santa Claus was dead.

"Well, maybe you can ask down the line of wagons." Travis gestured as he finished his eggs. "Maybe there's some family that would like to have five more children."

Violet cocked her head to one side and tears flowed down her pretty cheeks. "We been asking. All these people are dirt poor, that's why they're going on the run, trying to win some land. None of them need any more mouths to feed."

"Well, neither do I. Maybe I need to take you into town and turn you over to the authorities. As a Ranger, that's probably my duty."

Now all the children were crying and a couple walking past turned and glared at Travis.

The woman said in a huffy voice, "Some people just shouldn't have children if they're going to mistreat them."

The couple walked on and Travis felt like a villain. He couldn't take five young kids on the run with him, especially with the authorities looking for them. He'd be breaking the law that, as a Texas Ranger, he'd sworn to uphold. "As you can see, I've only got two horses and there's six of us."

"We could double up," Violet said, hope in her blue eyes.

"No, you see, I've got one horse and a spare. The idea is that if Mouse gets tired, I can trade off and ride the Appaloosa. The first and fast ones in get the land."

"Oh." Violet's slight shoulders fell and she looked sad. He hated himself for making the kid unhappy, but none of these children were his responsibility.

"Harold"—he nodded to the Chinese boy—"get a bucket of water to put out the fire. Then I'll give Violet whatever food I've got left and we'll part ways with no hard feelings, okay?"

Harold went off to get the bucket of water and Violet began to clean up the dishes. Travis noted her shoulders were shaking as she worked. The other children were crying softly.

"Look," Travis tried to explain again, "I've only got two horses, not a wagon. I can't take all of you with me."

Violet wiped her eyes. "You want me to re-bandage your wrist before we go?"

"I can't ask you to do that." She was a sweet youngster, he thought, and he felt guilty that she was offering to doctor his swollen wrist at the same time he was running them off.

"I owe you something for all the food we ate." Violet dug in his saddlebags and got fresh bandages and a small bottle of whiskey.

Travis brightened. "So you didn't trade it all away after all." He could already imagine a good slug of it and what it would do for his aching head and his throbbing arm.

"What's this?" She held up a small wooden horse.

"Put that back in my saddlebags," Travis ordered. "My stepdaddy, Colt, made it for me when I was a little kid. I carry it for good luck."

She didn't say anything, put the toy back in his saddlebag, knelt before him and pushed up his sleeve, began to unwrap his wrist.

He looked down at her. She had the softest, smallest hands. It had been a long time since he'd had any contact with any woman besides his mother or whores. Before that, there'd been Emily, but that thought only brought him anger.

"It still looks swollen and discolored," Violet murmured. "I hope it isn't going to get infected."

"Germs," said Kessie importantly. "If it gets infected, we may have to cut it off. You got a butcher knife?"

Travis glared at her. "No, I won't let a bunch of kids cut my hand off."

Harold said, "My ambition is to be a doctor."

"I still won't let you kids—"

"How does it feel?" Violet asked. She looked up at him and her mouth looked so soft and inviting.

What's wrong with you, Travis? This is a kid, not a woman. "Not too bad," he lied, but he could feel sweat breaking out on his forehead. His right wrist was throbbing like a war drum.

"You don't have to lie to me," Violet scoffed. "I don't know why men always got to pretend nothing hurts."

She opened the little bottle of whiskey and he smiled. Yes, she knew what he needed, all right. He started to reach his left hand for the bottle just as she poured most of it all over his injured right wrist.

"Ow, my God! Girl, are you trying to kill me?" He jumped up, shaking his wrist.

"I told you I needed to disinfect it," she answered.

"And a waste of perfectly good whiskey," he complained.

"Oh, stop being such a baby!" Violet caught his hand and yanked him back down.

"Did you save me even a drop?" he asked.

She handed him the almost empty bottle and started wrapping his wrist.

He held it up to the light, then held it to his mouth. There was one or two drops left and he savored it. "Waste of perfectly good whiskey," he muttered.

Harold and Kessie had wandered away from camp and now Harold came running from the direction of the creek. "Sheriff's coming!" he yelled. "He and his deputies are asking all up and down the line about missing orphans."

Violet looked up at Travis, her young face twisted by worry. "Please don't let them take us! Please!"

"You're fugitives from the law and you ain't my problem."

"Aren't," corrected Kessie.

Boo Hoo began to cry and that started Growler barking.

How in the world had he gotten mixed up in this mess and now what was he to do about it?

Chapter 4

Travis looked down into the young girl's face. "Now how am I supposed to stop them from taking you kids?"

Violet grabbed his big hand in hers. "You're a Texan. Can't you think of something?"

"I'm also a Texas Ranger and sworn to uphold the law. I can't go up against authority."

"I thought Texans could go up against anyone. Please, Mr. Prescott." The young girl held on to his hand and her eyes were bigger and sadder than a doe's. "You don't know how awful it is in an orphanage."

"Okay, I'll do this much. You take all these kids and go hide somewheres. I'll head them off." Why was he doing this? He was a confirmed bachelor and had no way to take care of five tramp kids, but there was something about the way they all cried and the way that young girl, Violet, looked up at him as if he could change the world.

The kids needed no further bidding. They scattered like scared quail. In moments, he couldn't see hide nor hair of them. Even Growler was gone, no doubt with the little blond toddler. Travis took a deep breath and began to straighten up his camp. When he looked down the row of wagons, he could see a man with a star on his chest and two deputies walking along, stopping to talk to people. He put on his own Texas Ranger star and tried to look casual as he leaned against a tree. The men were coming this way.

Travis happened to look up and there were little Boo Hoo's drawers flapping in the breeze just above his head. *Oh, Lordy.* He reached up and grabbed them, stuffed them in his vest pocket as the trio sauntered up. "Howdy, Sheriff, what can I do for you?"

The sheriff nodded, held out his hand. "I saw you face down that killer yesterday, Ranger, mighty excitin'!"

Travis blushed, and offered his left hand awkwardly. "Just doin' my job."

"Fastest draw I ever saw," volunteered the short deputy with the gapped teeth.

"Used to be," Travis said before he thought.

"Big shame." The sheriff nodded his white head toward Travis's swollen wrist. "What you intend to do now?"

Travis shrugged. "I don't know, maybe go back to Waco and sit behind a desk, maybe take part in the land run, not quite sure yet."

The fat deputy said, "Those takin' part in the run are already startin' to move up. It's a few miles south and the race starts at noon tomorrow, ya know."

Travis nodded. "Yeah, I was just thinking it over and breaking camp."

"Oh, I know this is a waste of time, but you see anything of some kids?"

Travis looked out over the landscape and reached in his shirt pocket for his makin's. "What kids? Some youngster lost in all this crowd?"

"Oh, some run off from the orphan train—ones that nobody wanted. They was bein' sent back to New York City," the sheriff volunteered.

"That's kinda sad," Travis answered and returned to rolling his smoke.

"Ain't it? Reckon no one wants to live in a big city when they can live in the west. Oh, there's a girl named Violet missin', too, and she might be with them, but I can see they ain't here."

"Now that's a fact." Travis stuck the cigarette in his mouth and scratched a match on the seat of his pants.

"Well, we won't keep you no longer." The sheriff touched the brim of his hat with two fingers. "Good luck to you, Ranger, whatever you decide to do."

"Good luck to you boys, too." Travis nodded and everyone sauntered away.

He leaned against a tree and smoked, watching the lawmen move down the line of camps, stopping to ask about the missing children. So the kids were all rejects that no one wanted. Well, he could understand that. Hadn't he always been the half-breed with two white younger brothers? His parents loved him, but sometimes that didn't make up for always being the outcast everywhere he went.

That's why he'd gone after the prettiest girl in town, Emily, the blond beauty every man wanted. But Emily had made him the butt of ridicule. That's why he became the best pistol shot in the state and a Texas Ranger. People had to look up to him after that. He had the best horse, the finest pistol, everything had to be first-rate. His pride became his armor, but sometimes, he still felt like everyone was laughing at him. And now with his damaged wrist, he wasn't the fastest shot or even a Texas Ranger anymore. He was a half-breed with a bum wrist. He couldn't go back to the ranch; there wasn't enough land to support his brothers' families and him, too.

Travis watched the lawmen walk on down the line and disappear. He finished his smoke and checked his watch. Almost two o'clock. If he was going to take part in the run, he'd better move on south. He didn't know what had happened to the kids; maybe they'd found a family to take them in. At least, they hadn't come back, so they were no longer his responsibility. He began to pack up his camp and saddle the horses. He didn't want to admit he'd kind of miss them all, especially that mouthy young girl with the pretty eyes and soft Southern drawl.

"Are they gone?" Violet peeked out from behind a tree.

Travis turned. "Oh, I thought you kids had found someone else to take you in. Where's my dog?"

"Here." The blond toddler came through the woods, her hand on Growler's head as they walked.

The other three came from a different direction.

"Oh, by the way," Travis said and reached in his pocket, "you almost got tripped up because Boo Hoo's drawers were still hanging in the tree." He held them out.

"Oh, my!" Violet's face colored and she took them and grabbed Boo Hoo's hand. "Here, let's go back in the bushes and put these on, okay?"

"Growler come, too, Feathers?"

"Yes, Growler can come, too," Violet said.

Travis looked at Kessie. "Why does she call her Feathers?"

"I wouldn't have the faintest idea; she's certainly not a bird." Kessie shook her red hair.

Anyway it didn't matter. Here he was almost ready to ride out and all the children were back. They were like wood ticks; he just couldn't shake them. They were determined to stick to him.

Violet came out of the bushes with Boo Hoo and Growler. "Are you going to leave us behind?"

Travis scowled. "We've been through all this already."

The children started crying again and Growler looked like he'd like to bite his owner.

Violet said, "I reckon we'll either starve to death or end up back in that orphanage."

"That ain't my lookout. I'm going on the run."

Big tears started in the blue-violet eyes and ran down her pretty face.

Travis sighed. "Don't cry, honey. Maybe I could help you find someone to adopt you."

She looked hopeful and snuffled.

He reached in his pocket and handed her his bandanna. "Here, blow."

She blew and gave him his bandanna back. "You know, mister, I heard the capital of that new territory is going to be Guthrie. If me and the other kids could get to Guthrie, where there's a new town and lots of new businesses, maybe we could find work."

"I could read to those who can't," Kessie piped up.

"Me and Limpy could clean stables or feed horses," Harold said.

Violet added, "I could probably get housecleaning jobs or maybe work as a cook in a café—"

"You're too young." Travis shook his head. "Besides, a pretty kid like you could get into trouble. There's some bad men in a lawless land that wouldn't care if you're young."

Violet blinked her eyes. "Mr. Prescott, I don't know what you're talking about."

Of course she didn't; she was an innocent child. "Never mind," Travis said. "The problem is getting you kids to Guthrie in the first place."

"If we had a wagon, we could follow you and meet up after you'd staked your claim," Violet said.

"But we don't have a wagon, and I travel alone," Travis reminded her.

She looked up at him, all eager and hopeful. "But we could get a wagon by trading."

"Trading what?" Travis shook his head. "You don't have anything and all I got is two horses."

"That extra one, that Appaloosa, is fine and has the fanciest saddle I ever saw," Violet pointed out.

"Are you loco? That's my spare horse," Travis snapped. "If Mouse gives out, I'm looking for this one to pick up the slack and get me there."

Violet sighed loudly and lowered her head. "Well, come on, kids. I reckon we got no other choice but to move on. Maybe we can find some acorns or scraps other campers left."

"We just had breakfast," Travis reminded her.

She didn't answer, merely motioned all the tearful children to join her and started walking slowly out of the camp, Growler following along next to Boo Hoo.

"Growler, come back here!" Travis called. The dog stopped, looked back at him and continued walking after the bedraggled little group.

Damn, they had taken his whiskey, eaten up his food and caused him to lie to another lawman, and now they were stealing his dog. "Wait a minute!" he yelled. "Maybe I can figure out something."

Violet turned and gave him a sad smile. "We don't want to be any trouble, mister."

"Trouble? Damn it, you've been nothing but trouble since I laid eyes on you."

"I wish you wouldn't swear in front of the children," Violet admonished him.

"Have you always been such a nag?" Travis snapped. "I swear, you're worse than some housewife."

"I'm just trying to look after the children," Violet answered meekly.

Travis's head was splitting and his wrist hurt. "If I find a way to take you to Guthrie, do you promise that'll be the end of my obligation?"

"We promise!" shouted all the children.

"Oh, kind sir," said Violet, "if you can just get us to the capital, we'll find jobs and you'll be done with us."

"I don't see how that little one can hold a job," Travis said and watched Boo Hoo hang on to his dog's neck.

"I'll take her with me," Violet said.

"Now how is a schoolgirl going to look after a toddler?" Travis asked.

"I'll just do the best I can," Violet answered, wiping her eyes.

None of them looked old enough or strong enough to hold jobs, Travis thought, but maybe they had a better chance in Guthrie than they did here.

I'm about to do something I'm going to regret, he thought. "You kids sit down under these trees," Travis ordered, "and I'll go see if I can make a trade for a wagon and team."

Violet watched him reach for the fancy saddle.

"Hey, kid," he said to Limpy, "bring that Appaloosa over here."

Limpy grinned and used his crutch to hobble over and untie the spotted-rumped horse. "I always wanted to be a cowboy and saddle a horse."

"You did, did you? Well, here, I'll show you how." Travis took the horse by the rope. "Now first you grab the horse by the forelock and the bridle in your other hand." He winced suddenly and Violet realized he had forgotten about his damaged wrist.

"Limpy, help him," she said as the Ranger bent over, cursing in pain.

"I can do it myself," the half-breed muttered, but the thin, crippled boy took the bridle from the man's hand and put it on the horse. "That's right." He nodded with approval. "Now throw the blanket up on his back, close to the withers."

Limpy looked blank.

"His shoulders," Travis sighed, "up almost to his neck."

Limpy hesitated, then put the saddle blanket on.

"Great." Travis nodded. "Now the saddle."

However when Limpy tried to lift the saddle, his crutch went out from under his arm and he stumbled and fell. He scrambled to his feet, his face blushing red. "I'm sorry," he said. "I tried; I really tried."

"Yeah, you did, kid," Travis said. "I like a kid who's game."

Harold stepped up and helped Travis lift the saddle onto the Appaloosa's back.

"Now we pull the belly strap tight," Travis said and did so with his left hand. Then he swung up on the Appaloosa.

Violet said, "I'll go with you."

"There's no need." He scowled, looking down at her.

"But you might not come back," she protested.

"I am a Texan and I have given my word to try to get you to Guthrie," he snapped.

"Maybe I can make a better trade," Violet said and held up her hand.

He hesitated and then he took it. He had big strong hands, she thought as he lifted her up lightly behind his saddle. She leaned her face against his broad back and put her arms around his waist. He felt so big and strong and she had a feeling he could take care of a woman. If he would marry her, they could raise these four kids and have one big happy family. But that wasn't today's problem. "Let's go."

He started off riding down the line, feeling her warmth against his back and her small arms around his waist. It unnerved him because it had been awhile since he'd had a woman and this young girl's soft warmth could be felt through his shirt. He reminded himself again that Violet was just a kid, although a pretty one. He didn't like the thought of what might happen to a pretty young innocent like this one if he abandoned her. Now why was that his business?

Well, it wasn't, he assured himself, except as a Texan and a gentleman, he felt honor-bound to protect women and children. Certainly this innocent girl, in spite of her mouthy ways, needed protecting against lustful men.

He rode down the line and came to a small covered wagon.

Violet tapped his arm. "That'll do, stop here."

He craned his neck and looked back over his shoulder into those big eyes. "Don't you think I oughta decide that?"

"I was just saying." She blinked those long eyelashes demurely. "But you're the grown-up."

"Damned right." He dismounted and without thinking, held up his hands to her.

She slid off and he winced. "Oh, I'm so sorry, I forgot about your wrist."

"I know I'm going to regret this, I knew it last night," he whispered between gritted teeth.

A man came out of the covered wagon. Violet stepped forward and gave him her most winning smile. "Oh, mister, you look like the kind of man who's going to win the run tomorrow."

He smiled at her and ran his hand through his graying hair. "Well, honey, I'd like to think so."

Travis stepped up and yanked her back beside him. "Doesn't look like you've got much of a rig to run with."

The man still had his eyes on Violet. "Maybe not, but it's the best I could do."

Travis looked at the ox grazing nearby. "That what you got to pull that wagon? Why, you won't get there 'til next week."

Violet smiled at the man again. "You look like the kind of man who ought to be riding a spirited stallion."

"You think so, honey?" He grinned again at Violet and Travis cleared his throat.

"Now forget about the young lady, mister—?"

"Brown. Clyde Brown." He shook hands with Travis, but his gaze was still on Violet.

"May I call you Clyde?" Violet smiled at him and patted his shoulder.

"You sure can, young lady."

"What she means to say—" Travis began.

"What I meant to say," Violet said, "was it seems like a shame a tough hombre like you has to go in an oxcart when you really belong on a stallion."

"Now you spoke a true fact." The man licked his lips and leered at Violet.

Travis put his big arm around Violet's slim shoulders. "What my little sister means to say, Mr. Brown, is that we just happen to have an extra horse. 'Course it's a fancy Appaloosa with a lot of silver on its saddle, so I reckon that wouldn't interest you."

Violet wiggled out from under Travis's arm. "Oh, I'll wager a fine man like Clyde could handle a spirited stallion, couldn't you, Mr. Brown?"

Clyde reddened with pleasure. "Oh, miss, I can't afford a fancy horse like that one."

"But—" Travis began, but Violet cut him off.

"Now, Clyde, you just mount up there and see what you think."

As Travis watched, dumbfounded, Clyde mounted the stallion and sat there proudly. "Miss, would you like to ride up behind me?"

"No, she wouldn't," Travis snapped, "but let's talk turkey."

The other man frowned. "I don't think I want to talk to you, mister. I want to talk to this young lady about making a deal."

"She's just a girl," Travis protested. "You can't do business with a young girl. Horse trading is men's business."

However, in the end, Clyde did business with Violet and Travis stood there like a wooden cigar-store Indian while the girl cajoled and charmed the man into throwing all his gear into the deal.

When they drove away fifteen minutes later in the ox-drawn covered wagon, Travis complained, "You took everything he had, even the change out of his pockets. Good thing he wasn't wearin' false teeth."

"I could have traded him out of those, too," she said.

"Remind me never to get into a trading deal with you."

"Oh, don't be so huffy," Violet answered. "He's got a much better chance in the run now and we've got a rig that will carry all the kids."

"And leaves me without a spare horse," Travis grumbled.

"Isn't Mouse fast enough for you to race on ahead and get a claim?"

"Maybe," Travis said. "This is just until we reach Guthrie, right?"

She nodded. "Just get us to Guthrie and we'll try to make out on our own."

He glanced sideways at her. She seemed even smaller and more defenseless. He didn't have any confidence that this bunch of children could make it alone, but of course, that wasn't his problem. He had enough of his own. Right now, his wrist was throbbing and he had to clench his teeth to hold back a gasp.

They drove into the camp and all the children ran to meet them.

"An oxcart?" Limpy asked.

Kessie frowned. "Oxen are slow. They can't outrun a turtle."

"How are we going to get a claim on a farm if we're slow?" Harold asked.

"No." Travis shook his head. "No, you don't understand; I'm the one racing for a claim. You all are going to the territorial capital and that's where I leave you."

"Oh." The children all looked downcast and he felt guilty as hell.

Violet said, "Don't worry, kids. Mr. Prescott is going to at least take us that far and it's good of him to do so, isn't it? We can make it on our own."

They all nodded and Travis felt like he'd stolen candy from the baby who was clinging to Growler's neck.

He wished he had a drink to quell the pain. "Look, here's what we do now: let's break camp and head south. I have to be waiting at the starting line by noon tomorrow when the gun goes off."

They gathered up the blankets and pans, and Travis saddled Mouse with the boys helping him. It occurred to him that he could help that crippled kid by making him a shoe that would make the short leg as long as the other, but of course, that wasn't going to be his problem after tomorrow when he left them all at the capital.

Violet got in the wagon seat of the oxcart. "I think I can drive this. Now all you children get in."

They all got in as Travis mounted up on Mouse.

Boo Hoo began to cry. "Doggie, my dog, Feathers."

Violet looked uncertainly up at Travis. "Do you mind?"

"I reckon not. I don't know what the world's coming to when a dog that's walked all over Texas now has to ride in a wagon like a baby carriage."

Violet snapped her fingers at Growler and he hopped up into the wagon and licked the tears off Boo Hoo's little face.

"Damn," Travis muttered. "What have I let myself in for?"

"Mr. Prescott," Violet said primly, "please don't swear in front of the children."

And so they started off south toward the Kansas state line, an injured Texas Ranger on a big gray stallion, and an

ox wagon full of kids with Growler's head poking out the
back as he barked happily.

They arrived at the northernmost starting line down in
Indian Territory about dusk. Travis looked up and down the
long line of wagons and frowned. "My Lord, there must be
thousands of people hoping to get a claim and there aren't
that many available."

"I got faith in you." Violet shrugged and climbed down
from her seat driving the ox wagon. "All out, kids."

She felt such relief at being out of Kansas without being
caught and returned to the Diamond Horseshoe that she
wasn't too worried about the odds of getting a claim. The
big Texas Ranger looked capable and responsible. She was
already thinking he'd make a great husband for some lucky
girl, even though he did have a few rough edges.

He grimaced as if he was in pain as he dismounted.

"Your wrist hurting?"

He nodded. "It's better than it was yesterday. I wish I
had more laudanum."

"Oh, Mr. Brown did have one small bottle of whiskey
in his wagon," she whispered so the tired children now
clambering out of the wagon wouldn't hear. "Have a few
swallows later."

His brown eyes lit up. "Young lady, that's a rip-roarin'
idea."

She turned to the children. "All right, Harold, you and
Kessie pick up sticks for a fire. Limpy, you help me un-
hitch the ox and stake him out to graze, and Boo Hoo . . ."
She looked at the little girl. The baby was already fast
asleep under a tree with Growler curled up next to her.
"Never mind."

The Ranger said, "I think I'll take my rifle and see if I
can get a couple of squirrels or a rabbit or two."

She watched him mount up and ride off. She wasn't sure how things would go from here, but at least she and the children were safely out of Kansas and with these thousands of people spread out as far as she could see, it would be difficult for the law to find four runaway children and a missing saloon girl. Duke would be furious when he got back from St. Louis, but maybe not mad enough to spend a lot of time looking for her. At least if she made it to the new territorial capital, Guthrie, she had a lot of options. Of course, there was still the problem of what to do with these pitiful ragamuffins.

In less than an hour, the Ranger came back with three fat rabbits and Limpy hurried over to help unsaddle the gray stallion. "I love horses," he said, stroking Mouse. "I wish I knew how to ride."

"I'll teach you," the Ranger began, then looked at Violet and stopped.

She remembered then that they were all supposed to make their own ways once they got to Guthrie. "Never mind, honey. Just stake Mouse out in that tall grass over there. Once we get those rabbits cut up and roasted, we'll eat."

All the children gathered around the small fire, their eyes wide with anticipation as Travis cut sticks and showed the children how to put the meat on the sticks and hold them over the fire.

Even little Boo Hoo came awake and toddled over to join them without crying. Violet made a pot of coffee and everyone ate. Then she gave the scraps to Growler.

Travis leaned back against a rock and sipped his coffee. In spite of his throbbing arm, he felt good that he'd managed to bring in enough meat to feed everyone. This must be what it felt like to be a husband and father, he thought, watching the children beginning to doze off on the grass. Of course, he was a confirmed bachelor, he reminded himself, and he'd be rid of the five when he went into Guthrie to file his claim.

Violet watched him, wishing he was her man. She had never felt so safe and secure as she did at this moment. She wanted to curl up next to him as he sat by the fire, but of course she didn't. After tomorrow, she reminded herself, he'd go on his way and she'd be on her own as she had been since she was a small child on the docks at Memphis.

As they sat around the fire sipping coffee, she could see hundreds of campfires along the starting line. All these people had hopes and dreams just like she did.

"Young lady," Travis said softly, "you and these kids had better bed down. Tomorrow is a long day."

She smiled up at him. "I want to thank you for everything you've done for us."

He flushed and stirred uneasily. "It weren't no big deal. You know what they say about us. 'A Texas Ranger knows what's right and goes right ahead on.'"

"Even if the odds are overwhelming?"

"Even if the odds are overwhelming." He nodded.

She wanted to go over to Travis, sit down close and lean back against him, enjoy the fire and the evening with him, but of course she couldn't do that. "We'd better bed down. Tomorrow's the big day."

Travis was up early, thinking about the run into the Unassigned Lands. It was to start at high noon and settlers would rush in from all four sides. The earliest ones in would get the best land, although, there were thousands more settlers than there was available land.

He watched Violet asleep with her arm thrown across little Boo Hoo. His dog lay next to the toddler. The little rascal had completely stolen his dog's heart and turned the grouchy old mutt into a pet. But he couldn't be angry. He had grown used to having these ragtag orphans with him, especially that mouthy one, Violet. *If only she were a few years older . . . What are you thinking?* he scolded himself. *She's just an innocent kid. What you need from women, you can get for a dollar at any passing saloon.* Soon he'd be back to his old ways of riding alone. Solitude suited him just fine.

Violet woke up and yawned, and he thought how cute she was as she scrambled to her feet and began to make coffee. "I didn't mean to sleep so late," she apologized.

He shrugged and sat down by the fire, rolling a cigarette as he watched her hustling around. "No hurry. The gun doesn't go off 'til noon."

"You'll ride in ahead of us?" She looked up at him with those incredible violet eyes.

"Yep, and you can follow with the ox wagon. We'll meet up in Guthrie when I go in to file my claim."

"How will I know how to get to Guthrie?"

"I reckon there'll be signs everywhere."

"Sure." She paused in dishing up some fried eggs for him.

He hesitated. "That's where we part ways, remember?"

She nodded and he swore he saw tears in those big eyes. "Mr. Prescott, you will help me try to find people to take in these children, won't you?"

"That wasn't part of the deal." He thought about total strangers taking in Harold and Kessie. Who would want poor Limpy? And who wanted a toddler who kept wetting her drawers? He'd have to be really careful who he let take Violet. She was too pretty and innocent, and he didn't want any man . . .

Boo Hoo sat up just then, rubbing sleep from her blue eyes. "Doggie goes with me."

"That's my dog," Travis said and then stopped. How in the hell was he going to separate those two?

Violet fed everyone breakfast and then began to clean up the camp. She didn't say much to the Ranger because she didn't know what to say. She wasn't sure what lay ahead in Guthrie, but at least it was better than the life she'd had as a saloon girl back in Kansas. Maybe she would find four nice families to adopt her kids. Her kids. They were beginning to feel like hers.

A couple of hours passed and the whole line of thousands seemed to be restless. The Ranger saddled his horse, and Mouse, as if sensing there was a race ahead, stamped his hooves uneasily.

He and the boys harnessed the ox and hooked it up to the wagon. Then he mounted Mouse and Violet walked over and looked up at him. "All right, you get a claim and we'll see you in Guthrie late this afternoon."

The young girl looked so vulnerable staring up at him that his heart went out to her. What kind of job could a pretty young thing like that get in a rough, wild, lawless new town? He didn't even want to think about it. Maybe he could find a preacher's family to take her in. He didn't even want to admit to himself that he felt responsible for her. He touched his fingers against the brim of his Stetson by way of farewell and yelled to the children, "See you in Guthrie this afternoon!" Then he whistled to Growler. "You going with me, boy?"

The dog hesitated, ran to him, then turned and raced back to the blond toddler. Boo Hoo put her arms around the dog's neck and he licked her face. Damn it, he knew now he'd lost his dog for good. He had never felt as lonely as he did at this moment.

Violet had gathered everyone up and was loading them in the wagon. "Good luck, Mr. Prescott."

"Good-bye." All the children waved to him.

"See you in Guthrie." He had mixed feelings about riding away and leaving them, but people were starting to gather along the starting line where the cannon was. Some had fine horses, some drove buggies or wagons. There were even several on foot or riding bicycles.

Damn, he should have hung on to that extra horse, it would have given him an advantage when Mouse tired out. He cursed himself for a soft-hearted fool for taking responsibility for all these children.

He had to hold Mouse back as the line straightened out and soldiers made ready to fire the cannon; the gray stallion was ready to race.

Then the gun boomed and with a cheer, the crowd of thousands was off, racing for free land in the Indian Territory.

Chapter 5

When the cannon boomed, Travis dug his heels into Mouse's sides and they were off like a shot. However there was no need to urge the big gray forward. Mouse liked to run and his long legs drummed like pistons across the flat prairie. Around them, dust swirled up like a brown cloud from thousands of other horses. To Travis, it seemed like the noise of all the shouting people, running horses and rolling wagons reverberated like thunder.

Where would the best land be? Maybe somewhere in the middle of the staked-out ground because the western-most areas were more apt to be without streams of water, land not good or rich enough to graze cattle or horses. The easternmost land would be covered in the scrub oak trees that grew from Texas on north. He'd been over this ground years ago during cattle drives with his adopted father, Colt.

He looked behind him as he rode. His big horse was already outrunning most of the line. He heard a shout as a racing buggy hit a gopher hole and turned over, spilling a man out onto the grass. Then a team of mules stopped and refused to move farther, hee-hawing in indignation as the irate driver cracked his whip over their heads.

The people running on foot were easily being left behind in the blowing dust. There were good horses galloping all around him as men rode the race of their lives, hoping to win a farm.

Travis's wrist was throbbing again, but he ignored it. He'd been in worse pain than this often over his career as a lawman. How many times had he been shot or stabbed and survived to fight again another day with nothing but a few scars to show for it?

The April day was warm and the prairie grass grew tall and green as he raced on. Scarlet Indian paintbrush and other wildflowers bloomed across the grasslands as he rode. It seemed quiet now that he was leaving the others behind. Somewhere in the distance, he heard a train whistle and knew that other settlers were riding the train into the Unassigned Lands, hoping to be able to jump off and stake a claim as the train slowed. He tried to imagine all the thousands of eager people coming in from all four sides of the Indian Lands, hoping to stake a claim for free farms.

Mouse was lathered and blowing now, and Travis slowed to a walk as he rode. He didn't want free land bad enough to ride his beloved horse to death, although he figured there were greedy men out there willing to kill their mounts to win this race.

It seemed quiet, although he could still hear shouts and running horses far behind him. Where did he want to stake a claim? He reined in and looked around. Up ahead was a green valley with a creek and a shady spot with dozens of big cottonwood trees; the perfect place to build a ranch house.

He rode forward, happy that now he'd have his own ranch. His folks' place was already crowded with his two younger brothers and their families. There was a big piece of land for sale next to theirs, but of course he didn't have any money to buy it. Well, he'd start his spread right here in the Indian Territory.

He grinned as he reined in, stepped down, reaching for his claim flag in his saddlebags, And then a man stepped out of a soddy built into the bank of the creek. "Hey, mister, I already got this place claimed."

Travis stared at him with disbelief. "You couldn't possibly have gotten here before I did. I've got one of the fastest horses in the race."

Then a thin, ragged woman came out of the shoddy, followed by six of the skinniest, dirtiest children Travis had ever seen. "Please, mister," she begged. "We need this land. We ain't got nothin.'"

Sooners. "Oh, I get it," Travis grumbled. "You sneaked in here before the gun sounded and staked this land."

The bearded man looked shame-faced and hung his head. "We didn't mean to do nothing wrong. We just need a farm so bad, and we only had one old mule, so we knew we couldn't compete. Please don't create no trouble for us, mister."

Travis looked them over and hesitated. This was the poorest, hungriest family he'd ever seen. He could make a fuss at the Land Office in Guthrie and probably get them thrown off this claim and he could have it. Did he need a ranch that bad?

"Please, mister," the woman whined again. "This is the only chance we got."

"You been in to Guthrie to file your claim?" Travis asked. He could still own this land.

The man shook his head and stubbed his worn shoe in the dirt. "I was afraid to leave my family alone, afraid some rough fellows might come along, and you know."

Travis looked at the woman. She might have once been pretty, but time and a hard life had worn her down. Still there were desperate men who would take advantage of a situation like this. What should he do? Well, there was only one thing an honorable Texan could do.

He said to the oldest boy who looked like he was about fourteen. "Son, you all got a rifle?"

The dirty-faced urchin nodded. "An old one, but no bullets."

"Now you do." Travis reached into his saddlebags and tossed him a handful. "You look after the family and I'll give your dad a ride into Guthrie to file his claim."

The whole family looked surprised.

The man said, "You'd do that?"

"I'm a Texan. Even though you're breakin' the law, I can't fault you, knowing how bad you need this farm. I'll give you a ride to the Land Office and you can catch a ride back. There'll be wagons comin' this way."

The woman started crying. "God bless you, sir."

Travis shrugged, embarrassed. "Don't take on so, ma'am. Can you and the kids get along for a day or two until your man gets back?"

She nodded. "Josh and me'll hold off any claim jumpers."

"Ain't you gonna keep racing?" a young girl asked.

Travis shook his head. "I reckon by now most of the good land is gone and my horse is tired. Come on, mister." Travis mounted up. He reached his hand down to the ragged farmer and lifted him up behind him. They stopped at the creek to let the horse drink and then Travis started north at a walk.

So he had lost his chance at a claim. Funny, he didn't much care. He probably could still get some land that wasn't so good or a town lot, but that didn't interest him.

The man didn't say much as they rode and finally came into Guthrie. It was a wild, confused scene of tents and shacks being hammered together along a crooked dirt path that was meant to be a street. Uniformed soldiers rode

about to keep the peace. Already saloons and eateries
had set up with nothing more than a couple of boards set
up over barrels and a piece of canvas stretched to keep the
sun off.

Travis yelled at a passing soldier. "Hey, where's the
Land Office?"

The blue-coated soldier pointed down the row of tents.
"Can't miss it."

"Much obliged." Travis nodded his thanks and started
riding through the crowded streets. The Land Office had a
long line out in front and soldiers to keep order. He reined
in and let the skinny farmer slide off. "Well, here you go.
You got enough to pay the fee?"

"Yep." The man reached up to shake Travis's hand. "Just
barely got it. Can't thank you enough, stranger."

"You got anything for groceries?"

The man hesitated. "We're makin' out all right."

Travis dug in his pocket. "Here's a dollar. I ain't got
much more than that. Buy a few potatoes and some canned
milk to take back to those kids."

"I can't take your charity. You already done enough."
The man backed away, protesting.

Travis reached over and stuck the dollar in the man's
torn shirt pocket. "I insist. For the kids."

"Thank you kindly." The man's eyes teared up.

"Now get in that line and get your claim registered,"
Travis ordered and turned Mouse around, rode away.

The street was dusty and full of bustling people, some
of them camping and building fires right where others
were hammering boards together. "Is there a creek around
here?" He grabbed a passing farmer.

"Thata way." The farmer pointed. "Otherwise, you got
to buy it by the glass."

Travis saw the sign then: DIP OF WATER 50C. *Outrageous,*

he thought as he headed toward the creek. The sign said: COTTONWOOD CREEK.

There were families camped along the stream. Some of them looked sad and discouraged. As he let Mouse drink his fill, he said to a dispirited old man sitting on the bank, "You didn't get a claim?"

The old man shook his head. "They said there was three times as many people as there was land claims. I just wasn't fast enough. How about you?"

Travis hesitated, then took off his hat and splashed his face with the cool water. He wasn't about to tell about the poor Sooner family. "Me, neither." He took a long drink from the creek and put his hat back on.

He heard gunfire from the center of the makeshift town. "Sounds like some of the boys are already getting liquored up."

The old man nodded. "Reckon by dark, it'll be wild and wooly, even saloon girls coming in on the train, I hear. Don't think the soldiers will be able to keep a lid on it."

"Maybe not." Travis nodded and led his horse away from the creek. It might be hours before little Violet and the kids showed up here in Guthrie. He didn't really owe her anything; he could just ride on south to Texas. What he was going to do once he got there, he wasn't sure, but it was evident there was nothing for him here.

His wrist throbbed and he took Mr. Brown's small bottle out of his saddlebag and took a long drink. He heard gunfire again as he walked toward the center of the town of tents and instant shacks being constructed. At one tent, they already had a roulette wheel set up and scantily clad girls stood outside, urging men to come inside.

"Hey, honey." A painted girl with dyed yellow hair grabbed his arm. "Why don't you come in? I can show you a real good time."

"I bet you could." He shrugged her off and kept walking.

She had made him think of Emily. He gritted his teeth, hating loose women and everything they represented.

Yes, the old man was right; by dark, this instant town might be out of control, men drunk, guns firing, pickpockets working the crowd and fights in the street. Not a good place to leave a young girl and a bunch of kids to fend for themselves. Besides he wanted his dog back. He'd at least stay here until Violet arrived. Maybe he could try to help place all the children with decent people, if there were any in this wild mob. Travis found a big oak with some shade, staked Mouse out to graze and lay down in the grass, pulled his hat over his eyes. He was dog-tired. He'd sleep awhile and then start watching for the ox wagon.

It was almost dark when he felt a small foot nudge him gently. "Hey, Mr. Prescott, how'd you do in the run?"

He sat up and blinked. Looking down at him was the young girl and all the kids. "I was wondering when you'd get here," he said, stretched and stood up.

"Did you get a claim?" Kessie asked while Limpy stroked Mouse's nose and talked to the horse.

He was ashamed. He felt he'd failed at his responsibility. "No, I didn't. It's a long story that I don't want to talk about."

"You didn't?" Violet exclaimed. "You had such a fast horse."

"Yeah, but someone else needed the land worse than I did."

"You gave it away?" Harold looked up at him with big almond eyes.

"Well, sort of." He stared at Violet and something told him she understood without telling her. "So here we all are. Judging from what I've seen of this crowd, I'm not sure we can find enough good people to take all you kids."

Boo Hoo began to cry and hugged Growler's neck. "No, no, don't want a new family."

Travis shrugged helplessly at Violet. "Young lady, I've kept my promise to get you all to Guthrie. I doubt anyone's looking for you here. Now let's look around and see if we can find homes."

She looked crestfallen. "All right. There's bound to be some good people in this crowd."

They started walking, Violet leading the ox wagon and Travis leading his horse. Growler followed along behind as Harold carried Boo Hoo.

They passed a man building a house. He looked like a family man, Travis thought. He stopped. "Mister, would you like to adopt Harold here?" He put his hand on the boy's shoulder.

"An Oriental kid? Now why would I want him?" the red-faced man sneered. "There's a laundry being built down the block—Chinese, I think. Take him down there."

Harold drew himself up proudly. "I don't intend to do laundry. I want to be a doctor or a scientist."

The man laughed. "And he's fresh, besides. Get used to the idea, you little Chink, all your future is laundry or running an opium den."

"Why you—!" Travis drew back his fist, but Violet grabbed his arm.

"No, Mr. Prescott, let's not get into a fight. We'll find better people."

They kept walking.

Violet said, "Now there's a nice-looking couple. Maybe they'd like a little girl."

Travis looked. They were an older couple and perhaps a prosperous one. The man had muttonchop sideburns and wore a gold pocket watch and chain, and the lady wore a fancy bonnet. They walked over to them.

"Excuse me." Travis took off his hat. "We're trying to find a home for this baby girl. Wouldn't you like to have her?"

Boo Hoo burst into tears and hugged Growler's neck.

"Why the poor little thing," the woman clucked sympathetically. "Why, she's so sweet and we don't have any children. What do you think, Horace?"

Horace looked down at the crying child. "Yes, the poor little thing looks like she could use a home." He reached to take Boo Hoo's hand and she promptly kicked him in the shins so that he backed away.

Violet said, "She's tired, that's all."

"Not go without doggie," Boo Hoo wept.

The woman wrinkled her nose. "The dog? That scruffy mutt? We have to take the dog, too?"

"Now just a minute," Travis said. "Growler is a good dog and smart, too."

The woman made a face. "I can't stand dogs."

"Doggie, my doggie," Boo Hoo wept. "Feathers, don't make me go."

Immediately Violet knelt and gathered the sobbing child into her arms. "They'd give you a nice home, honey."

"No, no, no!" Boo Hoo screamed and now people were turning to look at the scene she was making.

Limpy came forward. and looked up at Travis, tears in his dark eyes. "Please, Mr. Ranger, don't let them take her."

"We'll give her a good home," Horace said.

By now all the children were gathered around Boo Hoo as if to protect her and Growler bared his teeth at the prosperous would-be parents.

"My heavens!" gasped the woman. "And the dog is a vicious beast!"

"Never mind," Travis said and bent over and picked up

Boo Hoo with his good arm. "I don't think you're the right people to adopt this little girl."

Boo Hoo put her arms around his neck and sobbed. Travis sighed. Her drawers were wet again.

He looked down at Violet and she smiled up at him. "Thank you," she whispered.

They all started walking.

"Well, hell," Travis muttered, "this ain't gonna be as easy as I thought."

"Please don't swear in front of the children," Violet said primly.

Behind him, he heard the defeated voice of Limpy. "We told you we was rejects. None of these people really want us."

Violet patted his thin shoulder as he hobbled along on his crutch. "I'm sure that's not true. We just haven't found the right families yet."

It was dark now and a rowdy, drunken cowboy galloped down the street, shouting and shooting his pistol in the air.

"This is going to be a rough town for a while," Travis grumbled, "in spite of the army. There's too many people to keep corralled."

Boo Hoo had gone to sleep against his shoulder. They walked past a tent where a small piano banged away and girls with too little clothes and too much paint on their faces tried to beckon him in. "Hey, big boy, we know how to show a guy like you a good time."

Travis brushed them off and turned to look down into Violet's fresh young face. "Don't look, young lady. Them's bad women and you're too innocent to know about the likes of them."

Violet looked up at him, feeling her cheeks burn. If he only knew her background . . . but of course he didn't and she wanted to keep it that way. She could probably go to work in that very tent at top wages and make more than enough to look after these four orphans, but what kind of a life would that be? Besides, it wouldn't include Travis Prescott. "I'll bet I could get a job there, maybe serving sandwiches or something." She looked up at him.

"Sandwiches?" he snorted. "That's not what they're selling. That's no place for an innocent kid like you. Now come on, let's get away from here."

In truth, if he didn't have these five kids with him, he'd welcome a drink and a hand of cards and maybe a few minutes on the cot with one of these painted whores, but he had little money and five responsibilities.

They walked the length of the town, looking over people they might consider letting adopt the children, but the more Travis looked, the worse all these people seemed to him. He couldn't imagine letting any of them have these kids. These were special kids and he decided none of these settlers was good enough to give them homes.

They had walked a long way. Boo Hoo was still asleep on his shoulder with Growler following patiently behind and Violet and the kids, Mouse and the ox wagon still trailing along.

They passed another makeshift saloon, and a cowboy stumbled out and tipped his hat to Violet. "Hello, there, baby, let me buy you a drink." He grabbed her wrist.

Travis stopped and glared down at him. "Listen, hombre, you let go of that innocent young lady or I'll wipe up this street with you!"

The man seemed to take one look at the size and expression of Travis and backed away. "Sorry, mister, I didn't know it was your daughter."

"He was harmless," Violet protested to Travis.

"Drunks need to keep their hands off nice girls," Travis growled.

"I'm hungry," Kessie said, chewing her nails.

"So am I," Harold echoed.

Travis stopped and looked at all of them. In the darkness, he could see how exhausted and hungry they all were.

Violet shrugged helplessly. "I'm sorry, Mr. Prescott. I really thought we'd find our own way and you wouldn't have to mess with us after today. I reckon you've done your part and can ride on."

"It's all right," he answered gently. "I ain't giving these kids to just anybody. These are really special kids and you all deserve better. Anyway we don't have to worry about it right now. Let's go to the creek and maybe catch some fish and bed down for the night."

"But I promised you once we got to Guthrie—"

"That's okay." He patted her shoulder gently. "Miss Violet, you're doing the best you can and it's a heavy load for a young girl. We'll camp and see what we can do about food."

They turned and he led them all to Cottonwood Creek.

"Limpy, you stake out Mouse and the ox, and Violet, will you take Boo Hoo? She needs dry drawers."

"Oh, dear." Violet took her and laid her in the ox wagon.

"Start a fire," Travis said, "and I'll see if the boys and I can catch some fish."

Kessie cocked her fiery red head. "You'll have to catch a bunch to feed this crowd."

"Maybe I can rustle up something else," Violet said.

"Don't get too far from camp," Travis warned her as he took some fishing line out of his saddlebags. "There's bad men who'd take advantage of a sweet, decent girl and I don't want to have to kill anyone or beat him up tonight. My hand's still too tender."

She had never had a man offer to fight for her. They had

fought over her, but never for her. "I'll be careful." She smiled at him.

"Kessie, you watch after Boo Hoo, and boys, come along and I'll teach you how to fish. You ever fish before?"

Both boys shook their heads.

"You need to learn a lot of things, seems like," Travis scolded. "There's just things men need to know."

"Is that stuff Texas Rangers know?" Limpy asked.

"Sure 'nuff." Travis nodded. "Did you know the first Rangers wore stars made out of Mexican five cinco silver pesos?"

"Really?" Harold asked as they walked.

They went down to the creek where Travis showed them how to catch grasshoppers and bait a hook. They returned half an hour later with a string of catfish and perch. Travis noted Boo Hoo's drawers were hanging from a nearby bush and Violet had a fire going and potatoes frying along with a pot of coffee boiling.

"Boy howdy." Travis grinned. "Where'd you get the extra grub?"

She hesitated. "I figured it was an emergency—the kids were hungry."

"Kids are always hungry," Travis said as he began to clean the fish and all the kids gathered around to watch. "Here, Limpy, take over. My wrist hurts."

"I don't know how," the crippled boy protested.

"Well, it's time you learned. Cleaning fish is something a man learns young. Now, young lady, where'd you get the potatoes and milk? I hope you didn't steal them; that ain't honest."

"Well, if you must know, I traded your last little bottle of whiskey for the potatoes and some canned milk for Boo Hoo." Violet took a deep breath for courage.

He glared at her. "You did what?"

"Now, Mr. Prescott, you can always get more whiskey—"

"I'm pretty much out of money," Travis snapped.

"Is whiskey more important than milk for a baby?" Violet stood her ground.

Travis hesitated, then laughed. "Kid, you remind me of my mother. She's spirited, too. I reckon she'd say I was makin' too big a thing of it. You're right. Boo Hoo needs milk."

"I got a little cornmeal, too," Violet said, "so I'm making hush puppies to go with the fish."

"You're right handy and resourceful," Travis said. "About like a Texas girl."

"Well, I'm a Southern girl from Memphis, I reckon it's almost the same."

He looked at his wrist and winced. "Take over then. The boys about got the fish cleaned."

"Then what?"

He shrugged. "I reckon it's too late to make decisions tonight. We'll sleep and then decide what to do tomorrow."

Little Boo Hoo stuck her sleepy head out of the wagon. "Stay with Travis," she whimpered. "Stay with Travis and Growler."

"Don't say anything that will make her start crying," Violet warned. "Hey, honey, we'll have some food in a minute."

Boo Hoo toddled over and climbed up on Travis's knee. She was wet, but he didn't move her.

"I want to look at your wrist after supper," Violet said.

"It's still sore as a pincushion, but it's quit swelling," Travis answered. "I reckon I'll never be able to shoot worth a damn again—"

"No cuss." Little Boo Hoo shook her finger in Travis's face.

"I forgot," Travis said. "Sorry."

The toddler leaned her small face against his wide chest.

Violet smiled at him as she breaded the fish and put it in the skillet. "You look like you're used to having a kid in your lap."

"Not hardly," he snorted. "Of course Boo Hoo is special."

"We ought to give her a better name," Violet said as she cooked.

"Growler," lisped the toddler.

"The dog's already got that name, honey," Travis explained.

Violet paused. "What about Bonnie? That was my mother's name."

"Where is your mother?" Travis asked.

Tears came to Violet's eyes. "She's dead."

"Tough luck," Travis's deep voice was sympathetic. "I don't know what I'd do without my ma. She'd like you, young lady."

Violet merely smiled and continued poking the frying fish. "So it's Bonnie then?"

"Sounds good to me." Travis smiled. "What do you think, kids?"

Boo Hoo laughed. "Bonnie. I'm Bonnie."

"That settles that." Travis nodded.

The young girl had pulled the crisp fish out of the skillet and fried her hush puppies. They didn't have much in the way of dinnerware, but they managed. Everyone dived in and there was plenty. Travis leaned back against a tree and watched them all eat. He couldn't remember a time he'd felt so satisfied and here he was stuck with five needy orphans and not the slightest idea what to do with them. Maybe in the morning he'd find some good families or a preacher to look after them. After that, he'd figure out what to do about his future, now that he was too disabled to be a Texas Ranger.

In the morning, as daylight broke and Violet poured coffee, he made a decision. "I saw some people building a church last night; I'm taking you all there."

Kessie's homely little face crumpled. "We're just getting used to you, Mr. Prescott."

Violet sighed and kept making biscuits. "Mr. Prescott is a Ranger, kids, and needs to get back to Texas."

Boo Hoo, now Bonnie, wrapped her arms around Growler's neck so tightly Travis thought she might choke the dog to death.

"Violet's right," he said as he sipped his coffee. "I'm a bachelor and got no use for a ready-made family. That preacher will find you all good homes."

No one said anything. Travis felt so guilty he could hardly eat. He knew he'd made the right decision, but then, why did he feel so bad?

After breakfast, they packed up the oxcart and Travis told the boys to put out the fire. "Man's got to know about putting out campfires," he said. "Otherwise, you might start a prairie fire."

"I reckon we'll never need to know that now," Harold said as he poured a bucket of water on the flames.

"That's always good to know," Travis insisted. "Now stir the ashes and make sure it's out."

Finally everyone was ready to leave. Travis mounted up. "It was down this way." He led off with the oxcart following him. He tried not to listen, but he could hear little Bonnie sobbing in the background.

Two blocks away, he came to the people building the church. Travis dismounted and approached the honest-looking man holding a hammer. "You the preacher here?"

"I am, brother." The man held out his hand and Travis shook it with his left hand.

"I've got these here five orphans I need help finding homes for." He turned and gestured toward the group standing by the wagon.

"Where'd you get them?"

Travis hesitated. "I found them in Kansas, they'd got separated from their folks some years back."

"A shame." The preacher nodded.

"Yep, and I'm on my way to Texas. I was wondering if I could leave them with you and maybe you could find homes for them?"

"I might could," the preacher said.

Travis took a deep breath. "Then it's settled. I'd give you some money, but I don't have any."

"That's all right, brother, the Lord will provide. Come on, you kids." He gestured. "My wife and I have a big tent you can move into."

Travis mounted up and reined his horse around, passing the children, who all looked up at him. There were tears in their eyes. Well, they would get over it. They were too young to know that they'd be better off with this preacher's family than tagging along with an injured Ranger who didn't know where his next meal was coming from.

As he passed Boo Hoo, she held up her arms to him, sobbing, and Growler barked and ran up and down as if not sure what to do.

He reined in and nodded to the oldest girl. "Good-bye, Violet. I hope you find a good home with lots of other young girls."

Tears ran down her face, but she managed to nod.

"Come on, Growler," he yelled and started off at a walk. Behind him, he heard Growler bark and little Boo Hoo sobbing, "No! No! Doggie! Doggie!"

He paused and looked behind him. He was a lonely man with little company but his horse and his dog, and now a toddler claimed his dog. Travis had never felt as alone as he did at this moment looking back at five children sobbing behind him.

"Oh, hell!" he muttered and reined Mouse around, headed back to the preacher. "I've changed my mind. I'm taking them to Texas with me."

"But they'd be better off here where I could find them good homes, brother."

He hesitated. "I know, but none of them look happy about it and besides, I've gotten used to having them along. I'll find them homes myself in Texas."

The children set up a cheer, and Growler barked and scampered up and down.

Violet came over to him. "Mr. Prescott, you're pretty soft for a Texas Ranger."

"Hell, I know it. Now get them kids in the wagon and moving before I come to my senses and change my mind."

"What are you going to do with us?" Violet called back as she scurried to obey.

He shrugged. "I'd take you and let Ma raise you, but the ranch won't support another family."

Violet couldn't contain her happiness. "You're gonna keep us all?"

"I didn't say I was gonna keep you." He shook his head. "What's a bachelor gonna do with five kids?"

Violet felt her spirits fall. "I was just hoping—"

"I figure once we get back to Texas, I'll draw the rest of my pay to keep you kids awhile. I'll bet my ma knows a lot of people and I'll get her to find homes for all of you."

"Yes, sir." Violet's heart sank. She had decided she wanted this man for her own and she wasn't about to be adopted. Either way, sooner or later, her age would come out and he'd be furious that she'd fooled him.

She didn't know how she'd manage it yet, but this Ranger wasn't getting rid of her. She intended to stick tighter than a cockle burr to him. She'd decided they belonged together.

Chapter 6

Travis started off south on his stallion with the kids in the oxcart singing behind him.

"Now that was a damn-fool thing to do," he scolded himself. "What in hell is a banged-up Ranger gonna do with five kids?"

Growler ran along next to him, barking happily. "Well, at least someone thinks everything's fine," he addressed the dog. "Was you really gonna desert me for a little girl?"

He reckoned he'd never know. He liked being in control and as a Texas Ranger, he usually was, but in four days, he'd gotten hurt, maybe permanently, collected five kids and an oxcart, lost his chance to claim a farm, and was now headed to Texas with little money and no idea what to do next.

Somehow, he didn't mind so much except his swollen wrist was throbbing again. Maybe that doctor was wrong. He could only hope.

Behind him, driving the oxcart, Violet called, "Thank you, Mr. Prescott."

"Don't thank me yet," he yelled. "I'm still thinking how loco I am. I ought to take you all back."

"Don't say that too loud, you'll have Boo Hoo—I mean, Bonnie—crying again."

"Oh, Lord, I hope not." He grinned to himself as he rode south, the oxcart bumping along behind. Actually, it felt good to have a little company, he'd been alone so long.

For the next few days, they headed south toward the Red River and paused to camp and cook whatever Travis could shoot or catch fish in a stream.

"Boys ought to learn to shoot," he announced at the campfire one night.

"What about girls?" Kessie asked. "Don't you believe in equal rights?"

He grinned. "You think you're big enough to handle a rifle, missy?"

Violet looked up from her cooking. "Oh, Mr. Prescott, I don't think a little girl should—"

"Well, now, if she's gonna be a Texan, she needs to handle a firearm. Who do you think stood off the Comanches out on those ranches when the men were away fighting the Mexicans and the Yankees?"

"I reckon you're right," Violet said.

"Me too! Me too!" said Bonnie.

Travis picked her up with his good arm. "Now young'un, you're too little. Wait a while."

Harold made a face. "I'm not interested in guns and stuff like that. I've decided I want to be a doctor, a scientist or an inventor."

Violet smiled at him. "What are you gonna invent?"

"What about a horseless carriage or a flying machine?" Harold said. "Somebody's gonna do it sooner or later."

Limpy snorted. "There'll never be a flying machine."

"Oh, I don't know about that." Travis leaned back against a tree and rolled a cigarette. "They've got those telephone things some places and I heard about lights that come on without putting kerosene in a lamp."

"See?" said Harold triumphantly.

"And girls are gonna get equal rights and do stuff, too," Kessie declared, "starting with voting."

"Voting, voting," babbled Bonnie.

Travis yawned and watched Violet. She was young, but sometimes, her face and expression looked older, more mature. He'd grown to like her. He wished she was older.

Why, you dirty bastard, he scolded himself. *You've been too long without a woman. Next time you hit a town, you need to find a whorehouse.* He didn't have much money. He shook his head. He was skilled enough with women that oftentimes, whores would make love to him for free.

They reached the Red River and he reined in and nodded to the kids. "The old Red lives up to her name. Look at that water, red as blood, and she's got quicksand, too."

Limpy hobbled to the river's edge and looked up at him. "How did you know?"

"I've done a few cattle drives through here with my dad many years ago," Travis explained.

"I'd like to be a cowboy," Limpy said. "But I guess with my bad leg, I don't have a chance."

"A man who can handle a horse don't need two good legs when the horse has four good ones," Travis assured him. "No cowman walks when he can ride."

"Will you teach me?" Limpy's dark eyes looked hopeful.

"Sure, I'll teach you as much as I can, until I find you a home."

Limpy's thin face fell. "I keep forgetting you're gonna give us away."

Now it was Travis's turn to feel sad and guilty. "Not unless I find you a really good home," he promised.

Violet got out of the oxcart and came over to stand beside his horse. "How do we get across?"

"There's places where there's no quicksand," Travis assured her. "Don't worry, little lady. I'll get you and the other kids across okay."

She looked up at him and he thought how beautiful those smoky blue eyes were. "Okay, Travis, I trust you."

At this moment, she almost seemed like a woman, the way she looked at him, and he reminded himself she was just an orphaned kid.

"There's a place downstream, and since we haven't had much rain, there'll be some dry spots in the riverbed."

He dismounted. "First we got to get the wagon where it'll float. Then Violet, you ride Mouse across and I'll drive the wagon."

"I—I'm not a very good rider." She looked scared.

"Mouse is a good horse, trust him." Travis stood looking down at her, and she looked so small and soft.

"Well, I trust you, so I'll do it."

"Good." He dismounted and put his hands on her small waist, hesitated, looking into her eyes. She put her little hands on his broad chest.

For a minute, she thought he was going to kiss her, the way he hesitated, and she wanted him to, but that would make a mess of things.

Limpy shouted, "You two gonna stand there all day?"

Travis jerked as if his mind was far away, and then he lifted her up into the saddle. "You don't weigh as much as a newborn colt," he murmured.

The touch of his big, capable hands had unnerved her and she hadn't wanted to leave his embrace. "You'd— you'd better get Bonnie."

He nodded and stepped away from the gray stallion. "Sure. She can ride over with you. I'll bring the cart."

"Isn't it heavy?" she asked. "Isn't it liable to sink?"

He shook his head. "We'll make sure it don't. Come on, boys, find me a couple of dead trees and we'll lasso them to each side of the wagon and float it across."

As Violet watched, the big Ranger pointed out two sturdy dead trees and the three dragged them over and tied them to each side of the wagon.

Then he spoke to the kids. "Boys, hang on to the sides of the wagon in case we run into quicksand. I'll lead the ox." He took big strides across the sand to the oxcart and took Bonnie in his arms.

"Doggie," she whimpered, looking back. "Doggie."

"Growler will be fine, honey," he assured her as he carried her over and put her in the saddle ahead of Violet.

"Mr. Prescott, be careful." Violet took the toddler.

"I'll be all right, I've crossed the Red before."

He walked back to the oxcart. "Kessie, you stay inside with the dog and I'll lead the ox across."

"I'm not afraid," the red-haired child declared.

"Good, that's a Texas girl. Now you just stay calm. The wagon will float, and if the current don't get us, we'll be across and safe."

Growler began to bark.

Kessie said, "I'm not sure I can keep him in here."

"Just hold on to him, he doesn't need to try to swim the river," Travis warned.

He turned and watched Violet knee the horse and start off into the water, holding on to little Bonnie.

She was a brave kid, Travis thought. Someday she'd make some lucky Texan a good wife and be the mother of some fine cowboys and Rangers.

"Keep moving," he yelled. "Don't stop and bog down."

He watched, holding his breath, and after a long moment, the gray stallion had crossed the water and walked out on the other side.

He looked back at Kessie holding on to the barking dog.

"All right, redhead, we'll cross now." He took off his boots and tossed them into the wagon, then he grabbed the ox by the halter and tried to lead it into the water. It stopped, not wanting to go. The boys looked at him expectantly.

Oh hell, now what was he gonna do? He stepped out into the knee-deep red water, and dragged the ox in by the sheer strength of his left hand. He was afraid to stress his right hand yet, even though he thought it was healing.

He was waist deep now, the ox swimming and the wagon floating, a boy on each side holding on to the logs.

"Hang on, redhead," he yelled and then the bottom gave way and he was swimming, and urging the ox forward into the dark current. The water was cold as death and red as blood, he thought as he swam. He remembered many a good cowboy had lost his life crossing this river. He saw Violet's anxious face on the other side and she yelled encouragement even as Growler pulled out of Kessie's arms and jumped into the water, swimming along beside him.

Bonnie screamed and began to cry as the dog began to float downstream. "Doggie! My doggie!"

"Dammit, Growler, you stupid mutt!" Travis cursed at him, but he couldn't stop now, he had to lead the oxcart across. He swam as hard as he could to make the other side while Bonnie cried and the dog fought the current. Then his feet touched bottom and he took a deep gulp of air, knowing he was almost safe.

"Here, boys, take over!" he yelled as the ox came up on the far bank, dripping water, and Travis turned and plunged back into the river, going in to save his dog. "Damn you, Growler, why don't you stay where you're put?"

The dog tried to swim toward him, but the current was pulling the brave little mongrel downstream. Travis made a mighty effort and grabbed the dog, then turned back toward the distant shore. He could see all the kids now, watching him with fear and concern. It occurred to him that if he drowned, he'd be leaving five helpless kids out here on the prairie alone, and that spurred him on.

Now Violet had dismounted and grabbed a lasso off his saddle and tried to throw the loop into the stream.

"Boys, help her!" Travis choked on the dirty water, hung on to his dog and kept battling toward the shore.

At his command, Limpy grabbed the rope, made a loop and tossed it. It came up short.

The shore seemed farther away and he realized the current was pulling him downstream. He hadn't realized how tired he was. Any other man might let go of the dog and save himself, but Growler was his buddy and he would rescue the spotted mutt or die trying.

Limpy made another loop and tossed it. This time, it landed in front of Travis and he managed to grab it, loop it over his body.

As he fought the current, Violet urged the big stallion to back up and the slack went out of the loop. Travis was fast running out of energy, but the lasso tightened around him and dragged him toward the shore. Finally he felt his feet touch bottom and he let go of the dog and fell into the shallow water and lay there, breathing hard.

Growler licked his face with a warm, wet tongue.

"You stupid mutt," he gulped. "You 'bout got us drowned."

Bonnie ran forward to put her chubby arms around the dog, who rewarded her by shaking his wet coat and getting everyone wet.

Violet backed up the horse and loosened the lasso. "Are you all right?"

He closed his eyes as she wiped his wet hair from his eyes. "I think so, just cold."

"I'll make some coffee."

"Sounds like a great idea," he gasped as he stood up, stepped out of the loop and stumbled over to sit under a tree. "Welcome to Texas," he announced. "I reckon this is as far as we go today."

Limpy used his crutch to hobble over to him. "Are you okay, Mr. Prescott?"

Travis grinned at him. "Call me Travis. You got the makings of a real cowboy."

"With a name like Limpy?"

Travis leaned back against the tree. "You're right. I think you deserve a new name, a Texas name. Let me think about it. Myself, I'm named for the leader of the men at the Alamo, Colonel Travis."

Violet had started a small fire with driftwood. "You take off those wet clothes and dry out," she said. "You boys stake out the livestock and see if you can catch some fish."

Growler bounced over to him and shook all over, throwing muddy water on Travis.

"Damn you, old dog," Travis swore. "I should have let you drown."

"And listen to Bonnie cry?" Violet snapped. "I think not. Here, give me that wet shirt."

He started to protest, then peeled it off, although he didn't think it seemly to strip half-naked in front of three young girls.

She took it. "I'll hang it near the fire to dry. Maybe you'd better take your pants off, too."

"In front of little girls?" He shook his head. "Hell, no."

"Mr. Prescott, you know what I said about swearing." She went to get the coffeepot out of the wagon.

He watched her go. Right now. she didn't seem like a kid, not the way she was taking charge.

She came back with the coffeepot and a blanket. "Here, wrap this around you. My, you've got a lot of scars."

He took the blanket and draped it over his wide shoulders. "Too many days as a cowboy and a Ranger."

"That river water can't be good for that wrist." She knelt

and took his wrist in her two small hands. "I'll wash the wound with whiskey after I make you some coffee."

"We don't have any whiskey, remember? You traded it."

"Oh, yes. Well, you would have probably drunk it up by now anyway." She shrugged and went to the fire.

"I would if I had some," he snapped.

She sneaked looks at him as she made coffee, realizing again what a big, broad-shouldered stud he was. His scarred, dark skin rippled over powerful muscles. This was a man who could take care of and protect a woman. She wished suddenly she could be that woman.

While Bonnie and Kessie played around the wagon, she took Travis a cup of hot coffee and put it in his calloused hands. "Much obliged." He nodded and sipped it.

He looked exhausted as he leaned back against the tree. She had to squelch an urge to stroke his weathered face, brush his wet black hair out of his dark eyes.

The boys came back with a string of fish and she fried them along with hush puppies made from the cornmeal.

They ate and as it grew dark, the children settled down around the sleeping Travis as if, instinctively, they knew he would protect them. She banked the fire and cleaned up the pans and dishes; then she took a cup of coffee and went over to sit beside him. In a minute, she would check his arm, but right now, she was enjoying the peace and security of the moment. She watched him in the glow of the crackling fire, pretending he was her man and these were her children. It was a nice dream and she imagined what it would be like to snuggle down next to him in the security and safety of his powerful arms. Men had always hurt her and used her, but she wasn't afraid of Travis. The Texan wasn't like the other men she had known. Tears came to her eyes as she wished things were different and that she could meet him again under different circumstances. He seemed to be a proud man, and she was certain he would be horrified if he found out she'd been a whore. She longed for a brand-new start and she'd like to make that with Travis.

Abruptly she heard a horse whinny and looked up even as Growler started barking.

Two men rode over the crest of the hill and down toward the river. Violet took a deep breath. They were tough-looking men who looked like they had ridden long and hard.

By now, Travis was sitting up and the kids were all awake. Little Bonnie had crawled into his lap.

Violet looked at the two as they rode into camp. Where were Travis's guns? Probably in the wagon.

"Hello the camp!" one of the men yelled. "Can we get down?"

Travis said, "Where you from and where you bound?" The tension in his voice let Violet know he was suspicious.

"Well, that ain't too hospitable for Texans." The men reined in. "You got some coffee?"

"We got some," Violet said and got up to get more tin cups. The two men sat their horses, staring at her like the men in the Diamond Horseshoe did. It made her skin crawl.

Both men looked rough, like they'd ridden a long way. They looked around as they dismounted.

"Well, girlie, you at least seem friendly." The bearded one leered at her.

"She's just a kid," Travis warned.

"Old enough for me," the bearded one laughed.

She was scared now, scared of the way the men were looking at her and what Travis might do. She didn't want the kids to get hurt. She handed each of the men a cup of the steaming brew.

Travis put Bonnie down on the blanket and stood up. "You didn't say where you're from or where you were headed."

The shorter man glared at Travis as if sizing him up. "No, we didn't. Don't figure it's none of your business, clod-buster."

Limpy said, "He ain't a clod-buster, he's—"

"Hush," Travis ordered. "You men drink your coffee and ride on."

"Tonight?" the bearded one said, sipping from his tin cup. "We're tired and we thought your fire looked inviting—"

"Make your own fire," Travis thundered. "Now you drink your coffee and git!"

"All right, all right!" the short one mumbled. "Ain't very friendly for Texans."

They stood up slowly, threw the grounds in the fire and tossed the cups to one side. Travis glared at them and the kids seemed to hold their breaths as the men backed toward their horses. "We didn't mean no harm."

"Keep riding," Travis ordered.

"That's a mighty fine gray, you got there." The short one licked his lips. "Would you be interested in—"

"No, I wouldn't." Travis stood there, feet wide apart. Limpy had come up behind Travis now and handed him his rifle. Travis cocked it. "You two get gone."

"We didn't mean no trouble," the short one whined. The two mounted up and took off at a lope down the river.

Violet stared after them until they were out of sight. Then she heaved a sigh of relief and walked over to Travis. "That was scary, Mr. Prescott. I'm glad they're gone."

The children began to laugh and talk.

Travis signaled for silence. "They may be gone, but they'll be back."

Violet felt her heart stop. "Are you sure?"

Travis nodded. "We've got something they want."

"Mouse," Limpy said.

Travis looked directly into Violet's eyes. "Him, too."

They wanted her. The knowledge sent a chill down her

back. *Don't be stupid, Violet,* she told herself. *You've bedded dozens of men like them. What's two more?*

Because she never wanted another man to touch her except Travis, and he would stand his ground to protect her, maybe even give his life, she thought, because he believed she was an innocent kid. She ought to tell him she wasn't worth a gunfight, but she didn't want him to know her secret past. She wished she were as fresh and unstained as the Ranger thought she was.

Travis motioned them all closer. "Listen up and listen careful. Here's what we're gonna do: we're gonna pile our blankets up like we're asleep and then we're gonna sneak off into those sand dunes by the river. Harold, get the rest of the weapons."

"None of us know how to shoot," Harold protested.

"If you're gonna be Texans, it's time you learn," he snapped.

Violet said, "What can I do to help?"

He looked at her. "Violet, can you handle a gun?"

"Not really."

"All right, you take the girls and hide in that grove of sand plum bushes over there until we scare them off."

Limpy shifted his crutch and took the pistol. His thin face looked pale. "I'll do the best I can, Travis."

"That's all any Texan can do. You're gonna make a fine man someday, Limpy. Now y'all do what I said and settle down."

Violet picked up Bonnie. "You sure they'll come back?"

Travis nodded. "Can you be brave and take the girls and run if we lose this?"

She took a deep breath. "I—I've got a little knife in my garter. I'll kill one if they try to hurt the girls."

He gave her a questioning look, but she decided this wasn't the time to explain why an innocent young girl might be carrying a knife.

She took Kessie by the hand and the trio melted into the darkness of the sand plum bushes.

Travis watched them go, then turned to the boys. "All right, men."

"We ain't men," Harold said. "We're just boys and they know it."

"In Texas, boys turn into men pretty early or they don't make it. Besides, we've got to protect the girls."

"Sure," Limpy said.

"Good. Now you two help me pile the blankets up like we're all asleep and then move over on the other side of the fire behind those sand dunes. If they come back, we'll catch them in a cross fire."

Limpy asked, "Can you handle a gun, Travis?"

Travis hesitated. "With my wrist? I'm not sure, but we don't have to kill them, we only have to scare them into running like scalded hounds. You afraid?"

The boys hesitated.

"Yeah," answered Limpy finally.

"If you're going to grow up to be a cowboy or a Texas Ranger, there's one thing you need to know." Travis checked his pistol.

"What?" Harold asked.

"A brave man is a man who knows the danger but keeps on coming. That's a Texas Ranger for you. Now get over there and keep quiet. It may be awhile before they come back."

The boys obeyed and Travis crouched down behind a small rise where he could watch the fire. His wrist was throbbing like it had been touched with a red-hot branding iron, and he cursed himself that he was so vulnerable when the kids needed him so much. He'd seen the way those desperados had looked Violet over and he wasn't about to let them take her for their lust. He'd die first.

* * *

He had almost dozed off in spite of himself when he heard the slight sound of a horse stepping on a breaking twig and Growler snarled softly. "Hush up," Travis ordered and grabbed the dog's muzzle.

Then he heard the unmistakable sound of a boot stepping on rocks. Of course, being half Comanche, he had keener hearing than most men. He could only hope the boys were awake and ready for this attack.

He saw shadowy silhouettes as the pair of outlaws crouched and sneaked along the ridge, coming down near the fire. They paused and the short one laughed softly. "I told you they wouldn't think we'd come back," he whispered.

"Shut up!" the other ordered. "We want that horse and that girl."

"We kill the rest?"

"Hell, yes. Let's not leave no witnesses."

Travis stood up suddenly and shouted, "Git 'em, boys!" and fired his pistol.

At the same time, Harold and Limpy let loose with a barrage of rifle fire.

"I'm hit!" the bearded one screamed.

"Let's get the hell out of here!" yelled the other, and they turned and ran over the hill.

Travis had fallen to his knees in such agony that he dropped the pistol. If they came back now, with his wrist throbbing and his hand paralyzed, they could kill him. He realized he was useless as a man and a Ranger.

Violet waited a long moment until she heard the two horses galloping away, and then she left the two little girls behind the plum bushes and ran to find Travis. "Are you all right?"

"Sure," he said, but she saw the sweat gleaming on his dark face in the moonlight. She fell down on her knees beside him.

"Is it your wrist?"

He nodded and she saw he was gritting his teeth. "You got any of that whiskey left?"

"Well, I do have a few drops," she confessed. "I'll get it." She ran to the wagon and searched around a moment before she came back with it. "You want I should pour it on your wound?"

"Hell, no, I need a drink."

She pulled the cork out and handed it to him. "I reckon you got a right to curse."

"Damn right, I feel like I've been bit by a rattler." He took a deep gulp. "I reckon I was foolin' myself that my wrist would heal up."

She wanted to reach out and comfort him, he sounded so bereft, but she stopped herself. "It isn't the end of the world."

"It is if you're a Ranger or a cowman. A Texan's got to be able to shoot." He took another sip. "You can call the kids in now. I don't think those hombres will come back."

Limpy and Harold crossed over to them.

"That was scary," Limpy said.

"But you boys didn't turn tail and run." Travis nodded. "That was mighty brave."

"We couldn't let them hurt the girls," Harold said.

Kessie came up to them, leading Bonnie by the hand. "Us girls can take care of ourselves," she snapped. "We just need to be taught to shoot."

Travis grinned at her. "You're right, Red, and I'll teach you how to shoot, but right now, we need to get some rest so we can move on."

"Maybe I need to stand guard," Limpy suggested.

Travis shook his head. "They won't come back. Which reminds me, I promised you a new name; Limpy seems bad for a brave Texan."

The tall, thin boy smiled. "What?"

"I think you ought to be named for one of Texas's

bravest and most famous sons, Sam Houston. How does 'Houston' sound to you?"

"Houston." Limpy savored the name. "I like it. You hear, everyone? From now on, I'm not Limpy, I'm Houston."

"Now let's get some sleep," Travis ordered. "If I remember correctly, there's a town only a few miles south of the river. We'll ride in there in the morning."

Everyone settled down, but Travis picked up his rifle and leaned against a boulder. If those rascals did come back, he'd be ready for them and anyway, he was too sad to sleep. He now had to face the fact that there was no hope for him as a Ranger. The doctor in Red Rock had been right; his wrist would keep him from being a fast gun. He had no idea what to do with his life or these five kids who were counting on him.

He watched the firelight play on Violet's brown pigtails as she slept. She was a brave, gritty kid and he had to admit he liked having her around. In fact, he was getting used to all the kids. Too bad he couldn't keep them, but it was loco for a bachelor with no home and no money to think about adopting five kids. Maybe in this next town, he could find good families to take them in and he and his dog could drift on, but he'd have to admit he'd be lonelier than he had been since the kids had joined him.

Chapter 7

The next morning they started off again and in the distance, Travis saw the town he remembered. "Hey, kids, there's a town up ahead. We'll pull in there."

Harold looked at him, distress in his big almond eyes. "You aren't going to give us away, are you?"

"Not unless I find some really nice families," Travis assured him.

Bonnie immediately set up a howl, and Violet gave him a murderous look. "Now look what you've done."

"I was only being honest," Travis answered. "She'd be so much better off with a family of her own."

"We got a family of our own," Kessie said.

"I reckon we do," Travis sighed, "but I got no way to feed five kids and anyway, I'm a loner. You need a better father than me."

Violet looked up at him with those large, sad eyes. "If we can find a way to make some money, could we all stay together?"

"I wish we could, but I can't make it as a Ranger anymore with this bad arm."

Violet said. "Maybe your wrist will heal on its own."

"Maybe." He hoped so, but in the meantime . . .

They drove into town with little Bonnie crying at the top of her lungs.

An old man turned around from loading a wagon. "What are you doing to that baby? You been beatin' her?"

"No," Travis said, now aware of how many people were turning to look at the wailing toddler on the front seat of the wagon. He rode up next to Violet and under his breath, he muttered, "For God's sake, can you make her stop?"

"No," Violet snapped. "She's afraid you're going to give her away."

More people were turning to glare at the motley crew with the wailing toddler.

"Why's that child crying?"

"That man hitting that baby?"

The men glowering at him along the street looked like they could turn into a lynch mob. Travis reined in in front of the general store and dismounted. "Violet, stop that oxcart and take all the other kids in for some peppermint sticks."

Immediately, Bonnie stopped crying. "Candy," she laughed. "Come, doggie."

Travis took a deep breath as all five trooped into the general store along with Growler.

"Hey," yelled a man's voice from inside, "you can't bring a dog in here."

Immediately, Bonnie began to wail again and Travis heard Violet say, "You better let her, mister, or she'll scream loud enough to wake the dead."

"All right, all right."

Travis tied up his horse at the water trough next to the ox and wished he had a cold beer. There was surely a saloon in town, but of course he had the kids to think about and not much money. So instead, he sat on the store's step and rolled a cigarette. He remembered this town now from early cattle drives with his dad: Pleasant Valley. He looked up and down the main street as he smoked. A railroad track ran right down the middle of the dusty street. Besides the general store, he saw a small hotel and a saloon across the street, along with a livery stable and a gun shop. The train station was on his side of the street along with the sheriff's office and a bank. Not much of a town, but there were a few houses scattered around and a sleeping hound laying out near the railroad tracks.

A plump old man with a star on his vest stopped and looked down at him. "You plannin' on stayin'? We don't get many new folks in town."

Travis grinned up at him and shrugged. "I don't know."

"I'm Sheriff McClain." He held out a meaty paw.

Travis stood up and shook it. "This a peaceful place?"

The sheriff nodded. "Only excitement mostly is when the southbound train comes through about four in the afternoon and the northbound train comes through about seven in the evening, but they hardly ever stop, except to pick up cows or drop off freight. Not many people get off or get on in Pleasant Valley."

"Sounds fine to me. Any work around?"

"I hear old Mr. Jensen might be lookin' for a part-time clerk. He owns the gun shop. You know anything about guns?"

"A little," Travis said. There was no point in mentioning he had been a Texas Ranger. "Got a school here?" Travis looked up and down the main street.

"Yep, off there to the west. There's a big park next to it, too." The old man pointed. "We also got a church and a library." His face was proud.

"I remember when this was a busy cattle drive town," Travis said.

"Yep, well, the town's gotten a little sleepier since then with the cattle all being shipped by train, but cowboys from nearby ranches still come into town on weekends and we have the best Fourth of July celebration in the entire county."

"That a fact?" An idea began to build in Travis's mind as he smoked. He was finished as a Ranger, and he was weary of drifting. Maybe he could get a job here and put the kids in school until he could find good homes for all five, although the longer they were with him, the more he hated to give them up. Maybe he might even meet a nice girl and get married, give his little brood a mother.

"You look into that job at the gun shop, you hear?" Sheriff McClain touched the brim of his Stetson with two fingers and moved on as Travis nodded.

Violet and the four younger children came out of the general store followed by Growler. The kids were all licking candy sticks. Little Bonnie held hers out to him. "Wanta lick?"

Travis grinned at her. She had candy all over her face. "Think I'll pass," he answered. "What I'd really like is a beer—"

"Mister Prescott." Violet's eyes turned a cold blue. "Are you a drunkard?"

"No, I'm not," he denied, "but just one cold beer—"

All the children paused and looked up at him.

He remembered then that they were short on money. "Never mind. Let's camp in this town tonight and decide what to do later." He sat back down on the wooden step.

Violet smiled. "It looks like a nice town and we're all tired of traveling. Why don't we stay?"

"Maybe not, young lady. I'm the grown-up here, and I haven't decided yet—"

Kessie nodded. "Looks like a good town to me."

Bonnie crawled up into Travis's lap and kissed him on the cheek, leaving sticky peppermint on his face. "Stay," she said. "Doggie wants to stay."

Travis laughed. "Well, that settles it then. If Growler wants to stay, I reckon we might."

It made him feel good when all the kids smiled.

"I hear there's a park down the street." He pointed west. "Now you all take the oxcart and go down there and rest. I'll see what I can do about a job."

The kids got in the oxcart with Violet driving while he mounted up on his gray stallion. Growler jumped up on the wagon seat in Bonnie's lap. As they started down the street, people came to the doors of small shops and houses to look out at them, obviously curious about new people in town. When they passed the saloon, loud piano music blared out the swinging doors and hung on the warm air. The faded sign read: CATTLE DRIVE SALOON. With its peeling paint and dirty windows, it had seen better days, Travis thought.

With the wagon headed for the park, Travis rode up to the gun shop and dismounted, tied Mouse to the hitching rail and went in. It smelled of gunpowder and pipe tobacco. An elderly gentleman smoking a pipe stood behind the counter. "What can I do for you, stranger?"

"Are you Mr. Jensen??"

The old man nodded and took the pipe out of his mouth. "Sure am."

"I'm Travis Prescott." He held out his hand. "Heard you might be looking for help."

They shook hands. "Sure am. Store's too much for me to be here all day, my age, you know. Need a good man who knows guns. Town's sleepy, but cowboys and ranchers always need ammunition and weapons."

They talked a while.

Finally, the old man nodded. "Travis, I like you. I'd like to have you take over. If it works out, I'll just pop in now and then and you can run the place."

"I've got a family," Travis said. "I'll need a place to live."

"There's an abandoned house across the street and

down about a block near the railroad station. I reckon you could fix that up. Talk to banker Clay about it."

"Much obliged, Mr. Jensen." He started out the door. "We'll try to get that house livable and then I got to enroll my kids in school. I'll be in touch." Travis touched his hat by way of leaving, grinned and walked out to mount his horse. Then he rode out past the old wooden schoolhouse to the park, where the ox was grazing and the kids played by a small lake. He dismounted. "Everything's all right, kids. I think I found us a house and me a job."

Violet ran to meet him. "I can hold a job, too."

Travis shook his head. "I admire your gumption, young lady, but you need to go to school with the other kids."

"School?" She blinked. She had never really been in a school. The little she knew she had taught herself. "I'm a little old for school," she said before she thought.

"At thirteen?" Travis laughed. "No, it's school for you and all these others, Violet. Now let's go look at the house."

Curious people watched them as they passed by.

Violet began to think this must be a nice town after all. However, when she saw the house, her spirits fell. It must have been abandoned for a long time.

Kessie said, "This doesn't look much better than a chicken coop."

Travis looked through one of the broken windows. "I think you're right."

"Oh, it's not so bad." Violet managed a smile. "With a little work and some cleaning, we'll do just fine. Look, here's an old broom and even some dishes left in the cabinets."

Growler ran past her, chasing a stray raccoon through the parlor and out the back door. Bonnie toddled into the room and looked around. "Home." She smiled. "Home."

"Yes," said Violet, "we're home. Now everyone start picking up and we'll have this place livable in no time."

"I don't know." Travis shook his head. "It's downright shabby."

She looked up at him, pleading with her eyes. "Please, Mr. Prescott, we can fix it up and make it a real home."

Even though she was just a kid, there was something about her that pulled at his heart. "All right, if you kids are willing. I'll go talk to the banker and you all unload the oxcart and start cleaning."

She grabbed the old broom. "By dark, we'll have this place turned into a real home."

Travis looked doubtful, but he nodded and went out the front door.

She watched him go, liking the way his wide shoulders moved when he walked. "Kids, by the time he gets back, let's have this place livable. Pick up trash and, Kessie, see if you can do anything with the kitchen."

"Why do the women always have to do the kitchen?" the redhead griped. "When we get equal rights, men are gonna have to do some of the cooking."

"But until then, let's get moving," Violet said. "You boys get some wood for the fireplace. I don't know about that kitchen stove."

"Me," Bonnie said, trying to take the broom from her. "Me sweep."

"Here, you can dust, honey." She put a rag in the toddler's hand.

Growler lay down in front of the fireplace and watched.

Violet started sweeping. It might not be much of a house, but she was happy. She had been watching Travis over the last few days and decided he was the man for her. He might be a little hard to tame and a little wild, but she could already imagine having children with the half-breed. In her mind, she saw a dark-haired little boy and maybe a girl too. Along with the four children she had picked up at the train station, they would have a large brood. Maybe her past was behind her and Travis need never find out. As far as Duke was concerned, he wasn't likely to ever find her in this sleepy Texas town.

Travis returned to say he had traded the oxcart and ox to the banker for a six months' lease on the house, and a cow. "Boys, let's put the cow and Mouse in that barn out back of the house. Can either of you milk?"

Both boys shook their heads.

"Well, it's high time you learned." The three of them went out the back door and soon returned with a foaming pail of fresh milk.

At four o'clock, the train roared through, headed south and then at seven, as it grew dark, the northbound train chugged through, rattling the windows.

"Damn!" Travis complained. "Now I can see why no one wants to live in this house."

"Mr. Prescott, please don't cuss," Violet scolded. "We can stand the train noise, can't we, kids?"

"Yes!" everyone yelled. "As long as we're together."

By dark, they had the place at least clean enough to make some pallets on the floor. Travis built a fire in the old stone fireplace and all the children settled down in front of it. He watched Violet putting on a kettle of stew and a pan of corn bread to cook in the coals. Soon they'd had all they could eat, washed down with fresh milk, and Growler cleaned up the leftovers.

Travis brought in a pail of water from the well out back and he watched her wash the little girls' faces while the boys gave themselves a quick wash. He thought how responsible the girl was, at only thirteen. And she was so pretty. If only she were older, he could fall in love with this girl. Then he reminded himself that, after Emily had broken his heart, he'd sworn to never take that chance again. He found an old rocking chair and pulled it up in front of the fireplace and sat down. He smiled and leaned back in his chair with contentment, holding his coffee cup. It was almost as if he were the father and these were really his children.

Violet sat on the floor near the fire and watched him. She had never felt so safe and protected. This big Ranger was a man she thought she could trust and really make a home with. The only problem was he thought she was a kid, and how could she explain this big lie without him ever finding out her terrible background? "Would you like some more coffee, Travis?"

"Sure." He held out his cup.

She got up, took his cup and poured it. When she handed it back to him, their fingers brushed. To her, it felt like a lightning strike, but if he felt it too, he didn't make any motion. Yet he was staring at her; she was very aware of that.

"What are you thinking?" she asked.

"Uh, nothing much." He looked confused as he sipped the coffee. "Tomorrow, I'll try to get the kitchen stove working and buy a couple of kerosene lamps on credit."

"I can manage with just the fireplace for a while if I have to." She wanted to sit down in his lap, but of course she didn't. She sat down on the floor next to his chair and leaned her head against the arm.

His big hand reached out hesitantly and stroked her hair. "You're a nice kid, Violet."

Her heart sank. She had created this mess herself. Now there was no way to tell him she was a grown woman without him asking questions she didn't want to answer.

The kids sat on the floor around the fire, Growler asleep among them.

Travis yawned. "You kids can start school tomorrow."

Houston said, "We're almost like a real family."

"Maybe so," Travis said softly.

"Then you need to get a wife," Harold said importantly. "To be a real family, you got to get a wife."

Violet felt like pinching the little boy for his observations. "I thought I was doing a pretty good job as a mother."

Travis laughed. "What he means, Violet, is that you're not old enough to be a wife. Anyway, we're doing just fine alone."

Harold said, "But if you found a lady you wanted to marry, wouldn't you?"

Travis laughed again. "She'd have to be mighty pretty."

"Prettier than Violet?" the boy asked.

"I think it's time we all went to bed," Violet interrupted and got to her feet. She didn't want the kids giving away her secret, if they even remembered it.

"I think she's right," Travis echoed. "You're all going to school tomorrow and I start my new job."

Kessie said, "Bonnie is too young to go to school."

"That's right," Violet agreed. "I'll stay home and take care of her."

"No, you don't, young lady. You're going to school with the others. Maybe we can talk the teacher into taking Bonnie, too."

"I hope she's pretty," Houston said seriously. "Then maybe you'll get married and we can stay together forever."

"Quit talkin' about marriage." Travis frowned. "I've had enough of women and their lying ways. We can do just fine without one."

Violet felt her heart skip a beat. She was the biggest liar of all. Travis was a proud man and he wouldn't want a saloon tart for a wife. However, sooner or later, he would figure out she wasn't really thirteen years old and before that, she would have to leave. She didn't want him to ever find out her sordid past.

The next morning, she fixed them all a good breakfast, with ham and eggs bought on credit at the general store; then Travis told everyone to get washed up for school. With Growler following along beside Bonnie, the group started walking down the street.

It looked like a typical one-room schoolhouse, Travis thought, white frame with Texas and American flags flying out front. He walked up on the porch and opened the door. About a dozen young faces turned to look at him from their desks. The tall, thin woman writing on the blackboard at the front of the room paused and turned. "Yes?"

Travis took off his Stetson and shooed the children inside. "Excuse me, ma'am, but we're new in town and I'm here to enroll my children."

The woman looked over her spectacles at him. "Usually, it's the mother who brings the children the first day."

He gave her his best smile. "I'm sorry, ma'am, but I don't have a wife. It's just me and the kids."

"Children," she corrected sternly and motioned. "Come in, come in." She gestured as if she was used to giving orders.

Violet pushed the reluctant children ahead of her, keenly aware of the stares of the other students. She thought the bony woman looked like a vulture glaring over her wire-rimmed glasses. The room smelled like chalk and old lunches.

The woman frowned down at all of them and then peered at Travis. "Are they all yours?"

It was evident they weren't, Violet thought, looking at Harold and then to Travis with his high-cheekboned face.

"No, ma'am, they're adopted."

The students at their desks tittered while the bony lady

slapped a ruler against a desk. "Be quiet, class, or I'll keep everyone after school."

"I just want to get them enrolled," Travis said and gave her an engaging smile.

"Humph. You do realize that there's only four weeks of school left before we break for summer?"

Travis gave the woman his most engaging smile. "I realize that, ma'am, but we just moved in and I'm sure you can teach them a lot in four weeks."

Her bony face now turned pink at the compliment. "Well, I guess I can. I am Miss Brewster."

"We are right proud to know you," Travis said. "This oldest one is Violet, the little redhead is Kessie, that tall one is Houston and this one"—he put his hand on Harold's thin shoulder—"this here is Harold."

"Harold?" Her eyes widened.

"I named myself," Harold explained.

The class tittered again and Miss Brewster rapped with her ruler as she faced Travis. "You expect me to teach that Oriental boy? There's a laundry just off Main Street—"

"No, ma'am," Travis frowned. "He wants to be a doctor or a scientist, not work in a laundry."

She looked over her spectacles at Bonnie. "This one looks too young to be in school."

Bonnie clung to Travis's hand while Growler lay down next to her and began to scratch a flea.

"It's outrageous that you've brought a dog in here," Miss Brewster said. "And that child is too young—"

"She's an orphan," Travis snapped, "and I got no place to leave her while I work, ma'am, and she cries if we try to take the dog away from her."

"Give me strength," whispered Miss Brewster under her breath, then she said, "I just can't—"

"I'd be so obliged if you'd help me out." Travis grinned at her. "I'm just a single man trying to raise five kids alone and I think learning under a pretty, smart lady like you would do wonders for them."

The bony Miss Brewster's face turned pink again and she appeared flustered. "Well, I might try it awhile and see if she's any trouble—"

Violet stepped in. "Ma'am, I'll make sure she's no trouble."

"But the dog—" began Miss Brewster.

Travis leaned even closer to the lady. "Ma'am, he's just a little dog. Don't you think you could find it in your heart not to notice him if he's laying under her desk?"

"Lying," Miss Brewster corrected. "Lying under her desk."

"So it's agreed then?" Travis stuck out his hand and took her limp fingers in his. "You're such a credit to the teaching profession, ma'am, I hope to see more of you."

Miss Brewster looked both flattered and bewildered. "But I'm not sure—"

"Thank you, Miss Brewster. You're as nice as you are pretty."

Violet watched the old maid teacher melt under Travis's smile. "Well, what is a teacher for anyway, if she can't help all the children she can?"

Violet snorted, but no one seemed to notice. Miss Brewster was smiling up at Travis like he was Romeo and she was Juliet. If that old maid thought she was going to grab Travis Prescott, she would have to step over Violet.

"All right, kids." Travis turned to his brood. "You all find desks and Miss Brewster will tell you what to do. I'll be at the gun shop when you get out of school. Have you all got your lunches?"

They all nodded. Violet stood there speechless and watched Travis walk out of the school, leaving her and the four children with Miss Brewster.

Miss Brewster pointed them all to empty desks. "Now children, introduce yourselves to the others."

Violet felt like an idiot as she managed to say, "I'm Violet."

Bonnie was too shy and Kessie had to introduce her. All the children laughed when Harold said his name.

The teacher looked down her nose at him. "Harold is indeed a strange name for an Oriental boy."

"It's a good name for a scientist or a doctor," he answered and sat down.

Houston was slow to come forward, leaning on his crutch. He whispered his name and Miss Brewster snapped, "Talk louder, young man. We can't hear you."

"I am Houston, named for Sam Houston."

The other children laughed and a fat boy on the front row said, "He's crippled, he don't deserve a good name like that."

"He does, too," Violet snapped. "He saved us from bandits down by the river."

Houston's thin face turned scarlet and he sat down while the other children tittered.

Violet wanted to grab the kids up and take them out of there, but of course, Travis wanted everyone in school.

Violet thought the morning passed slowly, but she had to admit that when the town children read she found the stories interesting.

At lunchtime, all the town kids gathered around the newcomers. "You all are tramps," a big boy taunted.

"And that Chink should go back to China," shouted another.

"I'm not from China, I'm from New York City," said Harold as a boy pushed him.

"Stop it!" Violet said. "Stop bullying or I'll tell Miss Brewster."

"Oh, you're just a girl," another boy taunted. "We ain't talking to you, missy."

Now they were crowding around Houston. "Hey, look, he's got a crutch. We don't want no cripples in our school."

Violet gathered her four together and faced the bullies. "Our father used to be a Texas Ranger, so you better leave us alone."

About that time, the bell rang and everyone had to go back inside, including the dog. Growler lay next to Bonnie's desk, snoring away, although he awoke now and then to scratch a flea.

Miss Brewster glared at the dog as if she was going to throw him out of her school, then seemed to remember. As the day ended, she patted Violet on the shoulder again. "Be sure and tell your father how much I liked the children. Maybe he can come up to school again and we'll visit about how much you're all learning."

"Yes, ma'am," Violet said as she gathered up her group and headed out the door. She had no intention of telling Travis anything. Miss Brewster might think she could interest Travis, but Violet had already planned that no single woman would have a chance with him—except herself.

Chapter 8

Violet carried Bonnie as she led the children home with Growler following along behind.

When they got inside, Houston grabbed her arm. "Don't tell Travis about the bully, will you not?"

"That little rascal ought to be spanked," Violet answered.

"But the boys will laugh even more if Travis comes up and tattles to the teacher."

"Okay." She turned to the others. "Here's what we do; we don't tell Travis about the bullies until we decide what to do."

"What can we do?" Harold asked. "They're bigger than we are."

"But not smarter," Kessie said.

"You're right about that." Violet nodded. "Now why don't I make a batch of cookies and then we'll clean our home some more?"

"Home," Bonnie lisped and patted the dog. "Our home."

"Anywhere love is is a home, right, kids?" Violet asked and hugged each of them.

"We all love you," Harold said. "I wish Travis would marry you and then we could be a real family."

That must have reminded Bonnie of their first meeting because she giggled. "Feathers, you are Feathers."

Oh, that would give it away. "No, not Feathers. I'm Violet, remember? And I'm young, young enough to go to school."

Houston grinned up at her. "Even with the bullies, this is better than the orphans' home. You think they'll ever come looking for us?"

She saw the worry on all four faces. "I'm an orphan myself and no one's come looking for me, so I think the orphanage has forgotten about you. Now you all get busy with the cleaning and I'll make some cookies. Harold, bring in some wood."

An hour later, they had accomplished a lot of cleaning and the fireplace crackled merrily even though it was warm outside.

"I hope they'll give me credit at the general store," Violet said. "I'll walk over and see. You all stay here and clean and study your lessons." She went out the door into the May dusk and up the street to the general store. The middle-aged man behind the counter was stoop-shouldered and wore his thinning hair combed and plastered over his bald spot. "Howdy, miss."

"Hello. Remember me from yesterday?"

He nodded and smiled. "How could I forget all them kids? I'm Herman Haskins, little lady. What can I do for you?"

"If you'll give me credit, I'd like some flour and some coffee, please."

He nodded. "I hear your bunch moved into the old, abandoned house." He dipped into a barrel, weighing the flour on his scale.

"Yes, sir."

"What a dump!" sneered a voice and she turned to see a big, freckled hombre leaning against the wall. He was almost as tall as Travis, but maybe only in his twenties. His clothes were dirty and he smelled bad.

"Now, Leroy, that ain't polite," scolded Mr. Haskins. "Go loiter someplace else."

Leroy ignored him and leered at Violet. "Hello, there, you pretty thing." He winked in a way that made her nervous.

She nodded and turned back to the counter.

"Don't turn your back on me." His tone was threatening.

"Now, Leroy," said the clerk, "don't bother the young lady. Can't you see she's just a kid?"

Leroy snickered. "She's old enough."

Violet took a deep breath and turned to face Leroy. "Did you know my daddy used to be a Texas Ranger?"

Leroy rubbed his unshaven face. "That a fact?" Then he turned and sauntered out the door.

She and Mr. Haskins watched him go.

"Watch out for Leroy," he warned her. "The Jenkinses have a bunch of sons, but Leroy is the oldest and no good."

"Thank you for the advice, sir." She gave him her sweetest smile. "Now I also need a small sack of sugar and some cornmeal."

"Your daddy got a job yet?"

"Looks like he'll be working at the gun shop."

The thin man nodded and measured the sugar and cornmeal out of the barrels. "I didn't see no woman with you when you came into town."

"She's dead," Violet said. "It's just us five kids and our dad."

"Such a pity about your ma." The stooped man took out a handkerchief and blew his nose. "Give your dad my regards and here's some peppermint sticks for the young'uns."

She shook her head. "I don't think we can afford—"

"It's a treat," he said. "Anything for a Texas Ranger.

They been defending this state for sixty years against bandits and wild Injuns."

"Thank you, sir." She took her purchases and the candy, and went out the door. In the distance, she heard the north-bound train whistle as it approached the town. Violet looked up and down the street for Leroy Jenkins, but he had disappeared. She took a deep breath of relief and walked down the dusty street toward home as the train rumbled through town without stopping.

She wasn't really afraid of Leroy, having handled many a drunk or an angry cowboy in her time. There was only one thing that worried Violet: running into someone from her past. Kansas was a long way away, she reassured herself, so that wasn't likely.

She went back to the house. All the kids were doing their homework as she put away her purchases. Then Travis walked in.

Without thinking, she ran to meet him and threw her arms around his neck. "I'm so glad to see you."

He was big and muscular, and she wanted to kiss him. Then she remembered that she was supposed to be a child. She stepped back and noted he looked uncomfortable. "I mean, we all are glad to see you."

The children gathered around Travis and he picked up Bonnie while Growler danced around his legs and barked. "Well, kids, how was the first day of school?"

The kids all looked at each other.

"Just fine," Violet said. "It's a good school."

"That old, skinny teacher told Violet to give you her regards," Kessie said.

"Oh, she did, did she?" He took off his Stetson and headed into the parlor. "She seemed like a nice lady."

Violet followed him into the room and took his hat. "The other kids call her 'Bones' Brewster behind her back."

He grinned. "That's not nice."

She hung his hat on the wall rack near the door, where his holster and Colt also hung, and looked at him. "You couldn't possibly be interested in an old pile of bones like her, could you?"

"Interested how?" He looked at her.

She felt flustered. "I mean, to call on."

"You mean like a sweetheart?" He threw back his head and laughed. "Not hardly. What even gave you that idea?"

Violet heaved a sigh of relief. "I only thought we all might be so much trouble you'd think about a wife."

"We're managing all right without a woman, aren't we? Now what about some dinner?"

"I was just about to start dinner."

As she turned to go to the kitchen, there was a knock at the door. Violet went to open it. A thin, homely woman in her thirties stood there with a covered basket. "Is Mr. Prescott home?"

"Can I help you?" Violet asked.

"Well, no, honey, I really want to see your father."

Violet managed not to slam the door in her face. She went into the parlor, where Travis sat with Bonnie in his lap and the children had all gathered around him. "There's a lady at the door for you."

"Oh?" He got up, put Bonnie down and came to the front door. Violet followed him.

"Hello."

The woman smiled at him. She had a big nose and warts on her face. "Mr. Prescott? Word's out all over town that you've just moved in, so I brought some food for your dear kiddies. I'm Miss Knowlen, the town librarian." She handed him the basket, leaning toward him.

"Why, thank you, Miss Knowlen, it's so kind of you."

Violet said, "I was already fixing dinner."

The homely woman reached out and patted her shoulder. "And now, dear, you won't have to. May I say, Mr.

Prescott, that it's very brave of you to try to raise children all by yourself? Mr. Haskins at the general store told me about you."

Violet said, "How nice of him to be concerned."

Miss Knowlen ignored her and kept her attention on Travis. "Being single myself, just me and my five cats, I know how lonely you must be. If there's anything I can do, just come to the library."

Travis grinned at the woman. "Why, thank you kindly, ma'am. I'm sure we'll be in the library a lot, studying."

Violet said, "Yes, we will. Now you probably want to get home before it gets completely dark—"

"Oh, I'm not afraid." The librarian was smiling up at Travis.

He said again, "Thank you so much for the food, ma'am."

"Miss Knowlen," the woman repeated. "Lavinia Knowlen. Remember I'm at the library any time you want to check out a book."

"Thank you, we'll remember, good-bye," said Violet and managed to shut the door.

"That wasn't polite," Travis said. "Why, I do believe she would have come in and eaten supper with us."

"I'm sure she would have, if we'd asked her," Violet said and took the basket. "Every old maid in town must know by now that a new man is here and you're single."

He laughed. "And they'll be saying my oldest daughter is quite rude. I'd think you'd be pleased to have women offering to take some of the load off you. It's a lot for a young girl."

"I don't mind," she said over her shoulder as she went to the kitchen. "We don't need anyone else, do we, kids?"

"No!" yelled all the kids in unison.

"Don't worry," Travis said, following her into the kitchen. "She'd have to be something special for me to court her and pretty as a new colt."

"Now let's see what our eager librarian brought," Violet said and opened the basket.

"Maybe she cooks better than you do," Travis said with a grin.

"You don't like my cooking?" She felt hurt and vulnerable. Cooking was not her strong point.

"I was just joking, young lady. You cook pretty good for a kid. Now let's eat."

The eager librarian had sent a chicken pot pie and a peach cobbler. They all sat down at the table and were just starting to eat when there was a knock at the door.

"I'll get it." Violet went to the door and opened it to a beautiful blond woman exquisitely dressed in light gray silk.

"Hello, dear, you must be Mr. Prescott's oldest daughter. He's so brave, raising all you children alone. Is he here?"

Behind her, Violet heard Travis coming from the dining room. "Why, hello, Mrs. Van Mayes."

"Hello, I was so happy to meet you at the gun shop today."

"Not as much as I was to meet you." He gave her that smile that so entranced Violet. "Children, come meet Mrs. Van Mayes. I think you've already met the oldest of my children?"

"I'm Violet." She didn't smile. This woman was not only beautiful, she had money. There was an elegant open barouche out front with a liveried driver.

A nervous giggle. "So happy to meet you and the other poor, motherless children," she cooed as the children gathered around the front door.

"Won't you come in?" Travis asked.

"No, I just brought a basket for these poor children. It's so brave of you to struggle along without a wife."

"I run the house," Violet informed her without smiling. "We make do just fine."

"So brave." The beautiful Mrs. Van Mayes dabbed at her blue eyes with an expensive lace handkerchief and reached to hug Violet, who stood like a stone, stiff and uncomfortable. "Well, I must be off. We'll see each other around town." The beautiful woman waved her handkerchief and returned to her expensive barouche with its fine black horses decked out in silver studded harness.

Violet closed the door and looked at Travis.

"She's a widow," he explained. "Came in for some cartridges for her ranch hands this afternoon."

"I'll bet the gun shop has never had so much business." Violet shrugged. "She looks rich."

"She says her elderly husband left her the biggest ranch in the county," Travis answered. "You notice she's still wearing light mourning."

"Ha!" said Violet. "She'd marry you tomorrow."

He started back to the kitchen with the big basket. "Well, she's beautiful—"

"And rich," breathed Kessie. "Did you see the jewelry she had on?"

"She could probably send you and Harold to college." Travis smiled.

Violet was stung. "So you've already given her some thought?"

"Of course not," he snapped as he opened the basket. "And anyway, the doings of adults is hardly the business of kids."

"You're very, very friendly to her," Violet said.

"Texans are always friendly," he said as he leaned over the basket and took a sniff. "Hmm, roast beef and apple cobbler."

"Wow!" said Houston, his eyes wide. "If this keeps up,

we won't ever have to buy groceries again and Violet won't have to cook."

Violet now felt threatened. "I doubt Mrs. Fancy Carriage cooked this herself. She's probably got other talents besides cooking."

"Like what?" Kessie asked. "Is she smart, too?"

Travis laughed. "She's beautiful, she doesn't have to know how to cook."

"Men!" Violet snorted and brushed past him, heading for the dining room.

Did Travis really like Mrs. Van Mayes? Violet could hardly eat all the good food the ladies had brought for thinking about it. Miss Knowlen wasn't a threat, but the beautiful, rich widow certainly was.

As they ate, Harold said, "If any more ladies come to the door, I hope the next one brings chili and some cookies."

Violet had a pang of jealousy. "There's no telling how many more single ladies are liable to show up with baskets."

"It won't do them any good." Travis buttered a piece of bread. "I've let everyone know I'm a confirmed bachelor."

"That's like waving a red flag at a bull," Violet snapped. "Everyone thinks she'll be the one to land you." *Even me*, she thought, but she didn't say that.

"They must be short of eligible men in this town," Travis muttered. "Usually respectable women won't give a half-breed the time of day."

Only Violet heard him; the others were eating and talking. She wanted to reach out to him, but then remembered she was supposed to be a child.

They ate and Travis and the kids played checkers while Violet cleaned up the dishes and Kessie complained about having to dry them. "It isn't fair. When equal rights come in, the boys will have to do dishes too."

"But right now," Violet said, "the boys do things like feed the livestock and milk the cow."

Finally they all went to bed. However, Violet couldn't sleep. She could hear Travis's gentle breathing from the next room in the warm May night and wished he was holding her in his embrace as they both slept. But he thought she was only thirteen years old while the beautiful, rich widow was evidently plotting to make him her next husband.

The following day at school, things did not go well. Violet thought Miss Brewster was too strict on Bonnie and scolded her when she wet her drawers. At lunchtime, three big, freckled-faced brothers, the Jenkinses, ganged up on Houston and Harold.

On the way home, Violet said, "They've got a grown brother too, Leroy. Maybe we should tell Travis."

"No," Houston begged. "It's embarrassing enough to get beat up without him finding out."

"I'll bake a pie," Violet said. "That should make you feel better."

"We've still got the pie the pretty lady brought last night plus all those leftovers," Harold reminded her.

Violet looked back. Bonnie was lagging behind, hanging on to Growler's neck. "Here, let me carry you."

She picked the blond baby up, and Bonnie laughed and said, "Feathers."

"No, not Feathers. Violet, remember?" Violet kissed the baby's chubby cheek and kept walking. What was she to do about the bullies? It wouldn't do any good to tell the teacher. She suspected Miss Brewster would say "boys will be boys" and shrug it off.

She was warming up leftovers when Travis walked through the door. "I've about got dinner ready."

The kids had all gathered around him and he hugged them before taking off his Stetson, hanging it next to his holster and plopping down in his rocker in the parlor.

"Don't make much of a fuss," he called to Violet. "Charlotte Van Mayes came by the gun shop and brought me a basket lunch so I'm not hungry."

"Charlotte? You call her Charlotte?" Violet fought the urge to stride in and dump the pan of leftover chicken pie on his head.

"She's very friendly," he answered. "She just insisted I start using her first name. She's from New York City. You know, I always thought Yankees were cold, but she certainly isn't."

I'll just bet she's not, Violet thought, but she didn't say anything.

Bonnie crawled up in Travis's lap. "She like doggies?"

"I don't know." Travis shrugged and picked up the weekly paper.

Kessie said, "It would be nice to be rich. We could have a big house and we could all have fine clothes."

"Yep, that would be nice," Travis agreed. "Business is picking up at the gun shop."

"I wonder why," Violet said and began slamming pans around in the kitchen. "Food's on."

Travis and the kids gathered around the table as Violet slammed plates and silverware down.

Travis scratched his head. "Now what's wrong with you, young lady?"

"Nothing," Violet snapped and sat down in a huff.

"I know enough that when a female looks like a thundercloud and says, 'nothing,' there's something."

All the children looked at Violet.

"Well," she said, "if all these women are going to keep feeding you, I reckon you don't need me anymore."

He looked sympathetic. "You afraid I'll send you to an orphanage? Don't worry, Violet. Even if I do eventually marry, there's always a place for you at my table. Why, the kids couldn't do without you, could you, kids?"

A chorus of denials.

That didn't change her mood any. She tried not to steal glances at him while she ate. He was so dark and handsome, and she could imagine herself as his wife, sharing kisses and caresses, making a home for the four orphaned children. But he thought of her as a kid. She had painted herself into this corner and now she couldn't see any way out of it without revealing her past. She began to eat, but the food lodged in her throat.

About the time they finished eating, Travis stared at Houston. "Are those bruises on your face?"

"I—I fell down," Houston gulped.

Travis stared at the two boys. "Harold, you've got a cut above your eyebrow."

"Uh, I fell down, too."

"Getting clumsy all of a sudden," Travis said. He looked at Violet. "You see this?"

She felt her face flush. "Uh, yes, they both fell at the same time."

"Fight," lisped Bonnie, "fight."

Kessie shook her head. "Hush, Bonnie."

"Uh-huh." Travis said and got up from the table. "Boys, you and me need to have a talk. This is man stuff, so you girls are excused."

"It wasn't their fault," Violet babbled. "They—"

"I said this was men's business," Travis thundered. "Come on out back, boys, and we'll talk."

He put his hand on each boy's shoulder and led them out in the backyard.

Violet, Kessie and Bonnie went to the kitchen window to watch.

Kessie asked, "You think he's gonna whip them?"

"I don't know." Violet shook her head, wanting to rush out and protect them. "It's men's business."

"Fight," lisped Bonnie, standing on her tiptoes to look out the window.

"Oh, you be quiet," Kessie ordered. "You gave away the secret."

Outside, Travis looked back toward the house. "All right, this is a discussion between men. What happened?"

Tears came to Houston's dark eyes, but he struggled not to cry. "There's—there's three Jenkins brothers, big boys. They called Harold a Chink and said he should go work in a laundry, that's all he was good for."

"And they make fun of Houston," sobbed Harold, "because he has to use a crutch. They took it away from him and pushed him so he fell down."

"Where was the teacher?" Travis asked.

"Inside, she didn't see any of it. Violet and Kessie tried to stop it, but the boys pushed them and said we were sissies who had to be rescued by girls." Houston hung his head.

"Okay, I'm gonna teach you to fight," Travis said.

"The teacher said fighting was for savages," Harold said.

"Well, but she's a girl and sometimes men just have to fight, especially a Texan, when some big galoot bullies them."

"Are we Texans?" Houston asked.

"You sure as hell are. You're in Texas, ain't you? You got generations of tough cowmen and Rangers, and men who died at the Alamo behind you, so you got to learn to stand your ground," Travis told him.

"Do Rangers fight?" Harold asked.

Travis nodded. "But only when they have to. The trick is to get so much respect, nobody would think of pushing you or insulting you."

"I don't know if we're big enough to do that." Houston's thin shoulders slumped.

"We'll work on that," Travis said. "First, I'm gonna do something about that crutch."

"I need it to get around," Houston said.

"I've shoed a lot of horses." Travis grinned and patted his shoulder. "I think I can build up your shoe so you won't need a crutch anymore. And Harold, you're smart so you ought to be able to talk your way out of a fuss. Let's go into the barn." He put his hand on each boy's shoulder and they walked toward the barn.

Inside, Violet took a deep breath. "Oh, he's taking them to the barn."

"You think he's gonna whip them with a horse whip?" Kessie asked.

"No, no," Bonnie wept.

"Don't worry." Violet bent and hugged her. "I don't know what he's planning, but I'm not gonna let him whip them. You two stay here." She took a deep breath and, squaring her slight shoulders, marched out the back door and into the barn.

The three were gathered around a workbench as she walked in. Travis looked up and frowned. "Young lady, I told you this was men's business."

"Please, Travis, don't whip the boys; it wasn't their fault—"

"Hush up, Violet." Houston grinned. "He ain't doing nothing but fixing my shoe."

"What?" She paused, baffled.

Travis nodded. "I figure if I can build up his shoe, he won't need the crutch no more and also, I'm gonna teach them to fight."

"Fight? Now that's not civilized—"

Travis came over to her, caught her by the shoulders and turned her around. "Go in the house, young lady. I'm the man of this family and I'll handle this. Sometimes men gotta fight, especially Texans."

"But—"

"Go in the house, Violet." Travis's voice was stern and brooked no argument.

She went back in the house.

Kessie looked up at her. "What's going on out there?"

"Well, for one thing, he's going to teach them to fight."

"Miss Brewster won't like that."

Violet shrugged. "He's a Texan and a Ranger, there's no dealing with him."

Back in the barn, Travis took a hunk of wood and a small whittling knife. "I'll make this just the size of your shoe and then nail it to the sole. That way, both legs will be the same length and you won't limp."

He glanced over. Both boys were watching him intently. "Now, since you're not going to limp anymore, I want you to walk with your head up and your shoulders back, just like Sam Houston would. You are Houston Prescott and that's a name that should be respected."

Harold asked, "Can we use your last name? We don't have none of our own."

"Well, now you do, Harold Prescott, and you treat my name with respect now that I've given it to you. There's generations of brave men behind that name and I expect you to do it proud. I'm a proud man and I expect my sons to make me proud, too."

"I can't fight," Houston said with dejection. "I reckon the Jenkins brothers will still beat me up."

"They may try, but I'm going to loan you my good luck charm. That ought to turn your luck around." He walked over and dug into his saddlebags, came back with a small, hand-carved wooden horse.

Houston took it, stared at it. "Is it really lucky?"

"If you believe it is, it'll give you power you didn't know you had."

Harold stared at the tiny horse. "Where'd you get it?"

"My stepfather, Colt, carved it for me when I was a little kid. It's always brought me luck. Houston, you just rub it when you need courage."

"Can I keep it?" Houston held it tightly.

Travis nodded. "Until you think you don't need it no more. I set a heap of store by it, so you take care of it now, you hear?"

The boy nodded.

"Now let's get back to fixing that shoe. I wish we had more money, then maybe some back-east doc could fix your leg."

"And your wrist?" Harold asked.

Travis shook his head ruefully. "My wrist will have to heal on its own, since we don't have money." He started carving the wood.

Harold said, "That Mrs. Van Mayes has plenty of money."

"And she's beautiful," Houston added.

Travis laughed as he whittled. "I don't think Violet likes her. I don't know about the other two girls."

"We like Violet better'n we like Mrs. Van Mayes," Houston hurried to assure him.

"But Violet is just a kid and sometimes a man and a family needs a woman."

"But Violet—" Harold began. Houston glared at him and the Oriental boy fell silent.

Travis wondered what that was about, but he soon grew engrossed in his handiwork and lost track of everything else.

Houston smiled for the first time in a long while and inspected the tiny wooden horse. "I'm Houston Prescott."

"And I'm Harold Prescott," the Chinese boy said.

Travis winked at him. "Good name for a doctor or scientist."

"I always wanted to be a rancher or a cowboy," Houston sighed, "but I reckon I can't do that."

"Why not?" Travis asked.

"I can't even ride a horse."

"I'll teach you to ride Mouse," Travis said. "And remember, all men are equal on horseback, you don't need two good legs. You could end up being the best cowman in Texas. "'Course I'll have to teach you to shoot and rope, too."

Harold asked, "When are you going to have time to do all that?"

Travis continued work on the shoe. "During lunchtime, out behind the gun shop. Besides, summer will soon be here and then you'll have plenty of time to practice."

Harold said, "I don't think doctors or scientists need to learn all that."

"I reckon not," Travis agreed. "Now, you two men go on into the house and go to bed while I work on this shoe. And we don't have to discuss this with the ladies, okay?"

Harold nodded. "They're just girls anyway."

Houston's thin shoulders straightened. "We're Texans and we can stand our own ground, right, Travis?"

"Sure as we're both named for Texas heroes." Travis grinned and continued whittling.

The two boys left the barn. Travis looked after them. It was dark outside and he'd have to light a lantern and work late to finish this shoe, but he could do it. He reminded himself that out of his next paycheck, he needed to buy each boy a pair of boots. All Texan men had to have a pair of boots.

* * *

It was late when he went inside. The house was quiet, but Violet was still awake, sitting in a rocking chair in front of the fireplace. "Oh, I thought everyone would be in bed."

"What went on out there?" she demanded and stood up.

"That's between us men," he said and set the shoe on the mantel.

Violet looked at it. "He won't have to use a crutch any-more?"

Travis shook his head. "Nope, and I told them both to use my last name."

"It's all right if we all use your name?" She looked up at him.

He nodded. "All my kids can use it, but of course, you have to make me proud. My family wouldn't be pleased if anyone shamed a name that's been around since we fought redcoats by the side of George Washington."

Without thinking, she hugged him. "And I thought you were going to whip them." She reached up and kissed his cheek.

He looked shocked and stepped back. "Now, young lady, it wasn't that big a thing."

Oh, Lord, had she given herself away? She stuttered, "I—I mean, you're just such a great dad to all us orphans. I can't thank you enough."

He shook his head. "Save those kisses for some young man someday when he's on his knees wantin' to marry you."

"Of course." She lowered her eyes demurely.

"I'm going to bed now. Young lady, you got school to-morrow. You need to get some sleep."

"Sure. You go on, Travis. I've got lessons to read."

He went into the bedroom and she sat back down in her chair and listened to him getting ready for bed and remem-bered how it had felt to hold him close, the taste of his leathery skin and the man smell of him. She couldn't read.

Instead she sat and rocked and wished she wasn't saddled with this secret and could go crawl into bed and make love to him.

In his room, Travis went to bed, but instead of dropping off to sleep as usual, he lay awake, staring at the ceiling. He had been thrown off guard when young Violet had put her arms around him and kissed his cheek. Even now he could remember the softness of her body against his, the sweet, warm smell of her, and he had had to fight the urge to grab her and kiss her.

He cursed himself. What kind of monster are you? She's an innocent little girl and you're a grown man. Maybe you need to visit the local saloon since you haven't had a woman in quite awhile. That would stop indecent thoughts about young Violet.

Yes, that's what he would do. Otherwise, things might get out of hand and he was a Texan. He had to protect this poor orphan child and vent his lust on those slutty saloon girls next time he got paid.

Chapter 9

Young Houston wore his new shoe to school the next day. He walked proudly without a crutch and without limping. "My name is now Houston Prescott," he said and squared his shoulders, "and I'm a Texan."

Of course the three Jenkins brothers, freckled-faced and tough, taunted him at lunch. "You ain't a Texan, you're a Yankee. We can tell from the way you talk."

Violet stood with the two boys and even Kessie and Bonnie came to stand with them. Growler lay down next to them, baring his teeth at the bullies. "We're Texans," she declared, "as much as you are."

"Yep," said Harold. "Our daddy used to be a Texas Ranger and he says we're Texans."

"Aw, he ain't a Texas Ranger, he just works in the gun shop," the youngest one taunted, doubling up his fists.

"He used to be," Kessie said. "But then he got shot by a crook and he can't be a Ranger now."

"Why not?" the middle brother asked.

"Because he can't draw fast now," Houston said. "But if you want to fight, we'll take you on like Colonel Travis did the Mexicans at the Alamo."

"Sure, unless you're going to hide behind your sister's skirts."

Harold said, "We ain't gonna hide behind a girl's skirts. Violet, you need to step away and let us men settle this."

"I thought you could use my help," Violet said.

"We men can handle this," Houston assured her.

"We'll clean up the playground with you or we'll sic our big brother, Leroy, on you," the oldest of this trio, Jethro, threatened. Jethro must have been fourteen or fifteen, Violet thought. She remembered meeting Leroy at the general store and the way he had leered at her. Now the three brothers advanced on the small group, the other children gathering around to watch.

About then the school bell rang and all the children trooped back inside.

The oldest Jenkins leaned over to Harold. "We'll get you some day after school. I'm Jethro. Remember that name."

Violet, sitting next to Harold, heard the threat and leaned over to whisper, "You stop beating up my little brothers."

He grinned at her. "You're purty and you got spunk."

She managed to smile back. "I'd like you better if you'd stop threatening my brothers."

About that time, Miss Brewster rapped on her desk with a ruler.

Violet leaned back in her desk. Jethro was just a boy, but she had been charming all ages of men since she'd been thrown out on her own when her mother died. She could tell the teacher or find out who the brothers were and go tattle to their mother, but that would bring even more shame and disgrace to her brothers, and besides, she didn't want to take a chance on running into that big oaf Leroy.

* * *

At home that night, she decided to trust Travis with this problem and quietly told Travis what had happened, all except about Leroy. She didn't want to start trouble with that crazy hombre. "The Jenkinses are big, tough boys and they say they're gonna whip Harold and Houston. I don't know what to do."

"You ain't gonna do anything, young lady." Travis leaned over and kissed her forehead. "This is something for men to settle. Girls need to keep out of it."

She was angry. "So I'm just supposed to let the boys get bullied and beat up?"

Travis shrugged. "I'm teaching them to fight."

"Oh, that's the way you men settle everything." She went off to the kitchen in a huff.

After supper, Travis corralled the two boys. "Let's go out back to the barn."

The three started out the door. Kessie laid down her book to join them, but Travis paused in the door. "Sorry, Red, this is not something little girls ought to get involved in."

"Now why not? Aren't I as smart or smarter than those dumb boys?"

Travis grinned. "Maybe so, but this is for men. Go help your big sister with the dishes."

The three males went into the barn.

"Now," said Travis, "I hear the Jenkins boys are bullying you."

"Who tattled?" Houston asked.

"It doesn't matter," Travis said. "The question is, what are you gonna do about it?"

"They want to fight us," Harold said, "but they're big and tough. I think we'll get beat up."

"Yeah," Houston admitted, "I'm afraid."

"Well, I reckon even Sam Houston was afraid at times," Travis answered. "There's nothing wrong with being afraid, but sometimes you have to go ahead on even if you're shaking in your boots. You see what's right and keep right on coming. Now that's real bravery."

Harold looked glum. "We don't know how to fight."

"I told you I was gonna teach you," Travis said.

"You know how?" Harold asked.

"Of course. Every Texas man knows how to fight. Texans been fighting all their lives." He stopped and looked at his right wrist. The wound had healed. Maybe the doctor back in Kansas didn't know what he was talking about. "First you double up your fists and put them up high to protect your face." He demonstrated.

Both boys tried to copy his movements.

"No, you got to double up your fists," Travis corrected, "like this. Now if he comes at you, you better be fast on your feet and be able to duck and punch."

Both boys tried to box.

Travis grinned. "Now you come in under his fists and punch him in the nose or kick him between the legs. That hurts like hell and they won't want to fight after that."

He had the two boys face off and practice their punches. "No, not that way, Harold. Look, let me show you." Travis crouched to get on Houston's level and they exchanged light punches. "Now you're getting it."

He brought his fist up to show Houston how to do a right cross and their fists collided.

A searing flash of pain went up Travis's arm from his wrist and he thought for a moment he might faint. He stumbled two steps and leaned against the barn wall, smothering a groan.

"Oh, gosh, Travis, I didn't mean to hurt you!" Houston's face turned pale.

He was still having spasms of pain. "It—it isn't your fault. It's this damned wrist."

"I'm telling!" Travis looked up to see little Bonnie

standing in the open barn door. Before he could stop her, she turned and ran for the house.

"Okay, boys," he murmured, striving to stand up straight, "we're about to have girls out here clucking around and scolding like hens."

Sure enough, in seconds, all three females were standing in the barn door.

Violet's pretty face was white. "Travis, are you all right? What happened?"

"Quit fussing over me," he gasped, "and help me sit down."

"Here, put your arm over my shoulder," she commanded, "and I'll walk you to that hay bale."

He leaned on her, liking the smell of her clean brown hair and the warmth of her petite body. "It's just that bum wrist. Houston accidently hit my hand and the fragment must have dug into a nerve."

She sat him down on the hay bale. "You men! Don't you remember what the doctor in Kansas said?"

"I thought he might be wrong," Travis admitted, enjoying her fussing over his arm. Her touch was gentle.

"Well, obviously he wasn't, so you'll have to be careful 'til you can have it operated on back east."

"Which is never," Travis griped.

"Then remember it can go out on you at any time and leave you almost helpless," Violet scolded. She looked up at him and he saw tears in those pretty blue eyes.

Houston said, "He was teaching us to fight."

"That's right," Harold chimed in.

"Can't men settle a dispute any way but fighting?" Violet was still examining Travis's wrist.

Her hair looked so soft and brown that he wanted to reach out and stroke it, but he didn't. "Sometimes there ain't no other way."

"We'll practice," Harold said.

"Not tonight," Violet snapped. "And such a poor example in front of the girls."

Kessie said, "I bet I can fight. I bet I could beat up those Jenkins boys."

Travis shook his head as he got to his feet. "No, Kessie. In Texas, ladies don't fight. Let Texas men protect you."

"Oh, ladies don't get to do anything fun," the redhead complained. "When I'm grown up, I'm going to change all that. Ladies ought to be able to fight, too, if they want to, besides voting and running for president."

"Here." Violet took Travis's arm. "Lean on me and I'll help you back to the house."

"Young lady, you're gettin' awfully bossy." Actually he didn't need her assistance, but having her close felt so good and comforting he let her help him. Then he reminded himself that she was just a schoolgirl and he shouldn't like her touch so much.

They returned to the house, Bonnie trailing behind with old Growler.

The next morning, before all the children left for school, Travis took Houston aside. "You ready for that fight?"

Houston looked nervous. "Yes, sir, but they're bigger than we are."

Travis winked at Houston. "Let them start it, but make sure you get in the first good punch. Texans never start fights, but they damn well can finish them."

Kessie came into the room. "What are you talking about?"

"Just men's talk," Houston said.

"Humph!" Kessie put her nose in the air. "I don't care anyway. I'm just waiting for Violet and Bonnie to get ready."

"Everyone got their books?" Violet called and the

children gathered up and went out, walking down the street, the May weather warm and pleasant. Travis left them at the gun shop and they walked on down the road to school.

Violet was nervous, sure the Jenkinses would pick on the boys today. "Now, Harold and Houston, you just ignore their taunts and don't fight them."

"We can't do that," Houston said. "We're Texans and nobody insults us without either paying for it or backing down."

Violet said, "I'll tell Miss Brewster."

"Don't you dare!" Houston said. "This is between men and you ain't a man."

"Thank goodness for that," Kessie snapped, marching into school and sitting down at her desk.

Violet wasn't sure what to do. She listened to Miss Brewster ringing the big school bell outside and saw the freckled Jenkins brothers come swaggering into the building. They looked toward Harold and Houston, and sneered.

It occurred to her that Jethro was the most formidable of the Jenkins trio. Maybe she could make him lose interest in fighting. As he sat down at his desk, she turned and gave him her warmest smile and battered her eyelashes at him.

The big, clumsy boy flushed furiously but focused his attention on her. As Miss Brewster started the class, he sent Violet a note down the row of desks.

Making sure Miss Brewster was intent on writing on the blackboard, Violet opened it. It read: *Can I carry your books home from school?*

She scribbled back. *Yes, unless you beat up my brothers.*

She watched him. He gave her a silly grin, obviously smitten with her, and sent her a note back. *I won't, but I can't speak for my brothers.*

She nodded and smiled at him. She thought maybe Houston and Harold could handle the younger boys. Of course the idea of walking home from school with Jethro didn't thrill her, but if it would keep him from beating up her little brothers, it would be worth it.

Come lunchtime, all the children went outside with their lunches while the teacher stayed inside to eat hers. Violet settled herself on the steps with her sandwich with Kessie and Bonnie near her. Bonnie was sharing her sandwich with Growler as usual.

Violet sighed. "Bonnie, honey, I wish you wouldn't do that."

"Dog hungry, too," Bonnie lisped and kept feeding him.

The boys had gobbled their lunches and disappeared around back of the old frame building.

Kessie said, "You know they're going to fight now."

"I'm doing my best to stop it," Violet answered. "Let's go around."

Sure enough, the boys were squaring off back of the building.

Violet fluttered her eyelashes at Jethro, the big one, and he stepped away from the circle and started over to her.

"Hey, Jethro, where you going?" yelled his younger brother. "We need you in this fight."

Jethro ignored his brother and came over to stand by Violet. "You're wearing a purty dress," he said and blushed again.

"Thank you," Violet answered.

"Jethro, ain't you coming?" yelled his brother.

"You don't need me to whip them two sissies," Jethro said, smiling down at Violet.

Violet looked up at him. "It's more fair that way," she whispered.

"Yes, ma'am." He grinned at her like an idiot, completely smitten.

And so the fight began. The two younger Jenkins boys

against Houston and Harold with all the children gathered in a circle, cheering them on.

"I'm telling!" Kessie started for the schoolhouse, but Violet grabbed her arm.

"They got to fight it out or this will never get settled."

Violet muffled the urge to run in and rescue her little brothers, but they seemed to be holding their own. Whatever Travis had taught them must be helping.

The Jenkins boy drew a line in the dirt with his boot. "I double-dare you two sissies to step across that line."

Of course no one expected Harold and Houston to step across, but after a moment's hesitation, they did so. A murmur went through the group of children.

"Okay," said the other Jenkins brother, "I double-dog dare you to step across this line." He drew a line in front of him with his toe.

Instead of backing away, Harold and Houston stepped across. The Jenkins boy swung at him and missed. Then Houston doubled up his fist and hit the other boy hard in the nose.

"No fair!" yelled the boy, with blood running down his face. "You didn't give me fair warning!"

"That was fair warning!" Houston said and grabbed him, hitting him again.

Harold attacked the other boy with both fists and soon, all four were rolling and grappling in the dirt, Growler barking and dashing in to grab the strangers by the pant legs. Big Jethro started as though to interfere, but Violet caught his arm and said, "Don't forget your promise."

He looked down at her, adoration on his ugly face. "You're so pretty, Violet. I do want to walk you home."

And so the fight continued until the noise finally reached Miss Brewster, who came running out the back door, waving her ruler and shouting for all this nonsense to stop. The circle of children melted back and the skinny teacher waded in and grabbed two boys, pulled them to their feet, then grabbed the other two by the collars and dragged them to their feet. "You little savages. You're all going to get a paddling for this!"

So four dirty, bloody little boys had to stand up before the class and get their rears paddled with Miss Brewster's wooden paddle.

Bonnie began to sob and Growler started barking so Miss Brewster paused. She yelled to Violet, "Can't you stop that racket?"

"When you stop paddling her brothers, she'll stop," Violet shouted over the wailing baby and barking dog.

"I can't stand the noise," Miss Brewster snapped and put down the paddle. "You four go to your seats and write 'I will not fight' five hundred times each."

All four boys sauntered proudly to their seats, the admiring glances of all the other children following them.

Houston whispered to Violet, "Who won?"

"I'd say it was a draw," Violet answered.

"We wouldn't have if Jethro had got involved," Harold whispered.

"You all stop that talking!" Miss Brewster thundered.

Violet wasn't about to let them know why Jethro hadn't gotten involved. She was satisfied that Harold and Houston had survived the fight and were going to be accepted by the other boys now. In the meantime, what was she to do about the lovesick Jethro?

After school, Violet started out the door, but Jethro caught up with her. "Violet, you said I could carry your books, remember?"

"Of course. You kids go on ahead." She motioned to the four, but Harold said, "You gonna let a Jenkins walk you home?"

"It's okay," Violet said and motioned them on ahead. Jethro took her books shyly and walked along beside her.

"Miss Violet, half the boys in school have taken a liking to you."

She blushed. "Oh, I'm sure that isn't true, Jethro."

"It is too, but I threatened to beat up any boy that wanted to carry your books," he said proudly.

"I really don't like fighting, Jethro. Let's not do that anymore, okay?"

"Okay, unless they want to carry your books."

They walked along in the May afternoon. She tried to think of something to say to the big oaf, but after all, he was just a boy.

"Miss Violet, there'll be a picnic in a few days to celebrate the end of school." He stopped and stubbed his toe in the dirt. "Maybe, well, what I'm trying to say is maybe you might go with me?"

What to say? "Jethro, I'm sorry, but our dad is really strict—"

"I would be too if I was your daddy," he blurted.

"What I mean to say is probably my family will all come together, but I'll see you there."

"That'll be fine. You will save me a dance, won't you?"

"Uh, of course." She didn't know what else to say. She didn't want to lead this hulk of a boy on, but on the other hand, she didn't want to make him mad so he'd beat up her little brothers again, or worse yet, call in his older brother, Leroy.

They had walked past the gun shop and had reached her house. They paused by the gate. "Well, here it is. Thank you, Jethro, for carrying my books."

"I'd carry you if need be," he stuttered and turned bright red.

"That isn't necessary. Well, I'll see you at school tomorrow." She pulled her books from his big hands, ran up on the steps and waved to him. "See you tomorrow."

She was fixing supper when Travis walked in. "Oh, hello, how was business at the gun shop?"

"Fine." He seemed grumpy. "Who was that big lout who was with you this afternoon?"

Was he jealous? He looked jealous. No, she thought, he was thinking of her in a fatherly way. "Oh, that was Jethro Jenkins, one of the boys from school."

"Boy?" Travis snorted. "I've heard about those Jenkinses. That one looked almost grown. I don't want him walking you home anymore, you hear?"

"Now just who do you think you are?" Violet's temper flared before she thought.

"I'm looking after you." He grabbed her by the shoulders. "And he's older than you. I know what he's got in mind."

"And what would that be?" She looked up into his eyes, saw the hesitation there, thought he might kiss her.

Instead he took a deep breath and stepped away. "Never mind, you're too innocent to know about such things."

If he only knew, she thought as she turned back to her stove, shaken because of that moment, knowing she had wanted him to kiss her. She realized she was falling in love with him. She didn't know what she was going to do, but there didn't seem to be a good answer.

Chapter 10

The next week, when Violet took the children to the library to check out books, Miss Knowlen cornered her. "How are all you poor children getting along?"

Violet managed a smile. "We're doing just fine, thank you."

"You know, the townspeople are beginning to talk. They think it's not a good idea for a man to try to raise all those children by himself."

"We're managing," Violet said again.

"Well, just remember, I'm always around to help. I did tell you I was unmarried, didn't I? And I'm only forty—thirty-five."

"I'll tell Travis," she said and retreated to the fiction section. True, she could barely read, but she was learning fast and she loved the romances where the plucky heroine landed the handsome bachelor at the end.

The following week, it was Miss Brewster, the schoolmarm, who caught her one morning out on the school grounds. "How is your father?"

"Just fine. He's working at the gun shop."

"Yes, I know." She frowned and her spectacles slid

down her nose. "Everyone in town is saying he should get married so he'd have a woman to help with all those children."

Violet squared her shoulders. "We're doing just fine alone, thank you."

"As many eligible women as there are in this town, he shouldn't have any trouble finding a wife. Of course, a well-educated one would be a big advantage in rearing children."

"Yes, it would." Violet ran into the schoolhouse to end the conversation.

She knew that often, the pretty rich widow, Charlotte Van Mayes, came by the gun shop. It was amazing how fast her cowhands went through ammunition. Violet noted the widow had stopped wearing mourning and was now wearing bright colors. Conveniently, the lady also often brought a picnic lunch with her, and so Violet's plain sandwich for Travis went uneaten.

Violet did a slow burn over all this, but of course she couldn't say anything because she was just a child. Sometimes she lay in her bed at night in the late May heat and thought about Travis. She hungered to go into his embrace and have him kiss her, really kiss her. In her dreams, he came to her room at night and she held up her arms to him.

"Make love to me," she would whisper.

And he would murmur, "I thought of nothing but you all day. I want to make slow, passionate love to you all night and at breakfast, let's talk about marriage."

"Marriage?"

"Yes, and then we'll adopt all the kids and have some babies of our own."

He would kiss her, putting his hot tongue in her mouth and kissing her breasts until she was gasping and aching with pleasure. And then she would wake up and find herself drenched with perspiration and hear Travis's breathing from his room across the hall. *Oh, what a tangled web we weave when first we practice to deceive*, she thought in helpless desperation and sobbed into her pillow.

As June came, Jethro Jenkins still walked her home sometimes, though she tried to discourage him. More than once, she saw his big brother, Leroy, watching them from behind a tree or fence. The way Leroy looked at her made her nervous, but she didn't say anything.

Pleasant Valley stayed its sleepy self, the hound dog sleeping in the middle of the dusty main street, the elderly, plump sheriff asleep in his chair out in front of his office. Most of the rounds were made by his young deputy, Williard, who was really one of the local ranch boys.

The only excitement of the day was when the southbound train came through at four o'clock in the afternoon, and the northbound train came through at seven o'clock in the evening. Both rarely stopped, so after awhile, Violet didn't notice them except that their passing rattled the house windows.

School came to an end the first week of June with recitations and songs in the morning and the picnic and dance planned for that afternoon and evening.

The children gathered around Violet as she packed the picnic basket. "Isn't this going to be fun?" she asked. "All the stores are closing early and tonight there'll be a dance and maybe even some fireworks."

The gun shop had closed for the celebration, so now Travis leaned against the door and watched her. She was pretty, no doubt about it. No, she was more than pretty, she was . . . he couldn't come up with a name for it. He'd come to depend on the young girl. Sometimes at night, he could hear her moving restlessly in bed and his desire rose as he thought about her. *You sick bastard*, he would scold himself, *she's just a kid. You either need to marry or go over to the saloon and take one of those gals upstairs.*

Still he never quite got around to doing that. He told himself it was because with all the expenses, he really couldn't afford it. However, when he thought about it, he realized the only female he wanted to bed was just thirteen years old. *You rotten rat.* He would turn over and put his pillow over his head and try to sleep, but it was difficult.

Now he watched her packing the picnic and said, "May sure went by quick, and now it's June and school's out today."

Kessie made a face. "I hope no dumb boy asks me to dance tonight."

"Don't worry," laughed Harold. "They won't."

"Now, boys," Travis frowned. "Don't tease your sisters. If no one asks them to dance, you do it."

"What? Me dance with Kessie?" Houston's face screwed up in disgust.

"It's only polite," Travis insisted. "You can't leave your sisters standing on the sidelines like wallflowers."

Little Bonnie patted Growler. "What's wallflower?"

"Kessie," Harold joked and immediately, the redhead whacked him with a dish towel.

"I don't want to dance with some stupid boy who will step all over my shoes," she complained. "And Houston and Harold don't know how to dance anyway."

"I've been teaching them a few steps," Violet said, wondering if Travis would ask her to dance tonight. She was looking forward to it.

Travis laughed. "Houston is becoming a crack shot and horseman since I've been working with him."

"And Harold has read every book in the local library," Violet said.

"Besides," Kessie sniffed, "dancing is for silly girls. I've got more important things on my mind."

"Like what?" Travis asked.

"I hear the Texas suffragettes are coming to town for the July Fourth parade," Kessie said. "And I plan to be in it."

Harold shook his head. "We'll all die of embarrassment if you do."

"Oh, I doubt that," Travis laughed and watched Violet put the icing on her chocolate cake. Without thinking, he walked up behind her and put his big hands on her slight shoulders. "I don't know what I'd do without you."

He felt her stiffen and realized the children were all watching. He didn't want to step back, but he did. He had had the sudden impulse to kiss the back of her brown hair.

Harold leaned against the counter and watched Violet icing the cake. "I bet I know who won't be a wallflower."

"Who?" squealed Bonnie.

"Violet, of course. Half the boys in school, especially that Jethro Jenkins, have been mooning after her like idiots."

Travis frowned. "Word around town is that those Jenkins boys, especially that grown one, are nothing but trouble."

Violet looked up at him and he thought she had never seemed so fragile and lovely. "I can take care of myself."

Travis felt annoyed . . . or was it something else? "I don't think so, young lady. Now if you have any trouble with any boy, you let me know."

Violet looked at him a long moment and he couldn't read her face. "I'm not used to anyone looking out for me—I've looked out for myself for so long. But I'm not expecting any trouble."

Travis said, "Boys, why don't we go on ahead and help the other men set up the tables?"

"I was hoping to lick the bowl when she finished," Harold said.

"Me bowl," Bonnie yelled. "Me and Growler bowl."

"See?" Travis laughed. "Besides, there'll be plenty of cake at the picnic. Come on, let's go."

The three of them went out the front door and walked down Main Street. It was a busy scene, tents and tables and a big wooden platform for the dance set up on the wide street on the other side of the railroad tracks. Here and there were booths where ladies were selling cookies and knickknacks and even a kissing booth for the more daring women.

"Now, boys," Travis said under his breath, "let's all watch out for Violet tonight. She's too young and innocent to know what some men are capable of."

"I think she can take care of herself," Houston said.

"No, she can't, she just thinks she can," Travis growled. "Now if we take turns dancing with her, that doesn't give any of the other galoots a chance."

"I don't wanta dance," Harold complained. "I want to play games and eat."

"Now you mind what I say," Travis scolded. "The men of her family have to protect her."

"Do we have to protect Kessie, too?" Houston asked.

Travis laughed. "I don't think Kessie is in any danger."

They stopped to help set up some tables.

"Howdy." The tall owner of the hardware store shook hands with Travis. "We got all the streets blocked off so no one can drive a horse and buggy into the crowd."

"Too bad we can't do something about the trains," Travis said.

"Well, we know exactly when it comes through and we can hear it for miles, so that's no problem."

Travis and the other men continued to set up tables and booths as Violet and the girls walked up with their picnic basket.

Violet watched in disgust as the pretty widow, wearing an expensive pink dress, complete with a matching lace parasol, stepped out of her fancy buggy and Travis hurried to help her alight. She fluttered her eyelashes at Travis. "Thank you, Travis. Lovely day, isn't it?"

"Ma'am, it certainly is." He touched the tips of his fingers to the brim of his hat.

Violet moved close enough to hear the conversation.

"Travis," the pretty widow said, "I plan to save you most of my dances tonight."

Travis turned beet-red and fumbled with his hat. "Why, thank you kindly, Mrs. Van Mayes."

"Oh, don't you think we know each other well enough that you can call me Charlotte?"

At this point, Violet couldn't stand any more. She walked up and said, "Travis, I could use some help with some things."

The pretty widow glared at her, but Violet pretended not to see.

"Sure, young lady, what do you need?"

Violet took him by the arm and led him away on some pretext about a table. When she looked back, Mrs. Van Mayes was still glaring at her.

"What did she want?" she asked Travis.

"Just visiting, friendly like most Texans," he said.

"She's not a Texan, she's a Yankee," Violet bristled.

"But she's a pretty one, ain't she?" Travis grinned.

Violet had a terrible surge of jealousy. "I think she's got her cap set for you."

"Oh, I don't know about that." Travis shrugged. "But everyone in town is saying I ought to get married."

"We're doing just fine," Violet said. "We don't need her."

"Why, young lady." He stopped and looked down at her. "I do believe you're jealous."

She felt the hot flush rise to her face. "Of course not. It's just that I don't think she's right for you, that's all."

He winked at her. "Missy, I've had a lot of experience with women; I don't need a kid telling me about them."

He was telling her to mind her own business, she thought as she turned away. How could she compete with the beautiful and rich girl? Especially since she was only thirteen years old. She went to help put cloths on tables while gritting her teeth in frustration.

"My, my, ain't that a sight?" Travis sighed, looking down the street.

Violet turned and looked.

Mrs. Van Mayes was walking down the sidewalk to another booth, her pink bustle wiggling enticingly.

"Well, could you stare any harder?" Violet snapped.

"I might could." He grinned and then turned back to help her set up a table.

"Who are those ladies?" Harold asked, shielding his eyes with his hand from the sun.

Both Violet and Travis turned to look. The gaudy, scantily dressed girls from the Cattle Drive Saloon had come out on the balcony of their building and were watching the proceedings with interest. They wore bright feather plumes in their hair and lots of paint on their faces.

Violet's face colored and Travis rushed in to answer. "Uh, those are girls who work there."

"What kind of work?" Harold asked.

Violet looked at Travis and shook her head.

Travis stumbled. "Aw, we'll talk about it sometimes."

"Like serving lemonade?" Houston asked.

Violet sighed with relief. "Exactly."

"Then why are they wearing a lot of face paint and not much clothes?" Kessie said.

"Feathers," Bonnie lisped.

"What?" Travis asked.

"Nothing," Violet snapped and said, "Bonnie, keep

Growler from getting up on the table and eating the fried chicken."

Houston was still staring at the saloon girls and one of them waved at him.

Travis said, "Now boys, you all just stop looking at them. They won't be coming to the celebration."

"Why not?" Houston asked. "I might like to try dancing with that pretty little blonde."

Violet seemed to be struggling for words. "Because they aren't welcome. The ladies of the town don't want them there."

"Why not?" Harold asked.

"Never you mind," Travis said. "Now let's help set up the dance floor over past the train tracks and let those ladies get back to serving their—aw, lemonade."

"Among other things," Violet said pointedly.

Harold was still watching the girls on the balcony. One of them noticed him staring and waved at him again. Now all the girls were waving at him.

Violet looked at Travis. "Can't you do something? People are noticing."

"Now what do you expect me to do? Go tell them to stop waving?"

Now Harold waved back.

Violet snapped, "I don't think they're waving at you, Harold. I think they're waving at Travis."

"Now can I help that?" Travis made a motion of helplessness.

"Then stop looking at them," Violet snapped.

"Now what's wrong with you?" Travis asked.

"Nothing."

"I don't know much about women, but I know when one says 'nothing' in that tone of voice, there's definitely something," Travis said.

Kessie sighed. "Can we all just forget about the saloon girls and spread our picnic?"

"Good idea." Violet sounded relieved.

Travis took a deep breath. A man had a right to look, didn't he? It had been weeks since Travis had had a woman and a couple of those girls looked eager and pretty. He didn't expect to have to answer to a slip of a girl who sometimes acted more like a wife than a child.

Violet stared up at the girls one last time. They made her uneasy because only weeks before, she had been an over-painted, scantily dressed saloon girl herself and she wanted to put that behind her, but this had reminded her of it all over again. Funny, one of those girls looked familiar, but it was quite a distance and she was probably imagining it. As heavily painted as they were, who could tell one from another? That was all she needed, to run into a girl who knew her from the old days.

"Are we ever gonna eat or are you gonna keep standing there lost in thought?" Travis teased her.

She started. "Oh, I'm sorry. I was just trying to remember if I brought the lemonade."

Travis grinned down at her. "If you didn't, there's a stand over there run by Miss Knowlen, the librarian, selling lemonade."

"The library can use the money." Violet nodded. "Go buy some and I'll spread out our tablecloth while you're gone."

Growler sat next to Bonnie.

"Hungry," the toddler complained.

"Here's a piece of chicken to hold you until I get food laid out," Violet said. "And don't give it all to the dog."

Travis sauntered down the row of booths with Harold and Houston with him. "We'll find the lemonade, boys."

They passed the kissing booth and Miss Brewster, the skinny schoolteacher, leaned out and called to him. "Hello, Mr. Prescott. How about a kiss for a dime? The school needs the money."

Houston and Harold both nudged him. "Go ahead, Travis."

About that time, the little Avery girl from school, with her black corkscrew curls, stuck her head up out of the booth. "Hey, Houston and Harold, come kiss me for a dime."

They started backing away, but Travis caught them by the collars. "Now remember, boys, it's for a good cause."

Both boys turned beet red.

"I don't want to kiss her," Harold muttered.

"I'd rather kiss Growler," Houston said.

"Oh, it won't kill you. Here." Travis dug in his pocket and handed them each a dime.

"No." They both shook their heads.

"Well, would you rather kiss Miss Brewster?"

Both boys took deep breaths. "Can't we just give her the money?" Houston asked.

"I reckon." Travis grinned.

Miss Brewster beckoned to him. "Mr. Prescott, don't be shy. The money's for a good cause."

Mrs. Van Mayes popped up suddenly beside her. "Sorry, Miss Brewster, but I think I can handle this." She leaned forward, her eyes closed.

Travis felt himself flush, but he took his dime, put it in her dainty hand and reached over to give her a peck on the cheek. Instead, the lady grabbed him and planted a hot kiss full on his mouth. It felt so good, it was a long moment before he pulled back, breathless and surprised. He didn't even speak, just stared at her while she gave him a bold wink.

Miss Brewster looked scandalized and for once, she was speechless. "Why, I never—"

"I'll bet you haven't," said the bold blonde.

Travis couldn't think of anything to say.

Next to him, he heard Houston and Harold. "Did you see that? Why, he even acted like he liked it."

Travis backed away as Mrs. Van Mayes whispered, "Why don't you come to dinner next week?"

"Uh, well, yes, I reckon we could." He glanced down at the boys, who were staring up at him. "Uh, boys, I reckon we'd better go find that lemonade." He turned and stumbled away, his mind still on the widow's hot, wet mouth. She was eager, all right; the way she had kissed him told him that.

"Did you like that?" Harold asked as they walked down the row of booths.

"Well, sort of," Travis admitted sheepishly. "You see, fellows, when you get my age, you kind of like a girl to kiss you."

"Then why haven't you kissed Violet?" Houston asked.

"That's different," Travis gulped, but in his mind, he suddenly saw himself kissing Violet. *You rotten bastard*, he scolded himself, *she's just a kid. You need to take your lust to one of the saloon girls.* He promised himself he'd do that one night next week. He looked toward the saloon. The girls had gone back inside and he could hear laughter and "Camptown Races" banging away on the piano inside.

"What are they doing in there?" Harold asked as they passed the saloon.

"Oh, drinking, gambling, having fun," Travis said.

Harold snorted. "What do you do with a girl to have fun?"

"Someday, when you're older, I'll tell you." Travis grinned.

They bought five cups of pink lemonade and walked back down the length of Main Street. In the distance,

Travis heard the southbound train coming. "Must be about four o'clock."

They reached their table just as the train came through town. It must not have had any freight or passengers to let off or pick up because it didn't stop.

"What took you so long?" Violet asked, waving her hand in front of her face and coughing over the black, sooty smoke drifting from the train as it went through town and on south.

"Oh, some stuff happened." Travis shrugged. "We got the lemonade."

"He bought a kiss," Harold volunteered.

Violet smiled. "From Miss Brewster?"

"No, he—" Houston seemed to see Travis putting his finger to his lips and stopped.

Violet turned to Travis. "Who else was in the kissing booth?"

Travis shrugged. "Oh, just some old widow. The money's for the school, you know."

Violet looked up at him. "Just how old was she?"

"Oh, old." Travis reached for a sandwich. "This looks like chicken salad. I really like chicken salad." He stuffed a bite in his mouth.

"Yeah," Harold agreed with a nod, "she's old, maybe even twenty-five or so."

Violet put her hands on her hips. "Who are we talking about here?"

"Uh, Mrs. Van Mayes," Travis said and reached for a pickle.

"That pretty blonde with the big ranch outside town?"

"Now, young lady, that's not really any of your business. Just think, if I got married, you'd have a mother and it would take a lot of responsibility off your shoulders."

"I haven't complained," she said.

"Yes, and that's noble of you." Travis took a sip of

lemonade. "But maybe the other children would like a mother."

Violet turned and looked at the other children.

"No." Kessie shook her head. "We all like things just the way they are."

"Well, maybe I don't!" Travis snapped. "Does it ever occur to you kids that I might get lonely?"

Harold looked up at him. "You got all of us, Mouse and Growler. Ain't we enough?"

"That lady's got a big ranch and a nice house," Kessie said. "Maybe that's why he might want to get married."

"I don't think so," Violet snapped. "She's awfully pretty. Was it a good kiss?" She stared up into Travis's dark eyes.

"I don't know, it was just a kiss, that's all. Good God, you act like a wife instead of a kid."

Houston said, "Maybe that's because she's had to act like a mother to all of us and run the house."

Violet picked up a sandwich. "Maybe I should help out the school by working in the kissing booth."

"No, you don't," Travis said. "You're too young."

The boys started to say something, and Travis figured it might be about the widow working the kissing booth, so he shook his head at them. "By the way, Charlotte invited us to dinner."

Violet scowled.

Travis appeared puzzled.

He said, "Violet, you know I would never marry anyone you kids didn't like."

"Good, because I don't like her."

"You don't know her." He took a sip of lemonade.

"I know she's chasing after you like a hound dog on a hot trail."

He grinned. "The chase is always the best part of it."

She decided not to say anything more; she could only make it worse. If only she could come clean with him about her real age and that she was falling in love with him. Would that make any difference to the big hombre, or was he stuck on Charlotte Van Mayes? She wished she knew.

Violet made her plans. She was going to dance with Travis tonight and maybe, maybe she might kiss him and confess about her lies. Did she dare? It might either be that or lose him to the beautiful widow.

It was a great afternoon, Travis thought. The food Violet had brought was delicious. "You know, kid, I could eat your cooking the rest of my life."

"That can be arranged," she said before she thought.

"What?"

She gulped. "I meant you could adopt all of us."

Along about sundown, the northbound train came through, rattling windows and bellowing smoke, but not stopping.

As darkness grew, the small band assembled on the platform and began to tune their instruments. The crowd put away their picnic gear and gathered around the wooden dance floor.

Travis looked toward Violet. He would dance with her first, of course, and then he might dance with the pretty blond widow, who was smiling at him across the crowd.

The band began to play a slow waltz. Travis turned to Violet, but before he could speak, that oldest Jenkins, Leroy, was by her side. "Dance with me, Miss Violet?"

She hesitated, a little cautious. "Of course."

And he whirled Violet out on the floor.

Travis watched, a little annoyed, but he wasn't certain why. That oldest Jenkins was a man and everyone in town thought him a little odd. Violet looked nervous. That was all it took.

Travis strode out onto the dance floor and tapped Leroy on the shoulder. "I'm cutting in."

"No," said Leroy.

"Let go of her and get off this dance floor," Travis ordered.

The man hesitated, then walked away, sulking as Travis took her in his arms.

She looked up at him, loving him as she had never thought she could love a man. "Thank you," she whispered and laid her face against his chest as they waltzed.

Now it was Travis's turn to feel uncomfortable. He didn't think it looked right to be dancing this close to a young girl, but it felt so good to hold her tightly, he didn't pull away. He put his face next to her head, and her brown hair smelled so clean and sweet he didn't ever want to let her go. He could hold her like this forever, he thought.

Then he looked up and realized people were staring at them and he knew he must protect the young girl's reputation. She was too innocent and naive to realize what dirty minds might think. He stopped dancing suddenly and led her to the sidelines.

"But the song isn't over," Violet protested, looking up at him.

He felt sweat breaking out all over his muscular body and his manhood pulsating. He was having thoughts he shouldn't have about this kid. "I—I thought Harold or Houston might want to dance with you."

He abandoned her on the edge of the dance floor and walked away.

Violet was both crushed and angry. She had never felt so much pleasure and so protected as she had in Travis's strong arms. What had she done to annoy him? Then when she looked across the crowd, she saw Travis asking Mrs. Van Mayes to dance. Violet's heart fell. She had no chance against that beauty.

She looked down to see all four children standing next to her and Growler by Bonnie's side.

She leaned over to Houston. "It would be nice if you asked Kessie to dance."

The boy made a face. "Must I?"

"It's good manners," she said, pushing him toward the red-haired little girl.

But Kessie shook her head. "I don't think suffragettes waste their time dancing. After all, the man gets to lead. Now what kind of equality is that?"

"Never mind," Violet sighed.

"Look." Harold's almond eyes widened. "Travis is dancing with that pretty lady in pink."

"I hope he puts one of his big boots on her dainty foot," Violet said under her breath.

Bonnie had Growler up on his back legs and was dancing him around the edge of the crowd as people smiled and laughed.

Violet didn't think the song would ever end as she watched Travis dance with Charlotte Van Mayes, but finally it did.

Then the band began an old sweetheart schottische: *Put your little foot, put your little foot, put your little foot right there. . . .*

The beauty in the pink dress was shaking her head and stepping back. Obviously, Violet thought, the Yankee girl didn't know the dance.

Violet took a deep breath, crossed the dance floor and grabbed Travis's hand. "I know this one. Dance with me."

"All right, young lady." He smiled as they stepped out on the wooden floor. The schottische was a Texas cowboy favorite and he enjoyed it. Violet danced well and when she brushed against him, it seemed to set his nerves afire. He reminded himself again that she was just a child and he needed to direct his thoughts elsewhere. The townspeople would string him up if they had any idea what he was thinking and he was horrified himself.

The band stopped and he walked her over to where Mrs. Van Mayes stood.

She gave Violet a condescending smile. "Travis, you dance so well with your daughter. Young lady, you must teach me that step."

Violet didn't smile. "I'm sure Travis would be happy to teach you."

Now the beautiful blonde turned her face up to the tall Texan. "I hope so."

Violet resisted the urge to kick the lady in the shins.

Both females nodded to each other. As Travis watched, he was reminded of two cats circling each other, ready to fight.

Mrs. Van Mayes said, "Violet, you're such a brave little girl to mother all those children. It must be very difficult."

"No, I really enjoy it," Violet answered.

The music started again, a slow waltz, and Travis turned to the pretty blonde. "Mrs. Van Mayes, may I have the honor?"

"Of course, Travis."

They whirled out on the dance floor, leaving Violet standing there, fuming.

Harold walked up beside her. "What are you scowling about?"

"That widow. Do you see how she's hanging on to Travis? Why, you couldn't get a grass blade between them."

"He is holding her pretty close, isn't he?"

An eager cowboy touched Travis's shoulder and he gave up his partner, but Violet thought he looked reluctant to do so.

He came back to stand beside her. "Damn, every man in town wants her."

Violet gritted her teeth and didn't answer for a long moment. "Why don't you dance with me?"

"Uh, I'm a little tired, young lady."

"You didn't look tired when you were dancing with Mrs. Pink Bustle."

"Oh, all right." She was annoyed at how much distance he kept between their two bodies as they danced. Probably he'd rather be dancing with the pretty blonde.

The night had grown dark in the summer heat with a few paper lanterns lighting the dance floor. Violet tried to snuggle up close to him as the band played "Genevieve, Sweet Genevieve."

He appeared startled as she put her body close to his and for a moment, he held her very close and she heard his breath quicken. His body became tense and she snuggled even closer.

At that moment, he took a deep breath and pushed her so that there was distance between them—so much that a horse could have walked between them. She looked up into his eyes and licked her lips, then parted them and fluttered her eyelashes very slowly.

She saw the sudden hot desire in his dark eyes and knew that he wanted her. She wanted him in a way she'd never known a woman could want a man.

"Damn it all to hell," he muttered and stopped dancing abruptly, took her hand and headed for the sidelines.

"What's the matter?" she asked innocently.

"Nothing a young girl would understand," he snapped. "Anyway, I need a beer." He handed her over to Harold. "Here, dance with your sister."

"I don't want to dance with him, I want to dance with you," Violet declared.

"No, you don't. It might lead to trouble."

"I don't want to dance," Harold complained, but Travis had already headed over to the beer booth.

Violet watched Charlotte Van Mayes start after Travis, but just then, Harold grabbed Violet and doggedly began pushing her around the dance floor. She could hear him counting under his breath.

"Honestly, Harold, you don't have to dance with me," she insisted, still trying to watch Travis. She saw him lean on the rail of the beer booth and gulp a mugful. "Gimme another!" he yelled.

About that time, Mrs. Van Mayes came up beside him and engaged him in conversation. He said something and the blonde patted his arm and laughed.

Violet sighed and stopped as Harold stepped on her foot again. "Harold, it's getting late. Gather up the other kids and we'll pack up the picnic stuff and go home."

"Aw, no one wants to go home yet," he grumbled.

"Well, there isn't anything else gonna happen tonight except a little dancing and most of the men getting drunk."

He looked toward the beer booth. "Including Travis?"

"Probably."

"Why?"

She knew why. She'd seen that sudden hot desire in his eyes as he held her close and abruptly pushed her away. "It's just something men do."

"I'll get the kids," Harold said.

"And I'll go gather up the picnic stuff," Violet said and started walking out into the shadows toward the tables.

To be in the shade, they had set up their picnic a long way from the others and it was dark and shadowy out here under the trees. She tripped over a rock and walked on, wishing she had a lantern.

A big shape suddenly stepped out from behind a tree. "Hello, Violet."

"Oh, Leroy, you startled me." She took a step backward. "Where you going?"

"To pack up our picnic stuff."

"I'll go with you."

She had an uneasy feeling about this. "No need to," she said brightly, "It's not heavy."

"Well, I'll carry it."

Way off in the distance, the music played faintly. People laughed and talked around the dance floor. She'd feel foolish screaming and even if she did, would anyone hear her? When Leroy stepped closer, she smelled liquor on his breath. She'd handled drunks for years as a saloon girl, she could certainly handle this brute.

"It's nice of you, Leroy, but why don't you go back to the dance? I can get the basket alone."

"No," he said and then he grabbed her.

Chapter 11

Violet started to scream, but the big lout clapped his hand over her mouth and pulled her close. She tried to bite his fingers, but he slapped her, and for a moment, she felt dizzy and staggered on her feet. Now he had his arms under her legs, lifting her, carrying her toward the creek in the shadows of the underbrush.

She fought him, but she was no match for his strength.

"Stop it, you bitch!" he snarled, "I'm going to lay with you like I've wanted to do since the first time I saw you. If I give you a baby, your pa will make you marry me and I'll have you for good and all."

She writhed in his arms, but he held her tightly and stuffed a dirty rag in her mouth. Violet managed to get one arm free and scratched his face, but he only laughed. "You're a little wildcat, ain't you? I think I like that. Now if you don't stop fighting me, I'll have to knock you out 'cause I intend to have you."

She could smell the reek of whiskey on his breath and knew he was very drunk. Oh, Lord, why hadn't she seen him as more of a threat? Now she was going to be raped and maybe murdered.

Think, Violet, think. Abruptly she went limp in his arms.

"Did you faint? Are you okay, bitch?" He paused and laid her down on the grass near the creek.

When she felt his hot hands leave her, she came alive suddenly, fighting and jumping to her feet. She gave him a hard kick to the groin. He swore and doubled over in pain.

I'm free, she thought, but even as she tried to run, he caught her by the ankle.

"No, you don't, you little tart!" He reached out with one big paw and caught the front of her dress, tearing it and pulling her back down on the grass.

She yanked the dirty rag out of her mouth and bit his hand as hard as she could and he slapped her until she saw stars. *Just relax and let him do it*, her brain told her. *Otherwise, he may kill you. It isn't as if you've never had a man before.*

No, the only man who would ever have her body again was Travis. She had vowed that and she'd go down fighting rather than be raped.

"What the hell's going on here?" Abruptly a big shadow stood over them.

For a split second, she thought Leroy had a partner, but then she recognized Travis's deep drawl and he reached down, grabbed Leroy by the collar, yanked him to his feet and slammed him against a tree.

She was crying with relief, hunched up in a small ball while Travis and Leroy fought. She couldn't seem to find the strength to get up and run.

Suddenly Harold, Houston and even Kessie, Bonnie and Growler were there.

"Bite him!" Little Bonnie yelled and the spotted dog charged in barking, attacking Leroy's legs as Travis hit him hard in the jaw with his left hand. Leroy fell backward and then stumbled to his feet and fled.

"I didn't mean nothin'!" he yelled back. "I wasn't gonna hurt her!"

Travis yelled after him. "You get the hell out of town or I'll kill you!"

Violet scrambled to her feet as Travis leaned against a tree, breathing heavily. "Thank God you came!"

"Are you all right?" Travis asked. "Harold saw him dragging you away and came for me."

She couldn't stop the tears. "I—I'm fine. My dress is torn a little, is all."

He bent over and picked her up in his strong arms. "I can buy you another dress."

She leaned her face against his wide shoulder. He swayed a little as he started walking in long strides. He was a little drunk, she thought, but oh, she was so glad to be safe in his arms.

"You kids gather up the picnic stuff and keep your mouths shut about all this, you hear?" Travis commanded. "If it got out, it might ruin Violet's reputation; people are funny about stuff like this."

She had no reputation to save, but of course he didn't know that. Violet felt guilty as she closed her eyes and relaxed, just happy to be in his embrace.

"Are you sure you're okay?" His warm breath smelled of liquor, but she didn't care.

"As long as you've got me, I'm fine," she whispered.

"Let's go, kids," he ordered.

They started away from the picnic area, Travis carrying her easily. From here she could see that the party had broken up except for a few men still hanging around the beer booth singing and talking.

He carried her through the shadows of the trees so that no one could see them as they returned to the house. Travis took her inside and stood a moment. "Houston, light a lamp and you kids get ready for bed."

Houston lit a lamp and in that small glow, Travis carried her in and laid her on her bed. He stood there in the semi-darkness looking down at her and she realized that her dress was torn so that it revealed a little of one of her breasts. She hurried to cover it up.

His craggy face looked troubled and confused as he stared and she felt the tension in that gaze. He looked hungry, hungry like a man who has gone without food a long, long time. Would he now make love to her? She looked up at him expectantly, waiting, wanting him as she had never wanted a man.

Instead, he cursed and left her bedroom, slamming the door. She heard his thundering voice to the children. "You kids go to bed. I'll be home after while." He sounded angry.

She heard him go out the front door, slamming it behind him.

Violet got up and hurried to the window. He was a little drunk, all right. She watched him stagger back to the party and get himself another beer. Some of the drunks had gathered and were singing "Jeannie With the Light Brown Hair." Travis joined them.

In disgust, Violet put on a nightdress, tiptoed in to check on all the children. They were all asleep. She was tired, too. It had been a long day and she'd been roughed up and terrified by Leroy. She doubted that man would stay in town; he'd be too afraid of Travis.

She went to bed, but she could not sleep. In her mind, she saw Travis as he had been just now, looming over her again, all hot, aroused male, eager to take her. She had yearned for him to reach down, grab her and pull her to him, but of course he had not.

Violet lay there, restless and listening for him to return.

Judging from the off-key singing out on the street, he'd be even more drunk when he got home. She turned over and fluffed her pillow, trying in vain to stop thinking of him, yet imagining what it would be like to have him naked and virile next to her, making passionate love to her on this hot June night. However, as a Texan, he was not about to despoil what he thought was an innocent, underage virgin.

"What a mess you have made of things and now there's no way out," she scolded herself.

Finally she could stand the waiting no longer. She got up, went to the window and peered out into the darkness. The wooden dance floor area and the picnic tables were shadowy and forlorn, but down the street, the saloon was brightly lit and music and women's laughter drifted through its swinging doors. The men who had been on the street were gone. Some of them would have gone home; others might be continuing their celebration in the saloon.

Had Travis gone in there? Was he even now upstairs, venting his hot desire on one of those scantily dressed whores? The thought made her grit her teeth. He was hers and she knew he wanted her, knew it from the way he had stared down at her as she lay in her bed looking up at him.

Jealousy began like a sharp-toothed coyote chewing on her insides. She had to know. Violet got up and dressed in her plain yellow dress and combed her hair into two pigtails. She tiptoed through the house, checking on the children.

Growler, asleep on Bonnie's little bed, raised his grizzled head and snarled, then recognized her and his stubby tail thumped.

"Be quiet, Growler," she whispered. "I'll be back in a minute."

Carrying her shoes to the door, she went outside before she put them on. The noise and music from the saloon was even louder now. Evidently, the beer and liquor were flowing freely. Well, the party was going to continue with one less man. She intended to bring Travis home.

Inside the saloon, Travis leaned on the bar and stared down at the voluptuous, red-haired woman looking up at him. "And what's your name, sugar?"

She looked up at him, rubbing her full breasts against his arm. "Sugar will do for now, big man, but my name is Kate."

God, he needed a woman. He managed to focus his eyes and take a good look at the whore. She was past her prime and deep wrinkles were only slightly hidden under the heavy makeup. Her hennaed hair had a few gray strands showing under the bright green feathered plume. What did he care? He could close his eyes and imagine it was . . . *You sick bastard, don't you even think of Violet that way.*

He put out his hand and stroked Kate's bare shoulder and then trailed his finger down her collarbone to the rise of big breasts in the gaudy green satin dress. "Can I buy you a drink, sugar?"

"You sure can and then let's go upstairs to my room."

He was having a hard time keeping his gaze straight. The room tried to spin a little when he closed his eyes. "What's that gonna cost me?"

"I hear you used to be a Texas Ranger, big man." She took his hand and put it on her waist.

He nodded. "I did, but I got hurt."

She leaned against him. "I hope it wasn't your pistol that got injured."

He laughed. "No, my arm. My pistol is loaded and ready to fire."

She reached up and kissed his cheek. "For a man like

you, the first one is free. I'll wager you're good for a dozen times a night?"

"Maybe only a half dozen, before I have to rest and reload," he confessed. He took a deep breath of her perfume. It was cheap, but earthy, like a bitch in heat. That made him think of Violet, who always smelled like soap and water, and the sweet scent of her long brown hair.

Violet. He remembered standing there, half drunk, looking down at her as she lay on her bed. He had never wanted a woman as much as he had wanted that girl.

You rotten bum, he scolded himself. *It took everything in you to walk out of that bedroom when what you wanted to do was take her quick and deep and fast, making her yours in the most intimate way a man can know a woman.* And she was just a kid. His want for her had begun to occupy his every waking moment and this evening, he had almost given in to temptation. Well, he was a Texan and a gentleman. He wasn't about to force himself on an innocent, underage girl.

Even as he looked down into Kate's painted face, he knew what the answer had to be: take out his lust on a whore or marry the pretty Mrs. Van Mayes. He couldn't live with his desire much longer. Thinking that, he reached down and kissed the whore's painted lips. The tip of her tongue reached into his mouth and he put his hand on her breasts and she only leaned closer, breathing hard.

"Not right here, Kate!" the balding bartender yelled. "Take your cowboy upstairs."

Kate broke away and laughed. "That's just what I intend to do. You ready, Ranger?"

"I'm past ready." He nodded and staggered away from the bar. She held on to his arm to steady him as they started toward the stairs.

Kate looked up as they started up the stairs. The other

whores leaned over the upstairs balcony, watching, and one called, "You get through with him, Kate, I'd like a ride."

"Naw, he's mine for tonight," Kate answered.

His vision was a little blurry, but he felt his manhood throbbing hard. He might be a little drunk, but the part he needed most was ready and willing. He looked back at the other men lounging against the bar and then up at the girls leaning on the balcony railing upstairs. Yep, there was enough of them that he could have a different one every night if he wanted. He reached down and kissed the red-head, but in his mind, the face he saw had large, almost violet eyes and was surrounded by soft brown curls. That made him angry. How dare Violet keep invading his thoughts? "Let's quit wasting time," he whispered. "It's been awhile since I've ridden an unbroken filly."

"Sugar, I expect you to give me quite a ride." She steered him carefully up the stairs with the piano banging away below on "My Old Kentucky Home."

Just as they started into Kate's room, the piano abruptly stopped mid-chord.

"What the hell?" Kate paused in her doorway as Travis grabbed on to the door frame to keep from falling.

He stumbled to the railing and looked down, tried to focus his eyes and see where everyone else was staring. In the swinging doors stood a small, slight figure. She wore a simple yellow dress and her brown hair was in pigtails.

"Daddy," she called. staring up at him, "I've come to take you home."

Men were laughing now. "Hey, Prescott, your little girl has come for you. You better forget about gettin' a little tonight."

He looked down at her, thinking he had never felt so humiliated. "Go on home, kid. I'll be home when I get damned good and ready."

"No, you got to come home now."

Behind him, Kate swore and stepped back in the shadows of the balcony so the girl could not see her.

Even as men laughed and Travis argued, Violet walked to the foot of the stairs and said to the astounded piano player, "There's five of us kids and he needs to come home. He has no spare money to spend here." Then she started up the stairs.

Kate retreated behind a pillar of the upstairs balcony, thinking she recognized the girl in the simple country dress. No, it couldn't be. She stepped back into her room, a little shocked and thinking she must be drunk herself. This pigtailed kid couldn't be who she thought it was.

The young girl never saw Kate as she came up the stairs, took the Ranger by the arm. "Come on, Daddy, let's go home."

"No," he said and shook his head, but the girl was persistent.

"Please, Travis," she whispered and led him to the stairs. They started down them, slowly and unsteadily.

Kate stared after them. Yes, it was Violet all right, Duke's favorite whore. How in the hell had Violet gotten from Kansas clear down here to Texas, and what was she doing in pigtails and dressed up like a schoolgirl?

Kate went to the balcony railing, frowned as she stared after the pair, who were now walking across the saloon floor toward the swinging doors.

Kate had been Duke's favorite, replacing a pretty blond girl named Emily, who had become a hopeless drunk and been thrown out in the street. But Duke soon tired of Kate and then she'd been replaced by the beautiful Violet and

Kate had had to move on to a series of lower-class dumps like this, the old Cattle Drive Saloon.

She hated Violet for replacing her and wondered now if Duke and his hired gun, Slade, knew where Violet was. Maybe there could be a reward in it for the person who told him. Kate smiled to herself, watching the men laughing below her as Violet tried to talk the tall Texan into leaving. Kate decided she would keep this information to herself until she could use it for her own benefit.

Travis could barely stand on his feet, but he was very aware that men were laughing all around him. "Violet, this is no place for a young girl."

"Or you either," she said firmly and began to lead him.

He turned and looked back at the whores on the balcony. "I'll be back, ladies."

"No, he won't," Violet said and led him out the door.

He stood outside taking deep breaths of the fresh air. "You just embarrassed the hell out of me back there, you know it?"

"I wouldn't be the first kid to drag her daddy out of a saloon."

"I'm not your daddy, damn it."

She started leading him toward the house. "You're drunk, Travis. Just come home and sleep it off."

"I was just going upstairs with a lady, and—"

"I know what you were going to do."

"No, you don't. A kid like you don't know anything. She just kissed me, that's all."

They had reached their doorway. Now they paused and she looked up at him. "A kiss? Is that what you're complaining about? I'll give you a kiss."

Before he was aware of what was happening, Violet put

her arms around his neck, pulled him very tight against her soft curves, and then she kissed him.

He couldn't ever remember being kissed with such passion and expertise before. He was astounded, and for a moment, he only stood there while the girl pressed her warm body against his and kissed him, really kissed him.

Then he took a deep breath and returned the kiss as her tongue went into his mouth and he felt its wet warmth against his lips. No woman had ever kissed him with such passion and he pulled her so tightly against him that she might not be able to breathe. He wanted to pull her inside him, kiss her deeper and deeper. Their tongues met and his hand went to her breast inside her dress and his manhood came up hard and throbbing. He had never wanted a woman like he wanted this one. He could feel her heart pounding hard against his chest and he pulled back so he could swing her up into his arms. All he could think of was getting her to a bed, a hayloft, anywhere where he could lay her down and make passionate love to her.

"Travis?" she whispered, looking up at him with those wide violet-blue eyes.

Her voice brought him out of his frenzied stupor. "What—what in God's name am I doing?"

He pushed her away from him, both of them breathing hard. "I must be very drunk or a very sick bastard to grab a kid like you and—"

"You're just drunk." She seemed to regain her composure and look around while adjusting her dress. "We'd better get inside before anyone sees us."

"God, yes. This town would lynch me in a heartbeat if they caught me fondling and kissing a thirteen-year-old girl."

"Forget about it. In the morning, you won't even remember this. Let's go in." She had him by the arm as she opened the door and they stumbled inside. "Be quiet and don't wake the kids."

He was drunk, there was no denying that. He stumbled along in the dark, letting her lead him to his bed, where he collapsed.

"I'll take off your boots," she said, "and in the morning, you'll be fine except for a hangover."

He closed his eyes to keep the dark room from swirling around his head. The gentle touch of her hands pulling off his boots was the last thing he remembered.

Violet stood up and looked down at him. He was already out cold. With any luck, he wouldn't remember the kiss in the morning. If he did, she'd lie and tell him he'd imagined it.

How could she have been such a fool? She had always wanted to kiss him and she'd given in to the temptation to keep him from thinking about the saloon girl he'd been about to bed when Violet had arrived.

Shaking with jealousy, she went to her room and got ready for bed, trying to forget that he had been about to make love to another woman. Violet had never wanted a man to make love to her before; she had just endured it as the price she had to pay to survive. But now she wanted Travis, and she'd painted herself into a corner. How could she let him know she was almost twenty without explaining? He would hate her for being a whore.

So there was nothing else to do but pretend she was only thirteen years old and one of the orphans. Sooner or later, he would want a woman again and head back to the saloon . . . or maybe he would marry one of the eager respectable women in this town. There didn't seem to be any good answer for this mess she'd created. Hot tears gathered in her eyes and ran down her cheeks. She dabbed at them awkwardly. She never cried, not since her little brother, Tommy, died at the charity hospital with her holding his small hand and begging him not to leave her.

After that, Violet had hardened her heart, knowing that to survive in this tough world, she would have to guard her soul so that no emotion ever came to the surface. Yet now here she was crying over a drunken Texas Ranger who she could never have. Tonight, she'd had just a glimpse of what love could be with a man she really loved and could never have. It hurt so much.

Violet drifted off into a troubled sleep and in that sleep, she dreamed that Travis had carried her into his bed and made passionate love to her, thrilling her in a way that she had never known.

She awoke at dawn, breathing hard and terrified that Travis would remember last night and ask questions. Oh God, what would she say if he did?

Chapter 12

Violet got up and put on the light yellow dress. Since Travis was working, she now owned two dresses. She picked up the blue one and sighed. It was torn down the front from last night's encounter with Leroy Jenkins, but maybe she could mend it.

The June morning was warm, and since it was Sunday, she went into the kitchen and began to mix flapjacks and fry bacon. Within minutes, the smell drifting through the house had awakened all the children and they were gathered around the table. Even Growler was there, sitting up and waving his paws in the air.

Violet laughed. "I've fixed enough so even the pooch can have some. Houston, run and milk the cow and feed the livestock. Is Travis awake yet?"

"Nope," answered Harold, "I walked past his door, but all I heard was snoring from inside."

"Him sick?" Bonnie asked.

"Uh, maybe," Violet answered, avoiding their eyes. "As soon as Houston gets back, we'll eat. Then why don't you all get dressed and go on to Sunday school and I'll join you in time for church?"

"Sure," said Kessie.

In a few minutes, Houston came in from the barn with a bucket of milk. Violet began to dish up flapjacks.

Harold had syrup on his mouth. "Travis going to church?"

"Uh, he may be too sick," Violet said, pouring foaming glasses of milk. She sat down and helped herself to a plate of flapjacks and reached for the butter and syrup. Biting into a slice of crisp bacon, she thought about last night and worried about how much Travis might remember this morning.

Kessie grinned at her. "You make a great mama, Violet. Wouldn't it be nice if we could live like this from now on?"

"We can't do that, silly," Houston corrected her. "We need a full-grown mama for Travis to marry."

Violet winced at the thought and poured thick cream in her coffee. "We're all doing just fine right now and if someday Travis wants to marry, he'll pick out a girl himself."

"You." Bonnie pointed with her spoon. "You Violet be mama."

"Stop feeding Growler all your bacon," Violet scolded.

Harold paused and cocked his head. "I can hear Travis groaning from the bedroom. What's wrong with him?"

"Maybe I'll give him some castor oil," Violet said, a little annoyed with Travis for last night's drunken spree. "Now if you kids are through eating, go out by the pump and wash the syrup off your faces, then get ready for Sunday school." She surely didn't want the children around if Travis came into breakfast and suddenly recalled what had happened last night. "Now go on with you."

Dutifully, the children trekked out to the pump to wash up and then into the house to get dressed for Sunday school.

"I'll be along in time for church," Violet promised and she heard the church bells tolling in the distance and pushed the kids out the front door. Then she thought to yell after them, "Don't let Growler into the building—make him wait outside. I don't think the preacher will like a dog lying under the pews scratching fleas."

The kids laughed and waved back, Growler trotting along beside Bonnie.

Violet closed the front door and took a deep breath. She heard Travis banging around in his room, putting on his clothes. She could only hope he remembered nothing.

She went into the kitchen and waited. In a few minutes, he stumbled into the kitchen, holding his head and groaning. "Damn it, I must have really cut the wolf loose last night."

"What?"

He blinked. "It's Texan for getting drunk."

"I believe you did," she said primly and poured him a cup of strong coffee. She thought a minute and added a splash of whiskey. "How about some breakfast? Maybe some nice scrambled eggs."

He looked toward the stove and shuddered. "I don't think so."

She handed him the cup of coffee and he took it with a shaky hand. "How about some flapjacks with lots of syrup and butter?" She gave him her brightest smile.

For a moment, he turned a little green, swallowed hard and then shook his head. "Coffee, just coffee."

He really had a hangover. Probably he didn't remember much of anything. She sighed with relief. "Are you sure? Poached eggs and bacon—"

"Please stop yelling," he grumbled, sipping the coffee. "You make my head hurt."

"I'll tell you what makes your head hurt." She put her hands on her hips, really annoyed with him. "Trying to drink a barrel of booze in that filthy saloon."

"Oh, yeah." His brow furrowed as if trying to remember. "And there was a girl in a green dress—"

"And about that time I came to take you home," she scolded. "A fine thing when a little girl has to come into a saloon to drag you out before you spend all your paycheck."

He was staring at her now, his cup halfway to his lips. He looked puzzled.

She felt a chill go through her heart. Did he remember after all? If he did, how was she going to explain it away? She should have kept her mouth shut, but she'd been so angry with him over those saloon tarts.

"I don't remember much," he mumbled finally and sipped his coffee. "One thing, I do remember is that redhead is a hellova kisser."

She felt like smacking him with the ladle in her hand. "Please spare these tender ears the lurid details of what you were doing or about to do when I came in there. I'm sure the men in this town are going to gossip like a flock of old hens over a kid coming into a saloon to get you."

"Yeah, I reckon so." He was staring at her again.

She turned away and put the ladle in the dishpan. "I've got to get ready for church. I've put a stewing hen in the oven for dinner and I'll throw together some banana pudding when I get home. You want to go to church? It looks good to have the whole family there."

"And deal with all those women who want to find me a wife?" He groaned again and held out his cup for more coffee. "Sometimes, Violet, you act more like a nagging wife than a kid. I don't feel like going to church and please don't insist unless you want to see me throw up during the service."

"I'll tell everyone you're sick," she said and marched off to her room, feeling relieved that he obviously didn't remember the kiss or pawing her breasts last night. She was still safe in her masquerade.

She washed and put her hair up with yellow ribbons, got her parasol to keep the hot June sun off her face and hurried to church as the bells began to chime. In the vestibule, Miss Brewster and Miss Knowlen waved to her and she nodded back. As she started to go in to the sanctuary, the banker's fat wife caught her arm. "Hello, dear, I've been wanting to meet you."

Violet managed a smile. "I know who you are, Mrs. Clay."

The fine jewels on the fat lady sparkled in the June sunlight. "I've been wanting to introduce my daughters to your father. Is he here today?" She craned her neck, looking around.

"I'm afraid not. He's sick today."

One of the fat daughters came up to take Violet's hand. "Oh, maybe I should bring him some chicken soup."

Mrs. Clay beamed. "Isn't that nice? Leave it to my girls to try to do their Christian duty. This is Clara and here comes her sister, Myrtle."

"I'm so glad to meet you." Violet offered her hand. They were probably both close to forty years old, two old maids looking for a husband. "I think he will be fine, but thank you very much. I've got a chicken in the oven at home."

Myrtle looked disappointed. "Oh, I was going to bring in supper tonight. I make the best liver casserole."

Violet imagined how the queasy Travis would face a liver casserole. "Thank you, but I'll manage."

Mrs. Clay patted her arm. "You're such a brave child,

but you know, your daddy really needs a wife. Everyone in town says that."

"Uh, I think the service is starting," Violet said and escaped down the aisle as the choir broke into a chorus of "Roll, Jordan, Roll." She spotted the kids and slid in beside them. When she looked down, Growler was lying beneath little Bonnie's feet under the pew. Oh, well, maybe no one had noticed him.

As everyone settled down for the sermon, Violet noted Bonnie was playing with Houston's small wooden horse and Harold was drawing on the back of a donation envelope. "What are you drawing?" she whispered.

"A ship," the Oriental boy whispered back. "Someday, people are going to the moon and I might design a ship to get them there."

It was such a preposterous idea that Violet managed to nod and not laugh. She didn't think anyone would ever even build a flying machine, much less a ship that would go to the moon.

The sermon was on Jezebel and how she had enticed men with lust and her terrible end. The subject made Violet uneasy and she tried not to squirm in her seat as the preacher talked about saloons, those dens of iniquity that should be closed and the loose women in them run out of town. When she looked around, it seemed most of the men in the congregation were squirming and looking guilty.

The June day was hot, with bees buzzing through the open windows and the scent of roses from outside the church mixing with the scent of candles and sweating bodies. The kids squirmed on the pew and Violet shushed them and Growler yawned and scratched again, his foot hitting the floor rhythmically until people craned their necks to look.

At last the congregate stood and the old organ wheezed

and began to play "Amazing Grace." Violet hoped no one would go down the aisle to get saved today. The kids were squirming and she was beginning to worry that her chicken in the oven at home might be burning.

There were probably a lot of people in the audience who needed to come forward and confess their sins, but the crowd seemed to heave a sigh of relief that no one did and the service could end.

Violet and the children lined up to shake hands with Pastor Smithe.

"Good service," Violet said.

"Good to see the whole family." He smiled and then frowned. "Where is Mr. Prescott?"

"Him sick," Bonnie volunteered.

"Really I think he's drunk," Kessie said in a hoarse whisper.

"Kessie!" Violet gasped. "Really!"

The pastor frowned. "People are saying around town that it's a shame a young girl has to run that house. There's plenty of eligible women in town."

She glanced back and saw Miss Brewster, Miss Knowlen, and the banker's wife and two fat daughters coming her way. "Reverend Smithe, I think we need to be going."

The pastor nodded his bald head. "Tell Mr. Prescott we missed him and, Miss Violet, would you try to keep the dog from coming to church? I doubt his soul needs saving." He looked down at Growler, who had stopped in the church doorway to scratch a flea.

"I'll do my best," Violet promised.

She and the children were about to walk home when Mrs. Van Mayes came up to her. "So good to see you children in church." The pretty widow looked around. "And where is Travis?"

Kessie began, "He's home and—"

"—not feeling well," Violet said and put her hand over Kessie's mouth before she could say more. "Come along, children, let's go home."

"I was going to invite you all over for Sunday dinner." Mrs. Van Mayes smiled, but her eyes were blue ice.

"I'm sorry, I've already got dinner cooking," Violet said. "A roasted chicken with vegetables."

"Such a brave little girl." Mrs. Van Mayes patted Violet's shoulder in a patronizing way that made Violet grit her teeth. "Your daddy should really get married so you wouldn't have to work so hard. It's not right, a mere slip of a girl having to take on the responsibilities of running a house and raising children."

"I don't mind," Violet said. "Come on, kids, let's go."

"Another night then," the widow said. "I'll contact your father."

"He's very busy," Violet said, snapped open her parasol and started walking away. "Bye now."

She glanced back. The pretty widow was staring after her and frowning. She wasn't fooling Violet. The wealthy beauty wanted a husband and she'd set her eyes on Travis. Well, that wasn't going to happen if Violet had anything to do with it.

They went home. The smell of chicken and vegetables wafted on the warm June air as they entered. Travis had gone back to bed.

Violet heaved a sigh of relief as she put on an apron and began making banana pudding for dessert. The kids would be thrilled because bananas were rare and such a treat, but Violet had saved her pennies to buy some. "You kids get washed up for dinner and one of you boys see if Travis feels like getting up."

"Is he still drunk?" Kessie asked.

Violet sighed. "Let's not be discussing this with the whole town, shall we not?"

"Drunk," lisped Bonnie, "drunk."

"I am not." Travis stumbled into the dining room and slumped down in his chair at the end of the table as everyone else sat down. He looked up at Violet and his expression seemed puzzled.

So he still hadn't figured out about last night. Good. Maybe he never would.

"How was church?" Travis asked as Violet served up the chicken and passed around the bowl of steaming vegetables.

Houston shrugged. "Something about a bad lady who was eaten by dogs."

Bonnie made a face. "Growler not eat lady. Growler like chicken." And before Violet could stop her, she leaned over and put her bowl on the floor so the dog got his dinner, too.

Travis looked puzzled. "Good Lord, what kind of things are they teaching these days in church, anyway?"

"Never mind," Violet said. "It was about Jezebel."

"Ohh." He nodded as if he understood. "Yep, bad ladies."

Violet felt her face burn. She had been a Jezebel in the past, but now she was trying to change her life and maybe God would forgive her if she did enough good deeds.

Kessie said, "Can I say grace?"

"Certainly," Violet said as she sat down at the other end of the table.

Kessie looked around at the family. "Everyone must bow their heads and close their eyes and, Bonnie, stop feeding the dog. Now, God is great, God is good and we thank him for this food. Amen."

"Wait, I want to add something," Houston said as everyone picked up their forks.

Travis nodded. "Go right ahead on, amigo."

"Thank you God for us not being in the orphanage and us having good parents like Travis and Violet. Amen."

"Pass the mashed potatoes." Travis smiled. "I think maybe I can eat a little now."

Violet looked around the table. She felt happy and fulfilled. Her family was all eating together and the only thing that would make her happier was to marry Travis and be a real mother to these orphans without him ever finding out she'd once been a saloon girl. "Harold, don't stuff your mouth so full."

"I can't help it," he choked out. "Everything is so good."

"Growler and me want more milk," Bonnie piped up.

Houston said, "Must she feed that old dog at the table?"

Violet shrugged as she got up to get the milk pitcher. "I've given up on that. Anyone want another biscuit?"

"I do!" yelled two children.

"Don't forget to save room for dessert," Violet reminded them. "It's banana pudding."

Travis's eyes lit up. "You got bananas? I thought I smelled something good."

"It's a wonder to me you can smell anything," Violet snapped before she thought, and went into the kitchen to get the bowls of pudding.

Kessie dived in and then licked her spoon. "Travis, we saw that pretty lady at church. She asked about you."

"Oh, who?" Travis paused in buttering a biscuit.

Violet sighed. She hadn't meant to mention the rich widow. "Mrs. Van Mayes."

Travis grinned. "She is pretty and rich, too."

"She invited us to dinner, but Violet said she already had dinner cooking," Harold volunteered.

"Well, that was nice of the lady," Travis said and returned to his biscuit.

Kessie said, "I'll bet she's so rich that her kids would all have ponies."

"Pony," Bonnie lisped, "pony."

The children looked interested, and Violet said, "Well,

now, Travis will give you all rides on Mouse. Hasn't he been teaching you to ride, Houston?"

Houston nodded. "I ride pretty good and I can shoot, too. I think I'm gonna be a cowboy—or a Texas Ranger like Travis."

Travis paused and his dark eyes filled with regret. "I used to be a Texas Ranger. Reckon those days are over for good. From now on, I reckon I'll just work in a gun shop."

Violet said, "Oh, don't give up hope, Travis. That arm might eventually heal up and you can return to the job."

"Maybe," he said as he ate, "but I can't take a chance that my arm'll go numb on me again and I don't have the money for surgery. Anyway even if I did, I'd spend it on Houston's leg or sending Kessie and Harold to college."

Violet sighed. "I wish we had enough money for both, but until then, we'll all just do the best we can and enjoy our happiness while it lasts, okay?"

Harold smiled. "Life don't get any better than what we got now, does it, Violet?"

"I reckon not." She got up suddenly to hide the tears in her eyes. Yes, life could be better if she and Travis were wed and she could make love to him like she dreamed of doing and give him a couple of kids to join the four they already had.

After dinner, the children set up a howl to go swimming in the little pond at the end of the creek in the park by the school.

"All right," Travis said, "but someone has to go with you in case you get into trouble."

"Can we skinny-dip?" Harold asked.

Travis scowled at him. "Not with girls going along. I'll sit on the bank in the shade and you all can swim."

Kessie looked at Violet. "You going?"

She thought quickly. If Travis saw her in wet clothes, he might figure out she was older than thirteen. "No, I'll go along, but I'll sit and watch, too."

Kessie frowned. "I hope I never get to be older. Ladies and big girls don't have as much fun as kids."

"Well, I might get too much sun and ruin my complexion," Violet excused herself. "I'll bring along some cookies and lemonade."

So in minutes, the group was walking to the pond in the park. Nobody had a real bathing costume, so they decided to swim in their old clothes. Travis walked beside Violet and took the basket from her hand as the kids ran on ahead, Growler barking madly. "Here, give me that. You're just a kid and too small to carry it. That's what men are for."

As he took it, their hands brushed and she could feel the spark that passed between them. Travis looked startled and scowled. "The kids are right, Violet. You work too hard for a young girl. I probably should take all of you home to my mother to raise."

"I thought you said your parents were barely getting by?" She looked up at him, wanting to kiss him.

He looked down at her, his face troubled, then started walking again. "That's a fact. I reckon then I ought to find good families to put all of you with."

"You could get married," Violet said and, without thinking, fluttered her eyelashes at him.

He looked alarmed and then cleared his throat. "I told you I was a confirmed bachelor. A girl named Emily broke my heart and dragged my pride through the mud."

"Haven't you gotten over her yet?" Violet asked as they walked.

"I reckon I didn't love her as much as I once thought I did, but I'm a proud man and having everyone laugh at me was more than I could handle. I don't ever want to be the butt of jokes or ridiculed again."

If he only knew Violet's background, he would throw her out in the street to fend for herself. "Sometimes one can be too proud."

"Maybe," he said, "but Emily left me with a distrust of women. I figure they're all liars and cheaters and I don't trust a one, except my mother, of course."

She smiled up at him as they walked. "Not even me?"

"Oh, well, that's different. You're not a woman, you're a girl, and you haven't learned yet about conniving and lying. Maybe you never will and someday, some boy will be lucky enough to get you for a wife."

"Oh." She didn't know what else to say. She'd woven this web of deceit and now there was no way out of it. Either way, she'd lose Travis.

"Now," he joked and poked her, "if I wait 'til you grow up, a half a dozen years from now, I might marry you myself."

"Would you?" She paused and looked up at him, wanting to throw her arms around him and kiss him, but of course she didn't.

"Be reasonable, Violet," he said. "By the time you're old enough to marry, I'll be much too old for you. You'll be looking at younger men while I sit in my rocking chair."

"I always liked older men," she answered.

For a moment, they stared into each other's eyes until the silence became uncomfortable. She wished she knew what he was thinking.

Then the tension was broken by Houston yelling, "What's keeping you two? We want to go swimming."

They finished their walk to the park. Travis spread a blanket and Violet made sure everyone knew to stay in the shallow water and not to jump off the rocks.

"Come on in," Kessie called.

Violet shook her head. "I'll just sit in the shade and after while, we'll have some lemonade and cookies. Make sure Bonnie doesn't get out too deep."

"Not deep," Bonnie said as she and Growler splashed in the water.

Violet leaned back against the trunk of the big cottonwood tree and Travis sat down next to her. Their arms brushed and she tensed, but he didn't seem to notice.

"You're a good kid, Violet," he murmured, "old for your age. You shouldn't have to be loaded down with the responsibility of looking after a house and all these kids. Everyone keeps saying I should get married. At least it would take a load off you."

"Who's been saying that?" she asked, looking up at him.

"Oh, everyone." He shrugged.

He was sitting so close, she could feel the warmth of his breath on her cheek.

"I don't mind," she said. "Better than having some mean stepmother who would mistreat the kids."

"I wouldn't put up with that." He shook his head. "I think of all of you as my kids now and nobody better even think about mistreating any of you."

She had never felt so loved and protected. She had to fight an urge to lay her head against his chest. The kids played and splashed in the water, and Violet thought she had never been as happy as she was now. She pretended for a minute that she and Travis were married and these were their kids playing in the creek.

He was looking down at her again, puzzlement in his dark eyes. He looked like he might be thinking of kissing her or maybe remembering kissing her last night.

"What's the matter?"

He shrugged. "I don't know. I had the strangest dream last night."

"Tell me about it."

He shook his head and stirred uncomfortably. "No, it's

not something for a decent girl. I reckon I need to stop drinking." He paused and didn't meet her eyes.

Abruptly there was a scream from the water and then all the kids were yelling and Growler barked excitedly.

Houston and Kessie were both screaming, "Harold's in trouble!"

"What the hell?" Travis swore and they both jumped to their feet. She saw in an instant that the Chinese boy had gotten farther down the creek and into a pool of deep water and was now thrashing around and going under.

"Oh, my God!" Violet took off running toward the water, but Travis grabbed her arm. "You stay here, kid, I'll go after him."

"But—"

He didn't let her finish before he was running for the water, stopping only an instant to pull off his boots.

Chapter 13

Travis dived into the pond, swimming rapidly toward the floundering boy. Ahead of him, Harold went under again and came up gasping and thrashing. "Hang on, kid, I'm coming!"

Behind him, he heard the dog barking and the others yelling and Violet shouting something about his wrist.

To hell with his wrist. It seemed to have healed up and anyway, he didn't have a choice. He couldn't let Harold drown.

He wasn't sure how deep the water was here, but he knew he couldn't touch bottom and Harold, with his thrashing, was drifting farther away from him. "I'm coming. Trust me!"

He reached out for the boy and saw panic in his almond eyes as Harold grabbed on to him in terror, pulling him under. Travis came to the surface and grabbed the child from behind with his right arm. "Stop fighting, I've got you."

Harold stopped thrashing, but he was still coughing up water as Travis swam toward the bank. And then the pain in his wrist kicked in at the strain of keeping the boy afloat and he flinched and almost went under himself. On the bank, he was aware of Violet's frightened face and her calling, "Travis, are you all right? Do you need help?"

His wrist sent shooting, throbbing pains up his arm, to his shoulder and all through his body. He gritted his teeth to keep from fainting, but he knew he was in trouble. If he could just get Harold to the bank, he might drown himself, but the boy would be safe.

"I'm coming in!" Violet yelled, stripping down to her cotton drawers and chemise.

"No," he gasped, still attempting to swim although every stroke sent agony coursing through his body. "I'm too big, you can't—"

But she was already in the water, swimming toward him and now she had Harold by the arm. "Travis, can you make it alone?"

"Maybe," he gasped, and then she was swimming strongly toward the shore with the child. Travis thrashed in the water with one good arm until finally he put his feet on the muddy bottom.

He took a deep breath and staggered out of the pond, stood dripping and gasping while Violet laid Harold out on the ground and applied pressure to his chest.

"Harold," she scolded, "didn't I tell you all to stay out of the deep?"

He sat up, still coughing. "I—I stepped in a hole."

She stood up and breathed hard. "Travis, are you okay?"

"Yeah." He took a good look at her standing there dripping in her wet underwear that clung to her form. Funny, she had more shape than most girls her age. He stumbled up the bank and sat down hard on the blanket. "My damned arm gave out on me. I hate being so crippled up."

"Here, let me wrap a towel around you." She knelt down before him and put a towel around his shoulders. Her wet clothes brushed his arm and he had a guilty rush because he felt a sudden desire for her. "It's a wonder I didn't have to rescue you both," she scolded.

He tried to take his stare away from her nubile body. "Where'd you learn to swim? I doubt most girls can."

She shrugged. "I was raised in Memphis, right on the Mississippi. My brother and I swam a lot, hanging around the docks." Suddenly she seemed to realize he was staring at the way her wet underwear clung to her curves and she grabbed for her dress, turned to yell at the children still in the water. "I think you all had better get out now before you get wrinkly and pruney."

"Is Harold going to be all right?" Houston called.

"Yes, he's okay. Now you all come dry off and have some lemonade."

Travis grinned at Harold. "Remind me to teach you to swim."

The other children came out of the water and Growler tagged along with Bonnie. When he got up to the blanket, the dog shook all over, bringing out screams of protests from Kessie.

Travis gave Violet a long look. "You look like a drowned rat."

"I know." She took her dress and slipped it over her head; then she poured lemonade for the kids and handed out cookies. "In all, it's been a pretty good Sunday."

Travis leaned back against the tree and sighed. "Except I found out that even if my wrist looks healed, it isn't."

"The doctor told you that, didn't he?" Violet chided. "You'll just have to be careful until you can afford surgery."

"Which is never," he muttered. "So I reckon I'll work in the gun shop from now on. I had hoped to maybe go back to the Rangers or own a ranch."

She handed him a glass of lemonade. "We'll just do the best we can, Travis."

He sipped it. "Thanks, young lady, for jumping in."

"I could tell you were in trouble," she whispered and without thinking, reached out and patted his wet face.

He caught her hand and for a moment, she thought he would kiss it. Then he seemed to think better and let go of it.

Houston said, "This was a fun day. It was almost like having real parents."

"It was nice," Harold coughed, "except for me almost drowning."

"It was still like a real family," Kessie said and lay down on the blanket.

Violet looked around. Little Bonnie had drifted off to sleep, Growler lying by her side, licking her face.

Violet smiled. It had been a great day. The only thing that worried her was the way Travis had stared at her with her wet underwear clinging to her body. Even though she was small-breasted, he might figure out that she was not a young girl. Then there would be hell to pay.

Travis broke into her thoughts. "It's getting to be late afternoon. I reckon we ought to be going." He stood up.

The children, all except Bonnie, scrambled to their feet.

Travis said, "Houston, you and Harold manage the picnic basket. I'll carry Bonnie."

Violet looked up at him anxiously. "Has your arm stopped hurting?"

He nodded. "Pretty much. Let's go home." He leaned over and picked up the sleeping toddler and cuddled her close; then he turned and started toward the house with Violet walking beside him and Growler at his heels. The other children trailed along behind, everyone sleepy and tired.

It was turning dusk when they got to the house. Travis carried Bonnie in and laid her on her bed. Growler hopped up on the bed and lay down next to her.

Behind him, Violet said, "I'll get the others ready for bed and put away the picnic things."

He turned around and caught her wrist. "Violet," he said, and the way he looked into her eyes made her uneasy. "I want you to start locking your door at night."

"Why?" She looked up at him and saw the passion and the need in his dark eyes.

"You don't need to know why. Maybe someday, when you're grown, you'll find out, but right now, I just think it's wise."

"But—"

"Don't argue with me, damn it!" he thundered so loud, it startled her.

He was afraid he might not be able to stop himself from coming into her room some night, she realized, and making love to her.

"All right." She turned and fled out down the hall and into the kitchen.

Kessie looked up from putting away the picnic things. "What's Travis shouting about?"

"Nothing you would understand," Violet said and began to busy herself at the dishpan. "Tomorrow, I'll take you all to the library. Would you like that?"

"We sure would, but see if you can get Bonnie to leave the dog at home. I don't think that old Miss Knowlen likes dogs in her library."

Violet turned to Houston. "Check on the horse and make sure it's got plenty of hay and water," she said, "and Harold can milk the cow."

"I don't think scientists milk cows," Harold complained.

"Well, this one has to or there won't be any milk for breakfast. Then you boys get ready for bed."

"Aw, why can't we stay up?" Kessie moaned.

"No one's staying up tonight," she said. "Everyone's tired and we're all going to bed early."

"Even you and Travis?" Harold asked.

"Yes, I said everyone."

The northbound train roared through at seven o'clock, shaking the house, but it did not stop. Violet hardly paid attention to the trains anymore.

In another hour she was in her own bed, but she couldn't sleep. She stirred restlessly, knowing she hadn't locked her door as she'd been ordered to do and wondering if Travis would come to her late at night. She wanted him in the most primitive way. The thought of him kissing her, caressing her breasts, set her very being on fire, and she lay awake a long time, hoping he would come and she could finally admit to him that she was almost twenty years old. Maybe in the throes of mutual passion, he would forgive her and make love to her. She lay there a long time and finally dropped off to sleep.

Travis lay awake a long time, thinking about Violet and the way she had looked with her wet underwear clinging to her body. A suspicion crossed his mind and he dismissed it immediately. There could be no reason for a girl to pretend she was younger than she actually was—or was there?

He was scared of the way he was beginning to feel about her. This was not only loco, it was sick. He couldn't fall in love with a young kid, it just didn't make any sense. Probably it was only because he was lonely for adult female companionship. There was plenty at the saloon, including that lusty redhead, Kate. His mind switched to Charlotte Van Mayes. There was a beauty who seemed hot and ready. Maybe he ought to marry her. At least it would give the kids a good home and pay for things they needed that he couldn't provide. However, as he drifted into a troubled sleep, the female in his dreams was Violet—so young and innocent.

* * *

Travis and Violet avoided each other's gaze at breakfast, but the kids were so noisy, talking to each other, that no one seemed to notice.

Travis said, "What're your tasks for the day?"

Violet kept her eyes on the biscuit she was buttering. "The kids want to go to the library and I've got a little shopping to do. What about you?"

"I expect things will be busy at the gun shop today," he answered, sipping his coffee. "Maybe I'll stop off after work at the saloon for a drink with the boys."

Now she did look into his eyes. "Just a drink? That's all?"

"Violet," he snapped, "I'm a grown man. I don't have to answer to a kid."

The children quieted.

Violet felt her face redden. "It's just that, well, we don't have enough money for you to spend much on . . . beer."

"You think I don't know that?" he snarled, getting up from the table. "But I ought to be able to cut loose once in a while."

Violet grimaced. "Very well. Give my regards to the girls."

Harold looked at both of them with his big almond eyes. "What girls?"

"Friends of Travis's," Violet snapped.

"Then why don't you bring them home for dinner?" Kessie asked. "Violet would be happy to cook some extra."

"I don't think so," Violet said.

"Damn it all to hell!" Travis shouted and stomped out the front door, slamming it behind him.

Houston looked puzzled. "What's he so mad about?"

"Nothing," Violet answered. "Drink your milk."

Kessie looked around the table and began to chew her

nails. "Have you ever noticed when grown-ups get mad, they always answer 'nothing' when you ask what's wrong?"

"Kessie, you are too smart for your own good." Violet got up from the table. "Now stop chewing your nails and help me do the dishes. Bonnie, stop feeding the dog your bacon."

"Growler like bacon," Little Bonnie said.

"Let him eat scraps," Violet said. "Bacon is expensive."

Harold had carried his dishes into the kitchen. "Travis forgot his lunch," he called back.

"Then you can go take it to him," Violet said.

He stuck his head around the kitchen door. "If we're all going out anyway, why don't we take it to him then?"

She hesitated. She was angry with Travis and didn't want to see him. "I'm busy cleaning up the kitchen. You take it to him."

Harold grabbed the sack and went out of the house while Kessie and Violet cleaned up the kitchen and Houston went out to take care of the livestock.

Travis looked up from cleaning a rifle to see Harold coming in. "Oh, howdy."

"You forgot your lunch."

"Oh, yeah. Just put it on the counter."

Harold came over and looked up at him. "Are you mad at her?"

"I could wring her pretty little neck," Travis said before he thought.

"Please don't. We all love her. Don't you?"

Travis looked down into the anxious face and smiled. "Of course I do. It's just something people say when they're mad." He paused. "Harold, did Violet come in on the orphan train with you kids?"

"Uh—" The boy hesitated, which gave Travis the answer he wanted.

Travis tried again. "How old is she, really?"

Harold backed toward the door. "I—I've got to be going."

"You didn't answer my question."

Sweat broke out on the boy's brown face. "Honestly, Travis, I don't know."

"But she's older than she says she is?"

"No—I—I don't know. Maybe. I got to go." He turned and fled out the door.

Travis stared after him. Could she really be older and, if so, why was she posing as a kid? None of this made any sense. About that time, a customer came in and Travis pushed aside his puzzlement.

The family was getting ready to go out when Harold got back.

Violet tried to be casual. "What'd he say?"

Harold shrugged, but he looked troubled. "I asked if he was mad and he said he'd like to wring your pretty neck. I gave him the sack and I came home. I don't know why you're mad at him."

"My neck, huh? Never mind," Violet said. "Just wash your face and comb your hair and we'll go to the library."

Houston had just come in the back door. "Aw, I'd rather hang around the gun shop and listen to the men talk about horses and guns."

"Well, in that case, go on. The rest of us will go to the store and the library." Violet brushed Bonnie's hair so vigorously that the little girl cried, "Stop! Stop! Pulling my hair out."

"I'm sorry." Violet paused and kissed the top of her blond head. "You've gotten it in such a tangle."

Kessie leaned on the chair and looked up at her. "It's because you're mad at Travis, isn't it?"

Violet swallowed hard. "Of course not. He's a grown man and can do what he wants. I reckon we're all lucky he took us in; most men wouldn't want a ready-made family."

Harold looked alarmed. "Is he liable to leave us or throw us out?"

That was Violet's worst fear. "I don't know. No, I don't think so—he's a good Texan. It's just that he's a man and men sometimes want . . . never mind. If everyone's ready, let's go to the library."

Houston went off to the gun shop and the rest of them headed for the library, where Miss Knowlen, in her staid black dress, met them at the door. "Is Mr. Prescott with you today?"

Violet shook her head. "No, he had to work. It's just us."

"Oh." The spinster looked disappointed. "Well, you kiddies head for that section." She pointed. "There's some books over there I think you'll like."

Violet started to go with them, but Miss Knowlen grabbed her arm. "Is your daddy keeping company with anyone?"

"No." Violet really didn't want to stay here for the grilling, but she had to be polite. "He just works and after supper, he may play checkers with the kids and we all go to bed early."

"Some of the citizens are saying that it isn't right for a man to have to raise all those children alone, especially a girl who's almost a young lady."

"We are managing, but thank you for your concern." Violet pulled away from her.

"I'm available some nights to come over and spiffy up the place and visit," Miss Knowlen said.

"How nice. I'll tell him." Violet smiled and fled over to help the children select some books.

They did a little shopping with all the single ladies inquiring after Travis and offering to bring in casseroles or come help with the children. Violet assured them all that they were managing just fine.

Miss Brewster was in the dry goods store and she called Violet "a brave, hardworking little girl" and allowed that Mr. Prescott should consider marrying to take the load off Violet.

At the butcher shop, old Mr. Anderson laughed and hooked his thumbs in his red suspenders that held up the pants over his fat belly when she told him about all the eager single ladies. "Poor Travis just don't stand a chance, young lady. Every single woman in town has set her cap for him and just watch, at the Fourth of July celebration, they'll all trot out their best food, hoping he'll take notice."

She had forgotten about the holiday. "That's only a few days away, isn't it? You suppose the general store will have fireworks?"

"Yes, indeedy. It's the biggest holiday we have in the whole county."

Kessie spoke up. "Here's a poster on your window about the suffragettes. Are they really coming to town?"

Mr. Anderson frowned. "I reckon so. Mrs. Van Mayes insisted I hang that and she's a rich customer. They are demanding to be in our parade."

"Good," Kessie announced. "I'll march with them."

Mr. Anderson scowled at her, then at Violet. "You raising a liberal?"

Violet shrugged her shoulders. "I sort of let the children do what they want."

He shook his head. "Maybe the local ladies are right,

maybe Prescott really does need a wife to keep you kids in line."

Violet stiffened. "Really, Mr. Anderson, I don't see anything so terrible about women voting."

"Aha! That's just a start. They want to change everything, take over the whole world, take control away from the men, where it belongs."

Kessie piped up. "And when women take over, things will be a whole lot better, I promise you."

"I think we'd better leave," Violet said and grabbed her package of pork chops off the counter.

Mr. Anderson yelled after them, "And don't bring that dog into my store again!"

Before Violet knew what she was up to, little Bonnie turned around and stuck her tongue out at the butcher.

Outside, she stopped and admonished the children. "We have to be careful what we say or do. Someone may decide we aren't a proper family and try to put us all back in an orphanage."

Harold looked up at her. "But you're a grown-up, Violet. They can't put you in an orphanage."

"Shh!" She put her finger against her lips. "Nobody knows that but us, right? Not even Travis is supposed to know."

Harold opened his mouth, then shut it and chewed his lip.

Kessie's eyes grew wide. "Violet, what do you think he'd do if he found out?"

Violet didn't even want to think about it. "I'm not sure, but I don't think it would be good, so we don't tell, remember?"

"Feathers," Bonnie laughed. "Feathers."

"Forget the feathers," Violet admonished her. "I don't ever intend to wear those again."

Kessie looked at her. "Why don't you and Travis just get married and adopt us all?"

Violet sighed and they started walking home. "It's not that easy. I think he would be furious to find out I lied and fooled him."

They walked the rest of the way home in silence. That was Violet's worst fear, that Travis would find out. He already distrusted women and first he'd be mad she had fooled him and then he would want to know the reason. Now just how would she explain that she was really a saloon whore on the run from the outlaw owner? That wasn't exactly the kind of girl an old-fashioned Texas cowboy wanted to take home to his mother.

At home, the children settled down to read while Violet did her chores. Late in the afternoon, Houston came home and into the kitchen for some fresh-baked oatmeal cookies. "That Mrs. Van Mayes dropped by the gun shop today," he announced.

Violet tried not to be jealous. "Oh? What did she want?"

"She invited us all to supper tomorrow night and Travis said we'd be glad to."

"He could have asked me first." Violet gritted her teeth as she got out her iron skillet and began to fry pork chops.

"Oh, and he said not to wait supper for him," Houston reported as he took a handful of cookies and headed back into the parlor. "He'd be going to the saloon after work and you were not to come drag him out."

Violet slammed the skillet hard down on the stove. "He needn't worry. I won't." She was so angry, she was chopping onions hard and furious. She pretended it was Travis's body under her knife.

From the other room, Harold called, "What's so loud in there?"

And Houston answered, "I don't know. Travis won't be home for supper and for some reason, Violet's mad about it."

Kessie's voice came through clearly. "Well, I don't blame her. She goes to the trouble to fix a good dinner and he goes to eat at the saloon instead."

If only it were the food, Violet thought as she worked on dinner. She had hot apple pie and plenty of gravy for the pork chops, but Travis would rather eat boiled eggs, pretzels and beer at the saloon.

Who was she fooling? What was really upsetting her was the thought of the dessert afterward when he was liquored up, one of the whores taking him up to her room when Violet wanted desperately to take him to her room and make love to him. Well, she'd made this mess and there didn't seem to be any way out of it.

The family ate supper in silence and then Violet went outside afterward and stood on the front porch. From here, she could hear the laughter and the piano banging away while the girls sang at the Cattle Drive. Travis was in there, probably drinking with one of those girls hanging on his arm and later . . . she didn't even want to think about later.

She went back in, slamming the door. "I think we all need to get ready for bed."

"It's still early," Harold protested.

"Then I'm going to bed alone!" Violet strode into her room and got ready for bed. Of course she couldn't sleep. It was a hot night in late June and the window was up. The music floated faintly on the warm breeze, and now and then she heard a woman laugh. She tried not to think what Travis might be doing at this very moment and despite herself, she felt the tears come. She loved him, and while she lay here alone, he was in the saloon, drinking and kissing the whores and having a great time. Men, they were all alike. Why had she picked this one to fall in love with?

She heard the children stirring around.

Little Bonnie stuck her head in the bedroom door. "You all right?"

"I—I'm fine, honey. Tell Kessie to put your nightgown on you."

Kessie stuck her head in the door. "You don't sound all right."

"Go to bed," Violet sobbed. "I'm fine."

She heard Kessie sigh and then the door closed. So this was what love was like: misery, because he was even now caressing and kissing another woman. She had never known such inner pain, not since her little brother died, and she was all alone in the world. And she didn't know what to do. She could leave and find a job in another saloon, a thousand miles from here, but then what would happen to the kids? They weren't really old enough to manage without her, even if Travis tried to keep them. No, she couldn't leave, but she was also certain she couldn't hang around and watch him marry another woman or make regular trips to the saloon whores. There just didn't seem to be any good answer. She buried her face in her pillow and cried.

Chapter 14

Travis closed up the gun shop and paused as he locked the front door. He could go home, but then he would be near Violet and that wasn't good. Besides, she was mad at him and he'd rather deal with a riled-up rattlesnake than an angry woman. He was a brave Texan, but not that brave.

Anyway, he had earned a mug of beer. Working in the gun shop wasn't nearly as exciting as being a Texas Ranger or a cowboy, and he was getting restless. As he walked, he flexed his hand. His wrist seemed to be okay today, but he could never be sure when it would go out on him.

Loud music and laughter greeted him as he went into the saloon. Yep, this was where a man ought to spend his evenings—plenty of beer, cigars, maybe a hand of poker and some loose women eager to take him to their beds.

"Hey, Prescott," Zeke, the old man who ran the livery stable, greeted him. "We ain't used to seeing you in here."

"Well, once in a while, a man needs to relax," Travis said and nodded to the balding bartender, who slid a foaming mug down the bar to him. But even as he sipped it, he felt guilty for spending the money. He knew Houston wanted a pair of boots and Violet needed some things, although she never asked for anything. She was one in a million. He'd get paid Saturday and then he'd buy her a bottle of perfume.

A couple of ranchers leaned on the bar near him. "Hey, Prescott, you gonna enter the shootin' contest July Fourth?"

He shook his head and sipped his beer. "Naw. I'm not much of a shot."

"Really? We heard you used to be a Texas Ranger," one of them said.

He couldn't tell them about his hand. He was too proud. "I never was much of a shot, even then."

"Well, that's still more'n a week away," one of the ranchers laughed. "You still got time to change your mind."

"I got one kid, Houston, who's a pretty good shot; he might enter." He sipped his beer and wondered what the kids were doing. Violet would be putting dinner on the table about now and she'd wonder where he was. Let her wonder. No man should have to answer to a kid. Still, as he stood there laughing and talking, spending time at the saloon didn't seem like as much fun as it used to be. He wondered what Violet had cooked for dinner. She could do a lot with a little piece of meat or a scrawny chicken and make it so good coyotes would fight a big grizzly bear over it.

Kate sidled up to him just then. "Hello, Travis."

The redhead had a big bosom, but she reeked of sweat and cheap perfume. That made him think of Violet again, who always smelled like soap, clean and warm. Damn it, why couldn't he enjoy even one beer without thinking of her?

Kate leaned against him, rubbing her body against his in her gaudy green satin dress. "Buy me a drink?"

"Sure, but just one."

She smiled up at him and he saw the paint on her face

that didn't quite hide her wrinkles. "After that, why don't we go upstairs?"

He shook his head. "Sorry, Kate, can't afford it."

She ran her tongue over her painted lips. "Who's talkin' about money? I like you enough to give you a free ride, cowboy."

The men around him hooted and hollered. "You can't pass up a deal like that, Prescott."

"Hey, Kate, if you're giving it away, I'll take some."

Kate ignored the other men and smiled at Travis as she sipped her drink. She ran one finger into the open neck of his shirt. "I just reckon you're a lot of fun for a woman."

He leaned against the bar, wanting her, wanting any woman. "It's been a while. It might be a wild ride."

"I'm a bronc breaker." She put her drink on the bar and took Travis's hand, led him away from the bar, through the rowdy crowd of men.

His manhood came up hard and throbbing as they walked toward the stairs. He took a deep breath and the saloon smelled like stale cigars, old beer and unwashed bodies. The piano banged away.

Kate led him up the stairs and to her room. She paused at the door, looking up at him. "When's the last time you had a woman, Travis?"

He was ashamed to admit it had been in the spring before he rode into Red Rock. "A while."

"Then you ought to be ready for a hard ride," she purred and led him inside, closed the door.

He sat down on the bed, watching her undress. She made quite a show of it, slowly peeling off her silk hose. "Unhook my dress, honey."

Her flesh was warm under his hands as he unhooked the bright green satin and his pulse began to pound.

She took the dress off slowly, revealing black lace

drawers and chemise. Then she smiled wickedly as she took off the chemise and stood there in nothing but her lace drawers. She had big breasts and just looking at her, he realized she was older than he had thought. Violet's breasts were probably small and firm and would be beautiful when she was all grown up.

Damn it. Why did he find himself comparing all women to that kid? He stood up and pulled Kate roughly to him and kissed her, feeling those big breasts pressing into his shirt. She smelled of sweat and cheap perfume.

"Easy, cowboy," she purred. "Ain't you gonna even take your pants off?"

"Sure." He started to unbutton his denim pants and his hands trembled with eagerness. Then, with dismay, he felt his manhood beginning to fade.

"What's wrong?" She must have caught the expression on his face.

"Nothing." But there was. For some reason, his body was not cooperating. He would not be able to perform. Nothing like this had ever happened to him before.

"Then get those pants off and let's get busy," she purred as she stepped out of her black lace drawers.

So here he stood with a naked, eager woman and he felt his manhood fading. He was both furious and confused. "I—I must be tired." He began to button his pants.

She reached out and caught his hand. "You're not gonna walk away, not when I've got such a hunger for you, are you?"

In his mind, he suddenly saw Violet's pretty face and blue eyes and four little kids sitting at a dinner table waiting for him to arrive. "I've got to go."

"What? You're walking out on me? What's the matter? Ain't I pretty enough? Am I too much woman for you?" Her voice rose and he wanted to be any place but here.

"Sorry, Kate, I changed my mind." He started for the door, but she grabbed his arm.

"You're making a fool of me. All the men will think I'm no fun."

"No, it's me." He paused with his hand on the doorknob. "I just remembered something."

"It's another woman, ain't it?" she shrieked.

No, not another woman, he thought, *a girl, an innocent young girl.* And he was the world's biggest fool for turning down this mattress romp with a hot, willing woman.

He took two silver dollars out of his pocket and tossed them to her. "Here, this is for your trouble."

She threw the money back at him, and it made a ringing sound when it hit the door. "I don't want your damned money, cowboy, I wanted you!"

He shrugged and started out the door, Kate still screaming at him. Men turned to look up as he came down the stairs with her shrieks and curses drifting loud and sharp over the music. Travis didn't stop to offer an explanation; he kept walking toward the swinging doors. He'd surely regret this later tonight when he was lying in bed unable to sleep, but right now, all he could think of was getting back to that tidy little house where people who depended on him were waiting. He crossed the dirt street and walked along in the growing dusk.

Opening the door, he walked in. "I'm home," he yelled and went into the dining room.

Everyone was seated at the table. All the little faces turned toward him, smiling. The face he wanted most to see was missing. "Where's Violet?"

"Her sick." Bonnie licked her spoon.

"Sick?" Travis asked.

"She went to bed." Kessie nodded. "I don't think she was sick. I think she's mad."

Violet came out of her room, scowling. "I was wondering if you'd be here for dinner. Houston said you went to the saloon."

"I'm a grown man," he bristled. "I don't feel I have to answer to a slip of a girl like you."

He sat down at the table and Violet went into the kitchen. "I'll get you some dinner."

He decided to ignore her cold tone. "Well, kids," he said, "what say after we eat, we play some checkers?"

No one answered. They were all staring at him.

Violet marched in and slammed a plate down in front of him so hard, it rattled. She sniffed. "You smell like cheap perfume."

"I reckon I do," he snapped back, "but that's not your business."

"You're right, it isn't. Would you like some coffee?"

"Sure." He picked up his fork. The plate was full of fried pork chops and potatoes. Violet could cook even better than his mother. The children didn't say anything. Violet brought in a cup of coffee and set it down so hard it sloshed into the saucer. Travis stuffed food in his mouth and ignored her. She had a lot of nerve to be angry with him. Right now, he could be rolling on a mattress with a hot whore who would give him the ride of his life, and he had, like a fool, walked away from that to come home to a young girl who was angry with him and kids who weren't his.

He took another bite and Houston said, "I told Violet we were invited to Mrs. Van Mayes's for supper tomorrow night."

Kessie popped up. "I don't think she wants to go."

Travis gritted his teeth. "Of course we'll go; we'll all go. We're not going to be rude and not show up when the nice lady has invited us."

"She doesn't want us, she wants you!" Violet called from the kitchen.

"I'm the man around here and I say we go."

Silence from the kitchen except for pans banging.

Little Bonnie got up from the table, came around and leaned on his knee. Growler lay down next to her. "Why Feathers mad?"

Feathers. Why did she insist on calling Violet Feathers? "I reckon I don't know."

"Yes, you do!" came the shout from the kitchen.

Kessie said, "There's apple pie."

"That's nice." He kept eating and thinking. Could the kid be jealous? No, of course not. He'd been like a father to her. Probably she was mad because they didn't have much money and he'd been in the saloon. Or maybe because she'd worked hard on dinner and he'd been late and let it get cold. The pork chop was really delicious. He finished the last of it and mopped up gravy with a piece of her homemade bread.

Harold said, "We had apple pie for dessert, you want some?"

"Sure," Travis said.

"I just gave the last piece to the dog," came the angry voice from the kitchen. She sounded like she was crying.

"You kids go into the parlor and get out the checkerboard. I'll be there in a minute," Travis said as he got up. He waited until they had all cleared out and then he went into the kitchen. Violet was wiping off the counter, with her back to him, but her shoulders were shaking.

"Kid, what's wrong. Are you crying?" He walked up behind her.

"Hell, no," she sobbed.

He was startled to hear her swear. "I'm sorry I'm late for dinner—"

"You think that's what's wrong? You're late for dinner?" She whirled around and her pretty face was streaked with tears that overflowed her violet-blue eyes.

He reached out and put his hands on her slight shoulders. "Young lady, I don't understand—"

"And you never will!" She pulled away from him and fled out of the kitchen and to her room, slamming the door so hard the house shook.

"Damn it, I reckon I will never understand women or girls either." He remembered the warmth of her shoulders under his big hands and the clean, sweet smell of her. He stomped into the parlor, where the kids had set up the checkerboard. Through the open window, he heard the faint music drifting from the saloon. Why had he turned his back on that much fun and hurried home, only to be greeted by angry tears from an orphan girl who had no reason to be mad at him? He'd only been behaving like most men, after all.

"All right, whose turn is it?" he asked as he settled down before the checkerboard.

"Mine," said Harold.

He groaned. "Oh, Harold, I hate to play you. You're so smart, you always beat me."

Harold grinned. "Best two games out of three."

"You still wanting to be a lawyer or an inventor?"

"Neither," decided Harold as he jumped three of Travis's checkers. "I think I want to be a doctor; maybe I'll come up with a cure for yellow fever."

"That's a tall order." Travis shook his head. "No one's figured it out yet and it kills thousands every year."

Kessie said, "Violet's mother and little brother, Tommy, died of it; did you know that? She's all alone in the world."

"I think she told me that," Travis answered and thought, *Poor, orphaned kid, trying to make her way in a tough world.* Probably a lot of men would take advantage of a young girl like that. He wondered again about what Harold had said, or not said, about her age.

He forgot about that as Harold beat him three times and then he played checkers with each of the others except Bonnie, who climbed up in his lap while the dog settled himself at Travis's feet. Her drawers were wet, but he didn't mention it. While he played, he listened for the sound of Violet's door opening, but it never did.

Finally, he yawned and said, "I think it's time for bed, everyone."

"Bonnie's already asleep," Kessie noted.

"I'll put her to bed," Travis said and gathered the toddler up in his arms and stood up.

While the children scattered to wash, he carried the toddler in and laid her on her bed, kissed her forehead while Growler curled up on the foot of her bed. He'd like to have a little girl just like Bonnie someday. In fact, he loved all these children like they were his own.

The children had all gone to bed. Travis walked through the house turning off the oil lamps and locking the doors. When he stood in the dark of the parlor, he could still hear music and laughter from the saloon. He walked to the open window and looked out. The glow of lights from the Cattle Drive shone out into the street and he thought about beer and poker and hot, lusty women like Kate waiting there. They seemed to be calling him.

After a long moment, he shrugged and walked down the hall, pausing at Violet's door. He knocked gently. "Violet?"

No answer. He opened the door and peeked in. She lay on her back with her brown hair loose around her shoulders, a blue nightgown against the white sheets. The moonlight revealed dried tears on her cheeks and he felt like a villain because he had made her cry. Her mouth looked so soft and innocent with no paint smeared on it.

He sighed as he closed the door and went to his room. The window was open in the warm June night and the sounds of the saloon drifted in. He walked over and closed the window, blew out the oil lamp. He stripped down to his drawers and got into bed. Now his manhood came up hard and throbbing. "Damn you," he cursed it. "Why didn't you act like that when I was ready to take a hot ride on Kate?"

His mind went to Violet again, lying there asleep in her blue nightgown and he knew he wanted her as a man wants a woman. "You're a sick, twisted bastard," he whispered to himself. *She's just an innocent kid . . . or is she?* He wished he knew for certain. What he was thinking could get him lynched by indignant locals, and then who would look after the kids?

Still it was a long time before he dropped off to sleep and when he did, the woman he dreamed of was the innocent young Violet.

He got up early, before anyone else, and made coffee, relieved not to face Violet. Then he left her a note:

Remember we are all due at Mrs. Van Mayes's tonight at seven o'clock for dinner. Go buy new clothes at the dry goods store. They'll give you credit. I'll be home early to get dressed. Travis.

Then he went down to the gun shop and opened up. It was going to be a busy day, men coming in for ammunition or to buy new weapons. The shooting match at the July Fourth celebration was something all the men wanted to win, and that was only a few days away now.

Violet was relieved when she got up to fix breakfast and discovered Travis was already gone. She furrowed her brow as she read his note. If there was one thing in the world she didn't want to do, it was go to the rich widow's for supper. The beauty was determined to have Travis; anyone could see that. She had plenty of money to look after the kids, and this situation between Violet and Travis was getting tense and awkward. She wanted to go into his arms, kiss him, make love to him, and he thought of her as a gawky kid. Maybe he would marry the rich widow and the kids would be looked after. Then Violet could just disappear. She wasn't certain where she would go or what she would do, but it didn't matter as long as Travis was happy and the kids were cared for.

She heard the kids rising and began making oatmeal and frying bacon. She had not slept well last night thinking of Travis at the saloon, no doubt in the arms of one of the whores. Well, what did she expect? He was a man, after all, and a virile one. He needed a woman in his bed. Violet realized that she wanted to be that woman. She was in love with Travis and he was taking his passion to other women. Maybe some night Violet just needed to climb into bed with him and deal with the consequences later.

Little Bonnie and the dog came into the kitchen, Bonnie still rubbing the sleep from her eyes. "You mad at Travis?"

"Uh, let's not talk about that. Here, sit down and I'll give you some breakfast." She felt Bonnie's drawers and sighed, wondering if she had gone to bed wet.

All the others were now piling into the kitchen.

Harold looked up at her with those almond eyes. "You still mad at Travis?"

"Why does everyone ask that?" she snapped. "It doesn't concern you kids."

Kessie picked up her bowl and spoon. "When you're mad at Travis, this isn't a happy house and we all worry."

Violet looked down at Kessie's fingers. Her nails were

chewed to the quick. "I'm sorry," Violet answered. "Now you all eat and help me clean up."

"Don't forget we're going to Mrs. Van Mayes's for supper," Houston said, his mouth full of oatmeal.

"As if I could forget. I hope you all use your best manners or she'll think we were all raised in a barn."

"I hear she's got a big house," Kessie said, "bigger and finer than this one."

Violet poured herself a cup of coffee. "I reckon it would be a very nice life for everyone to live at her ranch."

Houston stared at her. "You don't look very happy about it."

"Who, me?" She managed to smile. "Why wouldn't I want to live in her big, fine house?"

"Does that mean Travis would marry her?" Kessie asked.

Violet winced. "I reckon so."

Bonnie shook her head. She had oatmeal all over her face. "Want Travis marry Violet."

"That's not going to happen," Violet answered and got up quickly so the children wouldn't see her face. "Now you all finish up and we'll clean house some and then you can go outside and play—except you, Bonnie. I've got to give you a bath and wash your drawers." She got up and went into the kitchen, pretending to be very busy putting away things so she wouldn't have to discuss this with the children anymore. Yes, marrying the widow would give Travis a rich, pretty wife and a big ranch and a secure home for the children. Then why couldn't she stop herself from weeping?

She hated to spend the money, but she went to the dry goods store and bought everyone new clothes, including extra drawers for Bonnie and a cheap blue dress for herself.

The lady behind the counter had a pencil stuck behind one ear as she peered at Violet over her glasses. "Going someplace special, honey?"

"To Mrs. Van Mayes's house for dinner."

"My, my." The lady's eyes widened as she took the pencil out to write the ticket. "Hardly anyone gets invited to that rich Yankee's house."

"Yes, we're so thrilled," Violet said without enthusiasm as she took the package and left.

Evening came all too soon for Violet. She had the children all dressed and was putting Bonnie's hair in pigtails like her own when Travis came through the door.

"You still mad at me?" He grinned at her.

How could she be mad at him? She wanted to rush into his arms and kiss him, but of course she didn't. "I'm fine." She managed to keep her voice even. "You wash up and I'll get dressed."

He nodded. "Oh, by the way, we don't have to walk. She sent her butler to say she'd send her barouche to pick us up."

"What's that?" Houston asked.

"Silly," Kessie said. "Don't you know anything? It's a fancy open carriage. Rich people own them."

Violet managed to smile. "Won't that be a fun ride?"

Travis grabbed a towel and went out in the backyard to wash up. Violet stood at the window a long moment, watching him peel off his shirt and bend over the wash basin. Muscles rippled under his dark skin as he washed. He was all man and she had never wanted a man as much as she wanted this one.

Harold walked through the room. "What you looking at?"

"Nothing. I was just getting ready to go." She went into

her room and closed the door, leaning against it, feeling the flush on her face. At least Travis hadn't seen her watching him.

She put on the new blue dress and combed her brown hair into pigtails. If she left it down, she'd look older and she wasn't sure that Mrs. Van Mayes hadn't already guessed her secret.

At six thirty, everyone was assembled in the parlor, all combed and shiny. Violet said they should leave the dog at home because the rich widow might not like Growler on her fine carpets, and even though Bonnie threw a tantrum, the dog got closed in Bonnie's bedroom. Then there was a knock at the door and when Travis opened it, a snooty driver stood there.

"Mrs. Van Mayes sends her compliments and her barouche if you are ready."

"I reckon we are." Travis grinned and they all trooped out to the fancy open carriage. It had red leather seats and lots of shiny brass with two fine black horses to pull it.

"Oh, my," Violet breathed. "I never saw anything so fine."

Travis lifted each child up into the barouche and then he turned to Violet. "You ready?"

She nodded and he put his big hands on her small waist and lifted her. For a split second, she looked down into his face and he stared up at her, as if puzzled; then he sat her inside on the red leather seat and got in himself, sitting next to her. She could feel the heat of his muscular thigh through the thin blue fabric.

Travis nodded to the driver. "We're ready, my man."

The driver snapped his little whip and the fine black horses started off at a smart clip.

"Boy, this is the life," Houston said. "This must be the best carriage in Texas."

"I'll bet it is," Harold agreed.

Kessie looked around. "Wouldn't it be nice to ride like this all the time?"

"I want my dog," Bonnie sobbed.

Travis patted her shoulder. "He'll be all right until we get home and you can bring him some food, okay?"

That seemed to comfort her and she climbed into his lap so she could see the passing scenery.

In twenty minutes, they were driving up the circular drive to Mrs. Van Mayes's fine Victorian-style home. It had turrets and stained-glass windows and at least three stories.

"This must be the biggest house in Texas," Kessie said.

Houston looked around open-mouthed. "Wonder how much land she owns."

Travis frowned at him. "In Texas, it ain't polite to ask how much land or how many cattle someone owns."

The mustached driver looked back over his shoulder and smiled. "I believe the lady owns some ten thousand acres and several hundred thousand cows."

Even Travis took a deep breath at that.

As they got out of the barouche, Violet said, "Now, everyone remember to be on your best behavior."

Travis smiled at her. "It's nice of you to help the kids make a good impression on the lady."

"Of course." She forced herself to smile back although her heart was breaking. Here she would have to pretend to be a young girl while the pretty widow went after Travis, and of course that was why she had invited them all to dinner. Violet had seen the way the woman looked the Ranger over. She wanted him all right, and besides being rich, she was beautiful. What else could a man want?

They went up the steps and rang the bell at the massive leaded glass door as the driver took the barouche away to the stables.

After a moment, a dour butler answered the door and bowed. "Mrs. Van Mayes is awaiting you in the library, sir. I'll announce you."

They all stood in the fancy entry hall, staring in wonder as the butler disappeared and then returned. "Follow me, please."

Violet had never seen anything like this place. There were fine carpets, giant chandeliers, and big, carved dark furniture. They followed the butler into the library, where Mrs. Van Mayes, dressed in pale lavender, stood up and held out her hands to Travis. Her dress was cut daringly low, showing a full curved bosom. "Ah, so glad you and the children could come."

"Good of you to invite us. Kids, say howdy."

Violet and the elegant lady locked eyes and the widow's glare was as cold as marble. Violet curtseyed to her as a well-bred young lady should do, and the other girls did the same. The boys bowed low. "Evening, ma'am."

"Such nice children." Mrs. Van Mayes sat down and patted the cushion on the settee next to her. "You must sit and tell me how you are managing, Mr. Prescott."

He sat down next to her. "Just call me Travis, ma'am."

"Of course and you must call me Charlotte. Would you like a drink?"

"Well, ma'am, I reckon so." He ran his finger around his collar, evidently nervous.

"I'll ring for the butler." She got up, went to the wall and pulled a velvet rope. The dour, portly man came in promptly. "Jarvis, bring me some sherry and break open a bottle of my finest bourbon for Mr. Prescott."

"Very well, madam. And what about the children?" He peered down his long nose at them.

"Take the young lady and the others to the billiard room

and get them some sarsaparilla." She dismissed all the children with a nod.

Violet took a deep breath. "I'd just as soon stay here."

Travis frowned at her and the beautiful widow gave her a murderous glare as she spoke. "No, dear, be a good girl and run along so the adults can visit."

There was nothing else she could do but follow the children to the billiard room. In minutes, the butler brought them bottles of sarsaparilla. She decided it was too far down the hall to eavesdrop.

"How do we play this?" Houston asked.

"I reckon you hit the ball with the tip of that stick and try to knock it in those holes in the corners of the table."

Bonnie pouted. "Feathers, me can't reach and I miss doggie."

Violet sighed. "I'll hold you up so you can try to hit the ball." She lifted the toddler and showed her how to hold the stick. The children were soon engrossed with the game.

Violet fidgeted, wondering what was going on in the library, but there was no way to know. She could only imagine how the forward widow was coming on to Travis. She tried not to be jealous; after all, this would be a great life for Travis and the children. Darn it, Violet loved him and even thinking about him making love to Charlotte Van Mayes made her grit her teeth.

In a few minutes, the butler came back to the billiard room and bowed low. "Miss, Mrs. Van Mayes is ready for dinner. Please bring the rest of the children and follow me."

Violet nodded. "Come on, kids. It's time to eat."

Dutifully they followed the butler into the biggest dining room Violet had ever seen. The dark, carved table looked like it would seat at least a dozen people and there was fine china and silver reflecting the chandelier's candle glow.

The lady waited for Travis to seat her and then he walked down to the other end of the table and took a chair.

"Children"—Mrs. Van Mayes waved one bejeweled hand—"you may sit anywhere up and down the table."

Violet promptly took the seat next to Travis. "This one suits me just fine."

The lady frowned at her. "How sweet that you're so devoted to your father."

"He's not really my father," Violet said. "He's adopting all of us."

"Yes, I found them all." Travis grinned. "They needed a home and I took them in."

"What a big heart you have." Mrs. Van Mayes turned her warmest smile on Travis, then looked at Violet again and frowned. "It must be hard without a mother for a young girl like you."

"We are managing." Violet scowled back at her.

"But you are missing so much," the lady cooed at her. "You should be attending finishing school, learning French and embroidery, so you can move in the best circles and meet young men from the best families."

"She's a little young for that yet," Travis said.

"One is never too young to think about society," the beauty cooed and smiled again at Travis.

The children all seemed dumbstruck by the fine china, crystal and shining silver. They sat quietly, wide-eyed.

"And so quiet," Mrs. Van Mayes said with a nod of approval. "Most children are noisy and tear up things."

Violet looked at her. "You have no children of your own?"

The lady shook her head. "I wanted some, but you see, my husband died on our wedding night, so I've been alone ever since." She wiped her eyes with her napkin as the butler came in with a silver tray on which was the largest roast Violet had ever seen.

Houston looked at her. "What'd he die of?"

"Houston," Travis snapped, "you are being rude."

"I'm sorry."

He probably died trying to satisfy this lusty woman, Violet thought, but she didn't say anything as the butler paused by her chair. "Roast beef, miss?"

"Yes, please." She took the big silver fork and helped herself to a slice, plus some potatoes and carrots. She looked over at Travis. He was digging into that plate of food with approval.

At the other end of the table, the widow was inspecting the bottle of wine Jarvis had brought her. "Yes, this will do. See to Mr. Prescott's goblet."

And then to Travis, she said, "I do hope you like this wine. I had it shipped from France at great expense."

Travis smiled. "Ma'am, I don't know much about fancy wine, but if you picked it, I'm sure I'll like it."

The beauty blushed modestly and leaned forward so that her bosom showed in her low-cut dress. "Well, I do know a lot about wine." The butler walked the length of the table to pour Travis a glass. Without thinking, Violet held out her glass.

Mrs. Van Mayes laughed. "Oh, my dear, you're a little too young for wine yet. You need to learn so much. Have you ever thought about a finishing school? I attended Miss Pickett's in Boston and that would be a good place for you."

"I wouldn't want to leave the children," Violet said.

"Oh, but the boys might want to go to military school," the lady suggested as she sipped her wine. "And of course, that little one needs a good nanny."

The little one, Bonnie, scowled at her. "I want my dog."

"What?" The lady blinked.

Travis laughed. "She's got an old dog that she's never separated from. We made her leave him at home."

"Well, the poor little thing. Of course she should have her dog."

Travis paused in eating. "Mrs. Van Mayes—"

"Please call me Charlotte." She gave him a melting look.

"Charlotte, you see, I can't hardly afford to send girls to finishing school or boys to military school."

"Oh, but if they had a benefactor, that wouldn't be any problem." She gave all the children a smug, satisfied look.

Houston said, "I don't want to go to military school. I want to be a rancher or a Texas Ranger."

"I want to be a doctor or a scientist," Harold added.

The lady stared at Harold. "Where on earth did you get the Chinese boy?"

"I found him like the others," Travis said.

"Travis, you're such a kind, generous heart," said the widow. "How I've longed to meet someone like you. Wealthy widows have a difficult time in this world, everyone trying to take advantage of them when they don't have a man to look after them."

She was about as helpless as a black widow spider, Violet thought, but she kept her gaze on her plate. The food really was delicious and she wondered what it would be like to be rich. She already sensed the widow didn't like her and was thinking about shipping her off to school to get rid of her. Could she send her any farther than Boston?

"Of course"—Mrs. Van Mayes gave her a chilly smile—"there are grand schools in Switzerland, and some of the best families send their daughters there."

So there was a place farther than Boston she could be

sent, Violet thought. She glanced over at Travis to see if he understood what this woman was planning so she could have the man all to herself, but he was grinning like a coyote and staring at the lady like she was sugar candy that he intended to eat up that very night.

Chapter 15

It was the following Sunday after dinner at Charlotte Van Mayes's house. Violet had taken the children to church and convinced Travis to accompany them. She thought he looked grand, but he seemed uncomfortable and ill at ease in the stiff shirt and tie.

Everyone, particularly the single ladies, turned their heads, smiled and nodded a greeting as the little family found their way to a pew. The congregation seemed abuzz with the fact the family had had dinner with the rich widow.

Well, there wasn't much else to talk about in this sleepy town, Violet thought as she settled in and smacked Harold for pulling Kessie's red hair.

It seemed hot in the little church, even for June. Paper fans from the local funeral home fluttered at every sweating face as the choir sang "Amazing Grace."

Violet thought the children behaved well. She only once had to tap Houston on the shoulder for poking Harold, and even little Bonnie was quiet as she diligently scribbled on the back of a donation envelope. The windows were open and butterflies and bees drifted in and out of the building as the minister droned on and on, only interrupted by several old men who had dozed off and were snoring.

Halfway through the service, someone opened the big doors for more air and Violet heard titters and saw heads craning as Growler ran down the aisle, sniffing the wine-colored carpet until he tracked his way to Bonnie, who set up a cry and threw her arms around the dog's neck.

Even Travis frowned, but Violet managed to silence the greeting and settled the dog under the pew and the minister went on with his service.

Finally the choir led in an off-key version of "Shall We Gather at the River" and the service was over. Dutifully Travis led the little family out the big doors, stopping to shake hands with the minister. "Good service, Pastor."

The thin man looked over his spectacles at Travis and smiled. "Good to see you at services, Brother Prescott."

Reverend Smithe patted each child on the head. "Poor little orphans."

"We're not orphans," Houston said. "Travis has taken us in."

"And so kind of him to do so." The pastor nodded. "And you, young lady, so brave of a young girl to manage a house by yourself."

Before Violet could answer, Mrs. Van Mayes walked up, dressed in expensive green silk and smiling. "Yes, Pastor, isn't it brave of all of them to struggle along like they do? I think it's so admirable."

Violet frowned at her, but before she could say anything, Travis was tipping his Stetson to the lady. "Mrs. Van Mayes—"

"Charlotte, please," she reminded him with a dazzling smile. "We are good friends after all."

"Just wanted to thank you for the dinner the other night," Travis said. "The children were so pleased."

He nudged Violet and she curtsied. "Yes, ma'am," she answered, "so pleased."

"You're a brave little girl." The widow reached out and patted Violet's shoulder.

"I don't mind."

But of course, the pretty widow wasn't paying a bit of attention to her; her gaze was fastened on Travis. "How nice to see you in church."

All the other single women were now gathering around Travis to the point that Violet felt pushed to the outside of the circle and she stood there tapping her foot.

Kessie scratched herself. "Can we go home now?"

"That's not ladylike," Violet said. "Don't scratch."

"I can't help it; this petticoat itches and it's hot standing out here in the sun."

"Then gather up the rest of the kids and head home. We'll be there as soon as I can reclaim Travis."

"Who are all those old hens?" Harold asked.

"Shh!" Violet cautioned. "They're all interested in Travis."

"I thought he belonged to us," Houston said.

"Just gather up everyone and go home. I've got a roast in the oven and don't let Bonnie get into the peach cobbler before she eats dinner. We'll be there in just a minute."

The children trooped away toward their house down the street while Violet stood there patiently, as the ladies grouped around Travis, who ignored her.

Finally the ladies drifted away, all but Mrs. Van Mayes—she still chatted with Travis, who didn't seem to mind at all.

Violet tapped Travis on the arm. "I've got a roast in the stove. If we don't go soon, it'll be overcooked."

"Oh, what a shame." The pretty widow nodded to her. "I was just inviting your father to dinner."

Violet glared back. "I've already got dinner ready."

"Oh." The blond widow looked disappointed. "Well, it's

a lovely day. Mr. Prescott, why don't I drive over and pick you up later today and we'll go for a drive? I'd love to show you my ranch."

Travis seemed smitten with the woman. He grinned. "I'd like that. The kids would, too."

The lady bit her lip. "I was planning on driving the light buggy. Not much room for children, I'm afraid."

"Then the kids can go to the park." He turned to Violet. "You could take the kids to the park, couldn't you?"

Violet said, "I remember Mrs. Van Mayes has that fine barouche with the double seats. It holds everyone."

The widow gave her a steely look. "But it's my driver's day off and I couldn't possibly manage the barouche alone. No, I'm sorry, I'll be driving the small buggy."

Travis stared at the woman as if she were a steak and he was a starving hound. "I'm sure Violet will be happy to take the kids to the park." He poked Violet in the side and she grunted.

Mrs. Van Mayes smiled without mirth. "Children do get a little possessive of their parents sometimes, but they get over it. Good-bye, dearie," she addressed Violet. "So kind of you to take your little brothers and sisters to the park so your father can look over the ranch with me."

Travis tipped his hat to the lady, but Violet only nodded as the lady turned and walked toward her fine buggy.

The two started to the house.

"What's the matter with you, Violet?" he scolded. "You were barely polite to the lady."

"The lady wants to marry you. She's done everything but post a notice in the weekly paper."

He smiled. "You think so? Well, would that be so bad? She's beautiful and rich, too. Just think how well you kids could live in her big house. We're barely making it on my salary."

"You aren't thinking of us," Violet complained. "You're thinking how you'd like to get that beauty into bed."

"Violet!" He looked shocked. "Nice young ladies don't make comments like that. You shouldn't even know about such things."

She didn't answer for a long moment, thinking she didn't want to give her age and experience away. "All right, I apologize. I'll take the kids to the park and you can go riding with Mrs. Van Mayes. She's probably a better choice than some of those other eager hens."

Travis snorted. "Some of those women are old enough to be my mother. If this town is determined to marry me off, it ought to at least be a woman I like."

And can hardly wait to take to bed, Violet thought, but she didn't say that. She was so jealous, she was almost shaking, but of course she couldn't say anything.

They reached the house and Violet served dinner. Of course, part of Bonnie's went directly down to Growler, lying under the table, but Violet was too preoccupied with the elegant lady to say anything.

Travis dived in with gusto. "You know, Violet, Mrs. Van Mayes is right. You have too much responsibility for a young girl. It makes me feel guilty."

"I don't mind," Violet assured him as she poured gravy on her mashed potatoes and buttered her hot roll.

"And that's brave of you," Travis said, "looking after all these kids when you ought to be learning etiquette and French. I'll bet Mrs. Van Mayes can teach you a lot."

"Not as much as she can teach you," Violet said under her breath."

"What?"

"Nothing." She turned her head and addressed the faces around the table. "After we have pie, we'll all go to the park."

Bonnie had gravy all over her face. "Travis go with us?"

Travis shook his head. "Not this time, baby. I'm going for a buggy ride with a lady."

Harold made a face. "You'd rather do that than swing or go down the slide?"

Travis reached out and patted his head. "When you're a few years older, you'll understand." He got up from the table. "I reckon I'd better go comb my hair and put on a little rose hair tonic."

"Why?" Kessie asked. "The horse won't care what you smell like."

Travis winked at her. "But the lady might."

He left the room, whistling.

Violet felt like she was choking on her food.

Houston said, "He sure does seem happy."

"Don't he though?" Harold answered.

"Doesn't he?" corrected Kessie.

Violet sighed. "You two behave and I'll serve pie."

"Can I have Travis's pie?" Houston asked.

"Certainly not." She got up from the table. "He'll probably want it when he gets home."

Kessie looked at her. "He doesn't seem too interested in pie right now."

"Don't I know it," Violet snapped and went into the kitchen.

They were all eating hot peach cobbler when Travis returned a few minutes later. "How do I look?" His hair was slicked down and the scent of rose oil hair tonic drifted heavily on the warm air.

"You sure you put enough on?" Violet asked.

He didn't seem to notice her sarcasm. "I reckon so." He walked over to look out the front window. "Here comes Charlotte now." He went to the door and looked back. "Violet, you can take care of the kids?"

"Don't I always?"

He didn't answer as he went out the door.

Violet heaved a heavy sigh.

"Are you mad about something?" Houston asked.

"Me? Now why should I be?" She busied herself clearing off the table. "Just think how nice it would be for all of us if he married Mrs. Van Mayes. After all, she's rich."

Kessie stared at her and began to chew her nails. "We thought he was going to marry you."

"He doesn't even see me," Violet said and blinked away tears. "Now you all get ready and let's go to the park. I imagine they'll be gone a long time."

"Why?" Harold asked.

"Silly," Kessie said with great importance. "She's got a big ranch and there's a lot to show Travis."

"If you only knew," Violet muttered as she carried dishes into the kitchen.

Outside, Travis strode up to the buggy. "Well, hello again, Mrs. Van Mayes."

She leaned toward him so he got a good look at a great expanse of bosom in her pale green dress. "Please, dear Travis, call me Charlotte, all right?"

God, she was beautiful.

"Sure, Charlotte, although I feel a mite forward calling you by your first name."

"Oh, don't be silly," she sniffed. "Now hop up here and drive. I'm such a delicate little thing, I can hardly handle a horse."

"Of course." He climbed up into the light buggy and took the reins. He noted the seat was small but not so small that she had to ride with her thigh right up against his as she was doing. Her delicate hands touched his as she handed over the reins and he felt his manhood come up at her nearness. "My, you smell good—better than honeysuckle."

"Do you like it?" she murmured as he snapped the reins and they started off. "I had it sent from Paris." She leaned closer. "Take a deep whiff to make sure."

He took a deep breath. "I really do. I reckon it costs too much to get a bottle for Violet. She works so hard and never asks for much."

She patted his arm. "Yes, she's an adorable child. I'll get her a bottle of perfume myself, nothing too heavy, something a young girl would like."

He looked at her with admiration. "You're a great lady, Mrs.—I mean, Charlotte."

Her laughter sounded like a tinkling bell. "That's more like it, Travis. Now turn this buggy around and we'll go out and look over my land. I own ten thousand acres, you know."

"So I've heard." She was beautiful, all right, but his mind kept going to Violet.

"I've kept the foreman my husband had, but he's getting old and ready to retire. I really need a man who knows enough about ranching to take over. I'm just a helpless widow and everyone tries to take advantage of me." She wiped her eyes with a lace hankie.

"Never you mind, Charlotte. No one will take advantage of you when I'm around."

She scooted even closer. "Oh, I just knew you'd be a Texas gentleman who would stand up for helpless women. You know, I just don't know much about business and my husband left me with so much land and cattle."

"It's too bad your husband died. How long were you married?"

"Oh, only a few hours." She dabbed at her eyes. "Poor old Rufus had a heart attack just as he was getting into bed on our wedding night."

"Oh?"

"Yes. I'm an unplucked flower, so to speak." She blushed.

"You poor thing. It must have been terrible for you."

She sighed as the buggy trotted along. "Yes. It's been three years now and every sort of villain has tried to take advantage of a poor, innocent widow, but I just knew, as a Texas Ranger, you'd be my hero and protect me."

He flushed and glanced over at her. "I'd certainly do my best, Charlotte. It's too bad you don't have kids."

"But I could do so much for yours," she purred. "Why the boys could all go off to military school, I could hire a nanny for sweet little Bonnie and Kessie, and that oldest girl, I could send her to my old finishing school, Miss Pickett's in Boston."

"That's mighty generous of you, Charlotte, but I'd sure miss them if they were gone."

"Oh, but we could have children of our own," she said. "Dear me, I'm being so forward."

"That's all right, Miss Charlotte." He reached over and put his hand over hers.

"You don't mind?" She scooted even closer.

He began to sweat. If she scooted any closer, she'd be in his lap. She was so close he could feel her body warm against his, and her hand under his big one felt so soft, like satin. He began to imagine kissing her, holding her. His breath came quicker. He could have this woman, he knew by the things she had said, the way she pressed close to him. And she was beautiful, the most beautiful woman he had ever met.

Violet. Her big, blue eyes came to his mind suddenly. Well, Violet was pretty, but of course, she was just a kid. Someday, she would be a beautiful woman, too, but right now, Miss Charlotte was all woman and he knew that after a while, when they stopped the buggy, he would probably kiss her and she wouldn't mind at all.

* * *

Charlotte Van Mayes eyed the handsome, tanned man sitting beside her in the buggy. She wanted to add him to her possessions like her fine house, her horses and her wealth. She knew she was pretty and she had used that to her advantage all her life to get what she wanted and now she wanted Travis Prescott.

"It's a great day," he said and smiled at her.

"Yes, isn't it?" And put her hand on his knee. Of course he had that gaggle of assorted children that she had no intention of dealing with, especially that slant-eyed Oriental kid and that oldest girl, who seemed too possessive of Charlotte's future bridegroom. Well, she had already decided how to handle all of them. Travis might not like it, but she would convince him it was best for them all to be sent away. For the two youngest ones, she would hire a nanny who would keep them out of Charlotte's way until they, too, were old enough to send off to school. As for that damned flea-bitten mongrel, she had some rat poison she could slip into his food.

"Tell me about your ranch," Travis said.

She could see the sweat on his dark face. Evidently, sitting next to her was making him desire her. Good. She wanted a stallion of a man. This one looked like he knew how to handle women expertly, and she hungered for that. "It takes most of the county," she answered and moved her hand from his knee to his arm, feeling the hard muscle there. "We've been on it the past fifteen minutes. I really don't know how many horses or cattle I own. Why don't we stop in the shade of that tree?" She pointed to a tall elm. "So we can talk."

"Sure." He guided the buggy over to the tree and reined

in under the shade. "A big spread like that is hard to manage."

She moved even closer. "Especially for a poor widow," she murmured, looking up into his brown eyes. "Men always seem to want to take advantage of me." She fluttered her eyelashes and took a deep breath so that her bosom swelled out the green silk.

"That's a dirty shame," Travis declared. "I hate men who don't act like gentlemen."

She sighed and turned her face up to his. "I'm so alone in the world. I really need a husband to look after things, a real man who knows about ranching."

He licked his lips, looking down at her, and she could see the desire in his eyes. "I used to ranch before I became a Texas Ranger."

"I've heard you got hurt."

He nodded. "You got that right. I've got a bullet shard in my right wrist and every once in a while, it hits a nerve and I'm in pain for a few seconds."

"Can't anything be done about it?" She opened her lips a bit, looking up at him.

He laughed. "Yep, but I don't have the money. That's why I've left the Rangers."

"Travis," she purred, "I have money, plenty of it."

"I couldn't take your cash. They got a name for men like that."

"But if you were my husband . . ." She reached up suddenly and put her arms around his neck and kissed him.

He seemed startled at her advances, but he returned the kiss with hot passion, putting his arms around her and pulling her to him.

Now this was a real man. She put the tip of her tongue against his lips and he gasped and opened his mouth, letting her kiss him deeply. She put one hand on his thigh and felt the muscles tighten there and he breathed harder.

Then abruptly, he pulled away from her and scooted to his side of the buggy seat. "I apologize, Miss Charlotte, I know I was too forward with a lady—"

"I wanted to kiss you." She smiled up at him. "Oh, Travis, you and I would make sure a good team and I would love you like no woman ever has."

"But I've got the kids to think of—"

"And just think how nice it would be for them to have money and live in my big house. Why, I could be the mother they need."

"I don't know." He pulled out a bandanna and wiped the sweat from his face. "Violet has been doing a pretty good job of running the house."

"But is it fair to her? To have to be the mother and do all the housework and all that responsibility?"

He picked up the reins. "I reckon you're right about that. She says she don't mind."

"She's just being nice. I'm sure the poor dear child resents all that hard work."

"Let me think about this, Charlotte." He clucked to the horse and they took off at a fast clip.

Damn. She'd offered him wealth and passion. What else could this man want? The fact that he was hesitating only whetted her desire. She had always gotten everything she wanted until now. She wasn't sure how she would do it, but she was determined to add this big half-breed to her possessions.

They didn't talk much as they drove back, but she could see his mind was busy because his brow furrowed in thought. They pulled up before the little house and he reined in. There was no one on the street on this lazy late June day. She leaned over and kissed his tanned cheek. "I love you, Travis. There, I've said it. It might seem bold for a lady, but I think we were meant for each other."

"Charlotte—" He hesitated. "You're a beautiful woman, and I'm honored that you'd even consider marrying a poor cowboy like me."

She looked at him, wanting him. She smiled. "Then I'll consider that we are courting and we'll see where it goes from here."

He stared at her and she could see the desire in his eyes. This was a virile stallion who needed a woman and she could already imagine him naked on her silk sheets. "Miss Charlotte." He shook his head. "I don't think this will work out."

She was taken aback. "What? I thought—"

"I have responsibilities and besides, I wouldn't want anyone to think I was after your money."

"I never thought that, Travis. That's what I like about you. You're your own man." *But you'll soon be mine*, she thought.

Travis hesitated and shook his head. "What bothers me is that you keep talking about sending the kids away."

"It would be for their own good—"

"I love my kids and I want them with me, not stuck off in some distant school."

"Oh, for heaven's sake!" she snapped as he handed her the reins and stepped down from the buggy. "They aren't even your children. They're a pack of ragamuffins you've picked up along the way like stray puppies."

"Charlotte, they are my kids as far as I'm concerned, and besides, I don't think I can return your love."

"What? How dare you humiliate me in this manner!" She took a swing at him with the little whip and he stepped back.

"Good-bye, Charlotte."

"It's Mrs. Van Mayes to you, you ignorant cowboy." She whipped the horse and drove away in a cloud of dust.

Travis stared after her as she left. God, he had wanted to take her right there in the open under that tree and she had seemed to be willing. He must be a damned fool to pass up a chance like that. What had stopped him? Immediately he saw a face in his mind: a small face with large almost violet-blue eyes. The thought shocked him. Violet was just a kid, but her face had come to his mind just as he was about to pick up Miss Charlotte and carry her to the grass under that tree and take her with all the need and passion he felt at that moment. Now he was angry with himself for wanting a mere girl who was too young to even know what passion was. Maybe Charlotte was right; maybe he needed to send the innocent Violet away to school before his twisted mind forced him to take advantage of her. Did Harold know what he was saying about Violet being older? But how much older?

Quietly and lost in thought, he opened the door and stepped in, walking to the kitchen just in time to see Violet getting out of the washtub, her long brown hair hanging loose and partially covering her body.

She turned at his gasp of surprise and grabbed for a towel, but he'd already seen all he needed to know. "Holy mother of God!" he gasped. This was no kid, this was a full-grown woman.

Chapter 16

Violet froze only a split second, standing there naked as Travis stared at her, and then she grabbed for a towel. "You should have made some noise coming in."

He didn't answer. He stood there, staring at her as she shook her hair back, wrapped the towel around her and stepped from the tub.

"I'll be goddamned," he breathed.

"Don't swear," she said. "You shouldn't have walked in on me." Her heart was beating hard as she tried to brush past him and go down the hall into her bedroom, but he reached out and grabbed her arm.

"We need to talk, missy."

"Let me get some clothes on. Besides, I don't know what you want to talk about." She didn't return his gaze.

"You know about what. I reckon I've been a damned, blind fool all this time, thinking you were a kid." He pulled her to him and looked down into her face and she was afraid of the fury in his eyes and flinched.

"Don't hit me."

"Hit you? Why, you little wench, I ought to turn you over my knee and—"

"Please let me get some clothes on," she begged and the towel slipped and fell to the floor.

He yanked her up against his big body and she could feel the heat and the muscle of him. "You owe me an explanation. Just how old are you anyway?"

She hesitated, afraid of his anger. "I—I'll be twenty next week."

"Twenty?" He let go of her as if stunned and she took the chance to run into the bedroom and slam the door, lock it and lean against it.

"Violet!" She heard his big boots stomp up to her door and he banged hard. "Damn it, open this door!"

"Let me get dressed and we'll talk," she pleaded, "and you cool down."

"Cool down?" He banged on the door even harder. "You think I'll cool down! Let me in, damn it!" He banged on the door so hard it quivered and she thought it might give way. She grabbed up her blue dress, backing toward the window. "Just let me explain!" she pleaded.

He was kicking the door now, so hard she thought he would kick it down. "Let me in! You've been lying to me all this time and laughing because I was such a gullible fool."

She was terrified. Men had hurt her before and this one was bigger and madder than any man she'd ever known. "No, I didn't, Travis. Honestly I never laughed at you."

"The hell you didn't!" He kicked the door so hard the lock tore out and he stomped into the room, his brown eyes dark with rage. "You've humiliated me and the whole town will laugh when they find out—"

"Maybe they don't need to find out." She held the dress in front of her naked body and backed away. "Please, Travis, let me get dressed and we'll talk."

"We'll talk right now, missy, you lying little bitch!" He grabbed her arm and she dropped the dress as he pulled her naked body hard against him.

Violet trembled and shied away. "Please, please don't hurt me."

"Hurt you?" He sounded surprised. "What I feel like doing is spanking your drawers, you conniving little liar."

She was pressed up against him and she couldn't stop trembling. She tried to pull away, but he held her tightly. She had never seen such rage in a man's face and she was truly afraid of him for the very first time. Tears ran down her face and she tried to blink them away.

"Oh, that won't work, missy," he roared at her. "You think you can shed a few tears and I'll fold like a bad hand of poker?"

She burst into tears. "At least let me get dressed."

At that he stepped back and took a deep breath. "All right, damn it, get dressed. I can't think with you naked as a jaybird."

She sobbed as she slipped into her dress and when she looked up, he was still glaring at her.

"Where are the kids?" he asked.

"Out in the barn, playing," she sobbed. She didn't try to put up her hair, still loose around her shoulders.

"Do they know about this?"

She took a deep breath. "About what?"

"Hell, you know what. Do they know your real age?"

She didn't want to get them in trouble. "Sort of. They know I'm a little older, but they never asked much."

"And what about this feathers thing with Bonnie?"

He was already furious. If he knew about the scarlet plumes in her hair with the dance hall costume, he might be so mad, he'd be dangerous. "I—I told her I used to work on a chicken farm where feathers flew all over the place."

Silence.

"Travis? For God's sake, say something. You scare me when you just stand there glaring at me like that."

He didn't answer. She had hated lying to him, but she

loved him so and he would surely throw her out if he knew her background.

He turned suddenly and walked away without answering. She waited to hear the front door slam behind him, certainly heading for the saloon, but instead, she heard him sit down in that creaky rocker by the fireplace. He might beat her like other men had done, but she loved him enough to take the chance.

Taking a deep breath, she slowly walked into the living room. "Please don't be mad at me, Travis."

He came to his feet and grabbed her shoulders. "Missy, you owe me one hellova explanation and I hate liars."

She looked up at him and couldn't hold the tears back.

"I was on the run, just like I told you, and every man I met tried to take advantage of me, so I decided that the easiest thing to do would be pass myself off as a kid."

"Who are you running from?" His dark eyes were black with distrust and anger.

How she wished he would pull her to him, wipe the tears from her cheeks, and hold her close. His fingers were biting into her shoulders.

She couldn't tell him she was a whore—he would throw her out of the house—so she lied again. "A—A mean stepfather who tried to take advantage of me so I ran away and joined up with the other orphans. I didn't mean to fool you, Travis. I was just so scared and then I was afraid to tell you, afraid you'd be mad—"

"Mad! Missy, you don't know what mad looks like until you've seen me really mad." He snorted and turned to walk to the front window, his big boots stomping.

She stood there a minute, unsure whether to follow him or go back into her room. She had hoped that he would pull her into his embrace and stroke her hair. She had hoped he would whisper, "You know I'll always take care of you, Violet. I love you."

And she would lean her face against his brawny chest, her shoulders shaking with sobs. She would feel so safe and secure in his arms. No one or nothing could hurt her as long as she was held in Travis's embrace. She would turn her face up to his and say, "I love you, Travis."

"Hush, you don't know what you're saying. You're scared and upset," he would whisper as he put one finger under her small chin and lifted her face up to look down at her. "I reckon you had your reasons for fooling me and we'll just start fresh, okay?"

"Sure." She would look up at him, loving him as she had never loved anyone. Maybe they could go on from here without him ever finding out her past. Maybe he need never find that out. "I've wanted to kiss you for the longest time," she would whisper.

"And damn it, me you." He would bend his head and kiss her gently, a chaste, warm kiss that said: I love you and I will protect you and look out for you always.

She imagined she slipped her arms around his neck and molded herself against him as the kiss deepened. She could feel every inch of his hard body, including his aroused manhood throbbing against her, and she wanted him. She opened her lips and he plunged his tongue deep inside for a long moment as she breathed deeper. His hand slipped into the bodice of her dress and caressed her breast until her nipples grew taut with need and she moaned, urging him to go even further. "I want you," he gasped, "and I need you."

"Then take me," she urged.

He would pick her up, looking down at her. "I've been hungering for you almost since I met you and beating myself up because you're so young."

"But now you know my real age." She smiled up at him, her arms still around his neck.

"And I'd like to be your first man," he whispered and turned toward her room.

Her first man. She couldn't even remember her first man, but Travis need never know that. He was proud and if he knew her real past, she would lose him forever.

"Damn it!" Travis snapped. "Say something!"

That brought her out of her daydream abruptly. "I—I don't know what else to say. I've told you what you asked."

He scowled. "I got nothing to say to you, missy." His face was stone cold. "You're a lying little bitch."

She stood on one foot and then the other. "Do you want me to leave?"

"And go where?" He snorted. "You haven't got any money for a train ticket and I sure as hell don't."

"Maybe I could get a job and earn enough for a ticket."

"Doing what?" He snorted.

She was certain she could get a job at the Cattle Drive Saloon, but she didn't say that. "I just reckoned you wanted me to leave right away."

"And have all this come out and have everyone laughing at me and teasing the kids?"

"You want things to go on just as they were?" She couldn't believe it.

He shook his head and abruptly looked very tired. "I don't have a better idea right now. Maybe later we'll think of something."

She swallowed hard. "All right, if that's the way you want it."

"It is and we don't tell the kids."

"All right."

She heard noise from the back and the kids yelling and laughing as they came up on the back porch.

Travis glared at her. "You'd better get your shoes on."

"Sure." She ran for the bedroom as the kids entered the house. Violet began to braid her hair as she walked back into the living room. "Did you boys remember to milk the cow?"

"We did," Houston said as they all entered.

Violet managed a smile. "Boys, if you'll help me empty the washtub, I'll fix some supper."

Travis stood up. "I'll do it. It's too heavy for the boys." He strode to the kitchen.

"Gosh," Harold whispered, "what's wrong with Travis?"

"Yes," said Kessie, "he sounds like he could bite a nail in half."

"Hush," Violet whispered. "He's angry."

"Why?" Kessie asked.

"Never mind."

The boys had gone to help Travis with the washtub and Violet went to put her shoes on. She didn't know what would happen next. Maybe she should just crawl out the window tonight and try to hitch a ride on a passing wagon. She could probably find a job in a big saloon in Fort Worth or Dallas. The thought made her wince. She never wanted another man to touch her except Travis, and he hated her.

Travis came back in the house. "Maybe I can build a fire outside and we'll do a little barbecue."

Bonnie hugged Growler's neck. "Doggie likes meat."

"Good." He glanced at Violet and she looked away, continuing to braid her hair.

Houston looked at Travis. "How was the buggy ride?"

"Buggy ride?" Travis looked blank. Evidently, Violet thought, he had forgotten all about it.

"You know," Kessie said, "Mrs. Van Mayes, who's wanting to marry you."

Bonnie shook her blond curls. "Marry Violet instead."

"Oh, I can't do that," Travis snapped and glared at Violet. "She's much too young, aren't you, missy?"

She gulped. "Of course."

Just then, Kessie went into the hall. "Hey, what happened? Violet's door is torn up."

Violet tried to come up with an explanation, but nothing came. She looked at Travis.

"I did it," he snapped. "The rest is nobody's business. Forget about it, I'll fix it later."

Violet hurried toward the kitchen. "I'll fix some potato salad and beans to go with the barbecue."

She ran into the kitchen and leaned against the cabinet, shaking as the kids and Travis went out back, followed by the dog. If the kids had been a few minutes earlier, they would have seen the big fuss. Well, now that Travis knew her real age, what were they going to do? It didn't seem realistic that they could go on as before when she loved him so much and he was a virile man with a man's needs. And what did he intend to do about the eager Mrs. Van Mayes? What a mess, and Violet didn't see any good way out of it except maybe to leave. Yes, that way, Travis could marry the rich widow and the kids would be taken care of. She'd have to make plans.

They ate the barbecue outside on the back lawn, the kids so busy talking they didn't seem to notice that Travis and Violet hardly said a word. She heard the southbound train go by without stopping and wished she had the money to be on it, but there wasn't any spare money in the house.

It occurred to her that she could wire Duke and he would send her money for the northbound train if she'd come back to him. Violet shuddered at the thought. She'd rather be dead than return to the Diamond Horseshoe. Yet later, in the house about dusk when she heard the northbound train come through, she went to the parlor window and watched it pull into the station, pick up some freight and move on. Almost anything would be better than sharing a house with a man she loved who wouldn't even speak to her and now would never trust her again.

"What are you looking at?" Travis came to her side.

"The northbound train."

He was standing so close, she could almost feel the heat from his big body. Their arms brushed and the hairs on her arm seemed to stand up and she longed to have him put his arm around her, but of course, he did not.

"You thinking about taking it?" His chest brushed against her back.

"Maybe, but as you said, we don't have the money." She wanted to turn around and put her arms around his neck, but she knew he would push her away and rebuff her and she couldn't bear to be hurt like that. Besides, the kids might see it.

"Checkers," Harold said behind them. "Who's up for checkers?"

Travis turned away from the window. "Reckon I am."

She was shaking from having stood so close to him. She didn't see how she could continue to live here, loving him like she did and knowing he hated her. "I—I think I'll pop some corn. Who wants popcorn?"

A chorus of shouts went up behind her, all the kids offering to help, and she went into the kitchen, eager to have something to do to pass the time.

While Travis and Harold settled down with the checkerboard, Violet and the others went into the kitchen. She stoked up the old iron stove and got out her big skillet. "Now you kids watch out—I don't want anyone to get burned."

The kids and the dog gathered around the stove while she got out the grease and the can of popcorn. "Here's how you do it, see? You get the oil hot and put in the corn, then you keep sliding the skillet back and forth to keep the corn from burning until it pops."

In minutes, she had a savory skillet full of popcorn. "Now we'll add a little butter and salt." She put it in a bowl and carried it into the living room, where Travis and Harold were playing checkers.

Kessie laughed. "We're like a real family, aren't we?"

Travis looked at Violet and frowned. "Sure. Just like a real family."

She didn't like the way he was glaring at her. The children all dived into the popcorn with both hands.

"I'll make some more," she said and hurried back to the kitchen. She had thought his anger might fade, but he still seemed as furious as ever. As she started popping corn again, all she could think of was the coldness of Travis's dark face. In thinking about that, she wasn't paying enough attention to the skillet and she grabbed the iron handle and then shrieked in pain.

Immediately, children surrounded her and she heard the checkerboard being overturned as Travis got up and came into the kitchen. "What the hell's happening?"

"Her burned herself," Bonnie sobbed. "Feathers burned."

"I'm okay," Violet lied, but she was shaking as she plunged her hand into a bucket of cold water.

She couldn't hold back the tears as she held out her blistered hand.

"Damn it, how could you be so careless?" Travis reached for the butter and took her hand gently.

She looked up at him, tears in her eyes. "I—I was thinking about other things."

"Sit down," he ordered, "and you kids back away."

"Is she okay?" Kessie asked.

Travis was holding Violet's hand and she closed her eyes as he examined her burned fingers. "I think she'll be okay. Houston, get a clean rag and I'll wrap it up."

Violet tried to blink away the tears without any luck. Travis stared at her, still holding her hand. "It hurt?"

"Not much," she said.

"You know I hate liars," he said as he smoothed the butter on her fingers with a gentle hand.

"I know," and then she burst into tears.

"Gosh, she must really be hurt." Harold's almond eyes got big and round.

"Stop crying, missy," Travis ordered softly. "You're scaring the kids."

She closed her eyes as he deftly put a bandage on her hand, holding it in the palm of his big one. "Are you all right now?"

She nodded.

"I think you'd better go to bed," Travis said. "I can deal with the kids."

"Are you sure?"

He snarled, "Go on to bed."

She started down the hall. Behind her, she heard him telling the kids to put away the checkerboard and get ready for bed. Her hand was throbbing so she lay down on her bed fully clothed. Would he come see about her later? Was there any chance he cared anything at all for her? Of course not. Not only had she lied to him, but she couldn't compete with the beautiful, rich widow. She might have no choice but to run away.

No, she shook her head stubbornly. If she turned tail and ran, the kids would be at the mercy of that woman and they would all be sent off to boarding or military schools. As smitten as Travis was with the widow, he could be convinced that it was all for their own good.

She lay there, listening. Gradually the house quieted down. After a while she heard the sound of Travis's boots in the hall and he paused outside her door. She could see his big silhouette looming there. He knocked softly on the doorjamb, but she decided not to answer. She wasn't sure what to say to him.

He came into her room and he stood there, looming as a big shadow across her bed. "Violet? Are you asleep?"

She wanted to say, "No, how can I sleep when you hate me and I love you?" but she didn't say anything. She pretended to be asleep. If she answered or held out her arms to him, would he come into her room, kneel by her bed and embrace her, or continue the terrible row from this afternoon?

After a long moment, he sighed and walked on. She lay there listening to him walk down the hall to his room. Her hand had ceased throbbing and she wondered now what would have happened if she had answered. Would he have come in and made love to her now that he knew she was a grown woman? Most men couldn't pass up an opportunity like that, but maybe he was saving his passion for Mrs. Van Mayes. There was no way to know his true feelings. It was a long time before she dropped off to sleep.

Travis turned restlessly in his bed. He had conflicting emotions toward Violet now that he knew her true age, and he wasn't quite sure he believed everything she had told him. With Emily, he had had all the lying and ridicule he could take for one lifetime, and he didn't intend to let a woman do that to him again. In his mind, he saw Emily as she left him, bragging about her handsome gambler with his fine frock coat and the diamond horseshoe pin on his necktie. He realized now that maybe he had never loved Emily as much as he had thought. It was only that he had had so much pride in winning her hand in marriage and had suffered so much humiliation when she left him.

He tried to focus his attention on the beautiful widow, who might be delighted if he changed his mind, but his thoughts kept returning to the naked girl with long brown hair standing by the washtub. His manhood came up and throbbed hard. He hadn't had a woman in so long and there was a pretty little wench sleeping under the same roof with him. Immediately he felt like the worst kind of rascal. Yet he was a proud man and slow to forgive. The answer was to get enough money to buy Violet a train ticket and tell her to go away and never contact him again. He could marry the rich widow, and he and the kids could have an easy life with her.

And yet, when he finally managed to drift off to sleep, the warm thighs he dreamed of were Violet's and in his sleep, his hot mouth sucked her small, pert breasts.

Chapter 17

The next morning, Violet was awakened by the children running from one room to the other, laughing and playing tag. Little Bonnie and the dog both jumped on her bed, giggling and Growler licking her face. "Pancakes!" Bonnie shouted. "Want pancakes!"

"All right, I'll get up." Violet smiled as she swung her feet over the edge of the bed and sat there a moment as the toddler and the dog romped on through the house. She heard Travis banging around in the kitchen and she hurriedly dressed and went there. "I'm sorry, I must have overslept," she murmured as he looked up.

He didn't say anything, only frowned. "Since your hand is burned, I started breakfast."

"Thanks, but I'm not hurt; I can manage." Her arm brushed his and she stepped away. Now that he knew her real age, it was awkward to behave like an adult when he had always regarded her as almost a child. "The kids want flapjacks," she said, "so if you'll give me room, I'll get started."

"Sure." He didn't even smile as he walked out of the kitchen.

If he was going to keep this up, being cold to her, she

didn't know whether she could stand it and besides, the children would soon notice it and might start asking questions. The tense atmosphere in the house these last few days had led to Bonnie wetting her drawers again and Kessie chewing her nails once more.

She heard him talking to the children in the parlor as she got out the eggs and milk.

"Hey, Travis, are we gonna practice shooting today?" Houston asked.

She peeked around the corner to see Travis ruffle the boy's hair. "Yep. If you take that prize away from the men at the shooting match, they'll get the shock of their lives."

"Travis, won't you enter the contest?" Kessie asked.

He shook his head. "You know the trouble I have with my wrist. It hurts too much to risk it."

Harold grinned. "But if you did enter, you would win."

Travis smiled. "Well, I wouldn't be so sure of that."

Violet returned to her cooking, listening to the hum of conversation from the other room. They had been so happy as a family until Travis found out what a liar she was. Now she wasn't sure what to expect. She could only pray he didn't find out the rest of it.

She stuck her head around the door. "Flapjacks ready."

"About time." Travis scowled at her. "You should have let me do it."

"My hand's okay," she said as they all trooped in to sit down. She served up flapjacks with plenty of syrup and butter and big slabs of thick ham. "I'll get the coffee." She headed back to the kitchen. It felt awkward sitting down at the table, where she had to look at Travis ignoring her.

Finally she sat down. "Bonnie, stop feeding the dog all your food," she said and then concentrated on her plate.

"Growler like flapjacks, too," Bonnie lisped.

"Well, eat some of them," Travis said. "Now, Houston, don't forget to come by the shop at noon."

Houston nodded, his face happy. "How could I forget? Violet, did you know me and Travis been practicing? I'm going to enter the shooting match."

"I'm sure Travis will train you so well you're sure to win." She sneaked a look at Travis, but he kept his eyes on his plate.

"You men only have a few days," Kessie admonished.

"Is July Fourth that soon?" Violet asked. "Time sure does get away fast."

"And I'm gonna march in the parade with the suffragettes," Kessie announced.

Harold snorted. "Women ain't ever gonna get the right to vote, so you're wasting your time."

Travis looked up. "Well, I don't see why ladies can't vote. Some of them are smart as any man." He stared directly at Violet. "Although some of them are pretty devious and lie like a rug."

"What that means?" Bonnie asked, her round face smeared with syrup.

Violet felt her face flush and she got up from the table. "I'll get some more coffee."

"It means," Travis said behind her, "some women are big liars and keep secrets."

"Men do, too," Kessie said.

"Yeah, but women are best at it," Travis answered.

In the kitchen, Violet leaned on the stove and gritted her teeth. If this tension was going to go on every moment she didn't think she could stand it.

"What happened to the coffee?" Travis called.

"Coming." She carried the pot back to the dining room and squelched the temptation to pour it in his lap instead of his cup.

He didn't even thank her as he gulped the hot, strong brew. "Well, kids, I got to be leaving. Help Violet around the house and I'll see you boys about noon." He got up from the table and left, slamming the door behind him.

Harold looked at Violet with those big almond eyes. "What's wrong with Travis?"

"I'm sure I wouldn't know," Violet lied. "Now finish your milk and chop me some more stove wood. Houston, you can milk the cow and bring in some water so Kessie can wash the dishes."

"Why do the women always wash the dishes?" Kessie whined.

"Because, silly," Houston answered, "girls are too weak to chop wood and carry water."

"I'll show you how weak I am!" Before Violet could stop her, Kessie had dragged Houston from his chair and was pummeling him.

"Kids! Kids, stop it!" Violet jumped up, grabbed Kessie and pulled her away. "Now Kessie, if you want to trade jobs with the boys—"

"No, I'd rather do dishes."

"Then stop fussing, for heaven's sake," Violet snapped.

Bonnie looked up at her. "You mad?"

Violet sighed. "No, just didn't sleep well."

All four sets of eyes turned on her.

"I just didn't, that's all."

"Grown-ups," Harold snorted. "Both of them are grouchy this morning."

"Let's clear the table," Violet said. "And Bonnie, wash your face, you've got syrup all over it."

She walked into the kitchen, came back to see Growler licking the toddler's sticky face. "I said wash it."

"Growler wash it." Bonnie smiled.

"That's not what I had in mind." Violet grabbed a wash-cloth and pushed the dog away. "You three kids get on with your chores."

It took awhile to get the house in order. The late June

heat was oppressive and Violet opened all the windows to get a breath of air. The Fourth of July celebration was only a few days away and by then, she and Travis were going to have to come to some sort of truce. She couldn't stand to live under this much tension.

Kessie looked out the window. "There goes Mrs. Van Mayes in her fancy buggy."

"Oh? Where's she going?" Violet asked.

"Looks like she's headed to the gun shop."

Violet gritted her teeth. "Maybe she needs to buy a gun."

Harold laughed. "I don't think so. I think she drops in to visit Travis. Sometimes she brings him lunch."

"Is that so?" Violet snapped. "Well, she can't take him picnicking because he promised you boys he'd help you with your target shooting at noon."

"She brings a good lunch, Travis says," Kessie remarked.

"I pack a pretty good lunch myself, so I'll take him lunch." Violet marched into the kitchen and got out a fresh loaf of bread, some pickles she had made, the leftover roast beef and some oatmeal cookies.

"I'll take it to him when I go down for target practice," Houston offered.

"No, I think I'll take it down myself," Violet said as she wrapped the lunch up in brown paper and started out the door.

"It's a little early for lunch," Harold pointed out.

"I just want to make sure he doesn't get hungry," Violet said as she went out.

At the gun shop, Travis looked up as the beautiful widow, dressed in soft blue, entered the store. "Oh, hello, Charlotte. I didn't expect to see you again."

She smiled at him. "I've decided to give you another chance."

He shrugged, not wanting to start a row here in the store. "We're doing a lot of business here with the Fourth of July coming soon." He wished she'd leave, but instead, she came over to the counter.

"Travis, you intrigue me."

"Oh?"

"Every man in the county would love to marry me, but the only one I want is you."

He tried to busy himself with the display under the glass showcase. "You only want me because I'm not available, Charlotte. I've got a crippled arm and no money, plus a passel of adopted kids."

She leaned on the counter and he could smell her expensive perfume and see her big breasts in her low-cut bodice. "I have the money for the best surgeons in the world. I could pay to have that arm fixed."

"If it were healed, I'd return to being a Ranger."

She batted her eyelashes coyly. "You wouldn't settle for running my giant ranch?"

He shook his head. "You can't buy me, Charlotte."

"And that's why I find you so intriguing," she purred. "Anyway, that's not what I want to talk about."

"Oh?" He picked up a pistol out of a case and began to clean it.

"Well, you should know people are beginning to whisper." She lowered her voice.

"About what?"

"Mind you, I tell them they're wrong, but people are saying that it's not proper for a single man to be living with a girl who is in her early teens."

"They've got dirty minds!" Travis snapped and slammed the pistol down. "Violet is innocent and sweet."

She shrugged and turned away from the counter. "All I know is people are whispering."

"About what?" He was seething.

"Well, you know—"

"No, I don't."

"She's pretty and there's just the two of you, and—"

"And four other kids. This somebody had better not be smearing an innocent girl's reputation."

"Well, people will talk. I know it's innocent and you want to protect her and I'd like to help." She turned and looked out the window.

"How? What do you mean?"

"If you were married or had a housekeeper living there as sort of a chaperone, no one would think there was anything scandalous going on."

"There isn't." He ground his teeth in rage. "Who is smearing Violet's reputation? I swear I'll—"

"You can't fight the whole town." Charlotte smiled a little too sweetly. "What if I loan you Conchita, my old Mexican housekeeper?"

Travis snorted. "Violet does the housework with some help from the kids and she does a damned good job of it, too."

"That's not the point, Travis. Do you want to protect that girl?"

"Of course I do. In Texas, a man will fight to protect a woman's reputation."

"Then let me send Conchita to stay a few weeks. Violet will be properly chaperoned and the gossip will die down."

Travis sighed. "I really don't want your housekeeper."

The widow reached over to pat his arm. "I understand, Travis, but you'd do it to protect that young girl from ugly gossip, wouldn't you?"

He shook her hand off. "Of course I would. I don't want anyone talking dirty about that sweet girl."

"It's settled then. I'll pack her up and send her over tomorrow afternoon."

Travis snapped, "This town is getting too much for me."

"Don't be silly, dear. It's just like every other town; idle people need something to talk about and a grown man living with a young girl who isn't his daughter would cause gossip in any town."

"It's not like that, I tell you."

"I believe you." Her tone was soft, soothing. "But this will stop the gossip."

"I can't have your housekeeper forever. My house isn't that big."

"Well, maybe things will change. You might decide to get married." She smiled up at him and walked to the window. "Oh, here comes the sweet little thing now. I presume she's bringing you lunch, but in the middle of the morning?" She laughed.

Violet saw the fancy buggy tied up at the hitching rail, squared her shoulders and marched inside the gun shop.

Mrs. Van Mayes leaned over the counter, giggling at something Travis had said. "Oh, Mr. Prescott, you are so witty!"

"Isn't he though?" Violet said and slammed his lunch down on the counter.

"Violet, what are you doing here?" Travis frowned.

"I thought you might be hungry early," Violet snapped.

The pretty widow looked annoyed. "How nice that such a young girl is so thoughtful, but you needn't have bothered. I brought a lovely lunch for Travis."

The two women glared at each other and Travis cleared his throat in the silent tension of the room. "I'm mighty hungry today, I reckon I can eat two lunches."

"Or share it with the kids," Violet said. "Remember you

promised to help the boys with target practice during noon today?"

"Oh." Mrs. Van Mayes looked disappointed. "Travis, I was hoping you'd go driving with me at noon."

Travis shook his head. "I am sorry, Charlotte. I clean forgot I had promised the boys. Houston is hoping to win the shooting prize July Fourth."

"You know, I donated the prize—a fine black quarterhorse filly named Onyx."

Travis nodded. "Houston would love to have his own horse."

The rich widow fluttered her eyelashes at him and touched his hand across the counter. "And I'm sure, with your help, he will."

Travis blushed. "Oh, I don't know about that."

Mrs. Van Mayes frowned at Violet. "Well, now, dear, since you've brought your daddy his lunch, I guess you can run on."

Violet didn't move. "I thought I'd wait until the boys got here."

"Oh," the widow said. "Well, Travis, I guess I'll be running along. There's just so much to do on a big ranch, you know. I'll send Conchita tomorrow. Oh, by the way, there's a ladies' choice dance the night of the Fourth. I do hope you'll be my partner."

"Who's Conchita?" Violet asked.

"My housekeeper." The lady shrugged. "I'm sending her over to help you run your house."

"Thank you so much, but we don't need her," Violet said.

"But—" the lady began and Violet shook her head. "I said we don't need her."

"I think we do," Travis said in a harsh tone. "Now, Violet, since you're just a kid, I make the decisions at my house."

She gritted her teeth. "Whatever you say; after all, you are head of the house."

Mrs. Van Mayes smiled triumphantly. "I'll send her over tomorrow." She went out the door in a swirl of blue silk, her bustle waggling.

Violet looked at Travis. "What's she talking about?"

"Damned town is beginning to gossip about us," Travis told her, stepping around the counter.

"I don't give a damn if you don't," Violet said.

They stood facing each other and the air almost crackled with tension. She looked up at him, wanting to go into his arms, hoping against hope that he might reach out and pull her to him.

He hesitated. "Since when do you swear?"

"She's pushed me about as far as I can take, Travis."

He looked at her a long moment and she couldn't read his face. "I think you ought to run along home now," he said.

"Are we just going to continue like this?" She bit her lip.

"Damn it, what do you want from me?" he snapped. "You've lied so much, I don't trust you anymore."

"And you just can't forgive me and start fresh?"

"I don't know. I keep waiting for the other boot to drop."

She didn't meet his eyes. "Suppose there wasn't another boot? Suppose what I told you is all there is?"

"I've been made a fool of once by a woman, Violet. I don't think I could stand it again. Emily ran off with a gambler the night before our wedding. The whole town laughed at me."

"I love you. Nothing should be more important than love. Do you love me, Travis?"

"Hell, I don't know." He turned and went back behind the counter. She wondered if he had been about to grab her and kiss her.

The bell on the door jangled suddenly and plump old Sheriff McClain hobbled in. "Howdy, Travis, Miss Violet." He doffed his hat. "I need a little extra ammunition for the Fourth."

"You expecting trouble?" Travis asked.

He laughed and shook his head. "Never much trouble in this sleepy town. I got to be the one to start the three-legged race and the other events, that's all, so I need my pistol."

Violet realized she couldn't continue her conversation and she wasn't sure there was much to say anyway. "I'll see you at home tonight," she said to Travis and then nodded to the old man. "Nice seeing you, Sheriff."

She started walking home, lost in thought. There didn't seem to be a good answer for this mess of lies she had woven herself. They couldn't stay in Pleasant Valley and get married, even if Travis was willing, because it would cause too much gossip since she was supposed to be a kid. The only answer was for her to leave Pleasant Valley right after the Fourth of July celebration.

Tears blinded her as she walked up the dusty road toward home. He must not care about her after all. In fact, it would probably be a relief to him if she did leave town. Then he could marry the rich widow and they would raise the four kids at that fine ranch of hers. That would be best for Travis, and Violet realized she loved him enough to do whatever it took to make him happy.

That evening, Violet stepped around Travis as if walking on scorpions, and even the kids seemed to feel the tension in the house. Travis said little to her and she was afraid to ask what he was thinking, although once, when they bumped into each other in the kitchen, she felt the sparks fly between them.

He stepped back. "Excuse me."

She stepped back. "That wasn't your fault, I was clumsy and not looking where I was going."

For a long moment, they stared into each other's

eyes and she felt drawn to him by his animal magnetism. She looked up at him, wanting him to kiss her, wanting him to—

Then one of the kids came into the kitchen and the spell was broken. Travis fixed her broken door without ever speaking to her.

Violet hardly slept that night and she wondered if he was having the same problem.

Finally dawn came and she rubbed her swollen eyes, got dressed and went into the kitchen. Travis was there first, making coffee. He didn't speak.

"Travis," she began.

"Yes?" He fixed her with those burning dark eyes.

Did she have the nerve to beg him to love her? That might give her the courage to come clean with him and confess everything, even if it meant she would lose him.

"Hey," yelled Harold from the dining room, "what happened to the bacon and eggs?"

At that point, all the children began banging on the table with their spoons. "Breakfast!" they chanted. "Breakfast!"

Even Growler joined in by barking.

That broke the spell.

Travis grabbed the coffeepot and headed back into the dining room. "You all hush, she's cooking as fast as she can."

"Hold your horses!" She began breaking eggs into the skillet and slicing ham. She tried to get her mind off Travis as she grabbed up a platter and headed in to feed everyone, not looking at him.

He gobbled his food without looking up. "I'm expecting a lot of business at the shop today with the holiday right on us. Everyone wants to win that black filly."

"Okay." She didn't look at him. "Do you want me to bring you lunch?"

He didn't speak until he finished and got up from the

table. "Don't bother. Charlotte Van Mayes might come by with a picnic." And then he was out the door.

Picnic. Violet resisted the urge to run after him and scream curses, but of course the children were all staring at her so she only took a deep breath and sat down to eat.

"Can we go out and play?" Kessie asked.

"Sure. If everyone's got their chores done."

The children scattered to do their chores and then went out in the back to play in the barn.

Violet walked to the front door and stared out. The street was busy. She looked down toward the gun shop. She didn't know what to do about the competition, who was not that much older but much prettier and more elegant than Violet. Later Violet saw the widow going by and stopping at the gun shop.

Maybe she shouldn't, but Violet couldn't tear herself away from the window. Mrs. Van Mayes stayed at least an hour. Violet wondered if anything was going on there but lunch. She finally walked down the street and popped in. "Hello, there."

From the way the beauty started and stepped away from Travis, Violet wondered if she had interrupted anything.

Mrs. Van Mayes frowned at her. "I must be going. I'm in charge of all the decorations for the parade and I have to have a committee meeting." She turned back to Travis. "I've enjoyed our conversations so much. You've added interest to this dull little town." She turned, brushed past Violet and went out the front door to her buggy.

"You didn't need to come," Travis said. "I had lunch."

"I didn't bring any," Violet said pointedly.

"Well, I'm glad you came," Travis said. "That woman was taking too much of my time when I've had so many customers today."

Violet managed to keep her voice civil. "It didn't look like you were rushing her out the door."

"And what's that supposed to mean?"

"Never mind." She spun on her heel and went out on the front sidewalk, staring after the widow as she drove away down the street.

Violet was so jealous she was miserable. She had to do something to occupy her time. She went home and put some bread on to bake. It was hot in the kitchen and she felt perspiration running down between her breasts. She opened her blouse and fanned herself with an old newspaper, closing her eyes and pretending it was Travis blowing lightly on her bare skin.

After she got the bread out of the oven, she checked on the kids. They had gone down to the park to play.

It must be near time for the four o'clock train, she thought and then she heard it in the distance. She went out on the front porch and watched it rumble through town. If she had enough money, she would get on it and go away somewhere south, but she had stayed on because she loved Travis so. It was hot as a chili pepper, she thought, standing there long after the train had passed through. In this heat, everyone had taken refuge from the Texas sun either inside or out in the shade somewhere. The street was almost deserted.

She saw two men riding into town at a walk. They looked dusty and their horses were thin. They were strangers, she thought, and they looked like they had ridden a long way. They both had beards and wore pistols tied low. Outlaws or drifters, Violet thought as they dismounted and tied their horses up in front of the bank. She watched them walk up the wooden steps and try to open the bank's doors. Didn't they know that banks closed at three o'clock?

They banged on the doors, but no one came to let them in. After a minute, they walked back to their horses and stood there a while, looking up and down the street. Somehow, the furtive way they looked around told Violet they were up to no good. She wondered where the elderly sheriff was today. Of course he might not be able to handle these two lean, dangerous-looking hombres. Maybe they would just mount up and ride out of town.

Violet went back inside and closed the door; then she peered out the window. The two had mounted up and were riding down toward the gun shop. Her pulse picked up some. There was no way she could alert Travis that they were coming, but he could handle himself.

The two dismounted in front of the gun shop and hesitated, looking around before walking in. Maybe they just needed some ammunition or a new firearm, Violet thought. Somehow, she had a feeling that wasn't what they were after.

She glanced down the street to see old Sheriff McClain coming out of his office. He stood on the wooden sidewalk and looked up the street at the two thin horses. Then he started walking this way, the silver star on his vest reflecting the hot sun. *Good*, Violet thought. *Maybe they'll see the sheriff and drift on.*

Just as she thought that, she heard gunfire and the two thugs ran out of the gun shop.

Chapter 18

"Stop!" yelled Sheriff McClain and he waddled toward the two as they came out of the shop, pistols in hand.

There was nothing Violet could do but watch as the two turned and shot at the old man even as they grabbed their horses' reins. McClain managed to get off one shot as he fell and the two thugs mounted up.

She had to help the sheriff. In a panic, Violet ran outside, racing down the street to the wounded man even as the outlaws took off at a gallop, coming toward her. Then Travis ran out of the gun shop.

Now there were people sticking their heads out of buildings, coming out on sidewalks to gape at the noise and excitement. She was in the direct path of the outlaws as they raced away, but Violet was only intent on helping the bleeding old man lying in the street.

"Violet, damn it, get out of the way!"

She glanced back to see Travis in the middle of the street, pistol in hand. She froze next to the fallen sheriff, seeing the galloping horses coming straight at her. Past them she saw Travis taking aim with his pistol and the outlaws turning in their saddles to return fire.

Travis fired once, then again. One outlaw hesitated,

shrieked, then slid from his saddle. The other paused and for a moment it looked like he would keep coming, but then he fell from his terrified horse, which galloped on down the street past Violet, throwing a cloud of dust on her. She threw herself forward to shield the bloody old man. The young deputy ran out of the sheriff's office and some of the other men came running, too, standing over the injured outlaws.

"Someone find Doc!" the deputy yelled as people gathered around the wounded sheriff. Doc Adams ran out of his office with his black bag, bald head shining in the sun.

Violet looked toward Travis. He had gone to one knee, clutching his right wrist, his face a mask of agony as he dropped his Colt. Violet ran to him. "Travis, are you all right?"

She went to her knees and put her arms around him.

Sweat stood out on his face. "That damned wrist," he muttered, "went out on me again. Damn it."

"You got them, you got them both," she comforted him. "Here, let me help you."

"I can take care of myself." But he staggered as he tried to rise. She helped him to his feet and he leaned on her.

A crowd gathered on Main Street with Doc kneeling by the sheriff's side as the deputy put handcuffs on the two wounded outlaws and picked up the money bag.

Travis, aided by Violet, limped down the street to the crowd.

The young deputy yelled, "You all right, Travis?"

Travis nodded although she saw his face was white as milk. "I'm okay. How's McClain?"

"It'll take him a while." Doc Adams looked up from the fallen man. "But I think McClain'll make it."

One of the bleeding outlaws turned and snarled at Travis, "Damn you. We almost got away."

"I couldn't let you ride over this girl," Travis snapped.

"You're a hero, Travis," the newspaper editor declared as he began to scribble on his pad. "We need more men like you."

The crowd murmured agreement.

"Not one with a bum arm." Travis grimaced.

Old Mr. Jensen hurried up just then. "Travis my boy, you don't look good. Thank you for saving my cash. You'd better take the rest of the day off."

Travis looked like he might argue, but Violet said, "He's right, Travis. I think you need some rest."

"I'll lock these two up," the deputy declared, "and take them in to the county seat for trial in the next few days."

In the meantime, volunteers helped carry the sheriff down to his house and the crowd began to disperse.

Violet looked up at Travis. "You took a big chance, coming after those two."

"And you took a big chance getting out in the middle of the street. They would have ridden you down or grabbed you up and taken you with them."

"I was worried about the sheriff," Violet answered. She looked up. The saloon girls had come out on the upper level of the Cattle Drive to watch the goings-on. Once again, she thought she recognized one of them, but in this glaring sunlight, who could tell? "Let's go home, Travis."

She let him lean on her and they walked slowly down the street with the saloon girls calling to him. "Hey, cowboy, come on in. The drinks are on the house."

"Hey, big guy, come on in and I'll show you how we treat a hero."

Violet ignored them. "I've got some fresh baked bread," she said as she helped him walk down the street.

"Where are the kids?" The color was coming back into his face.

"At the park. They'll hear the noise and show up." She

helped him walk inside and sit in a comfortable chair. "Would you like some water?"

He nodded. "Really cold water sounds good."

She went out back and got a fresh bucket from the well, brought him a dipperful as she sat down on the arm of his chair. She felt so grateful that he wasn't hurt. "I'd hoped that wrist would get better with time."

He cursed under his breath and shook his head. "I reckon I can quit hoping I can ever go back to the Rangers."

"Something will change." She tried to sound hopeful. "And if not, we can stay here in Pleasant Valley."

He leaned back in his chair. "That's not the kind of life I had in mind, working as a clerk."

Without thinking, she reached out and brushed the dark hair from his forehead, looked into his eyes. "You know, Travis, I wouldn't care where we lived as long as we can keep this little family together."

He looked up at her and frowned. "You're just saying that because you feel sorry for me. I'm sure you could do better."

"Well, you've got that golden opportunity with the rich Mrs. Van Mayes."

He shook his head. "And be one of her possessions like her prize stallion or one of her thousands of cows? I don't think so."

"Her money would get your arm fixed and allow you to live in luxury."

"You think I haven't thought of that? They got a name for men who live off women."

Duke, she thought, but she didn't say anything. Duke had made her whore for him so he could live well. What a fool she had been to believe he loved her and go with him to the Diamond Horseshoe.

She leaned over and kissed Travis very slowly, her

mouth partly open. His big arm reached up and pulled her down into his lap, where he kissed her deeply and thoroughly. She put her arms around his neck and kept the kiss deepening, feeling his manhood rise up, urgent and rigid against her.

"I love you, Travis," she whispered. "I've loved you since the first time I saw you and you rescued us all."

He held her very close against him, but said nothing.

"Don't you believe in love?" she asked.

"I used to, before . . ."

"Are you not brave enough to take another chance?" She kissed his neck.

He sighed and pushed her away. "It's hard for me to trust a woman. They all seem to be cheating, lying bitches. I don't take ridicule easy. I don't know how much you've told me is true and what part is lies."

She winced, thinking how he would be humiliated if he let himself love her and then discovered she had been a saloon whore. Every man wanted a pure, lily-white girl that no other man had touched. "I still love you," she said and hesitated, waiting for him to say the same, but he did not.

After a moment of silence, she said, "I've almost got supper ready. You want some milk and hot gingerbread?"

He leaned back in his chair and smiled. "Sounds good."

"The kids will be home soon and they'll want to hear all about the outlaws."

Travis grimaced. "And let them hear how pain brought me to my knees out in the street before the whole town? No thanks."

"You nailed them both. That makes you a hero."

He snorted. "Everyday stuff for a Ranger."

She couldn't bring him out of his gloom, she thought

as she went into the kitchen to get some warm gingerbread and a glass of cold milk.

As she came back with it, she stopped and peered out the window. "Now who in the world is that?"

Travis took the milk and bread as he craned his neck to look at the plump Mexican lady alighting from a wagon out front. "Oh, remember? Mrs. Van Mayes is loaning us a maid for a while."

"A maid? Oh, yes, but what on earth for?"

He hesitated. There was something he wasn't telling her. "Well, I thought with all these kids, you could use the help."

She stared at the woman gathering her things and walking toward the door. "In other words, my housekeeping isn't good enough?"

"It's not that at all. Now just hush and smile, Violet. The lady is doing you a favor."

"Where is she going to sleep?" Violet went to the door as the woman knocked.

"She can have your room and you can bunk up with Bonnie."

"I don't like this at all."

"Violet, I've made this decision, so you be polite and grateful."

"Ha!" Violet opened the door then and smiled at the dour Mexican woman. "Hello."

The woman scowled. Obviously, Violet thought, she didn't like coming to stay in this modest house any better than Violet liked having her there. "I am Conchita, the housekeeper from Senora Van Mayes."

Violet gritted her teeth. "Do come in. We're glad to have you. Here, follow me and I'll show you your room." As she walked down the hall, Violet's mind was busy. Of course she knew the reason the widow had sent this woman. She wanted a spy in the house to report back to her and to make sure nothing happened between Violet and Travis. She couldn't imagine why Travis would go along with such a plan. Violet decided this couldn't last forever. "Here's your room." She opened the door to her own small room.

The housekeeper frowned. "Not as nice as I have at the ranch."

"I'm sorry," Violet said, "but we don't have the money Mrs. Van Mayes does."

"I will get settled and then I will make supper," the woman said, setting down her valise.

"I usually make supper," Violet said.

"And now I will do it," the housekeeper insisted. "Senora Van Mayes said you were a young girl trying to hold a household together. That is very brave of you, senorita."

"Hmm." Violet gritted her teeth and backed out of the room.

In a few minutes, the kids all showed up and gathered around Travis, making him tell about the outlaws coming into the gun shop and how he had wounded them.

Houston's eyes were wide. "Wow! Just like a Texas Ranger. Can we go down to the jail and see them?"

Travis frowned. "I don't reckon the deputy is letting people in. You all clean up for supper and I'll tell you stories about Pecos Bill and other tall tales of Texas."

There were noises of banging pots and pans from the kitchen and the children turned toward Violet with wide eyes.

"Mrs. Van Mayes has been good enough to loan us her housekeeper for a while," she explained.

"Why?" asked Kessie. "We think your cooking is good."

Violet glared at Travis and shrugged. "Thank you, but Travis and the pretty widow decided I needed help."

Travis squirmed uneasily. "And she does. You kids are a lot of work."

Bonnie climbed up in his lap. "Like Feather's food," she declared.

The other children nodded agreement.

"Hush," Violet cautioned. "You'll hurt Conchita's feelings. Now be nice and use your table manners. You don't want her to think we're a bunch of hungry wolves, do you?"

The Mexican woman stuck her head around the door. "Dinner is ready."

Travis picked up Bonnie and the whole family trooped in to the dinner table, Growler settling down beside Bonnie's chair.

The Mexican woman came in with a platter of chicken and paused in the doorway. "Dog eats with family?" She scowled in disapproval.

Travis said, "Dog is family, just ask little Bonnie."

The toddler nodded. The woman set the platter down and, with a noise of disapproval, returned to the kitchen.

Nobody said much; they seemed too self-conscious with the stranger in the house. Violet watched Travis. Kissing him had stirred her blood to the point she could think of nothing else as she sat down at the table and Conchita began to serve. Violet tried not to look at him, but once when she looked up, he was staring intently at her in a way that made her blush.

After the whole gang had wolfed down the chicken and hot gingerbread, Violet let Conchita clear the table while she sent the kids all outside to bathe in the big washtub. She had to bathe Bonnie, of course, and then wrapped her in a big towel and carried her into the house. She sat down in a chair with the curly-headed moppet in her lap.

Travis looked at her. "You know, you look natural with a baby in your lap."

"Not baby!" Bonnie declared, her lip sticking out.

"No, you're a big girl," Violet assured her, drying her off while the dog lay at their feet watching.

Violet laughed. "We've already got four."

"You ought to have one of your own," Travis said.

Violet looked down at Bonnie. The toddler was dozing off in her lap. "Someone's had a hard day," she murmured. She got up and carried the sleeping toddler into her room and put a nightgown on her. "Now you and Growler go to sleep. I'll be in later to sleep with you."

"Growler not sleepy," the toddler said, rubbing her eyes.

"You're both sleepy and even the big kids are coming to bed," Violet said, tucking the baby in. "I'll sleep with you tonight."

"Why?"

Violet sighed. "Because Conchita is taking my room."

"You sleep with Travis," Bonnie said.

Violet shook her head. "Afraid I can't do that," she laughed. "I'll be in after while, so you scoot over. Now good night." She blew out the oil lamp and went into the parlor, where Travis and the other children were playing checkers. She could hear Conchita cleaning up the kitchen and then the woman went into Violet's old room and slammed the door.

Houston looked up. "I don't think she likes us much."

"She's used to much better," Violet said.

"There isn't any place better than this," Harold declared.

Travis grinned at Violet. "You're right about that, partner. Now one more game and you kids go to bed."

There was a roar of disapproval from the children, but Violet said, "Come on, I'll tell you a bedtime story."

When she walked past Conchita's door, she saw the light was still on. She paused and knocked on the door.

"Si?"

Violet opened the door and peeked in. The woman sat knitting. "I was just concerned you weren't in bed yet."

Conchita frowned at her. "I like to stay up late."

"All right." Violet shrugged and closed the door. Then she went to get all the kids in bed and told them a story.

Afterward she looked into the parlor. Travis sat there reading a magazine about livestock. Violet noticed he was holding it upside down. She decided not to comment on that. "Are you going to bed?"

He looked up at her. "I think I'll read a while."

She started to go.

"Violet."

"Yes?" She turned to face him.

He looked up at her from his chair. "I can't promise you anything."

"I didn't ask you to, did I?"

"You never ask for anything. Surely you must want more than this—looking after an injured shop clerk and a bunch of kids that aren't yours."

"They're my kids," she answered emphatically. "I'd hoped you'd feel like they were yours, too."

He merely grunted and she sighed and went to her room to put on a sheer lawn nightgown and let down her hair. She got into bed with Bonnie and pushed Growler to the foot. It was a warm night, but a cool breeze blew through the window. It was almost dark and the northbound train whistled from the distance and slowly chugged into town. From her position by the window, Violet watched the train stop in the station. From here, she could see a woman on the platform waiting to board. It was a big thing for the train to stop, but a lady passenger was getting on. The red-haired woman wore a dark cotton traveling suit and when she turned her head, she looked familiar to Violet. Then as the train pulled out of the station again, heading north, she decided she had been mistaken. She didn't know that many people in town anyway.

She lay there a long time, enjoying the cool breeze

across her perspiring body as darkness fell completely over the town. She heard Travis get up and move around the parlor, then the thud as he took off his big boots. Now he would go out on the back porch and wash himself in the washbowl there. His black hair would be slicked down and his dark skin would be damp as he came down the hall, bare-chested.

She heard him pause at her door and she held her breath, hoping he would come in.

He didn't. She heard him sigh and then move down the hall to his own room. Violet was disappointed. She had wanted him to make love to her for so long and yet he held back. She began to think again about leaving right after the holiday. It would be easy to slip away at night, catch a ride on a passing wagon. The kids would forget about her and Travis would marry the rich widow and run her big ranch.

Violet lay there a long time, listening. She thought she heard Travis turning over and over in his sleep as if unable to rest. She was restless herself in a way that she had never experienced before. She had had a lot of men, but she had never wanted a man before she met this big Texas Ranger. If he wouldn't come to her, she would go to him. She had to know if he had any feelings for her.

She sat up in bed, wondering if he would rebuff her. That would be humiliating, but she'd never know until she tried. She got up and tiptoed through the darkness in her bare feet. She paused at his door. Did she dare chance it?

She opened his door, knowing she was standing there in the moonlight silhouetted in the filmy lawn nightdress. "Travis?"

"Yes?"

"Are you asleep?"

"No. What do you want?" He sounded guarded.

She shut the door behind her and tiptoed over to the

bed, sat down on the edge. "I—I can hear you turning over and over."

"I can't sleep."

"I can't either." She leaned on one elbow over him.

"You're taking a big chance coming in here, missy."

She picked up his big hand and kissed the knuckles. "I know."

His voice was angry. "You don't know anything about men, Violet. Go back to your own bed, before I—"

"Before you what?"

His big hand now encircled her small wrist. "I don't like silly, innocent girls teasing me."

"Suppose I'm not teasing?" She leaned over him and with a soft moan, he pulled her down to him, running his hand down to stroke her hips. His big hand was warm, possessive.

She lay on his chest, feeling the rippling muscles of his bare body through her sheer nightdress. It seemed to send flashes of fire through her nipples.

He breathed deeply, rapidly. "Missy, you don't know what men do to girls, and you're too innocent to find out without a white dress and a wedding ring."

"I don't care about those things."

"You will. You'll have regrets in the morning and then you'll go crying home to Mama that I had my way with you."

"I'm an orphan, remember?" She leaned over, brushing her breasts against his chest as she kissed him, putting her tongue against his lips until he opened them and sucked it inside while his big hands encircled her back and pulled her hard against him. His manhood came up, big and pulsating.

Her heart was beating so hard, it felt like a war drum inside her chest.

He rolled her over on her back and pulled down her nightdress, stroking her nipples until she trembled.

Then he froze and she too, heard the creak of a chair from her old room. "Conchita is still up," she whispered.

"Then you get out of here," he ordered, breathing hard, and rolling away from her. "I don't want your reputation ruined."

If only he knew she had no reputation left. "I'll go, but I don't want to."

Quickly she tiptoed down the hall and got into Bonnie's room just as Conchita came out into the hall. Violet peeked around the door and saw the woman go into the kitchen and heard the dipper clank against the bucket. What a time for the woman to want a drink of water.

With a sigh, Violet closed the door and got into bed with Bonnie. She was still breathing deep, thinking about kissing Travis. She had almost made love to him. What would it have been like? Wonderful, she was sure. Now it might never happen, not with Mrs. Van Mayes's spy living under this roof. What could she do to get rid of her? More importantly, what could she do to discourage the rich widow?

It was a hot night and her aroused passion had only made it worse. She felt the sheen of perspiration on her body. It was only three days until July Fourth and the kids were looking forward to it. Who knew what would happen after that?

Chapter 19

Kate stopped off the train in Red Rock, Kansas, and headed for the Diamond Horseshoe Saloon. She smiled as she walked, smug with her own cleverness. When she told Duke where he could find Violet, he would be pleased and reward Kate by giving her money or better yet, offering her the spot as his favorite at the Diamond Horseshoe. Once she had been his favorite, taking Emily's place, about four years ago. Then she herself had been replaced by Violet.

Around her as she walked down the hot, dusty street, little boys were amusing themselves by throwing firecrackers under horses' hooves and running away as the angry owners chased them. The Fourth of July was only a couple of days away and the town was crowded with revelers, especially the saloons. She flicked the red dust off her dark traveling suit and walked through swinging doors into the Diamond Horseshoe. It was crowded all right, smelling of cigars and stale beer, scantily dressed young women perched on the arms of gamblers' chairs as the piano banged away on "Camptown Races" in the background.

She looked around for Duke but didn't see him anywhere, so she pushed through the crowd toward the bar.

Once, men would have turned and ogled her, but now, she got scarcely a glance. There was a new bartender, a fat man with a pale face.

"Hey," she shouted at him, "is Duke around?"

He hardly gave her an interested glance as he slid a foaming beer mug down the counter. "In his office." He nodded toward the back.

With her heart beating hard, Kate elbowed through the crowds toward the back of the saloon. Duke's door was closed. She took a mirror out of her reticule and glanced at herself, tried to push faded strands of red hair back up into her bun. Even with the heavy makeup on her face, she noted the lines and small wrinkles. Well, she was still pretty and maybe Duke would be glad to see her. She took a deep breath and squared her shoulders before knocking.

"Who is it?" He sounded annoyed.

"It's—it's Kate."

"Who?" He sounded bored.

She got up the nerve to open the door. "Don't you know me, Duke? It's Kate." She gave him her brightest smile as she stood before him, and he looked up and blinked, wrinkling his face as if trying to place her.

"You know, Duke, I used to be your favorite. You called me the Flame from Maine."

He didn't remember her; she could tell from his blank expression. "Okay, Flame, what do you want?"

She must not cry. "Aw, Duke, is that any way to treat me? Four years ago, you couldn't get enough of me before you found that Violet slut. I replaced Emily, remember?"

He blinked. "Oh, okay. Yeah, I think I remember you. You've picked up a little weight."

"Not much, and I can still sing and dance just like when I used to be a star here."

He stroked his pencil mustache. "The years haven't treated you well, Kate. What do you want?"

She still had that valuable information. That might be her ticket to returning here. She needed some whiskey bad. "Aren't you gonna even offer me a drink?"

He sighed and the diamond horseshoe stickpin in his tie flashed in the light of the overhead lamp. "As I remember, Kate, you drank too much."

"But not anymore," she pleaded with desperation. "The Horseshoe looks like it's doing well."

He nodded. "It is."

She saw the flash of the pearl handle under his coat. "I see you're still carrying that two-shot derringer."

He looked bored and out of sorts. "Comes in handy sometimes. Enough with the small talk. What do you want?"

Any moment now, he'd toss her out of his office. "Duke, listen, I have information that might interest you."

He leaned back in his chair, his eyes suddenly bright as a snake's as he stared at her. "Now what would you know that might interest me?"

She licked her dry lips, needing a drink so much, her hands trembled. "Offer me a drink and we'll talk."

He gestured her to a chair as he stood up. "You better not be wasting my time. This is our busiest season, the Fourth coming up."

"I know, but this is something you'll want to hear." She moved forward and sat down across from his desk.

He grunted and walked over to the decanter on the sideboard, poured them both a drink.

She tried not to let her hand shake as she took it and tried to sip, but the need was too strong and she gulped it.

Duke laughed without mirth. "Stopped drinking, have you, you used-up slut?"

"I—I'm just thirsty, that's all. It's a long trip up from Texas and they won't serve women in the club car."

"Then you should go back to carrying a flask under the folds of your skirt like you used to."

She held out her glass. "I—I could use a little more."

"Haven't changed a bit," he growled and walked over to refill her glass.

She managed to just sip this one, although everything in her begged to gulp it. "I never drank until I met you."

"So what?" He shrugged and lit a fresh cigar. "You were just a farm girl until I put you to work in my saloon."

"And only sixteen," she reminded him as she drank the whiskey and pulled a cigarette from her reticule.

"They're always only fifteen or sixteen. I like 'em young. You sure as hell ain't sixteen anymore, Kate. You look like five miles of bad road. You now working some cheap crib somewhere?"

She waited for him to light her cigarette, but when he didn't offer, she lit it herself from the silver matchbox in her reticule. "I can still sing and dance, Duke. If I had some new clothes, maybe I could be the star here again."

He threw back his head and laughed. "Not likely. Now what's this information you have?"

She yearned for another drink, but she dare not push it. "That last favorite of yours, that Violet girl."

His face changed. "What about her?"

She looked into his eyes and realized he might really care for Violet—or maybe it was just that as she had been the star and favorite whore of the Diamond Horseshoe, he was angry that she had left.

"I know where she is."

Now she had his full attention. He came over and took the tumbler from her hand, refilled it and brought it to her.

"Duke, I remember when you used to look like that when my name came up."

He shrugged and smoked his cigar. His handsome face looked bored. "That was a long time ago, Kate."

"Only a couple of years, Duke," she pleaded, "and I was in love with you." She gulped her drink.

"You think I give a damn about that?" he snapped and ran his finger over his pencil-thin mustache. "All these pretty young girls are in love with me when I lure them to work here and then they get too old and I replace them, just like you replaced Emily and Violet replaced you."

She now felt like she had the winning hand, although she was a little bit drunk. "But have you replaced Violet?"

He shrugged and paced the floor. "No, she was special. Nobody could replace Violet."

"But you put her to work as a whore, just like the rest of us."

"Well, business is business. What makes me madder than hell is that I didn't throw her out, she left. Me, Duke Roberts." He thumped his chest almost as if he couldn't believe it. "How dare that little bitch walk out on me? She's got all the other saloon owners laughing at me behind my back."

Kate leaned back in her chair, smoking her cigarette, enjoying that she had upset him so. "She left with a man."

"What?" He wheeled around. "She was crazy for me."

Kate shook her head. "No, I was crazy for you, but you were too blinded by her big violet eyes to notice me once she came on the scene."

Before she could move, he strode over to her chair and grabbed the front of her bodice, half lifting her off the chair as the fabric ripped. "Quit playing with me, Kate!"

"I—I thought you might reconsider taking me back if I told you—"

He slapped her then, slapped her on both sides of her

face until he dropped her cowering and bleeding back into her chair. She began sobbing.

"Now stop that blubbering and tell me what you know or you'll feel my boots as I kick you out the door!"

She had dropped the cigarette and wiped her bloody mouth, crying. "All right, all right, Duke, just don't hit me again."

He walked over and stomped out her cigarette. "That's more like it."

Now she regretted coming here, but she had to tell him. She'd seen what Duke could do to women who didn't cooperate. "She—she's in Texas, with a guy, an ex-Texas Ranger, in Pleasant Valley."

"You're kidding me."

She shook her head, shying away in case he meant to hit her again. "No, there's a bunch of kids and they're all living as a family."

"Well, I'll be goddamned!" He stepped to the door, opened it and yelled, "Slade! Slade! Get in here!"

The sound of heavy boots, music and laughter from the saloon as the door opened and then Slade stomped in. "What is it, Boss?"

Duke closed the door. "You remember Kate?"

The ugly gunfighter scratched his head. "I don't know, Boss, there's been so many of them—"

"Never mind," Duke snapped. "Kate here says Violet is in Pleasant Valley. She ran off with a Texas Ranger."

"Now, Boss, I told you to forget about that one," the gunfighter soothed. "Ain't you got your choice of young gals all coming west for adventure and money?"

"But damn it, nobody takes something that belongs to me. I want her back."

Slade sighed. "Pleasant Valley? Ain't that in Texas?"

Duke cursed under his breath. "What do I care? I want her back, I tell you."

"But there's a big price on our heads in Texas," Slade reminded him, "and a Texas Ranger—"

"He ain't a Texas Ranger anymore," Kate said. "He got hurt somehow. He works in a gun shop as a clerk. The old sheriff is in bed suffering from a gunshot wound and the deputy ain't but nineteen years old."

Duke threw back his head and laughed. "It'll be like stealing milk from a baby calf. We take the train down to Pleasant Valley, grab her, and who's gonna stop us?"

"I dunno, Boss, with the Fourth coming up—"

"Aw, Frenchie can keep things running 'til we get back."

"What about me?" Kate asked.

"Aw, you drunken slut." Duke reached out and jerked her to her feet roughly. "Slade, have Frenchie give this old whore a drink for her trouble and toss her in the street."

"But I deserve more than that," Kate protested.

"Look, Kate, you're old, and—"

"I'm thirty," she protested.

"More like thirty-five and you look forty-five. My customers expect young, fresh gals." He pushed her ahead of him out of the office. "Come on, Slade, we got plans to make."

She was still protesting and wiping her bloody lip as the trio elbowed through the rowdy crowds up to the bar.

"Hey, Frenchie," Duke yelled, "give this slut a drink and then throw her out."

"You owe me more than that," Kate protested.

"Honey." He lowered his voice. "You're no use to me—"

"But I loved you."

"More the fool." He laughed and leaned against the bar. "Now take your drink like a good little girl and get out."

"But where can I go? I was just fired from the Cattle Drive Saloon in Pleasant Valley—"

"Drinking too much, huh? Go back to that Maine farm, you drunken whore, where you should have stayed."

She didn't argue, eagerly accepting the drink with a trembling hand.

Now there was a disturbance at a card table. Kate turned to watch a cowboy with too much liquor under his belt stumble to his feet and yell profanity at the dealer. "Damn you, I saw you slip that extra card outa your sleeve!"

Everyone turned to watch and the noise level dropped to a hush as the drama played out. Kate knew what was coming next; she'd seen it too many times in the past.

Duke, followed by Slade, walked slowly across the saloon to the card table, the crowds making way for them. Even the piano had stopped playing.

The cowboy wore a gun and he swayed on his feet as he looked around.

Duke walked up to him as the circle widened, and Slade stepped to one side. "Friend, I'm the owner of this place. You saying my card dealers are crooked?"

"You're damned right I am!" the cowboy shouted. "He just took my month's wages from me."

Duke smiled at him. "Maybe I can buy you a drink, friend, and then you can leave with better luck next time."

"Why, you cheap card sharp, you know your tables are crooked—" The cowboy tried to draw as women screamed and men backed away. Slade stood next to the cowboy and he reached out and knocked the barrel of the pistol up as the man drew. In a flash, Duke pulled the pearl-handled derringer from under his coat and shot the cowboy in the belly twice.

The cowboy grabbed for his belly, the scarlet blood

running out between his fingers as he dropped his Colt and staggered.

"You all saw it!" Duke shouted. "He drew on me first!"

All the customers nodded assent as the cowboy stumbled toward the door, still holding his belly with the blood oozing between his fingers.

"Slade, get him out of here," Duke ordered. "I don't want him bloodying up my floor."

Frenchie and Slade stepped up and caught the cowboy under the arms, half leading, half dragging him outside. He left a trail of blood on the scarred pine floor.

"Now, folks," Duke shouted, "sorry for that disturbance. Free drinks on the house!"

There was a roar of approval as the men all bellied up to the bar, pushing Kate aside. She looked toward Duke, but she could tell by his expression that she no longer existed as far as he was concerned. Maybe she never really had. She walked outside, knowing she was a little drunk. It was hot out on the wooden sidewalk with the coming July heat. The cowboy sat against the saloon wall, unnoticed by the crowds as his life slowly drained away.

She felt sorry for him, but she couldn't help him. She couldn't even help herself. She was sorry now that she had told where Violet was. The girl didn't deserve that. What was Kate to do now? She had used up her money getting to Red Rock in the vain hope that Duke might be grateful enough to take her back. She might have known he had no heart. He would do Violet the same way he had done her: use her until she was too old or bored him, then toss her aside.

She had had more to drink than she realized, she thought as she wobbled and started across the street. Maybe she could figure out a way to get back to Maine. There had been a farm boy there once who loved her. Maybe he loved her still. She kept that thought as she wandered out into the dusty street, smiling at the thought and ignoring the sudden screams of warning.

Too late, she looked up to see the galloping wagon loaded with liquor kegs coming toward her. She tried to get out of the way, threw up her hand to protect her face as the team struck her. *How ironic*, she thought as she went down. *How ironic, a liquor wagon.*

Then she was just a dusty, bloody bundle of dark fabric, red hair and broken flesh in the middle of the street in front of the saloon.

Duke looked up from the card table in annoyance. "Slade, see what the noise is outside."

The gunfighter walked through the swinging doors, returned, shrugging. "Nothing much, Boss. That slut that was in your office a few minutes ago wandered out and got run down by a wagon."

Duke yawned. "Is that all? I always knew she'd come to no good end. Oh, Slade, go see about getting us tickets. We'll go to Pleasant Valley for the Fourth of July."

"Boss, you know there's a reward for us in Texas—"

"We'll be in and out of that town before the law knows we're there. Someone has taken something that belongs to me and I want her back. You understand?"

"Sure, Boss. I'll take care of it."

"Then tell Frenchie we'll be taking that train south. We should be back that night."

"Sure, Boss."

"In the meantime, that new girl from Iowa, she's pretty good. I'll be up there in her room if you need me."

It was a sultry night as Violet stood on the front porch, leaning against a pillar. She was taking one last look before she left. Her little valise was at her feet. Things couldn't go on as they were, and maybe it was better for everyone if she left. By the time everyone woke in the morning and realized she was gone, she'd be miles down the road, or maybe even farther if she was lucky enough to catch a ride on a wagon.

She heard the screen door behind her open, but she didn't look back. She mustn't let this interruption interfere with her plans.

Travis said, "The kids all in bed?"

She nodded. "Took a real battle to get them there."

"Don't blame 'em." He came up behind her so close, she could smell the scent of him and feel the warmth of his big body. "After all, tomorrow's the Fourth and that's exciting—firecrackers, the picnic, the parade and all."

She hesitated. "Is Conchita asleep, too?"

"Yes." He chuckled. "I waited until I saw her light go out after I heard your footsteps." A pause. "What is this? A carpetbag?"

"I—I didn't mean for you to know until tomorrow. I left a note on the mantel."

"To tell me what?" He put his hands on her shoulders.

"After all my lies, and the mess I've made, I thought I'd move on."

"Move on?" He sounded genuinely alarmed.

"Well, after I've lied to you about my age and you can't seem to forgive me—"

"I can't help it, Violet. I don't trust you now."

She swallowed hard. If he only knew the rest . . .

"I'm a proud man, Violet, I can't help that. If the whole town finds out they'll laugh at me again as they did the time . . ." His voice trailed off. "It's bad enough to be a half-breed, but when the sweet girl I was gonna marry, Emily, ran off with a gambler the night before the wedding, it was more than I could take."

She blinked back tears. "That's the reason I'm leaving. I don't want you to be ridiculed."

His big hands pulled her closer. "What about the kids? What will I tell them?"

She closed her eyes, enjoying the warmth and the strength of him standing so close. "Well, you can keep Conchita or marry Charlotte—"

"It won't be the same." His voice was gruff and his fingers tightened on her shoulders.

She waited a long moment, waiting for him to say he loved her, that he wanted her to stay. Nothing.

"We can't go on like this," she said and tried to step away from him, but the porch balusters were in her way. "If I stay, sooner or later someone will find out my real age and then there'll be trouble."

"I reckon I've let my pride get in my way too many times, but I don't have much else. I can't even be a Ranger anymore."

She turned in his arms, looking up at him, and saw the tears shining in his dark eyes. "What is it?"

"I've never told anyone, but a year or so after she ran away with that gambler, Emily returned one night and begged me to take her back."

"And you were too proud?"

He nodded. "That bastard had turned her into a whore and that was all I could think of—other men kissing her, taking her. I told her to get the hell out of my life and go back to the gambler."

"Oh, Travis, I'm so sorry."

"You're sorry?" He laughed without mirth. "Never a day goes by that I don't think of her and my pigheaded pride."

"What happened to her?"

"One of the local cowboys said he saw her working in

the lowest crib on the Galveston waterfront. Later we heard she had drank herself to death."

He seemed to be in such pain that she reached up and kissed his mouth gently and he clung to her.

Now he stared down at her, his dark eyes intense. "We could go away. Maybe we could go back to my hometown. You could look after the kids and I could find some kind of job, I don't know what."

She looked up at him, loving him so much, but his pride stood between them. "You wouldn't be happy doing that, Travis. You'd only be happy as a Ranger or working your own spread. And I'm only adding to your problems. No." She shook her head. "It'll be better if I go."

"Damn it, can't you at least wait until after the Fourth? The kids are looking forward to it; don't ruin it for them. They're all so happy."

"I know." She felt herself wavering. "Kessie has stopped chewing her nails and Bonnie has stopped wetting her drawers, but I—I don't know—"

"You're stubborn." His face was set, angry. "Where will you go? What will you do?"

"I'll manage somehow." She tried to hold the tears back, but one escaped and ran down her cheek.

He pulled her to him, enveloped her in the embrace of his big arms. "If you do that, I'll worry all the time about you. I'd never get a night's sleep."

And she dared say it. "Because of Emily?"

"Damn it, maybe, but you're different; I care more about you than I did her. I can't bear to have you leave us." And his mouth came down on hers, eager, warm, possessive.

She knew she shouldn't succumb. It wouldn't help anything, but she couldn't help herself. She returned his kiss with all the fire and ardor she had given no other man. They clung together, kissing furiously until his lips went down her cheek, kissing away the tears and pausing gently on her throat. "I can't help it, Violet. I can't do without you. I'll give my notice at the gun shop and we'll leave town, get married, make a fresh start where nobody knows us."

She clung to him, wanting him, wanting to think this could possibly happen as his hand tangled in her hair and pulled her face to him where he kissed her deeply, hotly.

She returned his kisses, knowing this night was all there was for her. She must not take the risk that this proud man would ever find out she'd once been a saloon whore. She could only imagine his fury and his hatred if that happened, and sooner or later, it would. Someone from her past would recognize her and Travis's heart would close to her.

But she would have tonight. She would not think past this sultry darkness and the holiday tomorrow. She would have the memories to last her the rest of her life. She looked up into his dark, intense face. "Make love to me, Travis. Make love to me as I have dreamed you would do."

He hesitated. "Are you sure? A girl can only give away her virginity once and I don't want you to have any regrets."

Regrets? She had a thousand of them. She couldn't even remember the first time she had traded her body for food on the wharves at Memphis so she and her little brother, Tommy, could survive.

"I'm sure," she whispered. "I want to experience love in your arms, my darling."

He picked her up, turned toward the door. "We might wake up the kids, or even worse, Charlotte's housekeeper."

She kissed the side of his neck. It tasted salty and sun-tanned. "Then take me out to the barn."

"God, I want you like I've never wanted a woman," he murmured as he turned and carried her off the porch, around the house and into the barn.

The barn smelled of hay. The cow mooed and Mouse snorted a welcome. The moonlight filtered through the open barn door as Travis lay her on a pile of soft straw and stood over her. "Are you still sure, Violet?"

"I am very, very sure." She held out her arms.

He came down on her, still wearing his jeans, and she could feel the heat of his big, throbbing manhood.

"I don't want to hurt you," he gasped. "Sometimes the first time—"

"I'll be all right," she assured him and pulled her skirt up so that his big hand could stroke her thighs.

She unbuttoned her bodice and he hesitated, then bent his head to kiss her breasts. "God, I want you," he gasped.

"I love you, Travis," she answered and returned his kiss. She wished he had said he loved her, but he only wanted her as a hundred other men had. Tomorrow would be a different story, but she still had tonight. She reached to unbutton his jeans and put her hand on his hot manhood.

He groaned aloud and kissed her breasts again. "I never needed a woman like I need you now, Violet."

"And I need you, too," she whispered and fought back the tears because she loved him so.

His big hands stroked her thighs until they trembled and she kissed the hollow of his throat. "Make love to me, Travis," she said.

"I can do that," he gasped, "but first I want to kiss you and caress you as I have at night in my dreams." And he kissed her breasts feverishly as she spread her legs and he came between them.

His manhood was hot and throbbing, she could feel it against her thigh and she reached to guide him into position. "Take me, darling," she whispered. "Make me yours."

He came up on his elbows, hesitated and then came into her very slowly while her body reacted, wanting him so much. He had one hand around her, embracing her, and the other under her small hips as he began to ride her.

He was a strong stallion of a man, there was no doubt

about that. She'd had none bigger, but she loved this one with her whole heart and that made all the difference.

He began to ride her rhythmically while she wrapped her legs around his muscular body, holding him to her. She had never had sex like this and she expected she never would again. It was so different when you loved the man, really loved him.

His motion excited her and she felt her own need rise as they moved together.

"I want you, Violet," he gasped.

"And I love you, Travis," she answered as her excitement built.

Then he reached that pinnacle of desire and at the same time he clung to her, giving up his seed, something happened that had never happened before. Her own need built until it exploded, and she grabbed on to his body, convulsing as she clung to him. For a long moment, she knew nothing.

When she finally opened her eyes, Travis looked down at her anxiously. "Are you all right? I told you the first time would be—"

"I'm all right," she assured him and pulled his dear face down to kiss his cheek.

He brushed the hair away from her face tenderly. "That was the best I've ever had."

She almost said, "Me, too," then remembered she was supposed to be innocent. "Should we go back into the house in case the kids wake up?"

"I'd like to lay here all night and hold you, but I reckon we have to go in. I'll go in first and then you follow," he said and stood up, buttoning his jeans. "I'll bring in your valise and tear up the note. Nothing that happens tomorrow can beat this. I'm looking forward to loving you for a long, long time."

She smiled up at him and he turned and strode toward

the house. She lay there weeping softly because he didn't know there would be no more passionate love scenes. Violet dried her tears, pulled herself together and went into the house.

She went to bed but could not sleep. Tomorrow was the big day and she had a picnic to make. She would enjoy the day with the kids and then tomorrow night, she would slip away. Where she was going, she wasn't sure, but she had to leave and not take the chance that Travis would ever learn of her tawdry past.

Chapter 20

The fireworks woke Violet early. She wanted to lie there and remember last night in Travis's arms, but already, the children were bouncing on her bed, yelling. "Get up! Get up! It's Fourth of July and some of the kids are already shooting off firecrackers!"

She smiled and sat up in bed. "Is Travis up yet?"

"He's in the kitchen making coffee," Kessie answered, "and he's waiting for you to start breakfast so we can get ready for the day!"

"What happened to Conchita?"

"She packed up and went back to Mrs. Van Mayes early this morning." Harold grinned. "She said she never saw such an unruly household."

"And we love it that way, don't we?" Violet laughed. "All right. Now you all get out of here and let me get dressed. I'll be right in."

The kids left the room and she heard them pounding down the hall to the kitchen as she shut the door and pulled on her yellow gingham dress. She smiled as she thought of last night in Travis's arms. She had never been loved like that. Then she remembered that tonight, when the children were asleep, she would sneak away and out of Travis's life forever.

With a worried frown, she put on her shoes and headed to the kitchen to be met by the aroma of coffee and an array of eager little faces.

Travis grinned at her. "Hello, sleepyhead. You sleep in on such an important day?"

She looked up at him, searching his face, but it betrayed nothing. "Travis—" she began.

"Later," he cautioned. "We've got a hungry bunch here."

She waved the kids toward the table. "All right, who wants flapjacks and who wants biscuits?"

"Both!" yelled Houston, pounding on the table and his voice was echoed by the others.

"All right." She smiled and nodded. "Travis, get out of my way and I'll see what I can do."

"Music to my ears." He smiled and, taking his cup of coffee, retreated to the parlor. "Let me know when it's ready."

Did he care about her or had he only taken advantage of her vulnerability last night? There was no time to think about that, but she could think of little else as she cooked.

Outside, firecrackers exploded and she heard children already on the street, shouting and laughing.

"Hurry up," Harold begged, "or we'll miss all the fun."

"I hardly think so," she snorted as she scrambled eggs. "The party will be going on 'til midnight tonight."

"But without us," Kessie said. "Look out the window. You see the suffragettes gathering in the street?"

Travis called from the other room. "Violet, are you gonna let her march with those women?"

She bristled as she put the eggs and ham onto a platter and carried it to the dining room. "Well, I don't see what it would hurt."

"Ornery boys might be throwing rotten eggs or rocks," Travis complained.

"Oh, hush and come eat," Violet yelled. "She's not afraid."

Travis was still grumbling as he came to the table and sat down. "I'm not in a mood to fight anyone today. Pigheaded women. Who knows what they'll want next?"

Bonnie climbed up in his lap. "I want watermelon," she lisped.

Violet laughed. "See? That's what happens when women finally get equal rights; they want watermelon."

Kessie looked from Violet to Travis. "So is it all right if I march in the parade?"

Harold snorted. "You'll look like an idiot."

"She's just headstrong." Travis helped himself to the flapjacks. "Which is okay in this household. Mind you"— he shook his finger at Kessie—"I'm not sure I'm in favor of all this marching foolishness, but I reckon my girls are as smart as any man, so they ought to be allowed to vote."

Violet smiled at him as she poured more coffee, wondering if he was thinking about last night, too.

Houston said, "I'm gonna enter the shooting contest. I want to win that black filly."

"Pony," Bonnie said over a mouthful of food as she sat on Travis's knee. "Ride your pony."

"It won't be a pony, it'll be a real horse," Houston said, "and I'm gonna win it."

Violet looked at him. "Now don't get your heart set on it, Houston. Probably most men in town will enter."

Travis sipped his coffee. "He's a good shot; I've been teaching him at lunchtime. He might win."

Houston looked around the table, his mouth smeared with syrup. "And then I can be a real cowboy in spite of my leg, can't I, Travis?"

"Yep. A real cowboy. All you need now is a ranch."

"You'd have that if you married Charlotte," Violet said to Travis.

He frowned at her, then set down his cup so hard it rattled.

She waited, wondering if he would say something like "I love you, Violet. You're the one I want."

The only sound was the occasional firecracker outside and the noise of people gathering on the street. The racket through the open windows made the children gobble their breakfasts.

"Travis," Violet said, "you will watch the kids and not let them do anything dangerous that might blow off a finger or something?"

He frowned at her. "Now what kind of question is that? You kids will be careful with the fireworks, won't you?"

All four heads nodded. "Can we go now?" They were already scampering away from the table.

"I reckon." Travis grinned and stood up and looked around. "Where's Growler?" he asked.

"Hiding under the bed," Bonnie lisped. "Him scared."

"Well, leave him there for the day," Travis said. "You coming for the parade, Violet?"

"I got to pack the picnic first," she answered.

"See you outside then." Travis nodded and got up. The kids gathered around him with excitement as Violet began to clean off the table. Usually the kids would have helped her, but today they were too excited. She heard them all go out the front door as she cleared off the table and began to fry chicken and make potato salad for her family. Her family. She had long ago began to think of them that way, but after Travis had made love to her last night, did he feel the same way, or was she just a convenient female? She wasn't sure she wanted to know.

She soon had her picnic basket packed and went out the door to join the crowds gathered along Main Street. The parade was starting from three blocks down the street in front of the livery stable. She looked around for Travis and didn't see him.

Then the band music began, maybe a little off-key, but playing a march loudly. Mr. O'Neal, the pompous owner of the hardware store, was the drum major and he marched out in front of the band as they came down the street. Violet looked around for her kids. She saw them then, halfway down the block and across the street. Travis stood with all the kids but Kessie. He had Bonnie up on his broad shoulders. The kids waved at her, but Travis seemed preoccupied. The band marched past, and then the Men's Athletic Club. Violet thought the most athletic thing any of them had done in years was hoist a beer in the back room of the pool hall. A wagon pulled the suffragette group and she looked anxiously for Kessie. Some of the people around her booed and yelled, "Liberals! Get back in your kitchens!" at the ladies as they waved their VOTES FOR WOMEN signs.

There were horses in the parade and a couple of men dressed like clowns. Some mischievous boys ran out and threw firecrackers under the horses and sent them neighing and rearing.

The Women's Social Club came by riding in Mrs. Van Mayes's fancy barouche and of course, she was among them, along with Mrs. Clay, the banker's wife, and her two ugly daughters; Miss Knowlen, the librarian; and Miss Brewster, the bony schoolmarm. CULTURAL EVENTS AND CIVILIZATION FOR PLEASANT VALLEY read their banner.

Charlotte waved at Violet and she pretended not to notice.

Once the parade was over, everyone gathered in the park for games and contests. There were booths where one could win a toy bear by knocking over the wooden pins with a ball, and all sorts of other games, a booth to buy tart, cold lemonade and slices of watermelon. The suffragettes had set up a booth handing out their litera-ture, and that's where Violet found Kessie.

A group of toughs had gathered to catcall the women and throw horse manure at them.

"Stop that!" Violet yelled. "Stop that!"

"And whose gonna make us, lady?" one of the rough boys yelled back.

She looked around. She knew there were no lawmen here. The sheriff was still laid up from his brush with the gun shop robbers and his deputy had driven the two outlaws over to the county seat for trial and hadn't gotten back yet.

Travis strode up just then. "You boys stop it. These ladies got the right to pass out their papers. They aren't hurting anyone."

One of the Jenkins boys acted as if he might start an argument, but another whispered, "That's the one who stopped the robbery. I hear he used to be a Texas Ranger."

"Aw, he's got a crippled arm," jeered another. "He ain't no problem."

Travis advanced on the boys. "You want to try me?"

The boys turned and ran, blended into the crowd.

Violet smiled, "Thanks. I was afraid it might get rough."

He didn't smile. "Get Kessie out of that booth so she can help you with the picnic."

Violet glanced up at the sky. It must be about noon and the weather was getting hot. "Oh, I reckon it is about time to eat."

Mrs. Van Mayes hurried up and grabbed Travis's arm. "Why don't you and your children join me? I'm sure my servants have packed a lot of delicious food."

Travis hesitated. "I think I'd better eat with Violet and the kids."

The lady shrugged. "I'm sure her cooking won't be anything fancy."

"Maybe not, but it suits me," Travis said and picked up Violet's basket.

They started toward the picnic grounds with the kids running ahead of them through the crowd.

"Thank you for that," Violet said.

"Don't mention it." He caught her elbow as they walked.

She waited for him to say something about last night, but he didn't. Maybe it hadn't meant as much to him as it had to her.

They laid out their picnic on a blanket on the grass in the shade of a big live oak tree. Around them, other families had spread their food and children ran between the blankets, playing tag and yelling to each other.

Violet opened her basket and looked up at Travis. "I hope you're not disappointed. Charlotte probably had a lot of delicacies and all I've got is fried chicken and chocolate cake."

He grinned at her. "It doesn't get any better than that. You sell yourself too short, Violet."

She began to lay out the food. "Later, I'd like to talk about last night."

"There's nothing to talk about," he murmured. "Do you regret it?"

She shook her head.

"Neither do I," he answered and sat down on the edge of the blanket. Then he turned and yelled at the kids. "Hey, if you don't come on, I'll eat every bite."

They all tumbled onto the blanket like a bunch of puppies, laughing and romping.

"Watch out!" Violet cautioned. "You'll spill the lemonade."

"Settle down," Travis said. "There's a whole afternoon ahead and skyrockets tonight."

Each child grabbed a piece of golden fried chicken.

"Oh, good," Harold said. "Is there fried potatoes?"

"No, potato salad," Violet answered, "and homemade pickles and fresh bread."

Kessie looked around at each one as she ate. "We're just like a real family."

"We are a real family," Travis said.

Violet didn't say anything, wondering if Travis had any idea that she was going away tonight as he slept. "Who wants lemonade?"

Of course everyone did. She didn't realize how thirsty she was until she tasted the cool, tart juice and the sugar on the side of the glass.

Bonnie said, "Save some for Growler."

"Of course, honey." She grabbed the toddler and tried to wipe off her greasy face. "You look like you need a nap."

"That sounds great," Travis said and spread out on the edge of the blanket, put his Stetson over his face.

Violet sipped her lemonade and smiled at the children. Now they had chocolate cake smeared across their mouths, but she didn't say anything. No matter what happened in the future, life was good today and she wouldn't think past that.

At about one o'clock, the horse racing and the shooting matches began while the ladies sat in the shade and visited and small children like Bonnie napped on the blankets under the trees.

Of course the shooting match, with the fine black filly as a prize, was the major event of the day. Most of the men and some of the boys had entered this contest at the edge of the park.

People began to gather to watch this big event. Targets had been set up at the end of the park and dozens of men and boys lined up with their rifles to take their shots.

Violet gathered up her picnic and Bonnie was awake now. Violet looked at Travis. "Has Houston got a chance?"

Travis nodded. "He's pretty good for a boy. I've been

teaching him. Having a bum leg doesn't stop him from being a good shot."

"He's just so determined to have that horse," Violet said. "I don't want him to be disappointed if he doesn't win."

Travis shrugged. "That's part of becoming a man. You can't have everything you want, you can only try your best."

"That's right."

She left her picnic basket by the tree and took Bonnie's hand as they walked over to watch the men lining up to shoot.

Some of the boys hooted when scrawny Houston stepped up to the starting line. He was the last one to compete and Travis was whispering to him earnestly.

A boy yelled, "Hey, crip, you think you can shoot?"

Houston looked back at him. "I think I can," he said softly. "I want that horse."

"Now, young man," said the livery store owner, "you'll have to beat my score. I'm a pretty good shot and I want that horse, too."

Banker Clay asked, "Mr. Prescott, are you gonna try?"

Travis shook his head. "Everyone knows about my wrist. Besides, Houston is planning to win."

More catcalling and laughter.

Travis knelt down by Houston's side. "You calm?"

The boy shook his head. "No, not at all."

"Don't let them rattle you," Travis whispered. "Concentrate on your aim and everything I taught you. Someday, knowing how to shoot may save your life or someone you love."

"Will it make me a real cowboy?"

Travis nodded. "A cowman's got to protect his livestock, you know."

Houston hefted the rifle and put it to his shoulder.

Travis whispered, "Remember to notice the wind and how it'll affect your shot."

Houston nodded and the crowd grew quiet. Somewhere in the crowd a dog barked and a baby cried.

There was a long moment of silence as Houston aimed and then he squeezed the trigger.

The sound of the bullet echoed and re-echoed through the hot afternoon and a judge yelled, "By God, he's hit the center of the target!"

A roar and a cheer from the crowd as one of the judges announced, "The finalists are Houston Prescott, Zeke Tubb, the livery store owner, and Jake Gray, the rancher."

Violet blinked back tears as Houston looked toward her proudly and she nodded encouragement. Travis put his arm around the boy's shoulders and the crowd watched as the other two took their shots. The livery stable owner, Zeke Tubb, missed the bull's-eye.

The old rancher hit the bull's-eye but off center. Now it was time for Houston to take another shot.

Travis put his hand on the boy's frail shoulder. "You're named for a great Texan, now show them how it's done."

The crowd grew so quiet it seemed to Violet that everyone was holding his breath. She, too, held her breath and hung on to Bonnie's hand as the other children gathered around her. She knew how much that horse meant to Houston and they certainly couldn't afford to buy one for him if he didn't win the fine black filly.

She watched Travis standing by Houston, whispering advice and then the boy put his rifle to his shoulder and aimed. The whole crowd seemed breathless in waiting and then Houston squeezed the trigger.

After a split second, there was a roar from the crowd as a judge announced, "It's dead center! Dead center, ladies and gentlemen. Houston Prescott has won!"

There was a roar from the crowd as Houston rushed to throw his arms around the black filly's neck.

Violet was so happy, tears began to run down her face.

"Why you sad?" Bonnie asked and put her chubby arms around Violet's neck.

"I'm not sad, I'm happy for Houston," Violet explained, and then she and the kids ran forward to hug the skinny boy and congratulate him.

"I did it!" he said. "I did it!" He looked almost as if he couldn't believe it himself.

"Yep." Travis slapped him on the back. "Yep, you did it. You're a credit to the man whose name you bear. Now you take her home and put her in our stable, you hear? Next year, we'll breed her to Mouse and you'll have the start of a fine horse ranch."

"Wanta ride," Bonnie begged. "Wanta ride."

In the end, Houston had to give all the children rides before he headed home to put the new horse in their barn.

"Speaking of Mouse," Violet said, "aren't you entering him in the race?"

Travis shook his head. "The Prescotts have won one big prize today. It don't seem fair to win them all."

It was late afternoon as Travis took Violet's hand in his big one. "It's been a long day."

It's not over yet," the kids insisted, gathering around them. "There's still the evening dancing and fireworks."

She felt the warmth of Travis's calloused hand on hers and couldn't have been any happier. "As soon as the afternoon train goes through, they'll lay out the wooden dance floor."

Travis laughed. "It'll be too hot to dance until after the northbound train goes through at seven."

Harold said, "Who wants to dance anyway? All we want to do is shoot fireworks."

"Then I'll help you do that," Travis declared. "Just watch out and don't scare any horses or hurt anyone."

The kids began to light firecrackers as Violet picked up her picnic basket and started for the house, holding Bonnie by the hand. There were still crowds of people on the street, anticipating the dance tonight.

Away off in the distance, she heard the whistle of the southbound train. "Come on, honey. Let's go home and take a nap. There won't be much happening until after the trains run."

Bonnie began to protest. "Don't want to go to bed. Want to stay and shoot firecrackers."

"You're too little. None of the little kids are shooting fireworks."

"Bonnie not little, Bonnie big."

"Not big enough," Violet said and put down her basket, picked Bonnie up, started for the house. In ten minutes or so, the southbound train would be rolling in.

She carried Bonnie into the house and took her to her bedroom. Growler came out from under the bed to meet them. "It's almost over, Growler," she comforted him. "In a couple of hours, the noise will all end."

Growler obviously didn't believe her. He went under Bonnie's bed as the toddler lay down on it.

"Don't want to go to nap," Bonnie whined. "Don't want to nap. . . ." Her voice trailed off and she was asleep, smudged face and all.

Violet patted her and made sure she was sound asleep. Then she went out the front door into the crowd. She'd find Travis and the kids and see if they needed anything.

People were still milling around downtown, watching for the coming train. When it was gone, they'd begin to lay out the dance floor and then at seven, after the northbound train was gone, there'd be paper lanterns and dancing and skyrockets.

She saw Travis and waved at him. He grinned and nodded as he started toward her, the kids running way ahead of him as they pushed through the crowds. The southbound train from Kansas was chugging toward the station now as the kids crossed the tracks and ran toward her.

The engine hissed and threw cinders and soot as it chugged into the station and slowed to a crawl. Then at the station, it ground to a halt with a shudder and the smell of burning wood.

Must have some passengers getting off for a change, Violet thought as the crowd gathered around out of curiosity. The old conductor stuck his head out the door and when it finally stopped, he got the little stool, put it on the platform and yelled, "Pleasant Valley! Everyone off for Pleasant Valley!"

There was a stir inside the coach and Violet paused, only mildly curious about who might be coming to visit the little sleepy town. The kids were almost to her side now.

One man came out onto the platform, stood looking around. Then another stepped out and joined the first. Violet stood staring at them, both big men with cold, hard faces. For a split second, she thought the late-afternoon sun had played tricks on her and she took a closer look. The sunlight reflected on the cruel, handsome face and the diamond stickpin shaped like a horseshoe. With horror, she realized her worst nightmare had come true. The two men were Duke and his hired gun, Slade.

Chapter 21

Duke stood on the back platform as the train came to a shuddering halt. There was a big crowd around the station on this July afternoon.

He heard Slade come out behind him as Duke looked around, seeking a familiar face. Then he saw her standing near the tracks in the heat of this Texas holiday. She had her hair in two ridiculous pigtails and wore a yellow gingham dress. Violet. He smiled and nodded at her.

Violet felt her face blanch as she looked up at the gambler. Oh, dear God, surely it couldn't be, but the cold-eyed man was nodding to her, so it was too late to hide. Behind him stood his gunfighter, Slade. Now they were stepping down from the train.

She managed to lick her dry lips as the children gathered around her. "Kids, get to the house, right now, I mean it."

The children peered up at her, seemingly startled at her harsh tone, and scurried toward the house. What was she to do? She knew that it was no accident Duke had showed up in this sleepy town; he had come for her. How on earth had he found her?

As Duke and his henchman started down the steps and onto the station platform, the crowd seemed to part and watch with interest. New people in Pleasant Valley were unusual.

Violet took a step back. What should she do? The pair were walking straight toward her. Out of the corner of her eye, she saw Travis crossing the dusty street, his face relaxed and smiling as he walked.

In seconds, he would be standing by her side, no doubt thinking about the evening dance. Duke and Slade were also walking toward her. The gambler had a look of triumph in his black, beady eyes such as a snake might have when about to strike and swallow a small bird.

What to do? If she ran, it would only prolong this encounter, and where could she run to anyway? She dare not go to the house, leading the killers to the children. And then Travis was standing by her side. She could feel the reassuring heat of his brawny body against her arm.

Duke's lean face broke into a humorless grin. "Well, hello there, Violet. Kate told me I would find you here."

She glanced sideways at Travis, whose weathered face furrowed. "You know these men, Violet?"

She shook her head, wishing she did not know them, wishing they were back in Red Rock or any place but here, her secret refuge that was a secret no more.

"Oh, come now, Violet, don't pretend you don't know us." Duke had his hand out as he strode toward her.

The crowd had grown silent, listening with curiosity.

She felt Travis tense. "The lady says she doesn't know you, so maybe you'd better get back on the train and leave."

She saw Duke's thin fingers tense as he reached to touch his thin mustache and saw Slade's hands twitch.

She knew what would be coming next: Duke would provoke a fight with Travis and his gunman would reach out and strike Travis's pistol as he pulled it. In that split second, Duke would shoot Travis with his hidden derringer and then claim self-defense. He could get away with it, too, because there were at least fifty people gathered around who would see Travis draw first.

She hesitated and took a deep breath. Out of the corner of her eye, she saw Travis's hand resting on his gun belt. Maybe Travis was faster, maybe he could kill the pair and her secret would be safe and life could go on as it had been. On the other hand, Travis had that bad wrist that might go numb as he drew and between Duke and Slade, he wouldn't have a chance. They would shoot him down like a stray dog.

"Don't be so unfriendly and pretend you don't know us." Duke nodded and smiled as he and Slade now stood facing them on the wooden sidewalk.

They were maneuvering as always so that Slade would be in a position to knock Travis's pistol barrel down. It would happen fast if she didn't stop it. She knew at that instant that she loved Travis and would do whatever it took to save his life.

Travis's voice was stern and gruff. "You two move on. The lady says she doesn't know you."

Except for the puffing of the engine, the street had grown eerily silent. People crowded close out of curiosity at the drama unfolding here.

Now Duke's face was cold and expressionless. "She's going with us. Or are you going to try to stop us?"

She must save Travis's life, no matter what it cost her. She reached out to stop Travis from drawing. She would do anything, anything to save her love. "Yes, Duke, I—I'll go with you."

Travis looked shocked. "Why, Violet? Who are these two hombres?"

"Allow me to introduce myself," Duke said and smiled as he stepped closer. "I'm Duke Roberts of the Diamond

Horseshoe and Violet here works for me as a whore, don't you, honey?"

She threw up her arm to stop Travis from lunging at the man. "Yes, it's true. I work for Duke. I—I'm one of his saloon girls."

"And you want to go back to Red Rock with us, don't you, sugar?"

She forced herself to smile and lie because she knew if she didn't, Travis would give his life to protect her. "It's true, Travis, I'm just one of his whores. You thought I was an innocent young thing, didn't you? Well, I'm not. What a laugh. I'm just a saloon slut and I've gotten awfully bored looking after you and those ragtag kids."

She heard the murmur of dismay through the crowd and when she glanced over at Travis, he looked like he'd been punched hard in the belly. His face had turned white and twisted in pain. "What? You must be joking—"

"No, I'm not. I've been fooling you. I—I was about ready to go back to Red Rock anyhow."

"Well, I'll be damned," Travis gasped. His hand slid down his gun belt to hang by his side.

She swallowed hard. He believed her and as bad as it hurt to see his stricken face, she had just saved his life.

"Duke," she said and stepped over to stand by his side, "there won't be a northbound train 'til seven. Why don't we go over to the hotel, have a few drinks and wait for it?"

He grinned and shrugged. "If it's all right with your cowboy friend here."

"I don't give a damn what that stupid ass thinks. I had him fooled all along." She took Duke's arm.

"Yeah." Travis's voice was bitter. "I reckon you've made a fool of me. You can go to Red Rock or to hell for all I care."

She couldn't bear to look into his eyes. She had hurt him to the quick, but at least he was alive.

"Come on, Slade," Duke snickered. "The lady's got a good idea. Let's go over to the hotel and relax until the train comes. You folks can all go back to your celebrating now, but if you're ever up in Red Rock, you can lay this beauty for five silver dollars."

Someone in the crowd laughed and there was a buzz of conversation. *Damn, did she have us fooled. We all thought she was an innocent schoolgirl. Reckon Prescott did, too. Look at his face.*

She managed to keep from sobbing as Duke led her across the street to the hotel, Slade trailing along behind them. Silent crowds parted as they walked to let them through. She glanced back once at Travis. He looked wounded and furious and she remembered that another girl had hurt him once. Now Violet had wounded him even deeper. He would never forgive her for this public humiliation, but she had saved his life, so that was all that mattered.

As they entered the front door of the hotel, Duke laughed. "Well, sugar, you must really care about that big cowboy, you kept me from killing him."

She shrugged as if it didn't matter. "I was getting tired of this sleepy town," she lied, "and these silly, hick dresses."

"You do look like a yokel in that gingham," Duke agreed. "I got you a better outfit in my carpetbag. Here, take this upstairs and put it on." He opened up his valise and pulled out a scarlet dress and matching feather plumes.

"Great." She managed to keep her face immobile. "Then we'll have a few drinks and some supper."

Slade peered out the front window. "We gonna have any trouble with that crowd out there?"

"Naw." She started across the lobby. "They're all so shocked, it'll take days to get over thinking the innocent schoolgirl is really a saloon whore, and you saw how humiliated the cowboy was."

"Was he ever!" Duke snorted. "He looked like he'd like to kill you and me, too."

"Yeah, but there's no point in spilling blood on the Fourth of July," she said as she started up the stairs.

"Don't this town have any lawmen?"

She turned on the stairs and looked back. "Yeah, but the sheriff is laid up from a robbery a few days ago and the deputy has taken the robbers over to the county seat, so there's really no law in town right now." She decided not to mention that Travis had once been a Ranger.

"That's good," Slade grunted as he walked toward the dining room. "There's a big bounty on us in Texas, you know, and I was afraid someone might try to collect it."

Duke lit a cigar. "I told you we could get in and out without any trouble. Most of these hicks don't know there's a reward out for us and those who might don't have the courage to try to stop us."

"I'll be down in a minute," Violet said and, grasping the skimpy outfit, went upstairs to a room.

She spread it out on a bed and sighed. She should have known there was no chance of changing what she was or escaping her past, even though she'd tried. She wished now she had left town yesterday so that Travis would never have found out that she was worse than this Emily he'd loved. It had only been a stupid dream that Violet might walk away from her past and start a new life with a good man.

She went to the window and looked out at the sun slanting in the west. The southbound train was pulling out, puffing and throwing soot and smoke as it left. Now she had almost three hours ahead of her before the northbound train picked them up and took them back to Red Rock and her old life. She thought about climbing out the window and running, hiding. No, she shook her head. Now that Duke had found her, he wouldn't let her escape again. She had no money and no way to get out of town anyway. Anything she did might endanger Travis and the kids so she would accept her fate.

With a sigh, she put on the skimpy outfit and the red feather plumes. Then, choking back her tears, she went slowly down the stairs.

People standing about in the lobby stared at her and made way as she squared her shoulders and walked into the dining room. There were a few people having an early supper. She sauntered over to Duke's table, ignoring the shocked stares of the diners.

"Hey, sugar, you look great—just like old times. Sit down and have a drink."

She forced a smile. "I'll have a smoke, too, Duke."

He brought out his silver cigarette case. "I got to hand it to you, sugar. I thought you might have run off, and that hurt my pride. You know my girls never leave me."

"Aw, I was just bored." She took the cigarette and let him light it for her. "I thought it might be fun to see how average women lived."

"And?" Slade asked.

She swore and took a deep puff of smoke. "Hard work and plenty of it. I tried to figure out how to get back to Red Rock, but housewives never have a damn dime of their own."

"Glad you came to your senses." Duke grinned and signaled the waiter. "We'll have a bottle of your best whiskey and then three big steaks."

"Yes, sir." The hotel owner, who knew Violet, looked at her in surprise and disgust as he turned away and hurried to fill their order.

Violet laughed to keep from crying. "He's one of the locals I fooled into thinking I was an innocent schoolgirl."

"Damn fool," Duke said. "You're the best whore in Kansas, that's what you are, Violet. I'll give you a roll tonight myself on the train and then starting tomorrow, that little sweet butt of yours will be back earning money for me. Half the men in this hick town will be looking for an excuse to come to Red Rock and enjoy your charms."

"Sure." She winked at him and took a deep puff of her cigarette. She'd rather die than let any man make love to her again except Travis, but she couldn't say that. Now she knew why so many of the saloon girls drank themselves senseless every day. She had found real love and now she had lost it again. There was nothing ahead in life but misery, entertaining crowds of men who wanted to fondle her and rape her, and none of them, including Duke, gave a damn about her. And now Travis didn't either.

Travis. She must not think about him or she wouldn't be able to keep up this charade, that she was happy Duke had rescued her. She had less than three hours to pretend, and then she would be on that northbound train with Duke and his henchman. Travis and the kids would be safe and nothing mattered after that.

Travis had watched Violet walking away with the gambler in disbelief. Around him, people were tittering and whispering. He felt fingers pointing and people stealing curious looks. It was far worse than what had happened with Emily.

He watched the trio walk into the hotel and disappear. He stood there, staring after them, feeling like he'd been shot in the gut. She wasn't an innocent. She was a saloon whore, the worst kind of woman on the frontier, and she had boasted about lying to him, fooling him. The train conductor yelled, "All aboard!" The train shuddered and then began to chug out of the station, headed south into the hot afternoon. The crowd began to scatter.

The joy and excitement seemed to have gone out of the

Fourth of July celebrations. A few people still stood about on the streets, but many of them had drifted away, into homes or businesses until the street was almost deserted.

With a sigh, Travis walked slowly home. The kids were all waiting for him inside, gathering around him, their faces hopeful and anxious. He noted Kessie was once again chewing her fingernails and the youngest sobbed softly. He took off his gun belt and hung it on the rack by the door, feeling no emotion, nothing but a numbness in his gut.

He picked Bonnie up and hugged her. Her drawers were wet. "Are you going to become Boo Hoo again?"

The toddler wept against his neck. "Gone? Violet gone?"

He sat down in a chair, feeling as if he didn't have enough energy to do anything else. "Yes, I reckon she's gone, Bonnie."

The toddler burst into a fresh bout of weeping while the dog sat at his feet and whined.

Houston said, "You ain't gonna let them take her, are you, Travis?"

"She's going of her own free will." Travis reached absently to pat the dog.

"How can you let her?" Harold demanded. "We don't want her to go."

He was angry now, angry with Violet for causing all this pain. He realized part of the pain was his. "You kids don't understand. She's not what we thought she was."

"We don't care!" All the kids set up a howl. "She's Violet and she looks after us and loves us and we all love her, too."

Travis frowned. "I used to think she loved us, but now I know she was just making fools of us. She don't love us at all."

"She does, too," the toddler wept. "Violet. We want her back."

"Damn it!" Travis couldn't control the anger and the anguish in his voice. "Don't any of you understand? She's decided to go back to Kansas. I can't stop her."

"No, no. She wouldn't go if you asked her not to," Kessie begged and chewed her nails.

"Naw, she'd laugh at me," Travis argued. "All she cares about is nice clothes and fun and plenty of money."

Houston sat down on the arm of the chair. "I've saved forty-five cents, and I'd give it to her if she needs money."

"You don't understand," Travis said again. "She's going back to the life she loves. Her time with us was one big lie."

Harold looked at him, tears in the almond eyes. "She always acted like she wanted to be here with us. She was the best mother ever."

"I thought she was, too," Travis said, "but I reckon she made fools of all of us. As far as a mother—" He thought about it a minute. There was nothing he could do but ask the town ladies to find homes for all these kids or take them home to his own mother to raise. He shook his head. His parents couldn't take on the expense of four kids, even though they'd want to try. Their small ranch didn't make that much money.

"Can we do anything to stop her?" Houston asked.

Travis snapped, "There's nothing we can do. She's decided to leave. Now, you kids see if you can rustle up some grub. She'll be leaving on the seven o'clock train and I don't want to hear any more about it."

The children wiped their eyes and started toward the kitchen, all except Bonnie, who continued to cry.

Travis sighed, remembering Bonnie's past. Would she go back to being Boo Hoo and crying all the time? He felt helpless without Violet. He loved kids, but he didn't know how to handle four kids without her.

In a few minutes, Kessie called from the kitchen, "I got milk and some bread and butter. There's some leftover cold chicken from the picnic."

"Good." Travis stood up. "We'll do just fine by ourselves. We don't need Violet."

That unleashed fresh tears from little Bonnie, and even Growler looked up at him like he'd like to bite Travis.

They all gathered around the table and looked at each other morosely.

Harold said, "Are you gonna marry Mrs. Van Mayes?"

The other kids all moaned aloud and Travis sighed. "I reckon I could. It would give you all a home." Somehow, the idea seemed distasteful.

Nobody said anything as Kessie brought dishes and leftovers. Travis picked at his chicken, but he had no appetite and he noted none of the kids were eating. "You kids should eat something."

"You aren't eating anything," Houston said.

"Yes, I am." Travis took a bite. "Hmm, this is really good. Everyone eat up."

"What time is it?" Kessie asked.

Travis pulled out his pocket watch. "Almost five thirty."

"That still gives you over an hour to talk her out of going," Harold said.

"Damn it!" Travis swore, standing up suddenly and upsetting his chair. "How can I get you kids to understand that I've got my pride? You don't understand what kind of a woman she is—why, the whole town is shocked and gossiping about her. She's no good and I ain't gonna make a fool of myself again." He stomped into the parlor and looked out the open window. The sun was moving toward the west, but it was still hot as a chili pepper outside and there weren't many people on the street. He stared toward the hotel and wondered what was going on over there.

Oh God, he'd be glad when that northbound train came through and she was out of this town and out of his life forever. He sat down in his chair and tried to roll a cigarette, but his hands shook and finally, he gave up and threw the paper and tobacco down in disgust.

Bonnie toddled into the parlor and stood looking at him. Her little face was streaked with tears. He held out his arms to her. "Come on, honey, I'll hold you."

She shook her head and burst into tears. "Violet! Want Violet!"

"Well, damn it, you can't have her!" he exploded. "Don't you understand? She's leaving us. Maybe she never cared about us to begin with."

At that, Bonnie ran from the room and into her room, slamming the door.

"Well." Kessie looked at him. "Now you've really got her crying."

"It's not my fault," he snapped, angry with Violet for all the pain she was causing. He hadn't realized how much he would miss her and she wasn't even out of town yet. "You kids get a checkers game or some cards started."

"Will you play with us?" Harold asked.

"Sure." He had to have something to occupy his mind until that train took Violet away. He tried to play checkers with the kids, but he couldn't keep his mind on what he was doing and even Kessie beat him.

The freckled-faced girl gave him a sympathetic look. "You miss her too much already to keep your mind on the game."

"Naw," he said and shook his head. "It's been a long day and I'm just tired." He glanced out the window as he saw the shadows of evening lengthening. He would not let himself pull out his watch, but he knew it wouldn't be long now. There was no one on the streets. Somehow, the town had lost its interest in the Fourth of July or maybe they were expecting trouble. Well, there wasn't going to be any. After what she'd admitted, to hell with her and good riddance. She'd made a bigger fool of him than Emily had.

Then he heard the far-off whistle of a train and the kids all ran to the window. "It's coming! It's coming!"

He pulled out his watch and stared at it. Ten minutes to seven. It was right on time.

"Can we go watch her get on?" Houston had tears in his eyes. "Maybe when she sees us, she won't go."

"Hell, no, you can't," Travis snapped. "We don't want her to think we give a damn whether she goes or not."

"But we do care," Harold argued.

The train whistled again, drawing closer now, and little Bonnie came running from her bedroom. "Train! Train coming!"

All the children were gathered around the open window now, looking out. Travis tried to force himself to stay in his chair, but he finally stood up and walked to the window. Out of the hotel came three figures, two big men and a woman dressed in gaudy red.

Kessie gasped. "Look how Violet is dressed. Why is she dressed that way?"

Travis stared. His darling, innocent Violet dressed in a scanty scarlet costume, red plumes in her brown hair as she sauntered across the dusty street with the gambler and his gunman.

The train whistled again, even closer now as the trio crossed the street and stood at the train station down the block. They could still see her from here.

"Feathers," whispered Bonnie. "Feathers."

"What?" Travis asked and he looked and saw the scarlet,

gaudy plumes in Violet's hair. Feathers. Bonnie had known all along.

The late evening sun shone on the feathers and on the diamond stickpin in the gambler's tie. A diamond horse-shoe, Travis thought and then it dawned on him so that he laughed without mirth. "Of course, it's the same hombre, the one who took Emily." And now the rotten bastard was taking Violet.

The train roared toward the station, slowed and then stopped with a shower of black smoke and soot. The con-ductor took the carpetbags from Slade and their tickets as they stood on the station platform, making ready to board.

Violet looked back at the house one last time and Bonnie whimpered, "She's crying! Violet don't want to go! She's crying!"

"What?" Travis stared out the window. Sure enough, he could see Violet's face and it was twisted in misery with tears from those blue eyes coursing down her cheeks.

In that split second, he made a decision. In his heart, he finally admitted to himself that he loved Violet and he couldn't let her go, no matter how flawed she was.

"Damn it!" he swore and grabbed for his gun belt hanging on the wall.

The kids all looked at him.

"What are you doing?" Harold asked as Travis buckled on his Colt, took out the pistol, checked it, slid it back in the holster.

"They'll take her over my dead body!" Travis declared and swung open the door.

"What about your bad wrist?" Kessie asked. "It'll get you killed."

A Texas Ranger is a man who knows what's right and keeps right on coming.

"It may, but I can't let them take her without a fight. You

kids stay here!" he ordered, and then he stepped out on the porch and began striding toward the trio.

Violet gasped and put her hand to her mouth. "No, don't!"

The two men with her turned to face the big man striding toward them, staring at him in disbelief.

The gambler yelled, "What the hell do you think you're doing, plowboy?"

"You took Emily, you bastard," Travis shouted. "But you ain't taking Violet."

Violet stuttered. "No, Travis, I—I want to go with him."

"Stop lying!" Travis yelled. "Even Bonnie knows the truth." He kept walking, aware of the way Slade's hand hovered over his gun belt, the shadowy faces of people in nearby windows watching the drama. "Step away from her, you sleazy bastards, and fight like men!"

Duke's handsome face paled. "I ain't wearing a gun, cowboy."

Violet gasped, knowing they wouldn't give him a fair fight. Slade would grab his gun hand and Duke would shoot Travis down with that hidden derringer. She couldn't let that happen.

Travis came up to them now and there was a split-second pause. Out of the corner of his eye, he was aware Slade was moving toward Travis's right. Then Duke's hand went inside his fine coat even as Violet threw herself against his arm, grabbing his hand. There was a sudden burst of noise and acrid gunpowder. She screamed in pain and then crumpled, still hanging on to the gambler's hand, struggling with him over a tiny derringer.

Travis couldn't shoot without hitting Violet. He stepped forward suddenly, hitting the gambler hard on the chin.

"Travis, look out!" Violet screamed and he was abruptly aware of the sudden movement of Slade. Travis slapped leather and abruptly, Slade reached out and knocked the Colt down, spoiling Travis's aim and sending agony rushing through his right hand. He stumbled, knowing he was a split second too late even as the bleeding girl struggled with the gambler, turned the derringer against Duke's fine frock coat and pulled the trigger.

Through a cloud of pain, Travis heard the derringer go off again and the look of horror on Duke's face as he froze and stumbled forward, even as Violet fell, the wooden sidewalk bright with her blood.

Travis was on his knees, struggling to overcome the pain and bring his Colt up to pull the trigger.

He saw a flash of movement as Slade drew and fired, and Travis fired, but he knew he was a second too late. He felt Slade's slug tear into his side and he staggered, struggling to keep his pistol firing, but it fell from his useless right hand. Travis knew terrible pain and heard heavy boots walking toward him as he fell to the sidewalk.

A big shadow loomed over him and Travis struggled to reach his pistol, but his fingers had gone numb.

"Now, you plowboy," growled Slade. "I'm gonna finish you off!"

Travis tried to grasp his pistol, but he couldn't control his right hand and his wrist felt on fire. He heard Slade's trigger being pulled back. So this was what it was like to die. It didn't matter now if he died with his darling Violet already dead, trying to save him, but who would take care of his kids? Yes, his kids. He had to keep them together and care for them. He tried to cock his own pistol as he heard the other man laugh.

And then there was a sudden sound, not a pistol but

the crack of a rifle. Travis looked up and saw the surprised expression on the gunfighter's face and the sudden spurt of blood running down his denim shirt. Slade grabbed for his chest as if he could hold back the bright river of red. "A kid," he whispered. "Best gunfighter in the west taken by a kid." Then he staggered and crashed down.

What? Who? Travis used his last ounce of strength to turn his head to see the children running down the street, following Houston, who carried his rifle. "I got him, Travis! Travis, are you all right?"

"Violet," he whispered as he crawled toward her and took her limp body in his arms. "Get Doc Adams," he gasped to Houston. "She can't die—I love her so." Then he collapsed into darkness.

Epilogue

Long Horn, Texas
July 4, 1890

"Come on, slowpoke." Violet moved her fat baby boy to her other arm and gestured to the big man sauntering toward her. "Everyone will be in town before we get there."

Travis grinned at her as he walked up to the waiting buggy. "No hurry, Mrs. Prescott. The celebration will last all day."

"But the picnic basket's in the other buggy and I'm getting hungry."

"You want me to take Tommy?"

She nodded and handed their baby over to her husband. Tommy had a tight grip on the little wooden horse.

Travis put his arm around her and kissed her. "Well, I see Houston gave him my lucky piece. Did Mom and Dad go on into town with the kids?"

She nodded as he helped her up into the buggy, then handed her their baby boy and climbed up next to her. "The kids were all so excited about the fireworks, they wanted to go early. Of course, Houston insisted on riding Onyx."

He laughed. "He's making a real rancher, that one, and Onyx's foal looks just like Mouse. Houston's got the start of a good herd."

They drove past their pasture and the big gray stallion raised his head and nickered.

"Sorry, Mouse," Travis called. "You'll have to enjoy your time off and I'll bring you an apple later."

She smiled at him, loving him like she'd never thought she could love a man. "I'm glad we can afford to send Harold and Kessie to college when the time comes."

"Have I told you how much I love you?" He smiled at her as they drove along.

"Not since breakfast."

"I never knew I could be so happy," he murmured. Tommy gurgled and Travis reached out to cluck him under the chin. "We've got a big family, Violet, honey, but I want even more."

"Five kids aren't enough for you?"

"Naw, let's have a dozen." He winked at her and then snapped the reins at the bay horse and they drove along toward town. "Where's Growler?"

"Hiding under Bonnie's bed. I reckon he'll come out when the fireworks are over."

"By the way, tomorrow, the Rangers need me again. Manhunt over near Abilene."

"I wish you wouldn't ride with the Rangers, but I reckon they need you."

"Someone's got to keep this state safe for honest people, honey, and the Rangers will probably still be doing it a hundred years from now."

She looked back at their ranch gate as they drove through it. "Who'd ever thought last July Fourth that a year later, we'd have our own big spread?"

"Well, the reward you and Houston got for killing those two thugs not only paid for all those surgeons back east, it bought the ranch next to my folks."

She leaned her face against his arm as they drove along in the summer heat. "Last year at this time, I thought we were both goners."

He kissed the top of her head. "Old Doc Adams was a better doctor than we thought and we were both so determined to live."

"Do you have any regrets about marrying me?" She looked up at him as they drove.

"Never!" he said and stared down into her blue eyes. "I love you, Violet, and let's close the door on the past forever. Nothing matters but the future, right?"

"And our love," she promised as she reached up to kiss him again and then cuddled little Tommy closer as they drove into Long Horn for the Fourth of July celebration.

Fans of Western historical romances
won't want to miss any of the books in
Georgina Gentry's exciting new series,
THE TEXANS.

Read on for a sample of
RIO.

*He's a man who burns as hot and free as a wildfire—and
where love is concerned, he's twice as dangerous . . .*

Rio Kelly knows what he wants when he sees it—and he
wants the ebony-haired, fair-skinned beauty with the
extraordinary blue eyes, Turquoise Sanchez. But in the
battle for her love, this bold vaquero is competing with a
Texas senator who's used to getting his way, at any cost.

Turquoise knows the sensible choice would be to marry the
wealthy senator and enjoy a lifetime of comfort and status.
But her heart has chosen differently. If she dares to follow
her passion—and defy one of Texas's most powerful and
ruthless men—she and her defiant cowboy are in for the
fight of their lives . . .

A Zebra paperback on sale now!

Mixcoac, Mexico
September 13, 1847

Padraic Kelly looked around at the cactus and barren land, then chafed at the hemp rope around his neck that also tied his hands behind him. The oxcart he stood in creaked under his feet as the animal stamped its hooves in impatience and the smell of blood and gunpowder.

In the gray light of dawn, the roar of cannons and the screams of dying men echoed across the desert battle-ground.

Ah, but by Saint Mary's blood, the delay would not be long enough for the thirty condemned soldiers. Padraic turned his head and looked down the line of other men standing in oxcarts, ropes around their necks. Some of them seemed in shock, some had their eyes closed, praying to the saints for a miracle.

There'd be no miracles this morning, Padraic thought bitterly and wished he could reach his rosary, but it was tucked in the breast pocket of his uniform. It was ironic somehow that he had fled the starvation of Ireland to come to America and now his new country was going to execute him.

The colonel walked up and down the line of oxcarts, the early sun glinting off his brass buttons.

"Beggin' your pardon, sir," Padraic called, "for the love of mercy, could ye hand me my holy beads?"

The colonel sneered, his tiny mustache wiggling on his ruddy face. "Aw, you papist traitor! You'll not need your silly beads when the flag falls. We're sending all you Irish traitors to hell, where you belong."

He should have known better than to ask the Protestant officer for help. Hadn't he and most of the other officers treated all the new immigrants with disdain and bullying, which was the very reason some of the St. Patrick's battalion had gone over to the Mexican side? It hadn't seemed right, fighting fellow Catholics just because America had declared war on Mexico.

A curious crowd of peasants gathered, most with sympathetic faces, but the American soldiers held them back. There was nothing the unarmed peasants could do to rescue all these condemned men.

Padraic mouthed a silent prayer as he stared at the distant castle on the horizon. The early sun reflected off steel and gun barrels as the soldiers of both sides battled for control of the landmark. Smoke rose and men screamed and Padraic held his breath, watching the Mexican flag flying from the parapet.

"Yes, watch it!" The colonel glared up at him. "For when it falls and is replaced by the stars and stripes, you cowardly traitors will die!"

The Mexicans seemed determined to hold the castle as the hours passed and the sun moved across the sky with relentless heat, throwing shadows of the condemned men in long, distorted figures across the sand.

Padraic's legs ached from hours of standing in the cart

and his mouth was so dry, he could hardly mouth prayers anymore. Behind him he heard others in the oxcarts begging for water. Padraic was proud; he would not beg, though he was faint from the heat and the sweat that drenched his blue uniform. He knew they would not give the condemned water anyway. Their guards did bring water to the oxen and Padraic tried not to watch the beasts drinking it.

In one of the carts, a man fainted and the colonel yelled for a soldier to throw water on him. "I don't want him to miss that flag coming down!" he yelled.

Padraic could only guess how many hours had passed from the way the sun slanted now in the west. The castle itself was cloaked in smoke and flames. He began to wish it would soon be over. Better to be dead than to stand here waiting all day in the hot sun for the hanging.

Sweat ran from his black hair and down the collar of his wool Mexican uniform. God, he would give his spot in Paradise for one sip of cool water. Well, his discomfort would soon be over. He didn't regret that he had fled the U.S. Army; he had done it because of his love for a Mexican girl. That love had transcended everything else. He did regret so many had followed him, some of them so young and barely off the boat. They had been escaping from the potato famine, but now they would die anyway.

The heat made dizzying waves across the barren landscape and he staggered a little and regained his footing. If he must die, he would go out like a man.

The crowd of sympathetic peasants was growing as word must have spread that the Americans were hanging their deserters. Padraic looked around for Conchita, hoping, yet dreading to see her. He did not want his love to see him die this way.

Hail Mary, Mother of God . . . He murmured the prayer automatically and he was once again a small boy at his mother's knee as they said their beads together. Now she would never know what happened to her son who had set off for the promise of America. It was just as well. He'd rather her think he was happy and successful than know he had been hanged like a common thief.

The riches of the new country had not been good, with so many Irish flooding in and everyone hating and sneering at the immigrants. If he could have found a job, he wouldn't have joined the army, but no one wanted to hire the Irish.

The fighting in the distance seemed to be slowing, though he choked on the acrid smell of cannon smoke and watched the castle burning in the distance. The Mexican flag flew bravely on the parapet but he could see the bright blue of the American uniforms like tiny ants as the invaders attacked the castle. It wouldn't be long now. The ropes bit into his wrists and he would give his soul for a sip of cold water, but he knew better than to ask. He closed his eyes and thought about the clear streams and the green pastures of County Kerry. He was a little boy again in ragged clothes, chasing the sheep toward the pens with no cares in the world save hoping for a brisk cup of tea and a big kettle of steaming potatoes as he ran toward the tumbledown stone cottage.

If only he could see Conchita once more. He smiled despite his misery and remembered the joy of the past three months. The pretty girl had been the one bright spot in his short, miserable life. He closed his eyes and imagined her in his arms again: her kisses, the warmth of her skin. He hoped she had not heard about the court-martial and the public hangings. He did not want her to see him die, swinging and choking at the end of a rope like a common criminal.

The rope rasped against his throat, the ox stamped its feet, and the cart creaked while Padraic struggled to maintain his balance. The colonel had stood them here all afternoon and now he almost wished the cart would pull ahead because he was so miserable, with his throat dry as the barren sand around him and his arms aching from being tied behind while his legs threatened to buckle under him. *No*, he reminded himself, *you are going to die like a man, and a soldier. You just happen to be on the losing side.*

In the distance, he could see the blue uniforms climbing ladders up the sides of the castle as the fighting grew more intense. Screams of dying men mixed with the thunder of cannons and the victorious shrieks as the Americans charged forward, overrunning the castle now as the sun became a bloody ball of fire to the west.

The ruddy colonel grinned and nodded up at Padraic. "It won't be long now, you Mick trash. I knew I could never turn you Irish into soldiers."

"If ye'd treated us better, we wouldn't have gone over to the other side, maybe," Padraic murmured.

The colonel sneered. "And look what you get! We're hanging more than the thirty I've got here. General Scott asked President Polk to make an example of the Saint Patrick's battalion. If it'd been up to me, I'd have hung the whole lot, especially that John Riley that led you."

"Some of them would rather have been hung than to have been lashed and branded," Padraic snarled.

"It's better than being dead," the colonel said. Then he turned and yelled at the soldiers holding back the Mexican peasants. "Keep those brown bastards back. We don't want them close enough to interfere with the hanging."

Padraic watched the peasants. Some of them were on their knees, saying their rosaries, others looking up at them gratefully with tears making trails down their dusty brown faces.

"Paddy, dearest!" He turned his head to see Conchita attempting to fight her way past the soldiers.

"Hold that bitch back!" the colonel bellowed. "Don't let her through the lines."

"Get your filthy hands off her!" Padraic yelled and struggled to break free, although he knew it was useless. Conchita was so slim and small and her black hair had come loose and blew about her lovely face as she looked toward him and called his name.

There was too much roar of battle now as the Yankees overran the castle for her to hear him, but he mouthed the words, *I love you. You are the best thing that has happened to me since I crossed the Rio Grande.*

She nodded that she understood and her face was so sad that he looked away, knowing that to see her cry would make him cry, too, and he intended to die like a man.

A victorious roar went up from the American troops as they finally fought their way to the top of the distant tower. It would only be a few moments now.

"Take her away," Padraic begged his guards. "I don't want her to see this!"

The colonel only laughed. "No, we want all these Mexicans to see what happens to traitors. Why don't you beg, Kelly? Don't you want your little greasy sweetheart to see you beg for your life?"

In the distance, the American soldiers were taking down the ragged Mexican flag, but even as it came down, one of the young Mexican cadets grabbed it from the victors' hands and as they tried to retrieve it, he ran to the edge of the parapet and flung himself over the edge to the blood-soaked ground so far below. The Mexican peasants sent up a cheer, which the colonel could not silence with all his shouting. The cadet had died rather than surrender his country's flag to the enemy.

Now the American flag was going up, silhouetted

against the setting sun. The peasants shouted a protest as soldiers climbed up on the oxcarts and checked the nooses. "No! No! Do not hang them!"

Conchita screamed again and tried to break through the line of solders holding back the crowd. "Paddy! My dear one!" She couldn't get to him, although she clawed and fought.

Padraic smiled at her and gave her an encouraging nod. If only things were different. He would have built a mud hut on this side of the Rio Grande and lived his life happily with this woman. If only he could hold her in his arms and kiss those lips once more.

Conchita looked up at him, her brave, tall man with his fair skin and wide shoulders. She made one more attempt to break through the guards, but they held her back. A roar of protests went up around her from the other peasants. He was her man and they were going to execute him and there was nothing she could do to stop it. She screamed his name and tried to tell him the secret, shouting that she carried his child, but in the noise of distant gunfire and the peasants yelling, she wasn't sure he understood, although he smiled and nodded at her and mouthed *I love you, too.*

"Your child!" she shrieked again. "I carry your child!"

At that precise moment, she heard the officer bark an order and all the oxcarts creaked forward. For just a split second, the condemned men swayed, struggling to keep their balance, and then the carts pulled out from under the long line of soldiers and their feet danced on air as they swung at the end of their ropes.

Conchita watched in frozen horror and tried to get to her Paddy as he fought for air, but the soldiers held her back. Her eyes filled with tears and the sight of the men hanging grew dim as they ceased to struggle.

"This is what the U.S. Army does to traitors and deserters!" the colonel announced to the crowd with satisfaction.

Conchita burst into sobs. She was in great pain as if her heart had just been torn from her breast. She did not want to live without her love, but she must, for his child's sake. She was not even sure he had heard her as she tried to tell him he would be a father. If it were a boy, she would raise that son and call him Rio Kelly for his father and the river that made a boundary between the two civilizations. And then she would go into a cloistered order and spend her life praying for the souls of her love and the other condemned men.

The soldiers were cutting the thirty bodies down now, and she broke through the line of guards and ran to her Paddy as he lay like a tattered bundle of rags on the sand. She threw herself on the body, weeping and kissing his face, but his soul had fled to his God and he could no longer feel her kisses and caresses.

Only now did she realize he had died smiling and so she knew he had heard her and knew he would have a child.